How They Became Birds

Three Novellas

Joshua Amses

Fomite
Burlington, VT

ISBN-13: 978-1-953236-27-2
Library of Congress Control Number: 2021945326

Fomite
58 Peru Street
Burlington, VT 05401
www.fomitepress.com
02-04-2022

Also by Joshua Amses

Raven or Crow
The Moment Before an Injury
During This, Our Nadir
Ghats

Contents

How They Became Birds

Even before the lawyer called, Benjamin had a feeling Aunt Lisa's death would leave him with something mediocre at the center of his life. There was room there, acres of it. He took the call in Marta's kitchen. The calendar on the fridge indicated it was somewhere in August. Benjamin was nearing the six-month anniversary of his unemployment in New York City. His lack of work imparted a weird resonance to the lawyer's call. It seemed to promise things great and small, and maybe some money.

"You got the valley," said the lawyer, like it was a diagnosis. In the rearguard of all this, Benjamin liked to think he'd seen it coming.

"Sell it," he said. "Send me the check with whatever your fee is taken out."

"Can't do it," said the lawyer. His name turned out to be Sherwood. "There's a codicil about it. Not my job anyway. Maybe we can find a way around all that when you come down here, but it's pretty clear she wanted you to have it."

"I'm not going anywhere right now," said Benjamin. That was true enough. Marta would have agreed. Where he wasn't going had been most of what she talked about lately, usually before bed, after her son, Rudy, was asleep, or listening to them argue with his ear pressed to wall of his bedroom, as Benjamin imagined it whenever Marta really let him have it. She argued constructively, sought equitable solutions and dynamic outcomes to problems of all kinds. Benjamin couldn't stand much more of it. But it was her apartment, so her rules. And since it was now August, his twenty-six weeks of workless benefits, or the checks he'd been duly signing over to her for the past six months, would be over soon. Or extinct, he thought glibly, remembering the valley Sherwood had mentioned. He hadn't been there since he was Rudy's age.

"Be that as it may," said the lawyer, sounding like he was winding up for something. "You're going to need to come down here eventually and sort it out. And when you do, you'll probably need me on your side to unravel this thing if you want to unload it like you said. So maybe let's be friends for the time being until we get it all worked out."

"Okay," said Benjamin, a reflex from his nightly councils of war with Marta.

"I'm going fishing in Florida next week," said Sherwood. "Be gone through the last week or so of the month. It'd be good to get this wrapped up before then."

"Okay," said Benjamin. Without a job, his time had no essential value to other people; he should probably get used to working with their schedules. Marta had made this point as constructively as possible the night before, and it remained fresh and unadorned in his mind.

"Anyway, it's summer now, and it's nice up here during the summer."

"I know."

"Of course you do," said Sherwood. "Didn't mean that to sound like there isn't some history up here for you."

"I don't know what you're talking about."

"Well, you have my number," said Sherwood, sort of like a

little league coach who'd given a benchwarmer a chance only to have it blow up in his face. "Call me when you're on your way. And I'm sorry for your loss; I don't know if I said that."

"My what?"

"Okay," said Sherwood, hanging up. Benjamin felt the call had gone as well as could be expected.

Rudy clattered through into the apartment, shirtless, fifteen, a skateboard under his arm. Benjamin couldn't tell if Rudy smelled more like alcohol or pot smoke, but it didn't matter. He'd given over control of what little money he had to Marta, so both items maintained an element of inessential luxury.

"Where's my mom?" asked Rudy, his head in the fridge, scouting around for something to drink.

"At work," said Benjamin, reciting lines once again; it was a conversation they'd had every day at about this time since school broke for the summer. Because he wasn't working, Benjamin knew Marta expected him to keep an eye on her son while she was, but he didn't see how that could happen. Rudy was too old for the stepfather thing to really take, and Benjamin didn't want to be his father in any case. Rudy was also already showing signs of being smart in way that meant there was probably a troubled future ahead of him. It often made Benjamin wonder exactly what he'd signed up for by hitching himself to Marta's wagon. He sometimes felt like he had more in common with her son than he did with her, and, though it went unacknowledged between them, he suspected Rudy felt the same way about him.

It hadn't always been like that. When Benjamin first moved in, Rudy had spent a lot of time testing him, and Benjamin was pretty certain he'd flunked overall. It was always when Marta wasn't around to notice, which left him feeling slightly victimized by her son's calculated displays of micro-dominance; peeing with the bathroom door open, smoking cigarettes on the fire escape, even bringing a girl back to the apartment. Benjamin was seated in the kitchen during this last one, eating a bowl of cereal for dinner, staring fixedly at the wall and listening to an opera unravel on the radio when a very pretty young lady wrapped in one of Marta's towels poked her head in the door and asked him for directions to the bathroom. Benjamin pointed with his spoon, dribbling a seminal constellation of dots on the tabletop, and she disappeared down the hall. A toilet flushed, a door opened, another door closed; Benjamin turned up the radio. Rudy walked the girl out an hour later in a sandstorm of giggles on her end, murmured half-truths on his, and stopped off in the kitchen on his way back to his room, standing shirtless in the doorway for a moment, clearly daring Benjamin to say something about it. Benjamin said nothing, as usual. He didn't think it was his role to provide any friction hereabouts, and didn't want to give Rudy the chance to shout at him about things the two of them already knew, and probably agreed upon: you're not my father, you can't tell me what to do, I don't need to listen to you. If Benjamin opened his mouth, the unvoiced sound of all this threatened to overwhelm the opera spinning to a close on the radio. Getting it all out there was likely a normal step in this kind of domestic arrangement, but it was one he hoped to skip entirely if he could.

Benjamin considered kicking some of this back to Marta when she came home, letting her know what Rudy had been up to while she was away, and washing his hands of the entire thing. But Marta was a nurse at a hospital in downtown Manhattan, and worked long shifts at odd hours, so she wasn't home very much, and he knew no matter what kind of fresh guidelines or censure she set down for her son, it would probably end up being his responsibility to uphold. This state of affairs sounded a lot like the way things were already, only worse. Benjamin wanted peace for himself and Rudy, or at least a ceasefire. So he kept his mouth shut until Rudy ran out of tests, eventually lapsing back into a more or less regular array of mid-adolescent bad habits: leaving the milk out on the counter, staying out late on school nights, or, at worst, the stray suggestion of pot smoke emanating from his room at the end of the hall. There it was now, piney and unmistakable, as Benjamin cradled the telephone in the kitchen. He turned on the fan above the stove, and flicked the switch for the overhead one in the living room as he trailed the odor down the hallway like a cartoon wolf.

Rudy's door was open, but Benjamin tapped lightly on the jam anyway before walking in as a kind of plangent herald of his arrival. Marta's son lay on his bed, blowing smoke from a joint into an oscillating fan aimed roughly toward the window, and reading a copy of *The Story of the Eye*. The walls and ceiling were a mosaic of skateboard posters, fliers from punk rock shows, comic book iconography here and there, other kinds of youthful insignias. Benjamin could recognize enough of them to feel at home. The family cat chittered at him from the exact right angle of Rudy's left knee as he settled into a rocking chair in the corner of the room. I've lived here for eight months, thought Benjamin. And the damned cat still thinks I'm a bird.

"What do you need, Ben?" asked Rudy, as if the two of them were roommates, which was probably the easiest way to describe the territory their relationship had run aground in after Benjamin dismissed himself from stepfather tryouts.

"I was wondering if I could have some pot," said Benjamin, trying and failing to disbar the mendicant intonation from his voice. He'd never asked Rudy for anything before, but he really wanted to get high after the phone call with the lawyer. He figured asking Marta's son for help was a better choice than huffing whatever was under the bathroom sink.

"Does this have something to do with who you were talking to when I came in?" asked Rudy. The joint swung toward Benjamin like a yardarm.

"Mostly," he replied, taking it, doing what had to be done, and passing it back. "A friend of mine died."

"Good friend?"

"Used to be."

"Sorry."

"She left me some property I don't want."

"So you're finally getting your own place?" asked Rudy. It was a good joke. They chuckled in canon over it.

"It's upstate," said Benjamin. "Around Lake George, pretty close to the Vermont border. I have to go up there to deal with it. I was thinking maybe you and your mom would like to come with me, get out of the city for a little while. Kind of a summer vacation."

"I'm already on vacation," said Rudy. "But you probably need her to pay for a rental car."

"Even if that wasn't true, I'd still want the two of you to come," said Benjamin. This was a lie. He decided to change the subject before it caught up with him. "How was your day?"

"Fine. This girl I know gave me this book about French people peeing on each other and cracking eggs in the toilet. And I learned three flip noseslides on the big hubba at the park. Going to see if I can stick it down something substantial tomorrow, maybe get some new street footy if this filmer I know is up for it. I got a few clips on my phone if you want to see."

"Sure," replied Benjamin. He was high as a kite, and watching videos of Rudy skateboarding sounded like just the thing. They sat side by side on the bed, going through the small library of clips on his phone with the cat snoozing by their feet in a diamond of sunlight, awakening only to cackle balefully at Benjamin and show him her fangs. It had been years since he'd been on a skateboard, but he still knew enough about the sport to appreciate how much better Rudy was at it than he had been.

He was also amazed by the technology Marta's son carried around his pocket; Benjamin's phone opened like a compact, and threw his voice back at him whenever there was a minor disturbance in the atmosphere. Most of the conversations he had felt like a tripartite negotiation, so he'd taken to giving out the house number whenever he had a reason to, mostly on job applications, though he'd had less of those to worry about lately. His pride was at an all-time low regarding gainful employment, and Marta was making decent money at the hospital and still doing her best to sympathize with him. The possibility of moving forward seemed remote. Benjamin liked to think he was now aware of his limits, and deciding to respect them from here on out was a mature choice. He'd even tried explaining this to Marta during what now seemed like the salad days of his joblessness, hoping to buy some time to enjoy the fruits of his non-labor, and maybe a low to medium dosage of Xanax from the hospital pharmacy, by being mistaken for depressed. Benjamin may have been depressed for all he knew, which wasn't much; but he knew enough to realize diagnosing himself wasn't a step toward the kind of recovery he was after. This was back in February; Benjamin imagined passing through the rest of midwinter into spring beached like a sea turtle on Marta's living room couch in a deep pharmacological hibernation, listening to the radiator tick and classical music on the radio while the frozen city went about its business outside; 'a

preferred activity' they would have called it at the job he'd lost
six months ago.

It seemed like a good, foolproof plan, and it nearly was. Marta
spotted his signal flare shining out above the rolling sea of in-
action he'd been sailing upon since January, and interpreted it
correctly as a cry for help. She'd even gotten out one of her old
medical textbooks, and gone through a depression checklist with
him, a spreading tree Benjamin was thrilled to find he hit almost
every branch of as they descended it together, seated head to
head on the living room carpet with the textbook spread open in
the center of the near perfect rhombus formed by the points of
their knees touching, like two people using a Ouija board. It felt
almost like intimacy, and Benjamin knew he was probably under-
mining the medical value of Marta's informal diagnosis by how
much he was enjoying receiving it. But he couldn't help himself;
his dreams were greatly limited by his circumstances, but they all
appeared to be coming true, even before Marta closed the book,
kissed his face, and said she knew some people at the hospital
who could probably help him. She would talk to them tomorrow.

Benjamin spent most of the next day cleaning Marta's apartment, as if the help she promised to return with at the end of
the day was a guest he was preparing for. In truth, he wanted
to leave things nice, the stovetop clean, the bathtub bleached,
the floor mopped, before rolling himself into the velvety anx-
iolytic cocoon wherein he expected to pass the lion's share of
the winter months, maybe to emerge a better man when spring
rolled around, or someone who was at least prepared to rejoin
the workforce. Either way, Benjamin was nervous and excited
for Marta to arrive, a compound of feelings he only recognized
as traveler's anxiety when it tailed out into the kind of worka-
day disappointment he associated with remaining in place, cer-

tainly more familiar ground, when she came through the door later that evening and presented him with the name and number of a nurse psychotherapist who had agreed to see him for free as a favor to her.

Benjamin did his best to shroud his disappointment in the appearance of gratitude, an appearance he fixed to his face like a bayonet as he read the name on the card Marta handed to him instead of the translucent orange cylinder of one milligram blue pills he'd been expecting all day, wondering if this friend of hers could prescribe what he wanted, but too afraid to ask. No departures from reality appeared imminent. In the end, he decided Marta was probably expecting him to handle this in stages, a tedious possibility. Benjamin said he would make an appointment in the morning, and never did, no matter how many times she reminded him, figuring he could live with the result of sidestepping her attempt to help him, no matter what it was. This turned out to be the slow withdrawal of her sympathy for his circumstances, and the more immediate and complete collapse of the cozy vision of himself overwintering on the living room couch.

So he'd spent most of what remained of that season and a good portion of spring holed up in a nearby branch of the public library in the middle of the day, wearing his only suit alongside bums trying to stay warm and retirees tipping toward senility, after telling Marta he had an interview, hoping this kind of Potemkin job fair might throw her off his trail long enough for things to get worse without it appearing to be his fault. The plan nearly failed. She'd almost caught him at one point, but he'd seen her coming through the front window, and hidden out in a remote corner beside the biographies, watching her return some books of his through a gap in the shelves. It was a close call, or seemed like one, until Rudy had actually caught him one day a few weeks after he'd brought the girl back to the apartment. Benjamin noticed a pair of skateboard sneakers appear below the copy of *The Education of Henry Adams* he was enjoying, and lowered it to complete a kind of behind enemy lines eye contact with Marta's son, who stood before him with a passel of comic books under his arm, ready for checkout.

They didn't speak, but Benjamin was left with the feeling that they'd reached a sense of mutually assured destruction, and he marked this as the informal beginning of the armistice between he and Rudy. Benjamin realized he was only beginning to enjoy the fruits of this a few months down the line as Marta's son spun a third joint into being on the back of a biology textbook as dusk bruised the sky outside the window. It was developing into a pretty night, so they took Rudy's skateboard to a small park across the street from the apartment after finishing the joint, and took turns rolling around, trading maneuvers in the twilight. Marta encountered them like this on her way home from work. Benjamin looked up from the skateboard beneath his feet and she was there, seated on a bench nearby, watching, smiling, not wanting to interrupt. It was an unusual moment, mostly because she seemed happy, and he had forgotten what that looked like. It seemed like the right time to mention the trip upstate, though Rudy saved him the trouble by bringing it up over dinner, slices and sodas in a booth at a nearby pizzeria, Marta's treat. Rudy sounded excited, which made Marta excited. She asked Benjamin what kind of property he'd inherited. The question stumped him, at first.

"You have to see it to believe it," he said finally, his lips pursed around a straw, trying to wash out some of the residual dopey dryness from his mouth. That settled it. Marta said she would find a rental car after dinner, and Rudy, his eyes like stop signs as he mowed through a tertiary slice of pizza, asked if they could do some shopping in the outlet malls in and around Lake George. For the moment, Benjamin noticed, they seemed to be functioning as a family. Marta's hand patrolled the interior of his thigh beneath the table, something she did only when Benjamin acted his age, but an overall sign that everything was all right. It reminded him of Aunt Lisa, or the sense of wellbeing her death had somehow bestowed upon them all. He was grateful for it, but what was the cost? Lymphoma, his mother had said. Benjamin didn't know what kind, but after they talked about it, he looked up the symptoms: drenching sweats, fever, itching, weight loss, feeling tired. That didn't sound too bad to Benjamin, but as he watched Marta and Rudy joke around ahead on the sidewalk after leaving the pizzeria, excited to be going on vacation, he considered the months Aunt Lisa had probably spent dying by herself in Glens Falls Hospital. She would probably have been about sixty years old. When his mother called, he was newly unemployed and had no money for a bus ticket. It had been too long anyway; she wouldn't remember him. But the call from Sherwood proved otherwise. Benjamin told himself there was no point in feeling bad about it. The ashes had already been tossed into Lake George, and there was really nothing left to feel after someone dies except what you felt when they were alive, no new ground to cover.

But what had he felt when Aunt Lisa was alive? Benjamin wondered. He didn't have to come up with an answer for the question to make him uncomfortable.

Rudy wanted to be a professional skateboarder. It was an ambition he'd never shared directly with Benjamin. He only knew it through osmosis, by way of Marta, who perennially sought his help in steering her son away from this singular goal. Benjamin always found himself caught on both sides of the argument whenever it came up, like someone straddling an expanding rift in the planet's crust. He knew Marta had a point, because she always had a point. Still, he couldn't help admiring and vaguely envying her son for his unwavering belief in himself; at thirty-two, Benjamin was coming up on a half-decade of disbelieving in himself, and the last year had only thrown his doubt into sharper relief. He remembered a conversation he'd had at work, shortly before he was let go. Someone, he couldn't remember who, asked him what kind of animal he was. A ghost, he replied. That's not an animal, someone else had said. Benjamin tried to think of another answer, but didn't come up with anything.

A week after Sherwood's phone call, Benjamin sat in the passenger seat of a rental sedan while Marta exited I-87, trying to remember what he'd wanted to be when he was fifteen. He studied the landscape through the car window, a place he hadn't visited since he was Rudy's age. Maybe it held an answer. The aggressive loops and scaffolding of an amusement park rose like a barbican against the evergreen horizon. Outlet stores and chain restaurants bloomed on either side the car. Blacktop stretched to the edge of the trees. Benjamin remembered feeling nothing when he was here last, shopping for beach food with Aunt LisWa. They were on their way to the lake for the day. He knew he only felt something now because she was dead, and had been kind to him. Too kind, his mother would say later. Benjamin didn't agree with her then, but he was only fifteen, and vulnerable to the prevailing interests of the adults in his life, his mother, his father.

And Aunt Lisa, of course; she bought two magnums of white wine at the grocery store that day, and had one of them open in the car before they even got to the lake. When they did, it was a twenty-minute walk through the forest to a rocky patch of secluded shoreline, a place she claimed no one else knew about, except the three or four nudists they shared it with, three middle-aged men, and one old woman. All of them spent the day avoiding the water, and striding back and forth in front of the blanket Aunt Lisa spread over the sand, stopping only to bend deeply at the waist to retrieve some curiosity from the shoreline, or plant a thorny foot atop a waterlogged tree trunk with their hands resting on their hips, surveying the wide blue featurelessness of the lake. Aunt Lisa told Benjamin the beach wasn't an officially sanctioned place of nakedness, so he didn't have to remove his swimsuit if he didn't want to, a relief he only felt the business end of after she had a few more glugs of wine and slipped out of her bikini top. He still remembered it, fluttering vividly to the checkered blanket, and watching her bare, suntanned back withdraw beneath the surf. She was probably Marta's age then, ranging toward forty, looking well overall. It was the first time he'd ever seen something like this. Then, as now, almost twenty years later, it helped to remind himself that Aunt Lisa wasn't actually his aunt. She was a friend of his mother's, someone who'd known him since he was born, and had probably seen him naked many times over the years.

I guess it's my turn now, he remembered thinking as she emerged from the water; her nipples were the size and color of strawberries. Benjamin suddenly felt like a mailbox with its flag up, awaiting collection, so he went in the water shortly afterward to cool off, and stayed in until he was almost hypothermic, trying to freeze out the puerile part of himself that was sort of hoping his parents would show up to rescue him from Aunt Lisa. Looking back on it, Benjamin figured he would have probably needed to age himself at least a decade in order to approach the situation with any sort of precision, but he thought he'd done okay anyway. He didn't refuse the wine she offered after he came out of the water, helped her refasten her bikini top when it was time to leave the beach, barely reacted when she said she'd had too much to drink, and asked if he was comfortable driving her ancient station wagon back to the Valley. It was the same question she asked hours earlier when she was already halfway out of her bikini top. There hadn't seemed to be much of a choice then either. What did he want to be when he was Rudy's age? Agreeable, he decided. It felt like the only accurate answer.

His head was a little foggy from the wine, but he managed to navigate the summer traffic and get them back to the Valley without a problem, rolling into the dirt parking area then as Marta did now, with Rudy pulled up between the seats, looking everything over through the windshield.

"What the shit am I looking at?" he asked Benjamin, not meanly at all. He sounded astonished.

"Language, please," said Marta. "But seriously, Ben. Is this really the place?"

"Sure is," he said, trying to tailor the enthusiasm in his voice to the mood of the other passengers, though he couldn't tell if they were excited or appalled by what they saw, so it ended up sounding way off-kilter, and a little like a question. He tried to imagine what all this must look like to them; a ten-foot-high wooden fence running off into the swarthy woodland to either side of an imposing pair of studded wooden gates, above which a now faded but once proud illuminated sign read: DINOSAUR VALLEY. Benjamin remembered how relieved he felt seeing it through the windshield of Aunt Lisa's Volvo when he'd driven them back from the lake, the letters blazing out of the darkness above the gate as he tried to find a place to park amid the cars in the lot. It was almost closing time. They threaded their way through a trickle of departing visitors toward the guest cabins at the rear of the property. There were eight of them, arranged around a swimming pool fringed by plastic palm trees and a belching plaster volcano lit from inside at night. A bathing Diplodocus statue emerged from the center, something for kids to climb on, jump off, or slide down, whatever they wanted. Benjamin was in cabin five. When they reached the door, Aunt Lisa said he looked sunburnt. She had something to put on it at her place. She lived on the very edge of the property in an old farmhouse that came with the place. She had been in the process of fixing it up for years without ever really getting anywhere. There were holes in the floor and wall, rooms half-painted, windows and doors missing. The whole mess was concealed behind a bamboo fence to give it thematic consistency. Benjamin remembered following her across the turf of a miniature golf course, an Allosaurus rearing out of the night from beside the penultimate hole as his earlier relief at having reached the Valley with her in one piece retracted in on itself like a dying star, boiling off until there was only the unexpected to expect, or whatever was on the other side of the door in the bamboo fence he waited beside, while she fumbled through her purse for the keys. He knew he couldn't go home, so he mostly wanted to go back to cabin five, call it a night.

But there were other things to consider then, or other opportunities to be agreeable, it seemed now, as Benjamin leaned on the hood of the rental car, watching Marta and Rudy examine the gate up close, like explorers encountering the ruined walls of a lost city. The only other car in the parking lot was a comfortable looking pickup, angled under some shady trees in a corner by the fence with a portly middle-aged man asleep in the front seat. This turned out to be Sherwood who apologized after Benjamin tapped on the window and woke him up. The lawyer removed a sheaf of papers from amid the fishing gear in the backseat, and a set of keys he handed off to Benjamin.

"What about selling it?" he asked, in between signatures.

"I'll do the best I can to help you there, and bill it to the estate," said Sherwood, flipping a page, touching the place where Benjamin needed to sign. "But I should be honest with you. It'd be easier to try and sell a national park. I guess she really wanted you to have this place, maybe make it work again."

"When was the last time it worked?"

"Well, I know she had a couple guests last summer, before she had to go to Glens Falls," said Sherwood, striving to be delicate in a way that made Benjamin wonder if he should appear to feel worse about things for the lawyer's benefit. "But that was during the biker convention at the lake, and most of the regular hotels were full, so she put a couple of the guys up here. She said they ate a lot, but were a pretty polite bunch otherwise. Spilled beer in the volcano though and blew out the interior light. That upset her."

"I'll bet. But aside from the bikers?"

"It's been tapering off for the past ten years, ever since the big amusement park went up close to the lake. That's the major family attraction in town. You probably saw it coming in. Fancy hotel, rollercoasters, water park, shopping. It's like a walled city, right off the interstate. Plenty of people never even make it to the lake when they see that."

"Is the property itself worth anything?" asked Benjamin, swinging the keys toward the gate.

"Something, sure," replied Sherwood. "But you'd have to clear it out if you wanted to build anything on it, and that'll probably cost as much to do as the property itself. But the short answer is yes. You got fifteen decent acres on a main road with the ski resorts on one side over by Killington and the lake on the other. If you could figure out how to make something out of the winter and summer traffic, you could do okay out here. But it's got to be more than mini-golf with a stegoceratops or whatever. People want more nowadays, I guess. Anyway, care for a tour?"

"I think I know my way around," said Benjamin. This appeared to disappoint the lawyer. Maybe he had been looking forward to it. No reason to let down the only man who could probably help sell the place off when the time came.

"But I guess it's been a while," said Benjamin.

"Well, sure it has," said Sherwood, raising his hand palm up between them. Benjamin was halfway to shaking it before he realized Sherwood wanted the keys. "She switched a lot of things around hereabouts over the years. You probably won't even recognize it!"

"Is cabin five still there?" asked Benjamin, but the lawyer was already shuffling through the key ring on his way to unlock the gate, and either ignored the question or couldn't hear it.

As it turned out, Cabin five was still there, at least in spirit. The number had been removed and replaced with DILOPHOSAUR. The others had also taken up the theme: ARCHEOPTYRX, CELEOPHYSIS, TRICERATOPS, and TYRANNOSAURUS-REX, of course. This last one was now some sort of honeymoon or deluxe suite, according to Sherwood, who marched around the edge of an empty pool, passing in and out of the Diplodocus' shadow as he did his best to read off the rest of the names, mashing the syllables with a kind of flourish. The Valley definitely lent itself to themed rooms. Benjamin was a little surprised Aunt Lisa hadn't gotten around to doing it earlier.

He lingered beside DILOPHOSAURUS nee cabin five as Marta

and Rudy followed Sherwood toward the interior of the park, testing the doorknob, finding it locked, and trying to get a look inside through a fissure in the curtains. There wasn't much to see, but Benjamin was sure what he was looking for, or trying to remember. Maybe the residual sensation of Aunt Lisa's hands sliding over his back, slick with Aloe Vera gel, over his shoulders, onto his chest; cooling his body, unsettling his mind. He remembered how her fingers seemed to carve troughs in his skin at the place where wings would attach if he were bird, or that's what it felt like when he returned from the farmhouse behind the fence. She asked if he wanted to stay and drink more wine. He declined, saying he was tired and maybe a little sick from the sun, thanks anyway. He was supposed to be there, in the Valley, for two weeks, and this was only day three. Benjamin figured whatever was rushing his way would probably get him eventually, but that didn't mean he needed to lie down in its path and give up before he fully understood what he was giving up. Still, he thought about her all night in cabin five, sleeping in patches, like a soldier in a trench, his penis flat against his sunburnt stomach like the stock of a rifle.

When his mother called the next morning from Massachusetts, he'd lied to her automatically when she asked if he was having fun with Stephen, saying yes, absolutely; the two of them were getting along great, as usual. Stephen was the son Aunt Lisa had with a man no one had ever met. He was a year older than Benjamin, someone he had often been mashed together with whenever his mother and father wanted to take a vacation by themselves. Benjamin and Stephen hadn't seen each other for a while. Stephen's father was an archaeologist of some renown, and traveled a lot for work, all over the world. As Stephen had gotten older, he often went with his father on these trips, mainly to remote dig sites in South America or the Mideast. It was hard for Benjamin not to envy Aunt Lisa's son whenever he returned from one of these sojourns, already in the early stages of commanding the kind of long view Benjamin had been trying to freeze out of himself at the beach with Stephen's mother as she lay half-naked in the sand, lapping at the neck of a wine bottle.

The smallness of Benjamin's world only appalled him when someone else was around to call attention to it, and that was most of what Stephen did when they'd seen each other recently. He wasn't very interested in skateboarding anymore, had given up listening to punk rock for the kind of cross-pollinated club music that probably played everywhere in the countries his father turned him loose in after hours. These places obviously made Stephen very happy. Benjamin could tell whenever he talked about them, and it was hard to enjoy spending time with someone who would rather be somewhere else.

Still, Benjamin wanted to be agreeable, and when his mother asked if he'd mind hanging out at the Valley for two weeks while she and his father celebrated their anniversary on Cape Cod, he said he wouldn't. Stephen would be there, his mother assured him, as if this was some kind of incentive. The last time they'd hung out, Stephen told a story about an older backpacker girl from Germany giving him a hand job in a tent somewhere along the Inca Trail, which left Benjamin wondering what there was to really talk about after that. Why didn't he know anyone else his age who'd received a hand job from a European? It was the kind of odd question he always found himself struggling to answer whenever he was around Stephen, a zone of inexperience Benjamin didn't relish, and had begun to dread whenever his mother made a playdate for him with Aunt Lisa's son.

It was a relief when his parents dropped him off at the Valley's gates, and Stephen's mother met them in the parking lot saying something about her son not arriving until tomorrow. She was picking him up at Floyd Bennett in the morning. With no one to make him feel small and unusual for the next twelve hours, Benjamin couldn't have been happier. His parents accepted this, and left, and he settled into a chair beside the pool, watching guests and absently reading a copy of *Martin the Warrior*, while Aunt Lisa went about her business in the park. They reconvened for dinner, pizza in Lake George. Benjamin noticed she appeared agitated then, shifting things around the table, checking her phone, drinking three beers during a forty-five minute meal, but he didn't tie it to anything that would affect him until the following morning came and went, and Stephen didn't arrive. The next day came and went as well with the same result. Benjamin didn't want to ask Aunt Lisa where Stephen was because he was happier without him overall, and didn't want to spoil the sang-froid he'd achieved around the Valley by slapping a time-stamp on it. It may have been selfish, but Benjamin was aware of his age enough to realize whatever Aunt Lisa may have needed to talk about, it wasn't in his wheelhouse. Still, after the Tar Pit Café had closed down for the evening, and the guests had gone back to their rooms, he'd gone in there for a soda to bring back to his cabin, and found Aunt Lisa at the bar, passed the midpoint on a bottle of scotch, a snowfall of cigarette butts at the foot of the stool she sat on. Stephen wasn't coming, she said. He'd decided to stay with his father. He was taking Stephen to Lebanon for a conference or something.

Benjamin tried to appear sympathetic to this news even though it overjoyed him. Aunt Lisa said she would call his mom if he didn't want to stay. Benjamin never understood why he'd said no to this idea. Agreeableness didn't quite explain it. Maybe there was something exciting in watching the person in whose care he'd been left unravel; it seemed to promise or suggest the kind of adventure he was always envying in Stephen, and suspected he wouldn't be allowed to have if his parent's knew about it. So he said he was fine with staying, got himself a soda from behind the bar, and took it to bed, lullabying himself with the fixed image of a black-haired girl about his age he'd watched earlier that day by the pool, sunning herself in a russet bikini; she hadn't appeared to notice him. But this was only his second day at the Valley, so maybe she would. But on the third day, he and Aunt Lisa went to the beach. Benjamin had other things to think about after that.

The Tar Pit Café had received a facelift within the past few years. Some of the goofier vintage fixtures had been removed and replaced with a sleeker variety. Plenty of prehistoric imagery remained around the place. It looked a little like a store in a natural history museum, not a bad way to leave things. Benjamin tested the taps behind the bar, as Sherwood rattled around in the kitchen, talking the entire time.

"The range is newish, or new enough. I'd keep that, and pretty much everything else in here. Just eyeballing it, I'm pretty sure you're up to code, and a commercial kitchen in good shape is a nice thing to have when you're selling a place zoned like this one is."

"There's still lots of beer and stuff here," said Rudy. He'd apparently found his way into a stock room.

"Sure is, but no food, I'm afraid," replied the lawyer. "Had to pass all that to the food shelf so it wouldn't spoil. There might still be some oyster crackers around here somewhere."

"How well did you actually know Aunt Lisa?" asked Benjamin from the dining room when Sherwood's face appeared in the service window.

"As well as anyone around here," he replied, adding: "Well, maybe a little better. I handled a lot of the paperwork for the place over the years, permits and stuff for things she wanted to do. And then there was the will. Knowing someone through their work isn't everything I suppose, but you get a sense of what they expect from the world."

"What did she expect?" ask Benjamin, watching Marta on the miniature golf course through the large glass windows of the dining room, appearing to practice her swing as the plaster Allosaurus reared histrionically behind her. She looked calm and relaxed and very beautiful. This is the woman who tolerates me, he thought, remembering he loved her, or remembering what it had been like before he did, the same thing. How must it have looked from her perspective? Pulling aside the curtain in the ER to find Benjamin seated in the shadow of Lawrence, a towering, twenty-one year old black man wearing a bulky pair of acoustic earmuffs, an assortment of favorite plush toys in his lap. Earlier in the morning, one of the interns at the group home where Benjamin worked and Lawrence lived had seen him swallow a paperclip in the staff office. Benjamin called the nurse practitioner the Achieve Network kept on retainer, who said X-rays were needed.

He explained all this to Marta when she appeared from behind the curtain while keeping one eye on Lawrence for any signs of developing agitation; increased rocking, certain non-verbal vocalizations, hitting people. The first two often heralded the last one, at least in Benjamin's experience. Ideally, he would have had a second person with him to help deal with things if they went that way, but the group home couldn't spare the staff. So here he was, alone in public with an unpredictable young man the size of a castle, who was already beginning to rock in his seat as Marta attempted to take his blood pressure. When the cuff tightened, the vocalizations kicked up a notch; the only place for Lawrence to go from here was to start swinging. Last winter, Benjamin had seen him punch a hole through the center of a television set in his room. Lawrence didn't speak, so they'd never figured out what the problem had been. Benjamin noticed a monitor of some kind against the wall of the alcove they'd been assigned in the ER, and hoped offhandedly that Lawrence might go for it first. The rocking was picking up; so were the noises. The cuff was around Lawrence's hitting arm; that probably wouldn't slow him down much. Marta was still struggling to get a reading, and Benjamin wanted to warn her without scaring her off, though the possibility of things turning out well for the three of them appeared to be in retrograde either way. Benjamin did the only thing he could think to do. He moved his chair to face Lawrence, and held the young man's hands, running a thumb over both palms in a kind of massage, repeating key phrases in a low voice until the rocking slowed down, and the noises tapered off. After a little while, Lawrence leaned his forehead against Benjamin's forehead, a sign things were now okay, or had at least returned to a brand of chaos they both trusted.

Marta worked around them, taking her measurements. Later, she told Benjamin watching this made her want to see him again, though it probably wouldn't have happened if he hadn't forgotten one of Lawrence's plush toys at the hospital. When she came by the group home a few days later to drop it off, Henry was reading on the porch while some of the residents played in the yard. He looked up from his book, and saw her standing at the gate. Benjamin assumed she'd come by to check up on Lawrence, and led off with a thorough summary of his recent bowel movements, very professional. Nothing had turned up on the X-rays, so if he had eaten something unusual, Benjamin was pretty certain it had passed by now without an issue. Would she care to see the log?

"The log?" she echoed, wondering what exactly he wanted to show her as she passed Lawrence his toy over the fence; he'd recognized her voice, and come outside to see about it. The two of them watched him lumber inside, the slow yet steady retreat of the one thing they definitely had in common. Meanwhile, Benjamin noticed she was pretty, and this reminded him he was lonely. He looked around the yard at the residents here and there, and saw no one who would judge him irrevocably, so he went for it. Did she live in the neighborhood? When she said she did, Benjamin asked if she'd like to grab a drink when he got off work. Marta said she had to go home and make dinner for her son, but immediately suggested a very exact alternate date. Her time seemed to be valuable; it made Benjamin wish he had a daily planner to consult before assuring Marta he wasn't doing anything during the time she'd suggested. But, even then, he suspected the kind of busy, organized person Marta appeared to be would be good for him.

And a year later, as he watched her and Rudy through the window of the Tar Pit Café, teeing up in the evening shade of the statuary Allosaurus, he knew remembering the time before he loved her made him love her more now, almost painfully. Maybe this was a good thing; or there had to be parts of it that were good. But he relied on her to help him recognize things like that, so there was probably a conflict of interest afoot, something he needed to work on by himself, an ugly thought. He hoped, in some way, he was still the man she'd found sitting with Lawrence behind the curtain in the ER, the man she wanted to see again, and not the anomaly that lied to her about job interviews and got high with her son in the meanwhile. He remembered how his skull felt, balanced in the bowl of her pelvis the day he'd returned jobless from a meeting with the Achieve Network's board of directors, a little frostbitten from walking across the Brooklyn Bridge in the middle of winter, something he'd done to clear out his head after leaving the administrative offices in Manhattan, and how the city seemed to lunge out of the gale blowing in off the East River. He had the sense he was only now unthawing from that walk, as he watched Marta and Rudy laughing and smacking golf balls together in the purple twilight. The sheet of glass separating him from them, the world outside perhaps, made Benjamin feel like he'd suddenly woken up on the wrong side of an exhibit. He remembered the same feeling or some inchoate form of it from day four in the Valley, when he passed cabin eight, the last in the crescent of bungalows around the pool, and noticed the black-haired girl removing her bikini top through the window; the curtains stood wide to either side of the frame, like courtiers receiving their liege. Her back faced him, so it seemed like a relatively minor display after seeing Aunt Lisa on the beach the day before. But he stood anyway, rooted in place like a flagpole, watching the girl's thin white arms join at the center of her spine as she fiddled with the catch on the swimsuit, the blade of either shoulder rising and receding beneath the skin as she shrugged it off, and disappeared into the interior of the cabin. The girl's bones looked like wings through the window, he had thought, walking away.

As with the day before, watching Aunt Lisa's tanned back sink below water, he had the feeling he was seeing something he shouldn't, but also couldn't look away from. Benjamin knew denying himself experience when he had none would only make him feel his age more acutely, the way he did whenever Stephen was around. The girl he'd seen changing through the window probably wasn't German, Canadian at best, the Valley was in upstate New York, not some South American pampa or whatever, and the possibility of peeling her away from her family long enough to get a hand job seemed remote. But the past four days in the Valley were turning into the longest period of his life he could remember being essentially unsupervised; he wanted to make the most of it. Aunt Lisa appeared to be developing as his ally in this, and after lying to his mother that morning over the phone, he seemed to have emerged as hers. She was a friend of his family, so trusting her had always been implicit, something he was raised with, and couldn't escape. But for the first time since he'd known her, Benjamin felt like he had a reason to, one of his own.

And fifteen years later, as he sat in the Tar Pit Café, watching night close in over the park, he knew he'd never stopped trusting Aunt Lisa. Then, as now, the reason was the same: her selfishness might make him uncomfortable, but it would never harm him. Could he say the same for himself? Benjamin didn't think so. He wasn't certain she'd died alone in Glens Falls, but he knew he'd passed up the opportunity to make sure she didn't by being there himself. And now, there was no one to forgive him for it. Only the ruin she'd left in his care remained, a kind of cenotaph marking the two weeks many summers ago when they'd briefly stepped out of the known world together, and all he could think to do was sell it. Benjamin couldn't identify the feelings he had about this as grief or guilt, but he figured both were probably normal under the circumstances. Still, his mind released a silent prayer for her ghost, like a smoke signal; he imagined it traveling laterally toward the lake, instead of up to heaven or the smoldering pit below. He saw no other place for her.

"Someone to agree with," said Sherwood from the kitchen. "Same as most people."

Benjamin didn't respond. He'd forgotten the question the lawyer was answering.

The tour ended at the Bone House, since it was getting late and Sherwood had some things he needed to do to get ready for his fishing trip in the Florida. They stood among the glass cases of specimens Aunt Lisa had collected during her travels with Stephen's father, things she'd mostly bought off fossil dealers in North Africa, Brazil, outer Mongolia. Benjamin wondered a little meanly if the lawyer was one of these himself; in the low overhead light, Sherwood looked like something dug out of a dry river bed.

"She always thought of this as the academic side of the park," he said, waving around the room, one of six, the walls and ceiling plastered over to resemble the interior of a cave. "Wanted the kids to learn something, probably the parents too, knowing Lisa. Better be careful who we sell this place to. She came by a lot of these though certain back channels, and only got them into the country because her kid's dad knew some folks in customs."

"Is it worth anything?" asked Benjamin, his eyes traveling over a polished row of Spinosaurus teeth in the tray beside them.

"I mean, sure, if you want to take the risk of finding a buyer," said Sherwood. "But you have to have papers for this kind of thing, and even then, no museum is going to cut a check for this stuff for someone who just walks in off the street with it in bag."

"So you're saying the best thing to do is leave it where it is?"

"Part of the charm, don't you think?" asked Sherwood, pushing open a fire exit. "Walk me to my car?"

As they walked outside, a few stray lights were on over the attractions here and there; the mini-golf was lit for the benefit of Marta and Rudy, who were still enmeshed in a game, the sodium vapor lamps between the cabins, and those below several of the plaster models roaring and grazing in turn on the way to the parking lot; Ceratosaurus, Ankylosaurus, Deinonycchus, Parasaurolophus.

"At some point, Lisa was thinking of getting animatronic ones in here, you know, so they'd move around," said Sherwood, as they walked past the models. "But she didn't think she could maintain them through the winter. That was before the amusement park over by the highway went up."

"I wish I knew what to do with this place," replied Benjamin.

"Well, that's what I wanted to talk you about," said the lawyer, as they left the gate. "Some of the guys I fish with in Florida deal in property. I was thinking I could float it to them while I'm down there, see what they think. Some of them got real weird taste in things, so this might be right up their alley. I know one guy just bought an old haunted mansion on an island somewhere in Maine. Says he's going to run luxury tours out there, put people up to commune with the spirits or whatever. Anyway, it seems to me this place isn't any weirder that that. So, if you want, I'll give it a try."

"Sure," said Benjamin, as they arrived at Sherwood's truck. "Do that."

"Fine, I'll do what I can to get the paperwork untangled in the meantime," said the lawyer, heaving himself into the cab and starting the engine. "What I would recommend for now is maybe rolling up your sleeves over the next week, and patching the place up a little. Nothing major. But those cabins could use a fresh coat of paint, pool could use a scrub, volcano needs a new light bulb, things like that."

"Why?"

"Well, we can sure try to sell it as is, but there's a little something called curb appeal, and I think you could significantly raise your asking price with a little work. Nothing too drastic, but it seems to me some cosmetic changes would go a long way, I think."

"How am I supposed to pay for it?" asked Benjamin. "I'm unemployed."

"Lisa left something in the estate for upkeep," said Sherwood. "We can use that, I'm sure. If you need a vehicle, you can take my truck if you give me a ride to the airport tomorrow morning. Trust me, do a little tune up, send me some pictures, and I can probably get someone up here by the end of the week to look the place over."

"That's a long way from where we started out. You made it sound like this place was unsellable."

"You mean back when you sounded like an asshole over the phone?" asked the lawyer, firing up the engine, closing the door, but lowering the window to continue the conversation. "It seems like you got some nice people in your life. Marta, and . . . the kid?"

"Rudy."

"Right. This could be good for all of you, if we do it right. It's easier to leave a man with an anchor around his neck when you don't know his people. If you do the stuff I mentioned, I'll help you do this, no problem. See you tomorrow at nine."

With that, the lawyer sped away, spitting gravel across the half acre of empty parking lot until he reached the road, the vehicle swinging left, west, toward town. As he walked back through the gate, Benjamin wondering what Marta would think of Sherwood's plan, but he didn't have the chance to ask her until much later in the evening, after they had gotten dinner in town, settled Rudy into a spare room in the farmhouse and settled themselves in the master bedroom, the place where Aunt Lisa had once slept. The house was less of a disaster area now. Most of the half-done renovations Benjamin remembered from his visit long ago had been completed. There were no holes in the floor, missing doors, pink insulation fluffing from between exposed studs. The entire place appeared to have been finished just in time for Aunt Lisa not to enjoy it; the toilet in the upstairs bathroom still had a price tag.

Benjamin lay in bed watching Marta undress beside the window across the room, the portside of her body glazed in cool bluish moonlight. Had Aunt Lisa stood there like that once as well? He couldn't remember; the past seemed to be suddenly overfamiliar, too close and too alive to be trusted completely, even here, in a garden of extinction. But he knew he'd been in this same position before, in the same bed with a pillow under his back, and his shoulders and neck resting against the wall, the sheetrock cooling the new sunburn he'd given himself after spending most of day five at the Valley beside the pool, awaiting the appearance of the black-haired girl in the russet bikini. She'd gone on a daytrip somewhere with her parents, and didn't appear until dinnertime, eating hamburgers and waffle fries with them in the Tar Pit Café. Benjamin lingered at a table by himself across the dining room, attempting eye contact while his body temperature ran hot and cold, and he fought the impulse to remove his shirt, which felt like a cilice against his dry, pebbled skin. His mind was hamstrung between the urge to vomit and the need to sleep. Usually he told his mother when he felt sick and she took him to the clinic to get checked out. But his mother was far away, and wouldn't be able to do anything even if Benjamin could reach her, except possibly foreshorten the newfound independence he was trying to make the most of by a few days. So after barely finishing his dinner, he went to see Aunt Lisa, who diagnosed him with mild sun poisoning, something she'd seen and experienced many times during her travels. She put him to bed in the room he now shared with Marta, so she could keep an eye on him, she said, draped a cool cloth over his forehead, and fired up the A/C unit in the window, which blew out all the fuses in the house. Aunt Lisa didn't have any replacements on hand, and it was too late to drive into town to get more, so he'd spent the night in her dark bedroom, watching a candle waver on the nightstand, sweating and shivering, passing in and out of febrile sleep. Occasionally, Benjamin awoke to light footsteps knocking down the hall, and her hand rising out of the darkness to cup his forehead, the rest of her in shadow, like the neck of the Diplodocus breaking the surface of the swimming pool beside cabin five.

Had that been all? This is what he couldn't be sure about. He seemed to recall the points of her body, elbows and knees, depressing the mattress during the night, the awareness of her beside him in bed, the cello-like rise and fall of her body turned away from him, outlined then by moonlight spilling through the curtains drawn against the window where Marta stood undressed now, halved by the same moonlight, as his neck and shoulders lay flat and cool against the wall behind the bed, once again. The overlay was imperfect enough to prevent Benjamin from feeling actively haunted by his own past, but not so imperfect that this didn't continue to seem like a possibility if he stuck around the Valley long enough.

How many cabins do I need to repaint around here before I stop feeling like my mental age is in retrograde? he wondered as Marta left the cleavage of natural light at the window and settled against him beneath the sheets. It seemed like it was time to either have sex or assess the day. Rudy was downstairs instead of next door. They had no reason to be quiet. Still, Benjamin decided to play it safe by mentioning Sherwood's idea.

"He said he was going to talk to you about that," said Martha, slipping her thigh over his. "I think it's a good idea."

"Wait. He talked to you first?"

"Sherwood just said he thought he could unload this place a little easier if he got someone to do some work on it. Painting and cutting the grass, whatever else. I told him you could probably handle that."

"Where was I when this was happening?" asked Benjamin, a little surprised to find plans already laid for him, and a little disappointed to see they already appeared to be in motion.

"Over by the cabins," replied Marta, leveraging herself atop him, her mouth dewy against his ear. "Peeking in the windows or something. I don't know what you were doing."

"I don't want to be here by myself."

"You won't be," said Marta, hunching above him for a moment as she maneuvered their parts into accord. "I have to go back to work, but Rudy's going to stay with you, and help out."

"Help out," echoed Benjamin.

"I'm glad you're okay with this," Marta continued, her voice acquiring a shaggy quality as she exerted herself above him in the dark. "I don't like him being alone all day, Ben, you know that. And he likes it here. The lake and the malls and all that. And he saw a skatepark in town when we were driving in. School starts in two weeks. I'll come down and pick you guys up a few days before. Now, will you fuck me already? I feel like I'm doing all the work here."

"Oh, sure, you got it," said Benjamin, heaving to; meanwhile, his mind remained on other things. What was he going to do with Rudy for the next week and a half? He knew the boy could entertain himself. He was more worried about the fact that Marta's son hadn't taken his supervision seriously in the first place, and any inroads he might have made in that direction were likely obliterated when they got stoned together last week. It wasn't that he couldn't imagine what Rudy thought of him; he could very easily imagine it. Marta's son had never called him a motherfucker, probably because he didn't need to. It was implicit in every interaction they had, a silent howl in the wilderness of their trustless coexistence.

It was also hard for Benjamin to envision a worse place to be stuck with someone who didn't respect him than Aunt Lisa's dinosaur compound, where every bit of prehistoric kitsch reminded him of what it felt like to be Rudy's age. Marta probably didn't realize that going back to New York by herself meant she was essentially leaving two fifteen-year-olds to look after each other.

But how could she not see that? wondered Benjamin, as her indistinct shape moved against him in the darkness of Aunt Lisa's bedroom, a woman he loved, yes, but also another, it seemed, there now: the revenant form of a woman he might have loved hanging somewhere nearby, adrift in the same darkness now as then, overseeing what remained of the man she had tried to make of him. And as he came, it was hard to avoid thinking about the morning after his fever broke. He woke up alone, naked, in the same bedroom, a little sticky, with no memory of having undressed himself. A note from Aunt Lisa fluttered beneath a glass of water on the nightstand, warning him to stay out of the sun. He still felt vaguely sick, but suspected the worst was over with. Looking back on it, Benjamin realized he had been right and wrong about that.

When Benjamin returned to the Valley the following morning after driving Sherwood to the airport in Glens Falls, a battered white Subaru was parked beside the fence, and a reedy man in a sport coat seemed to be awaiting him at the gate. He introduced himself as Orville Weller; from the Georgian, apparently.

"The what?" asked Benjamin, trying unsuccessfully to shift the paint cans he held from one hand to other so he could return Orville's handshake. The lawyer had been out shopping for the park the day before, and the back of his truck was full of painting supplies, stacks of shingles, power tools; Benjamin had no idea what to do with most of this crap, but had decided the first step in figuring that out was probably unloading it. Orville waited, his open palm hovering between them at around waist-level, not offering to help. Benjamin finally just gave up and dumped the cans on the ground, but Orville's hand had withdrawn into the pocket of his sport coat by then. It reappeared a moment later bearing a business card Benjamin accepted and returned without reading.

"The Lake Georgian. I write for them," specified Orville, glancing down at the paint cans beside Benjamin's feet. "Doing some remodeling?"

"I hope so," replied Benjamin, searching for something wooden to knock on, and giving the reporter a good looking-over while he was at it. Orville was about his age, maybe a little older; taller, meatless, with a kind of gallows bird look about him. A scavenger, at any rate, Benjamin decided, recollecting the paint cans in a way he hoped would signal to the reporter that there was plenty of work to be done, and he should be on his way, but adding, out of curiosity: "I'm not exactly clear on why you're here."

"He wants to come inside," supplemented Rudy through one of the ticket windows behind them; Orville and the boy had apparently been talking before Benjamin arrived. "I told him the owner wasn't here and he had to wait or come back."

"He did say that," said Orville, as if conceding something triv-ial, and almost, but not quite, winking in Rudy's direction for Benjamin's benefit. The reporter seemed to have mistaken him for the boy's father, and appeared to think complementing his son's pluck or vigilance or whatever in turning him away from the gate might end up getting him through it. "I decided to wait, as you can see."

"Well, we're closed, as you can see," replied Benjamin, who thought the whole song and dance was a little creepy and a back-door way to do things. "Come back when we're open for busi-ness and you'll have the run of the place."

"When will that be?"

"I don't know. Maybe never."

"But you're the owner now, correct?" asked Orville, crisply, like fire snapping.

"Nominally," replied Benjamin.

"You're Ben, right?" said Orville, appearing to enjoy the ex-pression of minor alarm this produced in Benjamin. "Please, don't be shocked; I didn't mean to put you on edge. I do my research, and this is a small community. Word gets around about things. We figured someone would be stepping in to handle the Valley when Lisa passed; my sincere condolences by the way. She was a very dear lady. Very dear. The point is, you're new here, and you should think of me as a way to introduce yourself to the people who live here. The Georgian has been a voice in Lake George practically since the area was settled. The townspeople trust what we write. All I'm looking to do here is get the mea-sure of what you're plans are for the place, because the people I write for would like to know. It's kind of a local landmark. I re-member coming here when I was a kid to swim in the pool, play some golf, have a burger; they had great burgers. I think we're all hoping to see it open again, or at least hoping it won't be sold off for the land. Anyway, a little tour, and maybe an interview, just a few questions, would go a long way toward putting everybody in town at ease. Plus, nobody's been inside the place for almost ten years now. Just a look at the property would get in above the fold. I can see you're busy, and all I'm asking is half an hour, a few questions, a couple photos, maybe you and your son in front of one of the big lizards. I can have a photographer over here in ten minutes."

"They're not lizards," said Benjamin.

"Pardon me?"

"Dinosaurs are not lizards. They're reptiles, but they're more closely related to birds and crocodiles than anything else. In fact, they have their own class; Archosauromorpha, I believe. Did you know that?"

"No, I didn't," said Orville, wearily. "But it's not the kind of thing everyone knows, is it?"

"No, it isn't," agreed Benjamin. "But it would be if you spent any time here as a kid. There were exhibits on that all over the place when it was open. Lisa even did little talks about the difference between dinosaurs and lizards during dinner once a week. How they became birds; it was one of her favorite topics. People used to come in from town to hear her. You don't remember any of this, do you?"

"I was mostly here for the burgers and mini-golf."

"I don't believe you, Orville. You were never here. You're a liar."

"Well, does it really matter either way? I'm trying to help you! And your family over there!" said Orville, jerking his thumb over his shoulder, toward Rudy, still framed in the ticket window, looking astonished by the whole thing. "Can't you understand that? You want to make this dump a viable attraction again, then let's put it back on the map. It seems like you really love the place and want to preserve it, so why don't you just do the right thing, and let me in to have a look around, ask a couple questions, take a couple photos, and we'll call it a day."

"Actually, I'm looking to unload it the first chance I get," replied Benjamin, signaling for Rudy to open the gate. "Your paper has someone who handles real estate listings?"

"Sure we do."

"Then send them over," said Benjamin, as the gate creaked open. "You can come along, but you have to wait outside."

"I'm a respected figure in this community," replied Orville, his sport coat billowing like a muleta in the moist wind rippling out of the woodland abutting the parking lot; the green silk lining was looking a little careworn. "No one treats me like this around here."

"I know it's a little late in the season, but there's probably still plenty of hands to kiss over at the Diamond Point yacht club," said Benjamin, as the gate closed over him. "You want to come inside my dinosaur park, learn to do your research."

"I do do my research!" shouted Orville through the fence, as Rudy and Benjamin divided up the paint cans on the other side, and crunched along the gravel path toward the cabins. "You want a for instance? What you said about those cops in New York? It's a matter of public record now! How about if that was the story? Big City Cop-Hater Seeks Shelter Upstate. Front page, in this town, believe me. I can make that happen for you! I know all the members of the developmental review board! They can tie you and your fucking lizards up in red tape until you both go extinct! Think about it, you smug bastard!"

"Sounds like you're making friends again," said Rudy, as he and Benjamin set the paint cans down beside the swimming pool.

"I promise it won't affect you," said Benjamin.

"You said that last time. I had to handle myself at school because of it."

"As I recall, you got to spend your suspension at home with me and that girl from Canarsie. I can't remember her name. The squealer."

"It wasn't something I was proud of," said Rudy; Benjamin suddenly realized they'd stumbled into serious territory together, and he wasn't sure how to find his way out.

"Then why did you do it?" he asked.

"You're not my dad," said Rudy. He sounded more carefully than usual. "But you're with my mom, and it's been like that for a while. So, the way I see it, you're part of our house, and if someone has something they want to say about you, then they're talking about how I live, because you're who I live with. Does that make sense?"

"No. You broke the guy's collarbone in two places, and his nose. That's a lot to prove a point, in my opinion."

"No one said anything about you after though. So I took care of it."

"They probably did. You just weren't there to hear it, because you were suspended."

"Maybe. But no one said it to me. They learned not to after that."

"I want to say I'm grateful, Rudy," said Benjamin, popping the top off a can, and stirring the paint with a dipstick, feeling a little like one himself. "But I'm hoping to get to a point where you expect more of me than that."

"You didn't say I wasn't your kid," replied Rudy, looking at him. "To the reporter, I mean. He said it like two or three times, and you didn't set him straight. You did with the dinosaur thing, but not that."

"Why does it matter? It's all science anyway, Rudy."

"I just thought you would."

"You're probably a little too smart for anyone to seriously mistake me for your father," said Benjamin. "I love your mom a lot though. You know that, right?"

"Sure," said Rudy, tilting his head in the direction of the parking area, where the sound of a starter rolling over and failing to catch had replaced Orville bellowing at the gate. "Sounds like your friend might need some help."

The reporter was in the driver's seat of his Subaru, resting his head against the steering wheel when Benjamin tapped on the window. Orville rolled it down without saying anything, looking mostly at home with the kind of defeat that speaks for itself, a position Benjamin had wound up in enough times to be able to recognize it pretty easily in someone else.

"You got cables?" he asked.

"Sure," said Orville. "In the trunk."

"Sorry you couldn't leave the way you probably wanted to."

"My cellphone's dead, and I can't charge it without the battery, so it looks like you're the only help I have."

"Glad to do it. I'd prefer to help you on your way than have you hanging around out here all morning."

"It's my fault. Need to replace it, the battery, I mean. Working for the paper doesn't quite add up to what I thought it would when I was in college."

"I'll buy you a new one when I sell this place if you keep the boy out of it."

"I don't see how I can do that if I'm writing about you."

"Then write about something else."

"Like what? Do you think I'd come all the way down here if I had something better to do? The season's almost over, so the best I can expect from here until next June is maybe some local falling out of a deer stand, or an Anne Taylor Loft going in over by the interstate. If I'm real lucky, there might be another Sasquatch sighting in Whitehall, but frankly I'd be shocked if my editor ran another story on it. I need this more than you don't need it."

"You're right."

"I'm what?" said Orville, agog. It didn't seem to be the sort of thing he was used to hearing from people.

"Give us the weekend to get the place spruced up," continued Benjamin. "Monday morning should be fine to come by. You're writing about the Valley, and what it meant to Lisa. I don't want my name in it or any mention of the kid."

"What about pictures?"

"Take as many as you want. Just none of us."

"Can I say you're selling it?"

"Up to you. It doesn't matter to me. If you think the good people of Lake George have a right to know, go ahead."

"I don't think anyone even remembers it's here," said Orville, stepping out of the car to raise the hood. "I've honestly never been further than the parking lot. We used to bring girls down here in high school after it was closed up."

"Put that in your article maybe."

"Thanks for doing this. And listen, I'm sorry for what I said about the thing in New York. I read through everything when I was looking you up, and it seems pretty obvious to me you got a raw deal out of it. Seemed like the whole thing became about what you said about it instead of what actually happened. Shooting at a kid like that; you'd think people would be more upset."

"I don't want anything about that in your article."

"You got it," said Orville, crossing around the side of the car to get the jumper cables out of the trunk. "You can see a draft before it goes to press. I'll try to write something Lisa would've liked."

"Just write whatever you need to write to get yourself a new battery so we don't have to do this again on Monday," said Benjamin, walking over to fire up Sherwood's truck. They jumped the Subaru within a couple tries, and he and Orville managed to complete the handshake they'd been working towards most of the morning. Benjamin watched him pull out, in more or less the same place he'd stood just after dawn, watching Marta depart for New York in the rental car. He was a little embarrassed about how cruel he'd been to the reporter, and wished she was still nearby to contextualize this for him; doing it on his own had a plangent ring to it. He remembered a picture he'd seen in a magazine: a village somewhere in South America flooded to build a dam. All that remained was the church, or the steeple really, piercing the surface of the lake that had absorbed the village. When Benjamin tried to place his baggage from the shooting in the proper context without Marta around, he always imagined himself as the bell in that steeple, ringing loud and clear across the deserted surface of the lake.

She never told him it wasn't his fault, only that he'd been treated unfairly. This seemed true when he looked over the facts of the matter: Lawrence had eloped from the group home in the mid-afternoon while Benjamin was on shift, so he and another staff member, Manuel, went looking for him. It wasn't the first time this had happened. Benjamin and Manuel were certain Lawrence hadn't gone far. He turned up a few blocks away, barefoot on the corner of a residential street with the group home's television remote in his hand. When a car drove by, Lawrence aimed it at the vehicle with a kind of spastic flourish. Benjamin never found out who called the police, but they showed up shortly after he and Manuel. Benjamin remembered an NYPD cruiser blocking the middle of the street, doors thrown open, two officers with their guns out, yelling for everyone to get on the ground. Benjamin also remembered wondering if this order included him as shots were fired, five of them. Three went nowhere, one hit Manuel in the center of the hand he'd raised to forestall the officers. The last one hit Lawrence in the shoulder.

Oddly enough, the sound of the remote clattering to the sidewalk was the clearest recollection Benjamin had of the afternoon. An ambulance was called, and the three of them waited for it to arrive, handcuffed on the curb. Manuel was in too much pain to explain things to the officers, and he gave up trying to after a while. They were eventually released when the ambulance arrived. Benjamin rode with Manuel and Lawrence to the ER, yet again, until someone sent by the Achieve Network showed up to relieve him. Then he went home, and explained it all to Marta, who'd already seen a cellphone video a bystander had shot on the evening news. Apparently, someone in the neighborhood made a call; a black man in his twenties waving what looked like a gun at cars driving by. A mistake had been made; that seemed to explain it. Benjamin spent the rest of the evening watching himself on the television in Marta's apartment, begging the officers not to shoot, trying to explain what was going on without breaching confidentiality, and finally placing himself between Lawrence and the cruiser when the shooting started. One of the bullets flew right past Benjamin's stomach. He hadn't realized it at the time, but he could see it in the video, a riffle in the frame, tunneling toward him.

Thinking about it now as he stroked at cabin five with a paintbrush, Benjamin remembered that Manuel was the person who'd asked him the question about what kind of animal he was. It was the day before the shooting. Something with wings. That was what he should have said. It was better than a ghost. But

Manuel quit right after it happened, and Benjamin hadn't seen him since they'd shared an ambulance. Not that changing his answer would have mattered then or that it mattered now. But it was nice to finally have come up with something better, in case anyone asked him again.

Benjamin went back to work sooner than he should have. He'd been debriefed by the Achieve Network's HR rep, told not to talk to reporters, and cleared for takeoff, so to speak. But later on, Benjamin and Marta ended up agreeing that he probably needed more time to process his feelings about everything, feelings no one, aside from her and the reporter from the Daily News who appeared past the fence at the group home a day or two after he returned to work, had really asked him about. The reporter wanted to know what Benjamin thought should happen to the two officers involved in the shooting; a loaded question, he realized too late. Benjamin had been reading Nietzsche in the porch swing for most of the afternoon, trying to keep his mind off things. Marta laughed when he mentioned this detail, a little hopelessly, since she also knew what it probably led to: Benjamin telling the reporter he thought the two cops involved should have their hands cut off and hung around their necks and be marched through Time's Square.

Benjamin's quote made the front page, beside a not very flattering photograph of him the reporter had taken, and generated the kind of sensational publicity a non-profit usually appreciates. But the Achieve Network cut him loose a week later, citing general malfeasance or breach of contract or something, and he walked home across the Brooklyn Bridge in a snowstorm, tears freezing against his cheeks, melting into the couch cushions later that evening when laid with his head in Marta's lap, reciting everything.

But it hadn't been all bad, had it? He'd been invited to appear on one or two television panels to discuss police brutality, and even collected a decent speaking fee for doing a half-assed commencement address at a small liberal arts degree farm in the Berkshires. But mostly, it seemed like the city just shouted at him. Along with fire fighters, police were essentially minor league saints in post-9/11 New York City, and advocating their mutilation, even offhandedly, made you a kind of de facto terrorist. It was the sort of lesson Benjamin never would have learned without subjecting himself to its blunt end, and when he finally understood what he'd done to himself, it was four months later, a beautiful spring day in Brooklyn, and he was watching a potential employer study him across a desk like a sideshow fixture, his resume between them, unread. It's hard to imagine what you're doing here; that was what the guy said, and Benjamin took it to heart, ushering in his period of pretend job interviews, or days spent wearing his only suit and hiding in the stacks of the local branch of the public library, waiting for the day to end.

The upshot was that he got a lot of reading done, though he couldn't remember what he'd read anymore, so the possibility that he'd improved himself in any measurable way during this period had a mythological quality to it, something only worth being proud of if you could set aside the facts of the matter. Benjamin decided he was probably depressed, and reading to pass the time rather than out of love, so it wasn't surprising that nothing stuck with him, except something he'd come across about ornamental hermits. These were men hired during the 18th and 19th centuries to inhabit the vast gardens of aristocrats as a kind of eccentric curiosity. They received room and board, sometimes a stipend for their trouble; duties were confined to occasional question and answer sessions with guests, or dispensing wise council when the moment called for it.

44

At the time, this sounded like the ideal job for Benjamin, but Marta hadn't really agreed when he'd shared the idea with her later that day. He ended up wishing he'd scrolled back his excitement about it a little bit after noticing her reaction, and spent the rest of the week tapping away at a library computer, trying to comb together a body of research to get her as excited about his newfound career goal as he was. But no one appeared to be in the market for an ornamental hermit nowadays. The nearest analogue was an opening somewhere in the Midwest for a human scarecrow, a job Benjamin, who liked birds and didn't want to frighten them, could never see himself enjoying.

So the project withered on the vine without ever dropping to the ground, or so he'd thought, until he and Rudy had dressed up a couple the cabins with a fresh coat of paint and repaired to the farmhouse porch for lunch; tuna fish sandwiches, dill pickles, seltzer water, nothing fancy. But the gate in the bamboo fence stood open, providing an unbroken view of the property without any real sense of its limits, and suddenly, the dream Benjamin had imagined for himself many months earlier in the library seemed within reach.

This may be the closest I will ever come to pastoral functionlessness, he thought, or realized. Either way, the result was the same: he was grateful to be where he was, a sensation he only realized he had been missing out on after it dropped into place, like one of the pinballs rolling into the shooting lane on Dino Madness in the defunct arcade abutting the Tar Pit Café. Aunt Lisa knew it was Benjamin's favorite, and unlocked it for him whenever he came to visit the Valley, so he could play without paying, though she hadn't done it during the last time, his final stay there. Benjamin hadn't noticed until now.

Benjamin and Rudy put in a couple more hours scraping and painting the cabins before calling it day. It was midafternoon, a few hours before dinnertime, and Rudy asked if Benjamin could give him a lift to the skate park so he could roll around a bit, and try a few things. Benjamin still had to find a new bulb for the volcano at the hardware store in town, so it worked out. They got high in Sherwood's truck in the rec field parking lot with John Parr on the radio.

"You broke the boy in me, but you won't break the man," sung Benjamin, watching a team of teenage girls poke around a coppice of trees near the truck for a soccer ball gone astray as he tapped out a joint in the half-empty beer can bedewing his groin and passed it along to Marta's son. This seemed age-appropriate to him, something that was always under discussion when he worked at the group home. He knew Marta wouldn't agree, but there was a certain unrealism in her love for her son. Benjamin would have felt worse about projecting such a poor example of himself for Rudy to follow if he thought the boy had any real stake in being like him in the near or remote future. There was something Benjamin admired about the way Rudy didn't admire him; it allowed them to have a good time together when Marta wasn't around, and didn't prevent her son from being excited when Benjamin suggested they grab a pizza at a place up the road after he finished up in town, and Rudy finished up at the skate park. That was when the joint came out, already rolled, otherwise unbidden. A nice gesture, and one that left Benjamin feeling like he was probably off the hook responsibility-wise, since he hadn't asked Rudy to get him high, and it was essentially a gesture of gratitude, one that should probably be nurtured in a young person. It was the kind of thing Marta was always trying to root out and encourage in her son.

Benjamin watched the boy cross the soccer field toward the parabola of a skateboard ramp on the opposite side. A few of the girls looking for the ball popped their heads above the tall grass, watching him like deer. This made Benjamin proud in a second-hand way. He knew he had nothing do with Rudy's handsomeness, aside from being its keeper for the time being, but it was nice to turn the boy loose and see what happened, something he felt good about being part of.

"I'll be where the eagle's flying higher and higher," he sung to himself, as the song closed, and he jerked the truck toward the main road with one hand, trying to sweep the ashes from the mouth of his beer can with the other.

The hardware store turned out to be a bad idea. The clerk was patient enough with him, but Benjamin was way too high to clearly explain what he needed; a big light bulb for a small volcano wasn't cutting it. He'd also slammed on the brakes on the way over to avoid a woodchuck making its mind up in the middle of the road, and dumped half a beer down his shirtfront. The stain it left behind was roughly the shape of Lake George, and appeared to be giving people the wrong idea. Even so, the clerk had lined up a couple possibilities on the counter for him to choose from, a gesture that seemed thoughtful to Benjamin, even if it was meant to get him out of the store faster. He ended up buying everything so the clerk wouldn't feel bad, and charging it to an account Sherwood had set up under his name. A fleet of houseflies descended from the rafters and began orbiting Benjamin's head while he waited for the manager or owner or whoever he was to approve the transaction over the phone; the clerk clearly wasn't taking any chances. Benjamin tried to smile at him in a way that said he understood how he must look, beer-stained, pink-eyed as a lab rat, flies on his face, and that the clerk could take all the time needed to make sure the book didn't match the cover. But one of the errant bugs landed on his bottom lip, so the smile didn't turn out to be much of departure from what came before.

Still, Benjamin got what he came for, or some variant of it at least. Twenty minutes later, he was back at the rec field, watching Rudy from a set of bleachers abutting the skate park, sipping a third or fourth beer out of a paper coffee cup he'd found under the seat in Sherwood's truck. It was turning into a beautiful night, all rising mountains and falling leaves, with a pretty good breeze sweeping out of the trees from the direction of the lake. The skateboarders stood out like young ravens at dusk, hopping from place to place, making a racket, establishing a sort of hier-archy in the twilight.

It looked about right from where Benjamin sat, and reminded him of the last time he'd been here. It was also the last time he'd seen Stephen, the summer before the last summer, when he hadn't seen him at all. Aunt Lisa's son had tried a few things on Benjamin's board. He hadn't brought his own, or maybe he didn't even have one anymore. Stephen didn't seem into it anyway. He kept dipping out of the park every quarter hour or so to answer calls or texts, eventually disappearing entirely, wandering off toward the empty baseball field with his phone clamped to his jaw like he was nurs-ing a wound, speaking in a low rumble like the distant sweep of traffic on the interstate over the hill. Benjamin watched him go, wondering what had changed. He and Stephen had always had a good time together, he thought. Summertime at the Valley meant skateboarding, listening to punk rock, watching girls by the pool, maybe stealing a bottle of whiskey or something from the Tar Pit Café and playing pinball or a half-cocked game of mini-golf after their parents and all the other guests were in bed.

But at the airport in Albany the day before, Benjamin wouldn't have recognized Stephen if Aunt Lisa hadn't hugged him first outside the arrivals gate. He'd grown six inches since last summer, and packed on maybe twenty pounds of muscle, well on his way to being a great big thunder god of a man one day, and looking overall like one of the Lacrosse captains Benjamin went to school with, guys who were always burning out of the student parking lot, or hoisting squealing girls over their heads, or calling him a faggot in the cafeteria. Stephen was like a one-man wedding of everything Benjamin had trained himself to mistrust about guys his own age, even down to the topsiders sans socks, the popped frill on a pastel polo shirt, or the weirdly inclement odor of body spray socking in the backseat of the Aunt Lisa's Volvo as she piloted them all back to the Valley. Benjamin associated the scent her son gave off with being outnumbered or otherwise at risk of some low-grade intramural assault, the kind of day-to-day bad feeling he would have to return to when school started in two weeks, but had expected Stephen's company to be a reprieve from, in the meanwhile. Still, Benjamin wondered if he wasn't about to get a head start on the academic year as he watched his friend in the rearview mirror, sleeping off the flight from Santiago or Sao Paolo or wherever; even then, he didn't know where Stephen had come from, only that it seemed to have made him into a kind of chimera. Benjamin had heard travel supposedly broadened a person's horizons; did it also narrow those of the people who'd stayed behind?

It was a question he never really answered, but he felt like he saw the tail end of it the following evening, watching Stephen cross the baseball diamond with his phone pressed to his cheek, a guy who had bigger things going on than whatever regressive amusement Benjamin represented: skateboarding, dinosaurs, punk rock, other things people grew out of. Benjamin didn't have a cell phone, and didn't know who he would call if he did, so he ended up hovering around a water fountain by the parking lot, pretending to drink from it while examining his reflection in the window of someone's pickup, seeking out a hint of whatever was now different between him and the Stephen in himself. He saw nothing new. Bleached hair, dog chain necklace fastened with a drugstore lock, ratty black jeans upheld by a studded belt, sleeveless black Discharge t-shirt. An unremarkable little dissident, as Benjamin saw it, the opposite of whatever had stepped off the plane the day before in Albany, wearing Stephen's skin. Maybe it wasn't what changed, Benjamin thought, looking himself over. But that I haven't.

The gloominess of this conclusion seemed to somehow support its accuracy. The rest of the week limped along in agreement. Benjamin and Stephen were bunked up together in cabin five, coming and going like roommates for the most part. Stephen had friends in the area for the summer, people with boats and houses on the lake, so he wasn't at the Valley most nights. Benjamin had the cabin to himself, though he hadn't mentally budgeted for so much privacy, and had no idea what to do with it except drink too much free soda from the bar, watch something on cable, or read one of the bulging, oversexed, ultraviolent fantasy novels he'd only brought to the Valley to pass the time getting there from Vermont. Stephen often wouldn't show up from his nights out until midday and would usually go right back to bed when he got in, so Benjamin ended up spending a lot of time with his parents.

His mother and father passed their nights at the farmhouse with Aunt Lisa, and their days antiquing and hiking around the Adirondacks while she managed the park. Benjamin didn't know anything about antiques and felt out of place trudging up a mountain in his antisocial getup beside platoons of suntanned, white-socked day hikers in nylon baseball caps, and t-shirts advertising some sort of physical activity in support of a worthy cause; walking for lupus, running for diabetes, biking for cures of all kinds. But he loved his parents, and liked spending time with them, though he'd perhaps never been as grateful for their company as he was then, stumping along in combat boots and jingling chains after his father up Prospect Mountain, or providing an opinion of a pen and ink drawing his mother had dug out of a junk shop occupying one corner of Fort Ann's single intersection, above which a red light never stopped blinking. His mother always did this; asked him what he thought of something he knew absolutely nothing about, and took seriously whatever he said, as if Benjamin were her consultant rather than her son. He didn't mind, and always just said he liked whatever it was, since he figured his mother was showing him whatever it was because she did. In this case, the pen and ink was clumsy and overpriced, an action scene of Georgie, Lake George's titular monster and subsequent hoax from 1904, rearing out of the water, set in a crumbling frame.

A present for Aunt Lisa, his mother explained; something to thank her for hosting them all at the Valley. It looked kind of like a dinosaur, didn't it? Benjamin agreed, giving his valueless approval of the gift. Are you having a good time? his mother asked then. He said he was. It's nice to see so much of you, she continued, gently. Your dad and I weren't expecting it.

By this time, Benjamin had a sense of what his mother wanted to know. Are you having a good time with Stephen? she asked, doubling down on her first question. Yes, answered Benjamin automatically, not understanding why he felt like he needed to defend an idea of things they both knew was untrue, going ahead with it anyway, adding as a kind of supplement: I think he's just busy.

His mother nodded instead of replying; Benjamin realized later on, that evening to be exact, that this hanging phrase of his had probably told her everything she needed to know, and alerted Aunt Lisa to her son's apparent business. It was the only explanation for Stephen inviting him up to the lake to visit some of his friends when Benjamin returned from Fort Ann with his parents. It was around 5PM; Stephen was freshly showered, eating a hamburger on the edge of his unmade bed, watching a soft-core porno he'd ordered on the television; two stage lesbians entwined in a Jacuzzi, steam cloaking the salient features for the most part, palm trees nodding overhead. I'm going out tonight, he said, without looking away from the movie, speaking through a bolus of meat and bread. You can come if you want.

Benjamin was mortified, and wanted to say no, but figured it would only get Stephen in trouble with Aunt Lisa if he did. He was briefly furious with his mother for whatever she'd done to bring this about, and then furious with himself in turn for not swearing her to secrecy, though he knew it wouldn't have done any good. Sure, he said; that sounds cool, trying for the second time that day to uphold an idealized version of events in order to avoid dealing with how they made him feel. It almost went without saying that things between Benjamin and Stephen would never be the same after this.

You can borrow some of my clothes, said Stephen, finishing his meal and looking Benjamin over, eyeing the dog chain necklace fastened with the lock, in particular. You have a key to that?

Benjamin didn't. Stephen lent him a sporty pair of athletic shorts, some night-going sandals, a short-sleeve button-down shirt patterned with anchors. It made Benjamin feel like he was being costumed for a game of croquet, but he didn't say anything. He knew Stephen was trying to make him invisible, and might have been insulted by that if he didn't also want to be invisible, at the moment, or look a little less like whatever Aunt Lisa's son had fled from at the skate park a few days earlier. At the time, Benjamin still didn't know what this was. But later on, he decided it was probably a figment of the same historicity their parents were seeking to preserve at all costs by cajoling Stephen into dragging him along, a benign ghost of summer's past flapping featherlessly around the dinosaur park, and out, over the surrounding area, the way Benjamin would one day imagine Aunt Lisa's spirit rising at dusk, and flying out above the water, toward the coral bolt of a sunset withdrawing behind the mountains.

A guy in a newish Saab picked them up outside the gate a few hours later, and drove like a maniac all the way to one of the numberless modular summer palaces jutting out into the lake; a veldt-like floor plan, rising white walls, large picture windows aimed like a battery toward the water, a living room with a seventy-inch television where a hearth would normally be, a kitchen with decorative baskets hung from the beams, bathrooms with toilets serving up dishes of potpourri on the tank.

The driver's name was Dan, or maybe Darren; Benjamin didn't quite catch it when Stephen said hello, and hadn't been introduced, his presence apparently having been explained or justified in advance. The house belonged to Dan or Darren's parents, at any rate, who were off in Saratoga for some reason. No one knew when they'd be back, or seemed worried about it. Darren or Dan led them through the house and out the other side, across a patio where a fire groaned in a hibachi and a hot tub murmured, to a dock with a motorboat moored beside it. Small waves clucked against the hull. Three girls and two guys were already aboard, drinking beers, smoking cigarettes, maybe some pot, Benjamin wasn't sure. The girls were pretty and the guys all uniformly intimidating, struck in the same mold as Stephen, who knew them all from one of the boarding schools his father shuffled him between, and settled down athwart two of the girls. It was the last empty seat, and no one made room for Benjamin as he climbed aboard, so he ended up standing in the middle of everything with people talking past or through him, gripping part of the awning overhead like he was commuting by train the way he would years later in New York. Darren or Dan set sail, spinning the boat around the cove the way he'd nearly spun the Saab off the road driving up to the house. No one seemed worried about this either, so Benjamin tried to relax and drink the beer he'd taken out of the cooler at his feet, and appeared to be tending, since he was the only one standing up, and whenever someone wanted another beer, they tapped his leg. But it kept frothing over his chin whenever Dan or Darren hit a wave, and he eventually gave up until they returned to shore after about an hour, and settled in around the fire on the patio. At some point, the girls stripped down to bikinis and repaired to the hot tub, bobbing in the steam like ingredients in a soup, or the women Benjamin had watched earlier on the television screen in cabin five.

Something about all this felt inevitable to him. Maybe it was the kind of thing he'd been rocketing toward since meeting Stephen at the airport, the sense of nascent disharmony between them only shaking itself off then, not yet fully arisen and striding around the house and surrounding property like it owned the place as it was now, with Benjamin seated in the midst of its chosen route dressed like someone who would normally kick his ass. Realizing he'd lost a friend didn't hurt as much as realizing what he'd done to himself by trying not to, clinging to what had already come and gone the way his parents and Aunt Lisa did to get Stephen to drag him up here, so Benjamin could see the ruins for himself.

Benjamin considered calling his father to come pick him up, but he didn't know where the house was, and also didn't know how he could find out without alerting Stephen and his retinue to what he was up to, thereby making himself out to be the one kid who has to leave early from the slumber party due to home-sickness. He appeared to be trapped, a state of affairs Benjamin had trouble raging against, since both he and the adults in his life were equally responsible for it, a feeling he would also revisit the following summer. It was a relief when the people around him began pairing off or otherwise recusing themselves, one by one, or two by two, until it was only he and Stephen around the hibachi, the fire untended, fading to coals. This was when the story about the German backpacker and the hand job came out, apropos of nothing at the time it seemed, although looking back on it, Benjamin wondered if Stephen might have been a little embarrassed to be the only person left standing beside him, and needing something to show that even though they'd found them-selves in the same place, they were still leagues distant where it mattered. Or maybe Stephen was just drunk, because Benjamin was pretty drunk, and couldn't justify the state he was in without seeking out parity.

Sorry if this wasn't so much fun for you, said Stephen, sud-denly, after Benjamin finished congratulating him on the overseas hand job. They're kind of hard people to get to know. We proba-bly wouldn't hang out if it wasn't for school.

Benjamin shrugged, but didn't say anything. Stephen cupped an awkward hand over his knee, a gesture that remained a little too long to be strictly affirmative. Sorry, he said again, the hand sliding up a few inches. Benjamin still didn't say anything. He only moved out of reach when Stephen slid his hand a little underneath the cuff of the athletic shorts he'd lent him, and not because he was afraid of what might happen, but because he had to throw up, which he did in a bed of rosebushes under the dining room window. There were a lot of scenes missing after that. He threw up again somewhere inside, at least once, maybe twice, and awoke around 6:30AM the next morning, facing Stephen across a sea-like expanse of beige carpet in the living room, where they'd come to rest on opposing couches like Roman noblemen after a nightlong orgy. The TV was on for some reason, playing the weather channel. Lake George had a day of rain and scattered thunder showers ahead of it. Benjamin got up, drank water, and went back to bed, awaking four hours later as the promised thunder shook the house, and Dan or Darren shook Stephen awake. His parents were on their way back from Saratoga. Everyone had to leave now.

They got back to the Valley around noon. Stephen went off to bed down in cabin five, and Benjamin made the poor choice to have brunch with his parents, both of whom could see immediately that he was hung over. No more nights out with Stephen, said his father, sliding his plate of half-eaten scrambled eggs toward Benjamin. Eat that. You'll feel better. Can we agree now it was mistake?

Benjamin wasn't sure what his father meant by this, but his mother seemed to silently agree to it in a way that left him wondering whether the whole thing hadn't been an elaborate plot on her part, something designed to show him what he wasn't missing out on by getting him orchestra seats to it. He never figured it out, but it didn't end up mattering. Stephen was absent from cabin five for the next few days, up at Dan or Darren's house maybe, and ended up leaving the Valley abruptly to attend an orientation at a Quaker boarding school somewhere in Lebanon. His father was working in Beirut, and had managed to get Stephen a spot at the last minute. Benjamin hadn't gone with him to the airport. They shook hands at dawn outside the gate, and that was it. The possibility of them never seeing each other again hadn't been explicit, but Benjamin had the feeling that was how things might end up. It was hard to feel sad about it when they were both so clearly relieved.

But looking back over the way things turned out the following summer at the Valley, the relief Benjamin felt then seemed un-earned, and almost luxurious now, watching Rudy finally land a trick over the pyramid as the sun finally fell below the line of the Adirondacks. A few boards slapped a few copings, and a half-as-sed cheer erupted from the skaters standing. That appeared to be the note Rudy had been awaiting to end things on. He looked around, found Benjamin on the bleachers, and walked over with his board under his arm, proud of himself and unable to hide it.

"You don't usually see people roll out from those that way," said Benjamin, trying to stand up without wavering in the breeze like scarecrow. "You surprised me."

"You saw it," said Rudy; it wasn't a question.

"It looked like the exact right trick when you did it that way."

"I guess I just saw it like that. Before I even tried it, I mean. Like I saw myself doing it, and I knew I could, so that was how it had to be."

"You make any friends?" asked Benjamin, eyeing the retreat-ing shadows of the other skateboarders. They walked in almost single file across the rec field, like soldiers or pilgrims.

"The local guys are fine," said Rudy. "They just kind of do what the local guys everywhere do. They got three to four decent tricks on everything that's there, enough to string a couple good lines together, maybe a minute of footage if they push it and repeat a few things. But nobody's trying anything you don't see in a shop video. And everyone's chewing on someone else's style the whole time, but you get that in the city, too. I guess it's good. Means there's room for originality. You want to get that pizza or what?"

Benjamin managed to get them both from the rec field to the restaurant before realizing he was a little too drunk to drive back to the Valley, so it seemed like the right time to suggest a driving lesson for Rudy. He did fine. Benjamin offered minimal instruction, reminding him to use his indicators once or twice, but that was it. He realized as the unlit sign for the park hove into view that he had no idea whether the boy even had a learner's permit or whatever was required for this kind of thing in New York State. Benjamin was still using a Vermont license with his parent's address on it himself, something his mother renewed for him every few years since the paperwork was sent to her house. Added to this was the somewhat overworked paper cup of beer growing flat in the console and the weed stench coming from somewhere, maybe Rudy's pocket. And the car wasn't even theirs. Benjamin had no idea where to find the registration if they got pulled over. The list of things he probably shouldn't share with Marta had definitely sprouted a footnote, but her son seemed happy. That had to be what counted. Benjamin wondered if maybe this was because outlawry came naturally to Rudy, but figured a stepfather, even a part-timer as he seemed to be, probably didn't need to know everything. That was Marta's job. But if she saw him and Rudy in that moment, without any context to spoil it, Benjamin thought she would be happy, too.

So maybe he was on the right track, even if it swung through the Valley, a place he didn't expect to return to after his parents picked him up from it fifteen years ago, with Stephen nowhere to be found, and his mother sweating out a nasty hangover in the Tar Pit Café, her hands throttling a cup of coffee with a grease slick at the center, and a plate of pecked-at scrambled eggs cooling by her elbow. Benjamin sat near at hand; too close, he realized now. They had just returned from spending the weekend up the road in Saratoga. The motel they'd stayed in was having an issue with the plumbing, and the shower hadn't been working when they awoke that morning, so they probably looked a little dirty on top of everything else. A few pleasantries flew high and wide before Benjamin's mother asked where Stephen was. Whatever Aunt Lisa's answer had been caused the two women to withdraw. He remained behind at the table, his father studying him across it with what Benjamin realized years later was probably the first man-to-man look of his life. He saw pride in it, yes, the unforced sort that usually showed up after a job well done, mowing the lawn in under an hour, or getting all the wood stacked for winter, or returning home with a report card good enough to earn him a trip to the bookstore, an arrangement leftover from elementary school and still honored by his parents. But there was something else there, something Benjamin couldn't identify at the time; it reminded him of the conspiratorial aspect his father took on whenever he rented an R-rated action movie for them to watch, something he only did when Benjamin's mother was out of the house for the evening. Don't tell your mother. That was always the warning then, and it seemed to be resurfacing now, in a slightly altered form that his father was either unwilling or unable to spell out for him. Don't tell your mother. Benjamin knew his father wanted him to keep something from her, but there didn't seem to be much left to lie to his mother about after she returned from wherever she'd gone with Aunt Lisa, holding his luggage in one hand, his skateboard in the other, and said they were leaving.

Benjamin was relaxed on the ride back to Vermont. He knew he'd done something wrong, but was also aware that it was something his parents wouldn't punish him for, so he settled into reading *Martin the Warrior* in the backseat and watching the up-state scenery roll along. The antique shops and produce stands rose and fell away past the window, and the billboards dropped out of sight once they crossed the state border into Rutland with the day already drawing to a close, the sunlight fading against red industrial brick in the city center and brushstrokes of leaves beginning to turn here and there on the mountain road outside town. Summer was already beginning to end.

Meanwhile, priorities were being reshuffled up front. His father had adopted the role of scoutmaster from the driver's seat, suggesting things they could all agree on that had nothing to do with what everyone was actually thinking about; picking up pizza and a movie when they got close to home, taking it easy for the night, that kind of thing. He was already thinking several moves ahead. That left Benjamin's mother to shoulder the remainder of the guilt he knew his parents probably shared unequally over the whole thing, since it had been her idea to lodge him at the Valley while they were in Cape Cod. His father had been fine leaving Benjamin at the house in Vermont for two weeks by himself, and so had Benjamin. For a brief moment, he had seen himself read-ing fantasy novels all day and watching violent movies all night, eating frozen pizza and drinking soda until he exploded. But his mother was afraid he might get lonely. She knew her son too well to worry about him getting into anything more aberrant; or thought she did, until about an hour ago.

Over the next few weeks, Benjamin had several appointments. His mother took him to the doctor for what Benjamin realized later was probably a social disease screening, and several meetings with a therapist, Dr. Rumney. Benjamin ended up wanting to be like him, not because there was anything particularly great about the guy, but because his job seemed so easy. Dr. Rumney mostly just asked Benjamin what he wanted to talk about. Benjamin didn't want to talk about anything with a stranger but also didn't want to be impolite. He'd recently started listening to Joy Division and New Order, so they talked about that. Benjamin ended up with a couple good listening recommendations from Dr. Rumney, the Smiths, the Blue Nile, the Chameleons, music he still carried with him, but nothing in the way of whatever his mother expected him to get out of it. She ended the sessions after she overheard Tears for Fears playing in his bedroom, music she knew for once, and asked about it over dinner. Benjamin was entirely too candid, and that was it for Dr. Rumney. His mother settled into asking him if he was okay once a day, than once or twice a week, and then once a month, and then not at all after hearing him produce the same bland answer over and over again, like one of the tour guides the Valley employed during high season: he was fine.

Benjamin assumed if either of his parents wanted him to expand on his fineness, they wouldn't have sent him to Dr. Rumney. He didn't know what Aunt Lisa said to his mother when they'd left the Tar Pit Café together, but he was grateful to her for saving him the trouble of having to clarify anything on his own. The closest he ever came to a direct discussion of what happened with her was his father asking a general question about protection one Sunday afternoon on the way back from the video store. Did Benjamin use it? He lied and said he did, figuring his mother probably had something to do with this line of inquiry, and he didn't want to say anything that would make her feel bad, or worry about him. It was the first time in his life he could remember needing to be okay so the people around him would be too.

But was Benjamin actually okay? Over the next few months, the question would gradually lose its meaning without ever ceasing to stump him, just as it had the first time his mother asked shortly after arriving home in Vermont from the Valley. They were still in the driveway, unloading his stuff from the car. As she handed him his skateboard from the trunk, Benjamin realized he hadn't stepped on it once in two weeks, unusual for him. But he said he was fine anyway, though the truth, at that point, was that he badly missed Aunt Lisa. He hadn't changed his clothes from Saratoga, and something of her still clung to him, he was sure of that; a residuum of the motel maybe, green bottles arrayed on the nightstand with the security light from the parking area shining through them, staleness of the sheets thrown open, sweat that made them stick to his skin, her breath on his chest, awake with wine, a filament of empurpled saliva uniting his left nipple with her bottom lip before she combed it away. So maybe he wasn't categorically okay, or at least not in the opinion of someone like Dr. Rumney, who would appear later. But for now, he missed her. It didn't help that Benjamin had unearthed a perfectly preserved Deinonychus claw in his luggage, something she'd probably slipped in before his mother hauled it away. His favorite archosauromorph; Aunt Lisa knew that. He set it on his bed beside the jaws of a young shark his parents had brought back from Cape Cod, wondering why the adults in his life thought he craved the kind of fierceness these items represented. That territory seemed more appropriate to someone like Stephen, whose absence Benjamin later suspected his mother might have been trying offset by leaving him unbagged, though it never came to anything. Benjamin wondered what he was still doing weighing himself against Aunt Lisa's son. He wasn't certain he'd surpassed Stephen in terms of experience, but after last summer at the Valley, he hadn't been sure the two of them even wanted the same things, and this summer at the Valley without him seemed to prove it.

Still, as he looked over the fossils on his mattress, Benjamin mistook the bathos he felt at suddenly being supervised again for being in love, something he couldn't imagine Stephen getting caught up in. Over the next week, he tried calling Aunt Lisa a few times on the number for the Valley, the only one he had, reaching the guy at the ticketing counter, and leaving a message with him. His mother found out about this somehow, and warned him off long distance calls, saying they were expensive without saying why, though she really didn't need to. It was enough for Benjamin to see how much it cost his mother to even bring it up. Her guilt was suddenly a vector, something he had to work around if there would be peace not so much in the Valley, as after it. So he gave up, as he imagined Stephen would never do, and watched what he'd mistaken for love fade to dimness by the time school began, like the pulse of a lantern dropped down a well, remembering Aunt Lisa the way he had no other choice to; as someone he wouldn't see again, but recalled fondly. Benjamin had killed her off in his memory long before she died in Glens Falls Hospital.

Benjamin still had the claw somewhere; you don't get rid of something like that. He'd shown it to Nicole, the girl he'd started dating around Thanksgiving. She liked New Order and fantasy novels, but was indifferent to the claw. Benjamin figured that was okay. His parents liked her, and it seemed like they were all returning to the same page after what happened over the summer. He got his driver's license just before Christmas, essentially the same license he had now, and took Nicole wherever she wanted to go until she got hers a few months later, and dumped him for an older dropout who sang in a hardcore band. Seeing Nicole around town with him had stung enough to keep Benjamin at home, until his parent's sympathy for the situation grew equally intolerable and drove him out of the house.

He'd eventually ended up sitting in his car outside the gates to the Valley. They were closed, and the parking lot was empty. It was a cold day in early April. Aunt Lisa hadn't opened for the season yet. Drifts of peppery snow hugged the fence. A couple of ravens danced along the wire against an overcast sky. The sign had dropped a few letters. Whatever Benjamin recalled as festive and exciting about the place appeared to be in abeyance, or maybe it never existed to begin with. Either way, he was glad he'd realized the mistake he'd made without having to go farther than the gate. He didn't want to see what was on the other side.

Benjamin and Rudy worked through the weekend sprucing up the park. By the time Orville showed up on Monday morning, Benjamin thought things looked pretty good. The grass and weeds were cut back, the cabins had a fresh coat of pastel paint, and the models and caricatures dotting the grounds had been polished and straightened. As luck would have it, one of the bulbs the clerk at the hardware store sold Benjamin fit just right, so even the volcano was in working order.

"Looks good at night," he explained to Orville as they stood before the plaster eminence, dormant now in the daylight. "Really ties the place together. Too bad you can't see that at the moment."

"It might be nice to have a couple shots after dark," replied the reporter, pocketing a notepad he'd been scratching on for the past forty minutes or so as Benjamin steered him and the photographer he'd brought along around the park. The photographer was an intern from the local high school named Vincent. "Vince and I have to drive down to Whitehall in a few hours, so maybe we can swing by on the way back, if it isn't any trouble. Probably be around seven or eight."

"Should be dark enough by then."

"We can go through the pictures later too, if you have time. I'll have the text for you tomorrow."

"You get your car fixed yet?"

"Made an appointment with the garage. My editor threw me an advance on this story and the thing I'm doing later today, so that should cover it."

"If you end up a little short, let me know," said Benjamin as Rudy and Vincent appeared around the corner of the Bone House, the two of them tilted over the screen on the latter's camera; sliding through skateboard footage as they walked, no doubt about it. When Orville showed up, the boys recognized each other from the park a few nights back, and Rudy had volunteered to show Vincent around. Though it had nothing to do with him directly, this kind of happy coincidence springing up nearby made Benjamin think the curse he'd imposed on himself by returning to the Valley might finally be lifting. The thought comforted him until he remembered he still owned the place.

"That's generous," said Orville, prodding at the volcano like a piece of supermarket fruit. "And it feels a little like a bribe. We already have an agreement."

"Maybe I just need to make sure you're happy with your end of it, Orville."

"I just wanted something to keep the lights on, so we're good on my end," said Orville as Rudy and Vincent joined them beside the volcano. "I don't know what you're trying to protect around here, Ben, but you don't have to protect it from me."

"You mind if we take Rudy along on this Whitehall thing?" Vincent asked Orville before Benjamin could say anything else.

"No," said Orville. "Ben?"

"I don't know," said Benjamin. "What Whitehall thing?"

"A couple of guys looking for a sasquatch," said Rudy. His voice was full of mean-spirited excitement. "I guess they're filming a pilot or something. Vincent and Orville are going along to cover it for the paper."

"I thought your editor wasn't running that kind of thing anymore," said Benjamin to Orville, stalling until he could form a serious opinion about the mostly unserious matters suddenly at hand.

"He probably wouldn't if these Whitehall clowns didn't already have a deal with some basic cable network," said Orville. "Basically, it's a walk through the woods in the dark with three to four overweight pseudo-scientists waiting for twigs to snap without an obvious explanation. My editor thinks it'll be good publicity for the paper."

"You want to be part of this?" Benjamin asked Rudy. The boy just smiled. That pretty much locked it up. "Well, have fun. Try not to laugh at the folly of others. It only makes it stronger."

"We'll get him home before nine," Vincent assured Benjamin, who didn't really need assurance. Orville nodded in agreement. "You can come too, if you want."

"I don't think so," said Benjamin.

"Why not?" asked Rudy. "What else are you doing?"

"I was thinking I might take a ride up to Saratoga this afternoon," replied Benjamin, adding: "To visit an old college friend."

"I thought you went to college somewhere else," said Rudy.

"I did, Rudy. Sometimes people move away."

The reply came out a little more caustically than Benjamin meant it to, and pretty well paved over whatever was left of Rudy's interest in him coming along to Whitehall to knock around the woods with the sasquatch hunters or however they styled themselves. Benjamin felt bad about walling the boy off like that, but didn't see another way it could be. He'd been turning over the idea of visiting the motel in Saratoga for days, not seeing much of a chance of it happening with Rudy around all the time, until just now. Benjamin wasn't the best with mental notes, but he made one anyway, something vague about making all this up to the boy before his mother returned to stick her oar in at the end of the week. Maybe more driving lessons; Rudy seemed to like that. Or maybe they could rent a boat and some fishing gear, spend the day trying to yank something out of the lake. Or why not just sit the boy down with a bottle of whiskey in the Tar Pit Café and tell him stories about when Benjamin was his age, and waltzing across the Rubicon Aunt Lisa still seemed to represent, even in memoriam? That might brighten the corners a little. Maybe even throw a cape on old stepdad. Who could say? At the very least, it would clear Benjamin's head out, and give the boy an example of something to work toward, or flee from, depending on how badly he wanted a role model. But even if they didn't want role models, kids these days needed direction, didn't they? Marta would know. There had to be a way for Benjamin to run it by her without the question turning into a discussion about him getting a job. Maybe he could figure that out on the way to Saratoga.

"I have to run back to the office for a few hours, get started on this," said Orville, gesturing at the generality of park surrounding them, and then, to Rudy: "We can drop by to get you a little later."

"I got my board in the car," said Vincent, also to Rudy. "If you want to get in a session at the park for a few hours, Orville could probably pick us up there when he's ready to head over to Whitehall."

"Sure I can," said Orville, sounding ready to get going, edging his way toward the parking lot. Vincent fell into step behind him, and Rudy went off to the farmhouse to retrieve his skateboard. Benjamin was suddenly alone with himself for the first time all week, with nothing standing between him and the uninterrupted retracement of a time in his life when he could sit back and live through other people's mistakes without worrying about making any of his own. It had been a privilege; he saw that now. But the taste and shape of it hung near enough at hand to seem still catchable, a high-water mark burnt into the wall of his memory that he still stacked everything against without expecting to ever rise above it. So, he was content, because he had once been happy, even if his happiness only appeared in retrospect. Love had nothing to do with it; or it did, but only in its procrustean form, a feeling that spurred him beyond love, toward the reverence he now felt for his own past, the way he felt grateful for the memory of the sound of Aunt Lisa's mouth leaving his lips, or the vertebral swoop of her naked back sinking below the water of the lake, or the way she'd driven them like a maniac to Saratoga in a light summer dress worn without anything beneath it, the stubble under her arms, the sweat beading at her throat, the hem inching up over her thighs whenever she shifted in the driver's seat of her station wagon. She had Warren Zevon on the radio, singing a song about werewolves. It was possibly the best summer of Benjamin's life, and he had somehow found it all again; not the actuality, of course, but the way it made him feel to be there as a witness, near her, aging what felt like a thousand years in a single day. He knew he would never be happy like that again, tunneling beside her toward a cave-in, but it made him happy to know that his happiness was limited and therefore containable, a specimen he could look over all he wanted without it ever changing into anything else, joy trapped in ice like the bugs caught in amber on display in the Bone House. He was barely able to conceal the skip in his step as he walked off toward the Tar Pit Café to grab enough beer for the drive to Saratoga.

Benjamin got a little mixed up after exiting I-87 and was too afraid of getting caught with an open container in a car that didn't belong to him to ask someone who looked like they knew their way around for directions. So, he drove around for a while hoping something would look familiar, seeing all the things he hadn't seen when Aunt Lisa brought him here. Most of the town, as it turned out. It had pretty much been a straight shot from the interstate to the motel. How did she present the idea? It hadn't come on all at once. She'd mentioned needing to go up to Saratoga for some reason a few days before they left, once or twice, maybe sounding the shallows of his juvenile intuition, hoping he understood what was at stake, and might invite himself along without her having to do what she'd eventually done: more or less ordering him to join her, saying she wanted his company.

The day was already edging toward evening by the time Benjamin found a municipal kiosk with a map of the town on the edge of Skidmore's campus. Term hadn't begun, but a few early bird freshmen were already there, unloading boxes and dorm furniture from the back of the family station wagon with the help of one or both parents, maybe a sibling here or there, sometimes even a soon to be jettisoned boy or girlfriend held over from high school. Everyone looked eager to be done with what they were doing, and a little lost, which made Benjamin feel right at home as he looked over the map, unsure of how it was supposed to help people who didn't know where they were going. A red dot with a red circle engirdling it showed him where he was; maybe that was a good start. But he wondered why they didn't have one that showed you where you wanted to be. That would be nice, wouldn't it? Just a little dot to help you along, and instead of 'you are here' why not have it say 'you were here'? For how are we to know where we are if we don't know where we've been?

Benjamin noticed his inner voice had taken on a homiletic quality. It made him wonder if dipping into Rudy's stash before he left the Valley was such a good idea. Interstate driving made Benjamin nervous; he had no idea how to speed things up to get them over with, so the only choice seemed to be slowing everything down to a manageable crawl. He couldn't remember the drive from Lake George, and assumed it had been a success, even though he was now too high to find his way to the motel in any normal fashion, and would probably have to keep driving around until something looked familiar, or a bell rung in his head. What else could he do? Until today, the clearest image he had of Saratoga was of the interior of the motel room Aunt Lisa had rented for them; grey walls, green sheets, yellow curtains, a bathroom tiled in salmon, the thump of the ceiling fan, the smell a place takes on after smoking has been outlawed there.

There had to be something else he remembered, and there was, but it didn't appear until Benjamin was back in the car, heading through downtown Saratoga in the opposite direction he'd come, past businesses that probably couldn't survive anywhere else, hatters and saddlers, that kind of thing, even a Vespa dealership. This last one triggered something; Benjamin remembered sitting in the passenger seat of Aunt Lisa's Volvo, wondering the same thing he wondered now: why does a town that spends half the year snowed-in need a scooter store?

It wasn't much, but it was enough to keep Benjamin on course, and turned out to be all he needed. The motel popped up on the town's western outskirt, more or less as he remembered it: an acutely angled bank of double rooms, white with green trim, abutting a fabricator and a lesser golf course, almost hidden in a grove of willows beside the road. It was a weird place for a motel, not really near anything of special interest, and far enough outside town to seem like a sort of oasis. A small brook ran behind it, flowing out of sight; the roll of the water spilling into a culvert beneath the road reminded Benjamin of hearing a suggestion of it whenever Aunt Lisa threw on her dress and went out for a cigarette, the sound only reaching him in bed for the moment it took her to open and close the door to their room. Wind chimes chimed from somewhere inside the attached porch screening the office; he remembered that as well.

Benjamin kicked a couple of beer cans under the seat and got out of truck, trying to remember which room was theirs; there were eight, and he thought it might be the second or third in from the left, but he wasn't sure, so he loitered in the gravel outside windows, trying to get a look inside. But the yellow curtains were either drawn tight or pinned together within, and as he withdrew his cupped hands from the glass, he noticed a face scowling back at him above his left shoulder, an older man with a gray ponytail, patchy beard, sleeveless Judas Priest shirt, denim cutoffs.

"You a cop?" he asked as Benjamin turned around. It seemed like a weird question to lead with, but the guy presumably worked here, and probably knew his business.

"No, sir," he replied. "But I stayed here once. Had a good time."

"Glad you enjoyed your stay," said the guy as if he couldn't be less glad about anything; even though Benjamin had been at the motel before, he clearly wasn't a preferred customer just yet. "But I can't have you peeping in the windows. That kind of thing disturbs people."

"Who?" asked Benjamin, in earnest, glancing around. Sherwood's truck was the only vehicle in the lot.

"Me," replied the manager or keeper or whatever he was. "So unless you want a room, you should maybe go camp out in one of the mulch beds outside the Marriot if you want to look in people's windows."

"I just want to look inside. It shouldn't take more than an hour."

"Forty bucks."

"You're shitting me."

"I'm hoping that'll cover whatever you're planning on doing in there. Which one you want?"

"Second from the left," said Benjamin, a little defeated; he wasn't going to make the guy open and close every door in the place so he could hear what the brook sounded like from wherever the bed was in each room. He would never know which one it had been, so he might as well try and see. If it didn't feel right, maybe he could switch. "I'll get my wallet."

"I'll wait."

Benjamin crossed the parking lot to Sherwood's truck, and threw the door open hard enough to send a cascade of seven or eight empty beer cans clattering to the gravel. He combed them back into the cab, returning with his wallet, which he handed over to the innkeeper entire, as if it was something the guy had lost and Benjamin had found.

"I really just need to see your I.D. for now."

"Sure," said Benjamin, fishing around the folds for it.

"You just looking for a place to sleep it off?" the guy asked, his gaze ticking between Benjamin and the truck.

"More or less."

"You want to snooze in the truck, I won't bother you."

"I'd really prefer a room."

"Suit yourself," said the guy, producing a ring of keys from the rearmost pocket of his cutoffs, and popping open the door to the room Benjamin requested, number seven, as it turned out. "I'd rather have you in here than flying around on the road if you're doing it big like that."

"I didn't think it was all that unusual around here."

"It isn't. That's the point. Boy just got hit by someone doing what you're doing. I heard it over the scanner in the office."

"You have a scanner in the office?"

"Nice to know who's in the area when you have a place like this. Anyway, sad stuff. Pay on your way out."

Benjamin closed the door, and then opened it again almost immediately to go and get the rest of the beer and the pot out of the truck before he settled in. His phone glowed in the console; two missed calls from Orville. It was already dark out; the reporter probably wanted his pictures of the volcano. Rudy could let him in, if he needed to. Benjamin wasn't in any shape to rush back. He made another unreliable mental note to call the boy, let him know he would be back late, before turning his phone off, and returning to the room.

He laid himself out on the bed, above the covers with the lights off, a joint smoldering between his fingers, the beers arrayed on the nightstand like chess pieces. Aunt Lisa preferred wine. He should have picked some up. She'd forgotten it when they were here last, and had to leave to go buy a few bottles. He'd watched TV in bed, the local news, followed by a game show, waiting for her. He remembered she'd asked what he wanted for dinner, and he'd told her: pizza, almost a kind of reflex at that point in his life. That was how she came back, sweeping through the door of the motel room with the square box in one hand and wine bottle in the other, already open, a third empty, one of the thin straps on her dress descending the tanned shoulder it was meant to hang upon, her hair carelessly pinned back, wild and owlish. Why hadn't he gone with her? Because she hadn't asked him to. After the drive from Lake George, maybe she needed that moment to wait for something she already knew she had, the certain sweetness in having the thing you want trapped at the end of the line, awaiting you as well. They'd eaten the pizza in stages, he recalled, almost as if they were rationing it to keep up their strength. Later on, he'd peed sideways in the salmon tiled bathroom for the first time; finding out about his body and the weird things it could do. He looked over a wine stain in the shape of a mouth on his shoulder in the mirror above the sink, a stain that grew into a mighty bruise by the time he returned to Vermont. His shirt barely covered it, and the doctor his mother took him to glanced at the purple storm cloud beside his neck with a kind of admiration before drawing his blood. Had he ever been as proud of anything? Not nearly, as far as he could remember. The ceiling fan did as little then as it did now, throwing the humidity around the room. Benjamin removed his shirt, then his pants, then everything else; the sheets felt more or less the same against his skin. He tried to recall if Aunt Lisa drew her dress over her head or released the single strap still in place and let it fall to the ground after putting the pizza and the wine down on the dresser, beside the TV playing Jeopardy, the answers divorced from the questions finding him from moment to moment until the show ended. What is the Moa? Who is Abbot H. Thayer? What are corvids? The category must have been about birds. He'd been watching the show and answering out loud, the way he did with his father. Maybe that was why he couldn't remember how the dress came off. She was just suddenly naked, her body blocking Benjamin's view of Alex Trebek announcing a commercial break, the impact of it somewhat blunted after seeing her topless at the beach, but not old news by any stretch. She asked if he was okay, a question he would hear a lot in the weeks and months that followed. He said he was fine, as usual, striving to be agreeable. She crossed the carpet silently, and stood beside the bed, hand to hip, leg turned out a bit, wine bottle resting against a bare suntanned thigh. The fan cast her humidity toward him in regular sweeps of its blade; she froze like that for Benjamin he realized much later on. When he thought of that summer, this is what came rushing back first, not the moment it went wrong, not even close, but the moment when things began to recover from going wrong. Waking up beside her the next morning felt like the first day after an armistice; rebuilding was in the air. She had a headache from the wine, and no painkillers or anything, so Benjamin scooted out the door with a towel around his waist, got some ice from a machine athwart their door and the next one down, and wrapped it in a plastic bag and the same towel when he returned to the room, holding it against her head where it rested in the harbor of his armpit, the day beginning to smolder a little outside the window, the curtains flying out of the frame whenever the wind picked up, like the last feathers Icarus must have worn after plummeting to earth, still clinging to their wax embayment along his useless arms.

They weren't talking. They'd gotten a lot of that done the night before. I need this, she'd said, still standing beside the bed. I know, he'd lied, not knowing a damned thing about it, but this felt like the only agreeable response. I hope I don't look gross to you, too old, she said. I think you're beautiful, he replied, not lying this time. Despite the cigarettes and wine and whatever else of late, Aunt Lisa took care of herself. He was never awake to see her emerging through a postern in back of the park, fresh from running an old logging road behind the property, something she did every day, though not for the past two weeks. She ate a lot of food Benjamin considered boring; sheaves of greenery, like the stuff dangling out of the mouths of the larger herbivores mural-ized around the valley. What else? She swam in the lake most evenings May through October. He had no idea what she did when it got cold, but probably something; her long, thin muscles stood out in the dull light from the TV running through final Jeopardy, category: the history of aviation. Do you want to touch me? she asked then. He touched her instead of answering.

The next morning was unkind to Benjamin. He awoke around 5AM above the sheets, naked and sticky from the puddle of beer he'd passed out in, a stroke of luck as it turned out. His right hand rested in a burnt-out crater in the bedspread, about the size of the O in the sign back at the Valley with the remnant of his joint sat at the rough center like it had crash-landed there. This only appeared fortunate at first glance; after some thought, Benjamin decided it was more like breaking even, the more or less natural result of one bad habit climbing the coattails of an-other until both were pretty much neutralized. Still, as he got up to take a shower, images of himself returning to the park like an opera-less phantom sailed through his head, hiding his crisped face in a bag for the rest of his life, living off the kindness of Marta and the odd sideshow gig. Not hugely different from the way things were now.

Maybe everyone's just one accident away from things being exactly the same, he thought to himself as he flicked the light on in the bathroom, halogen on salmon, with a skunk stripe of greyish vomit adorning the wall of the shower stall. Apparently, he'd gotten up in the night; news to him. He ran the water for a while, but found the plumbing hadn't gotten much better since the last time he was here. Complaining about it seemed out of order after what he'd done to the bedspread. In any case, Rudy was probably wondering where he was, and he should be there, back at the Valley, when the boy got up.

The manager, as Benjamin had decided the guy must be, was up and around the office in the same getup as the day before, and didn't seem all that surprised about when his only tenant appeared with a folded-up room blanket in one hand and a credit card in the other.

"This needs to be washed," said Benjamin, setting the bedding on the counter between them, and then, rethinking it: "Or thrown out. I'll pay for whatever you decide."

"It got shit on it?" asked the manager; he seemed to be speaking from experience rather than meanness, just trying to cover all his bases.

"No. What? No, not at all. Just a large burn and some beer. But there is some throw-up in the shower, and I'm very sorry about that. I tried to clean it, but nothing much was coming out of the tap. I mean, your plumbing or whatever's not exactly robust."

"Robust?" said the manager, astonished.

"Right, I mean, I turned the nob, and got a dribble, but you can't seriously clean yourself up with that," said Benjamin, expanding on his point to encompass the mess he'd made: "Or anything else, for that matter."

"So you're saying the water pressure isn't strong enough to clean up your puke? Is that an official complaint?"

"No, I mean, yes, but just pointing out that I couldn't…"

"Well, sir, I'm sorry the facilities hereabouts were not up to your usual standard," interrupted the manager. "I'll kick it on up the ladder. Had we known you were coming around, we probably would've had a pressure washer standing by so you could swamp the place out after you finished up. Maybe call ahead next time. We'll really roll out the red carpet for you."

"Oh, fuck off," said Benjamin, brandishing his credit card, his patience gone. His head had started to pound with a kind of wicked cadence, and the rest of him wasn't feeling much better. "I'm a returning customer. You probably don't see too many around here by the look of things."

"You make any noteworthy messes the last time you stayed?"

"No. Well, maybe, but not the kind you need to worry about. In fact, I came here to think the whole thing over, see it again, I guess. I was only fifteen, so it was a while ago. I still feel bad about it though."

"The church where I go to meetings is probably good for a confession on a weekday if you want directions," replied the manager, plucking the credit card from Benjamin's hand like the last flower of the season. "Meanwhile, I'm charging you for the blanket, which you can take with you. We'll call it even on the puke mess, since I knew you were up to no good, but I let you stay anyway. That's sixteen and change plus forty for the room."

"Fine," said Benjamin, shocked to find the terms so reasonable. "Thanks. I honestly expected you to gut me a little more."

"I'd prefer to just eat the rest of the cost and have you out of here," replied the manager, swiping the card. "I'm supposed to be practicing forgiveness as part of my meetings. So I can forgive myself eventually or something. I guess that includes clowns like you."

"Why do you need to forgive yourself?" asked Benjamin, intrigued by the idea, wondering if there might be something about it he could drag back home with him, and maybe show off to Marta, a bit of souvenir wisdom cleaved from the natives.

"I got something that sticks around no matter what I do to shove it down, just things I look back on and know I won't ever get there again to say I'm sorry, or say I'm not sorry for how much I enjoyed myself. Not that it's any of your business, but I'm supposed to practice talking about it with people outside of meetings. It wasn't anything all that bad, just things I can't reverse on without sucking everything I've done since down with me."

"Like a toilet," said Benjamin, plumbing apparently still on his mind.

"You got it," said the manager, slapping the card on the counter, and poking the blanket off the desk with the blunt end of a golf pencil from the course next door. "I think I'm done practicing forgiveness and talking to strangers for the day. Whatever you need to relive from here on out, do it somewhere else. And take that with you."

Benjamin did as he was told, stuffing the blanket into to the cab of the pickup as he struck out for home, or the place that was standing in for it. It had been a good memorial, he decided. No dirt to throw or ashes to scatter, but he'd worked well enough with what he had on hand. Whether or not Aunt Lisa would be happy, Benjamin couldn't judge; but he thought she would understand. Cars ticked by on the interstate, barely bothering him.

He arrived at the Valley with dawn concluding above the mountains, and found Orville asleep behind the wheel of purple

Geo Metro in the parking lot. Benjamin knocked on the window to wake him up.

"Your Subaru finally go extinct?" he said jocularly.

"It's my editor's," said Orville, stepping out the car. "I had to borrow it."

Something dire and unpleasant in the reporter's face and voice set off a tinny alarm in Benjamin's already ringing head. Orville set his hands on Benjamin's shoulders, like he was a frame the reporter was trying to square, steadying him for whatever came next. It was the way Benjamin spoke to Lawrence when Lawrence was having a hard day, and reminded him of Marta in a crooked way, how they first met, all that. It moved him to ask about her. Orville said she was on her way; it took longer than it should have to contact her, and no one knew where Benjamin was, so they were operating with limited information and had done the best they could after it happened. What happened? Benjamin needed to be told again, but Orville said it might be better if the doctor explained it. By then, they were already on the way to Glens Falls, in Sherwood's truck since Orville's Subaru had proven unreliable, once again. Daryl Braithwaite sung about horses in the sky on the radio as camper parks and motorboat dealerships flew past the window, with dark and scrubby pine forest closing the gaps between settlements. Benjamin realized he was singing along and crying at the same time as Orville pulled into the parking lot for hospital customers; a new experience for the both them, it turned out.

Rudy probably wouldn't skateboard again; that was clear enough from the way the doctor looked at Benjamin when he asked. Time was overemphasized, or the need for it, at any rate. The boy's pelvis had been crushed, and a couple lower vertebrae. Hard to tell how that would turn out.

The truck had its hazard lights on, Orville said later, as they sat beside Rudy's berth in a not too bad room on the hospital's third floor. So, nobody paid too much attention to it when it came around the curve where his Subaru had died on the way back from the Sasquatch hunt. It had been uneventful, but the boys had a good time. They were somewhere between Whitehall and Fort Ann. Everyone was kicking around, trying to figure out what to do next when the truck flew into the back end of the Subaru on the shoulder, pinning Rudy in place. He was getting his backpack out of the trunk, and hadn't seen it coming.

It was a miracle the boy hadn't died, a nurse told Benjamin early on, while checking Rudy over. She'd also heard the driver had been drunk off his ass and was now in custody, so that was something.

"I know the arresting officers," Orville said when Benjamin asked him about it later that day, as they sat by the boy's bed, watching him breathe through a tube. "We went to high school together. Good enough guys. If you want to see her or anything before she gets arraigned, I could probably arrange that for you."

"Her?"

"The woman who owned the truck. She wasn't driving. Her kid was. She was passed out in the passenger seat. Barely even noticed when the kid slammed into us. A bottle of Smirnoff turned up when the police looked through everything. She said she was taking her son to do some back to school shopping at the outlets. That's about as much as anyone got out of her. They start up again at the end of the week. The schools, I mean."

"What happened to the kid?"

"I'm not sure. Probably protective custody. Mom's definitely going to jail, and it doesn't look like dad's in the picture. Seems like a nice kid though. Probably about Rudy's age. He said mom was giving him directions, telling him when to shift and stuff like that, but then she passed out; he flipped the emergency lights on, and was hunting around for the right gear when the truck came around the bend, not looking at the road. Anyway, if you have anything you want to say to her, let me know."

"Thanks, Orville. I think I'm going to pass," said Benjamin; he appreciated the gesture, but didn't know what to do with it. The boy's mother sounded like she probably had a miserable life before all this happened, and it was about to become even more miserable for her and her son. Benjamin didn't see what he could really add to that by shoehorning in his mostly guessable opinion on everything. Giving someone a piece of your mind always seemed like a great idea until you remembered how dumb indignation makes people sound and act, and how it all came back to the same basic problem of folks thinking the world was waiting to be saddled by them, and ridden off into a sunset where all their needs would be met unequivocally; how dare it spin on without them aboard?

Besides, Benjamin remembered wanting revenge after what happened to Lawrence and Manuel, and it took the taste for it out of his mouth. That hadn't landed him anywhere good, and had left a hole in his life large enough for the Valley to slide on in, creeping like a glacier through a trough of land until it was basically on top of him, blotting out everything else. If he'd had anything more important to do the day Sherwood called, he and Rudy would probably be back in New York right now, ignoring each other.

Instead, the boy's body was broken, crushed by another boy who might have been Benjamin fifteen years ago if Aunt Lisa's Volvo wasn't automatic, lying now in the same hospital he'd neglected to visit when she was dying in it, maybe in the same room for all he knew. Should he ask the nurse? Have the boy moved if the room he was now in turned out to be the place? The hospital must keep records of that kind of thing. Benjamin only believed in curses when they seemed to prove effective, and he was still deciding about this one. But he knew today was the second time he hadn't been here when he should have, and he didn't expect to ever forgive himself for that. But would Marta? That was a better question. They spoke briefly when she was just outside Albany, exchanged information and assurances, a dearth of the former adding to an abundance of the latter. She was a nurse, so she probably would know what to ask the doctor when she arrived within the next hour or so. Benjamin had only come up with the thing about whether Rudy would ever skateboard again, his first thought after seeing the boy as he was now, injured, graceless, his mother far away. The two of them stoned and mostly getting along, clattering around the park across the street from the apartment in New York would never happen again.

It made Benjamin wonder what he had done in a past life to end up back here in this one, a savagely self-centered question to ask, he realized, even if he'd been asking it of himself in one form or another for the past week; or maybe the past year, now that he thought about it. Vanity falls last and hardest; whatever remained of Benjamin's seemed to be rocking on its plinth, only toppling fully when Marta showed up around dinnertime, still in her work clothes, scrubs, looking right at home reading over her son's chart, speaking with the doctor when he appeared, putting everything in order for herself, as always, while Benjamin haunted the margin like a vulture, awaiting orders or consequences, whatever came his way first; consequences, as it turned out.

"Where were you?" she asked. They were outside, beneath the lee of the hospital's entrance, or the part of it set aside for smoking. Marta had quit long before Benjamin met her, while pregnant with Rudy. The cigarette she shared with him appeared to be the only thing she was enjoying, so Benjamin didn't mention it. "When I finally got a call, he'd already been here alone all night. They said no one could reach you, so no one knew to call me. Meanwhile, I'm at work, just working like on a normal day, while Rudy is here, by himself, probably wondering where the people who are supposed to care about him are. I just keep running over that, and it makes me want to scream at you, Ben."

"Orville was here."

"The creep in the blazer? Is that who you mean?"

"Right. Rudy was with him when it happened."

"Why was my son with this person instead of you? I'm still not clear on how that happened."

"They were going looking for a bigfoot in Whitehall. Or no, a sasquatch, pardon me; I think there's a difference. At any rate, a boy Rudy met at the skatepark was going along, too. I didn't have a reason to say no."

"Or go along yourself?"

"I guess I didn't see how it would make a difference, Marta."

"Because you would have been here when you should have been, dummy!" she said, not quite yelling yet, but gesturing as if she was. The filter flew from her fingers, vaulting out into parking lot, the lamps white above the cars at rest there, flooding the humid, windless night without displacing the low-frequency anxiety that hangs over places that never quite turn off, places where people are usually waiting for something; airports and hospitals, casinos and cruise ships. Marta flipped open her pack, almost empty, Benjamin noticed, and shook out another, adding: "Meaning: I would have been here when I should have been."

"I'm sorry I wasn't," he said, hoping the apology would hold its place long enough to keep him from saying anything worse, or more specifically true. Marta seemed to be angry at him for not having seen the future, or at least suspecting it of being up to no good, something that had never been a part of Benjamin's off-brand relationship with paranoia. But maybe that was how parents looked at whatever was up ahead; a series of threats to their children that were always clearly preventable after they'd flown past. Is this what his mother and father meant when they talked about learning experiences? It was a term he remembered well enough from the earlier years of his child- and young adulthood, though its usage had fallen off after the final summer at the Valley. That had probably been a learning experience for everyone involved in one way or another; Benjamin wondered if his parents had grieved in the same way then as Marta appeared to be grieving now; not for what had actually happened to him, or Rudy, but the many things they could have done to prevent it, whatever they'd learned to fear after it touched down.

Memory seems to be passive aggressive, overall, Benjamin noticed, as an ambulance flew past, bathing Marta in red, then blue, then red again, and then rose pink, as the vehicle docked somewhere behind them. She already looked furious, but the colored light made her seem like a cartoon character whose lividness mounts like mercury, from bottom to top, only to be disbursed in twinned plumes of steam from both ears, like the smoke now egressing her nostrils.

If only it were that easy, thought Benjamin, wondering if allowing Marta to offload most of the blame for the accident onto him would someone obviate her need to know where he exactly was while it was happening. Because she was vulnerable and would probably believe anything that came out of his mouth, he didn't want to lie to her now, and was hoping she wouldn't make him have to.

"I don't need you to be sorry," she said. "I need to know where you were."

"A motel. In Saratoga," said Benjamin; his hope from a moment ago actually seemed to invert. Only the truth remained, or the form of it he'd chosen to share. He didn't want to disappoint Marta ambiguously. "I was with someone there. I'm sorry."

"Who is she?"

"Someone I knew a while ago. We stayed there together before. I wanted to see if it was still the same."

"Was it?"

"I don't know. I was pretty drunk. That's why I didn't come back here until the morning."

"So why are you still here?"

"Because I love you," said Benjamin, noticing they were both crying a little. He wanted to be more specific, but knew that would probably make it worse. "And I care about Rudy."

Her cigarette hit his shirt in a scurry of sparks, like the tail end of a firework, the kind they shot off over the lake most nights during high summer. Benjamin found Orville sitting over an untouched cup of coffee in the hospital cafeteria, where he'd gone to give Marta time with her son, and had the reporter drive him back to the park in his editor's small purple car. Meanwhile, Sherwood had called four or five times. He was due at Floyd Bennet at 8AM. Benjamin knew he wouldn't be in any shape to meet the lawyer at the airport in the morning, but Orville said he would do it.

"Are you going to be okay tonight?" he asked Benjamin through the window, after watching him drop his keys four or five times outside the gate to the park. It sounded a little like the way his mother used to ask, expecting an answer that would set her mind at ease.

"I'm fine," said Benjamin, clinging to the libretto like a lifeboat. He got the gate open on the eighth try, but left his keys swinging in the lock. That was fine. There wasn't much to do. He went straight for the bar at the Tar Pit Café, not even bothering with lights, drinking straight from a bottle of gin in the dark, and listening to the same John Parr song on the jukebox until it drove him out the place, toward the farmhouse, her sanctum, a landmark he feared and loved in the same uneasy breath. On the way, he stopped off in the mini-golf shed for a putter, with some vague idea about smashing every window and wall in the house until it started to look the way he remembered it, but lost his nerve after caving in a panel in the dining room. With dramatic motions out, and Marta and Rudy gone, what was left? Only Aunt Lisa, he supposed, the tight corners of her body, the sweat pebbling her collarbone, the pulse ticking away in her armpit as she pinned her hair back before entering the water at the nude beach. He knew he didn't love her, because love went away; whatever he felt hadn't.

Benjamin awoke the next morning beneath the Allosaurus on the miniature golf course, thinking it had snowed during the night as he glanced around him, until he realized he was lying in a bed of plaster flakes thrown from the model looming overhead. The putter stuck out of the dinosaur's skull at an angle that read nine o'clock when faced straight on, and seemed to be pointing at Sherwood standing off to one side of the course, tanned the color of a breakfast cereal. Orville lurking nearby like a caddy. The toe of Sherwood's wingtip was pressing into the bottom of Benjamin's bare foot with a steady, almost clinical pressure.

"We should talk," said the lawyer, withdrawing his shoe when Benjamin opened his eyes.

"Maybe another time," he replied, not standing, but sitting up enough to rest his back against the flank of the dinosaur he'd partially destroyed during the night, its head and his poised for parallel extinction by the look and feel of things in daylight. "I'm not really feeling up to it."

"I imagine you're not. I heard what happened to the boy, and I'm sorry about that. But we should talk anyway. The reporter's got coffee on at the café. If you can't imagine drinking that, there's some ice water, too. Either way, we'll be down there when you're ready."

The lawyer and the reporter shoved off toward the cluster of buildings at the foot of the rise upholding the golf course. Benjamin stood up, hitting his head on the Allosaurus' underbelly, and stumbled after them, feeling a little like an avalanche when he hit the slope, his legs flapping underneath him. All the evidence at hand suggested it had been a shitty night, so Benjamin didn't expect what remained of the morning to radically diverge from this in any way. The only thing to do was get it over with.

"The good news is I found a buyer," said the lawyer when Benjamin fell into a chair across from him at a table in the café; the same table Benjamin and his father had shared while waiting for his mother to finish up with Aunt Lisa. Orville served coffee that neither of them drank while the same John Parr song played over the jukebox, unwilling to expire. "He's willing to go high on the place. Sees potential, I guess. At any rate, I need you to say yes, so we can move it along. I know you're hurting right now, but I think that makes what I said before about this being good for you and your people only more true. The boy needs care, and this could help with it."

"She doesn't want me to help," said Benjamin, dumping half a water glass down his shirt as he tried to sip it through a bridle of shaking hands. "That's all done. She doesn't want to see me."

"I'm sorry to hear that," said the lawyer. "Still, you said yourself you have no reason to hang around here."

"I'm thinking I might now. It might be the only place I have to go."

"You sell it, you create choices for yourself aside from that one."

"I think maybe it's where I'm supposed to be for a while."

"Orville," said Sherwood. The reporter appeared in the serving window as if summoned from a lamp. "Go out to my truck, if you don't mind. The papers are in a folder on the seat."

"I'm not signing anything until I meet whoever's interested," said Benjamin as Orville left the café. "If they don't keep it like it is now, I'll just have to remember it like it was. I've already forgotten so much. If I hadn't come back here, it would probably all be gone."

"Listen to me," said Sherwood, leaning in suddenly, no longer the bouncy, gnomish personality from a week ago, but a man reaching the end of the rope he'd allowed to trail in Benjamin's bullshit since then. "You're not going to meet them, because they don't want to meet you. This is business, not choice time. Orville will be back in a few minutes with what you need to sign. That's all the time you get to make a decision, as far as I'm concerned with the kid and his mom out of it."

"It's you, isn't it?" said Benjamin. "I'll sign whatever you want if you tell me why."

"You won't hear anything from me," said the lawyer. "But you weren't here to watch her die, so you have no call to pretend like what she left behind means more to you than it does to anyone else just because she left it to you. So you'll sign whatever I want because it's the right thing to do for her, especially since you can't seem to spend a night here without destroying something she cared about."

"You knew."

"We talked. She sought counsel afterward. Wouldn't you?"

"What did she look like? In Glens Falls, I mean."

"You want to know if she was thinking about you?" asked Sherwood, making little effort to conceal his disgust with the question, and maybe Benjamin in particular, as Orville reentered the café with the papers folioed under the sleeve of his sport coat. "Maybe you came up, but she had a lot else on her mind then. You will too, someday, I hope. And she looked beautiful, by the way. Like it was all happening overhead. When her boy came in from Bombay or Egypt or wherever to sit with her, you could see that was what she missed most. Not you. But I guess you were in there somewhere, because here we are, talking it through. Now sign the papers."

"Stephen was there?"

"Just sign," said Sherwood, sliding the folder toward Benjamin across the table. He obediently knotted his name beside each highlighted X, vaguely wishing for someone to announce the good news to, but knowing the one person he really wanted to share it with would have precluded the entire thing by being there to celebrate with him. Being thankful didn't quite cover it, so after Sherwood and Orville left, Benjamin went back to the room where he'd seen her body once rise and fall like a musical instrument, both in sound and shape, rebuilding the contour from memory as he fell in and out of sleep on the mattress, watching the rest of the day go by through the bedroom window where she may or may not have once stood in the moonlight; he still wasn't clear on that.

Rudy was able to do a little walking on his own by Thanksgiving, but he still needed Benjamin nearby to steady him if he got tired or his legs locked up. The pelvis was in good shape; everyone was still waiting to see about the vertebrae, but things were a little better than predicted, overall. A physical therapist, someone Marta knew, came by the apartment twice a week to put Rudy through the paces; it was ugly to watch, especially at first, so Benjamin usually left while it was going on. He'd wanted to be there, but he realized pretty quickly that the boy didn't want an audience for this part of his recovery. So he threw a leash on the dog, a wolfish brindle mutt he'd found at a shelter in Brooklyn and Marta had agreed would be a good thing for all of them, and took himself and the animal for a walk. After they'd returned to the city, having something they all could love without hesitation became important, and Marta didn't want another child.

The dog was older and good-natured, and gave Benjamin something to do when he wasn't looking after Rudy, or delivering the subscription newspapers that piled up on the stoop each morning. Whoever delivered them never got farther than the front door, so Benjamin had gotten into the habit of collecting these on his way inside the building after walking the dog in the morning, and cruising up and down the hallways, dropping the papers outside the right apartment. He'd been caught doing this once by an older Polish lady on the third floor, and was invited inside her abode to examine a troublesome light fixture after being mistaken for the superintendent, though he only realized it afterward. The lady fed the dog boiled cabbage out of a Tupperware container while Benjamin stood on a chair in her kitchen, tightening down a loose overhead bulb until it blinked on. It reminded him a little of the volcano at the Valley, the glow it had at night. Orville had never gotten a photo to go with his article, the text of which Benjamin had received and given his okay on without reading; that was the day before Marta showed up at the park. Sherwood was allowing Benjamin to remain there until all the paperwork went through, on the condition that he not destroy anything else; that seemed more than fair to Benjamin, though the temptation to smash all windows at the farmhouse was still there, so he'd dug around the place until he found an old sleeping bag, and set up camp in the Bone House, beneath a display of fossilized pelvises. He'd drink a couple beers and stare at them before going to sleep each night, thinking about Rudy, crushed in that way, wondering why he hadn't grown wings instead.

That was more or less how Marta found him the morning she came by. Benjamin hadn't locked the gate since Orville drove him back from the hospital; it was no mystery how she'd gotten in. Still, when Benjamin awoke in the mostly dark room and saw her figure seated on a bench beside the display case, he thought for a moment the ghost he'd been stalking since returning to the Valley was finally repaying his tenacity, or staying power, with a visit.

"I didn't think I would see you again," he said.

"I think you should stay with me," she said. "If you want to."

"Yes," he said. "I'd like that."

"I'm sorry I made you come back to this place," she said. "I didn't know what it meant to you. "

"I'm glad you did," he said. "I wouldn't know if I didn't."

Benjamin only realized he was speaking to Marta when she lit a cigarette, the flame drawing her face out of the darkness the way a single bright window seen from far off at night suggests a dwelling. He knew he'd just come far too close to something irrevocable, the final step backward into a footprint already filled by him long ago, when he'd turned his car away from the gate and drove back to Vermont instead of knocking to see who was home; it all rose for him now and scared him more than anything ever had before. In the next moment, he was out of the sleeping bag, naked and crying with his head against Marta's knees, apologizing like an open wound. She knitted her fingers in his hair, and told him he had nothing to be sorry about, like it was something they'd already discussed. That was when he knew she knew he'd lied to her about the other woman, but he wasn't sure how she knew until later on, when they were bypassing Albany, on the way back to the city. Rudy was in the backseat, blearily paging through a book of essays by Stephen Jay Gould, something the boy wouldn't have chosen for himself. Benjamin asked him where it came from; apparently, Sherwood brought it by the hospital during one of his visits. Benjamin didn't know what Sherwood told Marta, and was too afraid of finding out to ask; probably the same reason she never asked him what he had actually been up to at the motel in Saratoga. The silence between them on the subject was only rivaled in his memory by his parents' quietude after the last summer at the Valley. But in this way, he and Marta achieved peace. Benjamin hadn't decided whether to hate the lawyer for it or be grateful to him.

Between Rudy and the dog, Benjamin found most of his time accounted for. Otherwise, he listened to opera on the radio and went to the library whenever he could, though he rarely got anything for himself, and mostly brought back stuff he thought the boy might like. Benjamin hoped this might give them things to discuss other than skateboarding, still a sore topic; it worked maybe half the time. He'd had to help Rudy in the bathroom enough since the accident to leave their relationship relatively free of guile. But no girls stopped by to squeal through the wall, or ask where the bathroom was, and Benjamin felt bad about that. On the other hand, there was always pot, since it helped with Rudy's pain, and kept things light when they went on one of the walks the physical therapist recommended. He stayed close, even when the boy shook him off, trying not to talk to him the way he'd once spoken to Lawrence.

Things were not too different, overall, and mostly just slower. They got high and circled the park in the middle of the day like a retired couple, Benjamin keeping a hand on Rudy's arm as he stumped across the cobblestone. Sometimes they got pizza afterward, or watched a movie Benjamin brought home from the library. Yellow leaves flew past the windows, and it rained most evenings. Marta hated umbrellas, and often came home at night with her head wet. With the park sold, money wasn't an issue for the time being, so she'd been taking fewer and more regular shifts at the hospital. Benjamin responded to this, her renewed presence, by making dinner for them all each night, whisking a misty roux or plunging a fork into a quartet of oiled sweet potatoes as opera blew out of the kitchen radio, knowing she would be home soon with rain in her hair. He gained fifteen pounds from eating his own cooking and realized he was content, a feeling that almost felt leftover after everything else. He liked to eat too much and drift off on the couch with the dog's head in his lap, while Marta and Rudy watched a movie, and the sound of the world outside beat against the window like a pair of wings, drawn to the light, unable to reach it.

****

Orogeny

1.

"It's our task to launch the era of the innocent monster."
—Roberto Arlt, *The Seven Madmen*

Stanley Wysocki was a child with music in him. That's what his father said, and Stanley believed him. But what kind of music? Stanley wondered about that. He hoped for the sort that would throw open the land around him like a makeup case or like the shelves in his tacklebox, one tier after another, as it opened in his dreams. He called up the memory of them, those dreams of hidden steppes awakening, when his father said he had music in him. Stanley looked over the lake. The water appeared rumpled, ungently at rest. Lines fed beneath the surface from rods rigid along the gunwale, the rowboat a single point of hardness when seen from above, as an eagle saw it then, unfolding from the belt of trees on the opposite shore to bedevil a loon nesting there. The nest sat beside the remains of another boat, foundered in the shallows. The story was it had once carried a boarding party of picnicking nuns who drowned, leaving behind only the vessel that carried them to their doom. Even as a child with music in him, Stanley didn't see how it could happen in the two feet of water where the boat's skeleton came to rest, unless it had drifted there after jettisoning its monochrome crew, their sandwiches, tea thermoses, hymnals, whatever else; a guitar, perhaps, to accompany the hymns. Stanley imagined all of it swirling like rubbish caught in a tornado, but swirling down into the deep instead of up into the sky.

Three lines drew three identical circles in the lake's surface; Stanley's, his brother Titus', and their father's. Stanley had watched Titus' line diverging from his and their father's all morning, the red then white bobber bobbing as something attempted to drag it below, where Stanley imagined the nuns lay naked as roseate coral, the filament binding them ever closer as Titus reeled it in. His younger brother looked like he was flying a kite below the water. Their father saw this, and then Stanley's own line, looped in on itself like a chain of Venn diagrams, carelessness in one pan, distraction in the other, meeting somewhere along a spine of failure and passivity; it was easy to mistake Stanley for someone having a bad time.

Do you want to go back to the house, his father asked, gently; Stanley said he didn't. It doesn't seem like you want to fish, continued his father, still gently; Stanley said he didn't. Then why did you come? asked Titus, not so gently. His back cast seemed to underscore the question. Their father's silence echoed it.

Everyone remembers a moment when they tell the truth; this was Stanley's. He recalled it as an eagle-eyed portrait from above of the land at rest around him: the grey boat turning on black water against a brown bank of dark green, so thick in summer it nearly embowered the dirt road back to the house; the lake held them like ice in a cup. Why had he come along?

I wanted to see it from the water, Stanley said to his father, his brother. I dreamed there was a part you could only get to by water. And sometimes only if you knew the right song or music. Everything would change if you sang to the land. It would open, unlock, and be different, but not so different from the way it was before. I know it was just was a dream, but I wanted to see it the way it was when I dreamed about it. Where we are right now is how it looked before it changed.

Whatever that music is, I think you probably have it in you, said his father. Stanley hadn't considered this possibility. Titus submitted no opinion. Much later in his life, Stanley encountered music he wished would fit inside him; Liszt's transcription of The Solemn March to the Holy Grail, 'A Promise True and Grand' by Bukka White, certain figures or signatures of Mulatu Astatke or Bob Wills or Glenn Gould. Other things, as well, adrift, beyond capture. Taste was curated, the people around Stanley taught him this. Taste spoke for you, drew or repelled, looked a certain way on a shelf. By this measure, he had none. This didn't bother him. The music he longed for was inside him, as his father had said, and would open the land the way it opened in his dreams; he knew that. He continued looking for it outside himself anyway, overturning each stone paving his way for what he knew wasn't beneath it: a cue that would swing the jaws of a peninsula wide as a cattle gate, upraise an acclivity like a portcullis, open the evergreens like a pair of louvred saloon doors. It lived in him, this knowledge of possibility, like something trapped in the wall. He was fond of remembering it would never die there.

His father had a radio show every second Saturday, 6 to 10AM. The station was in the basement of a library attached to a small liberal arts college down the road from Stanley's house. He and his father awoke in darkness, and drove there together in the family Isuzu, eating buttered English muffins out of tinfoil, sipping coffee, listening to whoever was finishing up. It could be anything. Tuvan throat-singing, Teutonic electro-schmaltz, pitch-dark nationalist heavy metal from Scandinavia that sounded to Stanley like witches being burnt. The station didn't review content, so they never knew what they were walking into. This was a sign of tastelessness, Stanley would learn much later. For now, it was only a curiosity, something to mull over upon arrival after his father set to work raiding the station's jazz section and Stanley set to work pulling whatever looked like it might lead to the unlatching of the landscape he'd seen from the boat and knew from his dreams.

Nothing and everything stood in his way. He sat in an adjoining studio, playing through records, discovering things he liked (The Clash, The Church, The Cure) and things he didn't (Pearl Jam, Primus, Phish) without discovering what they were missing, or what they failed to throw back at him; not exactly a reflection, but a shadow, the kind flung upon a wall when headlights pass, there and lost again, like a saint's remains on a blanket, seen and withdrawn to the columbarium before the first photograph is taken.

The studio had a broad window looking out across a bare lawn into a copse of uniform trees. When the college was in session, Stanley occasionally saw revenant students at dawn rushing beneath the globe lights marking the path through the woods, on their way to classes and meetings to the sound of 'Straight to Hell' or 'Reptile' or 'Six Different Ways.' He associated these and other songs discovered this way with dark, furtive movements through forested interiors. None of them altered the landscape in any obvious way.

Sometimes footsteps creaked overhead in the library upstairs as students paced the shelves. Stanley would be one of them someday, the commuter variety. He attended the campus during business hours and fled back to his parent's house at dusk as if to avoid showing fellow students his true form. He felt no shame in landing his degree close to home the way Titus landed fish out in Montana. He'd seen photographs of his brother posing with cowpoke senators, ranching royalty, and other regional nabobs for a souvenir photograph with their catch of the day, paid well for leading those who could pay well to it like a hierophant. Stanley wasn't envious; he loved his brother and took pride in his success. It felt right for him to remain at home while Titus went west, awaiting the armature of the land they both grew up in to reveal itself like a not very good stage illusion, the sort of thing people hung around to see at the country fair; still, Stanley couldn't leave without seeing it for himself.

Titus was working on a degree in geography at the University of Montana; that was probably useful, or would be someday. Stanley's turned out to be in applied art through an error in the college's advising lotto. A few days before commencement, Stanley drove his father to a dispensary down the road from the college to locate something soporific. Prostate cancer, and what that involved had left his father sleepless and in pain. The Crash Test Dummies were on the radio. It made Stanley feel like he was unwillingly part of an opera. The land stood still as he waited for his father in the parking lot, crying until he almost threw up.

2.

"The force that circles the earth the most times is not electricity, but pain."
—Proust, *The Fugitive*

Across the road from Stanley's elementary school, brown beef cows browsed against a yellow hillside. He watched them through the library window, a place he came not from any particular love of books, but because it was the only location at school aside from the bathroom where he was permitted to go whenever he wanted.

Stanley's parents and his teachers decided he needed breaks. This was the behavioral plan they settled on after he slapped a girl on the playground. She'd slapped him first, but this didn't come up during any discussion of what his penance would be for returning fire. He apologized to his victim as if he was reading the topmost line on an eye chart, while the school principal. Mr. Duxbury, stood by in case Stanley decided to finish the job, and agreed to ask for breaks whenever he felt himself getting angry. The school therapist asked Stanley if he saw red. Stanley said yes, thinking they might be testing him for colorblindness or something, the way the school nurse came around once a year to check for lice; there was no going back after that.

Before the library was chosen for his place of banishment, Mr. Duxbury floated the gymnasium as a flagship location, perhaps because it was a windowless white box with mats hung on the wall, the sort of thing Stanley should get used to. He could play basketball with himself or kick a soccer ball against the fire door until the alarm went off or just listen to the radio in Mrs. Halloran's office. He liked music, didn't he?

Stanley's father fortunately headed off Mr. Dux, as he liked to be called, at the pass by suggesting the library instead. He'd tried to play catch enough times with his son to know Stanley lacked any natural competitive instincts, and only returned the ball to get it away from himself. His father couldn't imagine what Stanley would do if there was no one to throw it to. No one aside from Mrs. Halloran, of course. Stanley's father didn't see how there would be room for the gym teacher and his son in the bat cave she'd been given for an office. Picturing them listening to talk radio together between the bats and balls and whatever else

she kept in there gave him the creeps; he couldn't imagine what
the actuality of it would do to his son, who everyone agreed they
weren't trying to punish. Meanwhile, Mrs. Halloran supported
the idea in a way that suggested she had so much more to give
than her position required. That settled it. Stanley would go to
the library.

Astrid was the name of the girl he'd slapped. Stanley didn't
know if he was supposed to consider his crimes or not, but he
thought of her anyway during his breaks. She was smart, sharp,
prissy, a dentist's daughter. Stanley liked her very much before she
slapped him. He still liked her okay afterward. Everyone seemed
to believe she would do great things, Stanley included. Eventually,
everyone except him stopped waiting for them. By the time he
and Astrid made it to high school, she was pretty and a little wild.
She went to a lot of outdoor concerts, liked snowboarding, and
totaled three cars before dropping out in her senior year. Stanley
still liked her. He sometimes saw her in downtown Montpelier
with two or three older guys he didn't recognize. They surrounded her in a kind of formation, like bodyguards or disciples. She
was short, dreadlocked, buxom. He heard all kinds of things
about her. Astrid had an I.Q. of 160 and was pregnant. Astrid
gave someone a blowjob for a ride to a Phish concert and forged
knives in a smithy she built in her parent's backyard. Astrid was
fluent in French and had a tattoo on her lower back no one could
read because it was in French.

From her, Stanley learned the expectation of great things re-
sembles actually doing great things because people notice either
way; he watched Astrid for signs of change the way he watched
the land from the library window during his breaks after slapping
her; a yellow hill preyed on by brown cows, a wave of dark trees
crowning the acclivity, an abandoned thresher bricked red with

oxidization and blue with weeds, and nowhere the suggestion of keyhole to make it all spring open, as it did in his dreams. The book on his lap was a diversion, something to keep Mrs. Frobisher in her office, where she belonged. The school librarian had all the personality of the marooned farming equipment rusting on the hillside beyond the window, unwanted and unfed, dry, narrow, suspicious of the kind of changes no one really wants to make; Stanley was one of these. She dogged his breaks like she was following a sick animal, waiting for it to pass away so she could feed. Stanley found she mostly left him alone if he appeared to be reading, so he got into the habit of appearing to do this until it was time to take the school bus to Jean Bulow's house on the other side of the yellow hill.

The house was a slack-jawed ranch built into a hillside. It looked out on a fallow field that sloped to the road. Jean's child-care facilities were below grade, in the basement. Stanley and the other children hung their school things on a row of coat hooks beside the door after debarking the school bus. The basement had a wooden playhouse in one corner and a sticky tile floor, and a long snacking table at its center where Jean herself served apple juice and graham crackers each afternoon like a kind of sacrament. She had something wrong with her eyes, and wore large, tinted glasses inside and outside to treat or compensate for this ailment, whatever it was. The glasses blacked-out her eyes, and made her look like the angel of death. Would he like more apple juice? she asked Stanley, grinning like a skull. If he said yes, she would act as if she'd just remembered giving him a second cup and remind him that other people deserved to have some too. If he said no, the same thing would happen. A bitch, Stanley decided, flirting with the word, unable to fully imagine how it would sound leaving his mouth, but certain it applied here.

Jean smoked somewhere in the house. Stanley didn't know where exactly, but never in front of the children. It soured her breath, leavened her voice, and stained her knobbed hands the color of the hillside she lived in like a whistle pig. Stanley once had diarrhea in her house. He smelled cigarettes through the bathroom door, and knew she was about to bang on it in front of the other children and demand to know what he was doing in there that was taking so long; what if other people needed to use it? The stain he left in the toilet bowl and the scent of sickness in the air when he emerged did nothing to convince her; she couldn't see the stain because of her eye problem or identify the odor because of her smoking habit.

When Jean needed a cigarette, she would corral the children into the yard, and retreat to an upper story of the house where she puffed away in private and watch them through a high window. Stanley hated the yard. There were swings, a slide, and a fence he couldn't see over to remind him, he suspected, of where the immediate world ended. If he climbed to the apex of the slide, he could see the road, and would occupy it like a crow's next for as long as possible watching for his mother's car, until Jean's voice eventually shunted him off because other people were waiting their turn. In winter, the gray blue sky ceilinged the yard like a medical tent. No trees grew inside the fence as if the land had been salted, no grass either; in summer, it was shadeless and packed hard as a prison yard. No breeze reached it; the swings hung at rest from their crossbeam like fresh nooses.

None of this seemed to bother the other children backing up behind Stanley, who watched for his mother from the top of the slide in all seasons. A powder blue Subaru wagon turning at the base of the hillside, tunneling toward him the way the moon's reflection over water tunnels toward land. Jean lived on a lonely country road, the kind no one without a clear purpose would travel down, so the sound of a vehicle rising beyond the fence always sent Stanley rushing to the top of the slide, cutting the other children in line as Jean shouted at him from the deck's overbite, where she sheltered like a troglodyte. Stanley had done this enough times to know he had between ten and fifteen seconds before she reached him, more than enough time to get to the top of the slide and look for the powder blue Subaru turning at the base of the yellow hill; he knew his mother would protect him from Jean, so the risk he ran whenever a car engine broke the yard's defeated silence seemed worth it.

But the view from top of the slide was never what he hoped it would be: a pickup burping around a turn, a farmer rolling out of the surrounding fields on a tractor, the ochre high school bus dropping off students who lived up the lonely road at the bottom of the hill, Jean's son, Aiden, among them. Stanley learned disappointment from repetition, like a second language. He learned to hate the way other people live from the punishment that followed. Its predictability seasoned him. Jean's hand coiled in his coat, clawing him off the slide, the fence once again drawing up over the unrewarding view he'd defied her to gain, snacks cut off, toys embargoed. Nothing creative. Even when it came time to punish Stanley, Jean had the imagination of a stump. Still, it was more than enough to set him apart in front of the other children. He was on a break again, it seemed. Stanley used the opportunity to curate his hatred for her, and everything she appeared to represent: oversized pink and purple sweatshirts with seasonal or smartass sayings, a house that smelled a little like the lunchroom at school when meat was on the menu, the six-point buck's head jutting out above the fireplace he sat beside in timeout, the creature appearing to oversee him; why had his parents left him in the care of someone who hung dead things on the wall?

Stupid gross skull face bitch, Stanley often thought to himself, embellishing his foul name for Jean, the only one he knew, with care and even a sort of love, like someone tooling fine leather. She always made him sit on the lip of the unused fireplace in the basement playroom, watching what was probably supposed to look like fun; the other children playing, snacking, obeying Jean. Aiden usually arrived by this time, a middle-schooler in a baggy Aerosmith t-shirt, his hair cut like the cap of a mushroom, already fat in a way he wouldn't fully grow out of. Jean liked to put Aiden in charge of Stanley when he did something bad, going on and on to her son about how fed up she was. It was a term Stanley shoehorned in beside jeezum crow, another of Jean's favorites, as an enemy shibboleth, something he needed to watch out for. As far as he could tell, almost all the adults in his life aside from his parents were there to police and punish him arbitrarily. He knew he couldn't avoid this entirely by tagging them early on, but he could avoid being surprised by it, the way he grew accustomed to Jean's knobby hand falling upon his coat. He imagined himself atop a high dark hill, watching the numbers of people like her increase below, as he suspected they always would.

Aiden liked to take Stanley out to the yard after Jean remanded him to her son's custody. Ninja movies were popular that year, and Aiden needed someone to practice his karate on. He took classes twice a week, and was apparently a green belt. He taught Stanley how to stand still and wait to be kicked. Stanley taught himself to aim for Aiden's shin or balls whenever the older and bigger boy got a little carried away with his moves and flew at him with roundhouses and flying jump kicks that were supposedly used to knock people off horses. Their sessions in the yard always ended with Aiden coiled in on himself like a fiddlehead in the snow or dirt, depending on the season, clutching his ankle or groin and shouting for his mom, while Stanley ascended the ladder to the slide in the background to scour the horizon for the blue Subaru. Jean swept from the house to comfort Aiden, and shame Stanley for fighting.

Ma!, Aiden always said; He kicked me in the nerds, Ma!

Jeezum crow! Jean would answer, directing the rest of this to Stanley; That ain't fighting fair! You come down from there right now, you cheap little creep! You hear me? Come down right now and say you're sorry to Aiden!

Stanley's hatred for her blossomed in moments like these, threw out shoots. The scene between him and Aiden played out often enough for Stanley to wonder why it was allowed to go on at all. Maybe this was how people like Jean marked their days, by accumulating regular grievances. It seemed to be how Stanley was learning to mark his. He was a child, and lacked the power to move events. He was mostly at the mercy of whatever ripples older people threw out, identical moments looping like razor wire to bite into the days and hold them steady. Jean probably needed him to kick her son in the balls each afternoon so she would know things were still on track, that it was an hour or so before dinner, that her husband would be home from work soon, that it was almost time for a cigarette somewhere upstairs, where none of the children were allowed to go. Stanley had only been up there once when he was sick. Jean decided to quarantine him on a flowered couch under a blanket in the living room, an entire side of it taken up with what was once known as an entertainment center. He watched a TV movie about fighter jets with Horace, Aiden's older brother. Horace always wore camouflage pants tucked into combat boots around the house, and blaze orange t-shirts with the Vermont Air National Guard insignia on them. He lived in a concrete storeroom off the play area down-stairs. Stanley had never been inside, but had glimpsed the interior whenever Horace went in or out; a cot, one pillow, wool blanket, a television, a Nintendo, an overhead bulb sans shade. That was apparently as far as his needs went. Horace lived as if he was awaiting activation, or maybe further orders. Until that time, he mostly hung around upstairs, drinking the same apple juice as the kids below, and watching cable on the entertainment center. Since he and Stanley were both confined to their quarters in one way or another, Horace took the opportunity to go over the factual inconsistencies of the film they watched; it wouldn't happen like that because your afterburners would kick in, can't take down no plane I know of with a deer rifle, they're flying way too low to make that kind of call. Meanwhile, Stanley looked over Jean's inner web, or what he could see of it from the couch. Four or five rifles wracked above the dining room table. A loaf of white bread left out on a cutting board in the kitchen, a coil of stacked dishes rising from the sink. A sliding door with a view of where the lawn ended, maybe even an above ground pool out there somewhere. The upper floor also had a pet store smell; the place probably needed a dusting, or maybe a few less cats. Stanley didn't know how many Jean kept; he never saw them. But the creatures left evidence of themselves everywhere; tumbleweeds of fur tagging the carpet in the living room, motes of it hung like jellyfish in the snowy sunlight unrolling from the window above the couch, an ammoniac olfaction wafting from the dark end of the hallway where the bathroom was that indicated more than one kind of animal peed down there. Stanley fell asleep, and dreamt that Jean's cats were arrayed across the back of the couch, watching him sleep. They all had her face, and a small pair of dark glasses to go with it, each lens reproducing the image of him at rest, eyes closed and mind unaware, his reflection growing larger in the dream as the cats with Jean's face drew closer.

He awoke to the sound of Horace talking loud to someone in the kitchen and eating cereal off a legged tray, slurping the milk like soup, swallowing whatever came along with it whole like a sea monster. Something exploded on the TV, and a martial tune kicked in as Judd entered the living room with beer foam in his moustache. Horace's father looked like what Horace would eventually become: a midgrade state employee with an okay retirement plan waiting for deer season, saving for a snowmobile, reserving a cottage at Old Orchard for when summer rolled around; anything and everything to run out the clock. The only difference was the hitch Horace would acquire in his step after crashing a friend's dirt bike into a deadfall a few years later. Stanley only knew about it because Aiden was helping coach middle school soccer that year, and a few of the other players heard what happened, and said they were sorry. Aiden didn't seem to remember Stanley, or the damage the younger boy had done to his nerds long ago, and turned out to be a decent assistant coach. Stanley heard afterward that Horace spent a while in the ICU, had his leg rebuilt, lost a lot of blood, had a couple of seizures from a medication allergy no one knew about. Stanley saw him once outside the general store in East Calais, crossing the parking lot with a rack of beer under the arm he didn't need for his cane. Stanley felt nothing; feeling nothing made him feel peaceful. His hatred for the crippled man's mother and her shitty house had boiled off long ago, sent like steam to the stars. He hated other things now; the Algebra II teacher who always placed her large, red, moist palms over his knee, most of the third-tier liberal arts colleges he was applying to, his girlfriend's dachshund, who peed on the floor whenever he came over. It made what he'd hated before seem trivial; Horace hitching up a knee and farting like a flugelhorn when he noticed Stanley awake on the couch, Judd laughing, his jaws broad as a nutcracker's, dipping his moustache in his beer, trying to pop out one of his own to symphonize with his son, while Stanley lay paralyzed from the dream about cats with Jean's face, palming his groin beneath the blanket to make sure he hadn't wet himself in front of these two idiots. Judd changed the channel to a basketball game, still trying to sound off. Horace dug in a bag of chips like it held something alive he wanted to capture. The sound of them together, father and son, was like a fairground after dark, moving lights, rising smoke, sacrifices afoot. Stanley wondered if there could be anything worse than being sick in the house of someone he hated; being sick in the house of someone he hated when everyone was at home with nothing to do, he decided. He was too afraid to go to sleep because of the cat dreams. The only choices left were peeing where they peed at the end of the dark hall, or throwing up on himself.

Titus saved him from having to choose. His brother appeared at the top of the stairs, hand in claw with Jean. He came to see how Stanley was doing, she explained to her husband and son, rocking and hiccupping before the television as she led the boy over to Stanley on the couch. You okay? Titus asked, touching his brother's cheek; it's warm. I know, said Stanley. I'm sorry, said Titus. I'm all right, said Stanley; Go back downstairs.

Stanley would grow to love his brother more than himself one day. For now, Titus was still new, a divider of resources and splitter of affections. Jean adored him. It put Stanley on edge. She always tried to separate the boys whenever they fell under her jurisdiction, as if she were grooming Titus to one day be like the low-average morons she made her life with. Jean also liked to cap off everyone's day by delivering a report of Stanley's manifold villainies alongside a panegyric on Titus' overall goodness to their mother whenever the powder blue Subaru turned up, repeating herself through the car window the way all people who have no social skills and nothing to say anyway roll over the same ground again and again. The highs and lows of Jean's life took up so little space, but enough, as she saw it, to establish a clear and present polarity between the two brothers. She spoke biblically to their mother about them without realizing it, having no moral touchstone to call upon in moments like these aside from the subsurface religiosity, unlettered good sense, and dislike of anything new or different that helps the average American household limp along year after year. Jean spouted warnings like an oracle, pulled fables up by the roots, and generally deposited her views on the boys like stones to block their mother into the driveway, maybe until Stanley grew old enough to act on his hatred, and dispatch her by the mailbox.

Them boys you got, the one's good, that boy, your Titus, sweet as a button, lovely curly hair, such a nice boy. Always eats his snack, don't ask for more than his share, plays real nice with the others. He maybe could grow up to work for the state like my Judd if he plays all them cards of his right. But you better watch out his brother don't get in the way. I don't mean to speak bad about the boy, but he's always shoving his way up the slide, and kicking my Aiden in the you-know-whats, everyday it happens, and when he ain't doing all that, he's in the bathroom with the door locked, not coming out no matter how many times I tell him other people are waiting. I don't know what he gets up to in there, but you might want to have your husband have a talk with him about it, tell him there's a time a place for that sort of thing if that's the sort of thing you find the time and place for, because we all know what goes on with folks like that, what they turn into later on. I don't think I have to protect the other children from Stanley just yet, but you can be sure I might have to keep a pretty eye close on him in a few years, and you might want to also, because that's a sign of things no mother wants to think about. Now, your Titus on the other hand, sweet as a button, lovely curly hair, such a nice boy. Always eats his snack, don't ask for more than his share, plays real nice with the others . . .

It would have run on into the night if Stanley's mother allowed it. Instead, she rolled up her window up, saying she needed to get home, and backed out of the driveway. They regrouped in the parking lot of the general store down the road, the place where Stanley would spot Horace years later. His mother asked Stanley what happened. He said he hated Jean. His mother's response to this taught him that hatred is a fire best tended alone, where no one can see you feed it. Titus said he liked Jean. That didn't help. His mother encouraged him to experiment with pity, not in those words. But pity is faceted and self-reflective, which is why children don't feel it. Hatred is simple, and exists on a lower shelf. Stanley loved his mother, but didn't want to have to please Jean in order to make her happy.

Jean inadvertently saved him the trouble of having to do this by bumping him out of her house a few weeks before school broke for Thanksgiving. Titus could stay, but Stanley had to go. Jean heard about Stanley's breaks at school. She worried about the other children, or what he might do to them. Stanley was farmed out to another house at a different end of the same road, just over the yellow hill. The new place was closer to his mother's job, so Stanley was picked up first. He got to sit in the car in

Jean's driveway, listen to her sing Titus' praises; his hatred for her grew a pair of cloven hooves.

At one point, Judd appeared to demonstrate the high-five he taught Stanley's brother, stabbing his wide, meaty hand through the car window like he was trying to punch through a paper screen to get at a beer on the other side until Titus duly tapped it with his own. Moist-lipped and overloud celebration followed. Something about Jean's husband suggested a cage door left open to Stanley, the straw still wet within, no sign of Judd anywhere aside from a stray fart or happy gurgle from the woods where the furrows his knuckles had dug in the ground ended.

Years later, Stanley's father told him Judd had called the house one Sunday afternoon, saying he was taking Jean out for a drive, and was wondering if the two of them could stop by for a visit. It was clear they had no friends but didn't know it, so life was one big welcome mat stretching to the horizon. Lacking boundaries probably made them very happy, Stanley decided. He imagined Judd and Jean deployed in his parent's living room, no more than ten feet up the hall from where he slept, the former dribbling in his moustache as he demoed his high-five once again on Titus like the boy was a trained seal, the latter scenting the house's air like a coyote for a sign of Stanley's whereabouts, perhaps wishing she'd brought Aiden along to get kicked in the balls so she'd have a souvenir gripe to take back to her burrow in the yellow hillside. Stanley's parent's house had no gate, so barbarians had no reason to wait before striding on in and making themselves at home; leave the door open for a minute, and the frontier would come waltzing through, the near distance suddenly alive with constellated campfires, the clatter of weapons and armor and preparations, the land pulped and smoking, the way it looked after being logged.

Stanley imagined all this with the vividness of the age he was when it was almost at hand, when all horrors were easily realized instead of just day to day. His father didn't explain what he'd said to Judd to weasel out of the visit, though it was apparent from the way he told the story that he was still seeking humor in it years later, and needed his son's help in doing this. Stanley obliged and overshot, the way he had in the car with his mother a decade ago. I hated her, he said, adding: and her stupid husband. He remembered saying this to his father because he was seventeen and it was Christmas Eve, midafternoon, snowless that year, and they were having coffee on the deck after returning from a walk, watching over the land Stanley dreamed of even when it was right in front of him. Awful people, agreed his father. But you left me with them, Stanley silently replied, wondering how you could entrust your children to people you wouldn't have in your house.

Maybe because they're the only people who will have your children in their house, he decided, feeling an echo in the cavity his hatred had left behind like a prodigal wasp returning to a long abandoned hive, cruising the empty channels of the place, wings droning in stillness.

3.

"You're terrifying. Do you want to terrify people?"
"Yes. Everything around us is terrifying."
—Elias Canetti (in conversation with Hermann Broch),
The Play of the Eyes

Stanley loved the land, but hated the adults he shared it with. That was how he learned to love after his parents showed him what love was, the way you show somehow how to use a rifle before handing it over. His immediate world had yet to grow and take in the bordered vastness that would eventually make him feel like an adult, or someone who has lost their shelter. For now, the forest enclosing his house was unending, deep, and vital. It kept people away, people like Jean Bulow and Mrs. Frobisher and Mr. Dux, all the orderly, upright personalities seeking to arrange and control his life according to the mostly ambiguous grouping of letdowns that had made each of them into unremarkable grownups, spreading their wisdom like birdseed, invisible as soon as it hit the grass. Stanley believed they all wanted him to grow up to be like them; the possibility horrified him, so he fled from it as often as he could, to the school library whenever he needed a break, and into the woods sheltering his house at all other times.

He assumed the land held everything he read about; rabbits that spoke, mice with swords, people with destinies. Believing this comforted him the way masturbation would in a few years. He knew the names of nothing around him; the birds beating the spaces between nodding branches, the trees scratching the overhung grayness above, the striated rock exposed on a hillside above the lake spawned by a glacier. He was glad to know nothing about what he saw, to meet his ignorance on his own terms, the way he was never allowed to do at school. He went into the forest to hate limitlessly, and emerged refreshed. Slapping Astrid had been the biggest mistake he could remember; not because he felt bad about it, but because it allowed the adults in his life to believe in him agnostically. He knew they were waiting for him to prove them wrong or right about certain things. Building a mold for him to fall into, trapping the edges, hoping he would trip and fall in, make everybody feel smart. The forest and the water demanded nothing, even in the dreams he had each night; the sinking and rising of the studded

114

bank as it changed into a place he recognized without ever having seen it, the arm of the peninsula unyoking, the summer homes along the lake's southern edge drawing together as their foundations broke open and apart, the ridge above contracting like a squeezebox, unhinging its jaw, and unwrapping until he was alone with the empty broken homes along the shore. But always a single light on in one of them, when he dreamed about it, drawing him onward.

He watched it happen from different angles; the end of a dock, high on the ridge, the belly of a rowboat rocking on the beryline surf. Wherever he was, he made his way toward the single light, knowing there would be no one there, because he had reached it before, sifted the debris, a sensible place filled with old paperbacks, a creaking rocker, a lamp by the window providing the beacon he'd seen from wherever he was. The emptiness of what he dreamed swept over him like a panic, taking everything in and throwing it back with each contraction of the earth; it wasn't violent, because there was no one around except him to care. The dream awarded him this confidence, and he was grateful to be able to explore what had been thrown open without worrying how anyone else would feel about it. Music played; he could never identify it. Stanley would often bring his Walkman into the woods or down to the lake, loaded with a Chameleons or Lowlife cassette, things he taped in the basement of the college library where his father had a radio show every second Saturday. He still hoped to find the tune that would trigger the world to act in his waking life as it did in his dreams, maybe cracking the rim between the two.

Nothing took place, but his disappointment was patient and studied. The adults in his life taught him this skill. Even when nothing happened, Stanley knew he was still far away from the math teacher, Mrs. Cowie, who said 'nope' when he tried to answer a question in class, or Mr. Dux nodding like a woodpecker as he apologized hollowly to Astrid, or Jean cupping her hand over the spout on a pitcher of apple juice when he asked for more as if she was afraid he would attach his lips to it like a nipple if she didn't take precautions, her grim reaper shades catching the light and spitting a slightly diminished version back. Whore bitch with a crooked death's head dogface, thought Stanley, adding: wicked snatch. He'd learned some new words toward the end of his time with Jean, mostly from reading Stephen King and Peter Straub in the school library during his breaks, but was still having trouble using this new language with confidence.

Meanwhile, his love for the land killed everything he was supposed to respect, tamped it down like evidence stuffed down a toilet's weir. Watching the world grow and change each night while he slept left him wondering why the faces he saw each day at school stayed the same, refused to expand except when generating disapproval, and only then splitting the borders enough to redraw them, like a sandy shoal washed in and out by the tide. He'd stood on the sandbar at Race Point during a family vacation one summer at Cape Cod, watching the waves draw in and out, displacing nothing he could catch, yet reclaiming the imprint left behind with every rush toward land. He saw the faces of the adults he hated in the water, and his hatred was suddenly breathless, caught, vulnerable, flipping in the sand, gasping on the beach. His father read beneath an umbrella. His mother walked along tideline, collecting shells. Titus strode the dunes as if he'd conquered them. They were staying in a cabin on the bay outside Provincetown. The sheets were yellow, the linoleum gray. The yard gaped toward the water. Whitewash from the cottages flaked the sand and dune grass. Stanley's parents bought him a musket that clicked when he drew back the flintlock. He stalked the space between the bungalows every evening on patrol, envisioning Jean emerging from the scrub pine to forbid him from something and himself firing just one warning shot over her skeleton head before really opening up. He ate dinner with his family at various seafood restaurants, spent days at the beach, and wandered the streets of Provincetown at night, full up with drag queens and writers during the summer. Stanley appeared to be far enough from the people he hated to forget them; but he recognized their compound shape while malingering outside the window of a leather shop, looking over the mannequins, sliding through the impressions they left on him. How would Jean look in a studded harness? Bad. He somehow knew that for sure. But what about Mrs. Halloran? A hog in suspenders, Stanley figured; something out of Looney Tunes. Mrs. Cowie would probably count the spikes and divide by the number of dicks she'd lost time on. It was the kind of mean-spirited speculation that polluted his dreams, drew them back from the land like a leash.

He climbed the monument with his father and clung to the wall because the height scared him. He stood in the draft of a Portuguese bakery afterward until he felt okay again. The ocean spiked the air in the streets. He recognized the shade of the teenager he would become in the furtive outlines of skateboarders crowding up the brickwork outside city hall after dark. The week drew to a close, and he returned to Vermont. He imagined Jean and all the others missed his hatred for them, and the imagination of this brewed in him a hatred that would sink his first marriage, twenty or so years down the line, when he tried to explain it to his fiancée. She was patient as a statuary saint. The apartment they shared in North Chicago was filled mostly with things of hers, making their territory uneven. Outside the window, the city rose on the outlay of the lakeshore like a mountain from the bottom of the sea.

I think I love what hatred leaves behind because it leaves a trail I can follow, Stanley said, a few beers down the line, displaying his colors. The sound of sirens rising outside. That's like the definition of compassion, isn't it? Shit no, she said. Well, that's how I love you, he continued. Because of what's left on the tracks after what I hate rolls over it. If I thought like that, like you, you'd probably find me swinging from a rafter, she said.

Everyone has at least one friend they worry will commit suicide, so Stanley didn't see this as a big deal.

4.

"It's a matter of destiny . . . There are men whose destiny it is to bring unrest with them wherever they go, and it's no good barricading oneself in--there's no defense against it."

—Robert Musil, *The Perfecting of a Love*

Martina McDougall had a musical name; it rang out like part of a limerick, and seemed widowed on paper without a stanza beneath it. Stanley whispered her name like a benediction, sung it in his head, beat out its cadence on the brown vinyl seat of the school bus, hoping the music living inside him would answer back to reassure him the way his mother had that morning while dropping off him and Titus at school.

What if she hates me? he asked. What he really meant was: what if I hate her? She won't hate you, replied his mother, late for work. Jean hated me, he countered. No, she didn't, lied his mother. Then why can't I go back there? he asked. It's more of a little kid place, said his mother, lying again, but a better one this time. Wouldn't you rather be around people your own age? There was only one answer to that. Stanley didn't even bother filling in the blank as his mother shoved off, the powder blue Subaru sliding out of view around the shoulder of the gray hill helmeted by the school playground.

It was the first Monday after Thanksgiving break. His parents unveiled the new after-school arrangement over dinner the night before in a way that reminded Stanley of how they teamed up on the family cat to get him into his carrier whenever it was time for his shots. Stanley's mother coaxed with a treat, while his father grabbed with a pair of oven mitts. His mother had also spent most of the morning on the phone, scribbling on a notepad, so Stanley knew something was up. And the treat had already appeared; apple pie for dessert, his favorite. The oven mitts came out when he suggested walking home by himself from the bus stop between his second and third slice.

I'm not comfortable with that, said his father. Me neither, agreed his mother. It will save you guys money, said Stanley. Your safety is more important than that, replied his father. You might burn the house down, said Titus. Shut up, said Stanley. Don't tell your brother to shut up; he loves you, said their father, adding: we're finished talking about this.

The democratic façade Stanley's parents maintained whenever they made arrangements on his behalf had fallen, so he knew he'd lost. Stanley also knew they preferred his agreement on things of this kind, soccer camp, dentist appointments, playing trumpet in the school band, but would go ahead with whatever they'd chosen for him to do when his approval wasn't freely given. Maybe his parents really did think he'd burn the house down. At the moment, he wanted to, if only to clear the field of evidence of his defeat. That included the apple pie, a bribe he clearly saw now, sitting half gone at the table's center like a chart comparing the assurance of familiar horrors at Jean Bulow's house to the chance of things being even worse under the care of Martina McDougall. She had a nice name. Maybe she was a nice lady. He went to school with her son, Wendell. He seemed nice enough. Everyone said Wendell was retarded without getting more specific. Maybe they were right, and that was why he was nice. Stanley was eleven, so most of what he hoped for hung on the outcome of imbalanced, rudderless omens particular to him, the religious instinct making its own way after his parents threw up their hands over the matter. He scored his life based on the number of birds flying past the classroom window; fewer than five meant something bad would happen, more indicated the opposite. Or how many rocks he could throw onto the school roof during recess before one of the assistant teachers spotted him and put a stop to it; the more rocks, the better luck he would have that week. Or if there were any arrows sticking out of the decoy in the yard of the trailer up the road from Jean's house. Stanley counted them through the school bus window each afternoon, and made his divinations: three or more was very bad, less was very good, but if the fletchings were two or more colors, this was even better, because it obviated the potential badness of the first contingency, and offered up the possibility of expanding on the goodness of the third if one of the two or more colors was either red or blue. Yellow, however, sent everything back to square one, so you had to watch out for it.

Stanley rode a different bus to get to Martina's house, so he wouldn't see the decoy anymore, and had to come up with something else on the spot to help him predict the future. He settled for her name, repeating it, singing it, percussing it on the seat he shared with Wendell, who he'd been given over to by one of Mr. Dux's subalterns after school let out. Stanley's going to your house today, the lesser administrator said to Wendell; can you show him what bus to take and tell him when to get off so he doesn't get lost? At moments like this Stanley was aware of a great darkness within him, but he let it go, since freedom of choice was apparently not a gift bestowed during his last round with the decoy. Wendell was a little older than Stanley, and used to being assigned errorless or low ante tasks of this nature by the school faculty, delivering notes, handing out milk during snack time, counting his classmates when they lined up to go inside after recess. Whether or not Wendell was actually retarded almost didn't matter, since the apparently school-wide initiative to single him out this way made everyone think he was. Either way, the teachers and classroom assistants had set him up to become the semi-independent adult Stanley would often drive past years later, walking back to his mother's house from his part-time job at a food coop down the road, empowered to the point of no return. How much of it had been for him and how much for them? Stanley wondered whenever he passed by, sometimes stopping to offer Wendell a ride when the weather was bad. Wendell never said yes, and didn't appear to remember Stanley.

Maybe it was better that way. Stanley had no particular love for their shared history. Wendell tried to hold his hand that first day after the dipshit from the front office told him to make sure Stanley didn't get lost on the way to the bus. Even after Stanley made it to the right bus on his own, Wendell insisted on sitting beside him for the duration of the ride to his mother's house and loudly assuring Stanley every few seconds that they were almost there, even patting the top of his head, at one point; who knew where that gesture came from. Stanley remembered other people watching and listening from their seats nearby, our classmates; he didn't care about girls then, so his embarrassment was androgynous.

The rough start belied what followed. After they arrived, Martina McDougal served sandwich cookies for snack and chocolate milk, as much of either as Stanley wanted, and allowed him to play Sega Genesis in Wendell's room until his mother picked him up. Video games were outlawed at home, so this was a real treat for Stanley. Snow fell outside a window beside the television as an ebullient blue hedgehog rolled through a proscenium of golden rings on screen. Wendell sat nearby, watching and offering bad advice. Martina appeared at regular intervals to refresh their chocolate milk, and ask if Stanley was having a good time. He was; she was as nice as her name, it seemed, and may have even been pretty once. He knew he was on the verge of taking all this for granted, but didn't know how to pull back. Martina had to call him twice when his mother arrived, something that would never have happened at Jean's house, poised as he was to escape.

That night, Stanley dreamed of Martina McDougal wearing the studded leather harness he'd seen on display in Provincetown, and running on all fours through the shifting landscape beside the lake as he rode on her back. Martina sung a wordless, atonal music as she ran that seemed to stir the swaying ridgeline above the water, and the pronged peninsula reaching out into it; he watched them unwrap and change in ways he'd never seen before, the far shore splitting wide open until the horizon showed through to the other side, an endless gray curtain that could swallow ships. When her song paused, so did all this newness; he couldn't have that. Fortunately, the dream had equipped Stanley with a long-handled whip (a longeing whip it was called, he found out later, used to drive show horses) that he somehow knew to snap into her side whenever the music faded away. One crack was all it took to rewind the key, or slot the coin; from the smooth contour of her back, he watched a hillside across the lake melt like lava, and spill through the black spaded trees below into the water. He cracked his whip, she sung, and the world opened wide. It was everything he wanted. He could have ridden her forever.

Much later in his life, Stanley would recognize this dream as pre-sexual, and feel relieved that it hadn't formed the corner-stone of some weird fetish he couldn't escape from as an adult. Meanwhile, he awoke from it with an erection, laughing hysteri-cally. The dream left him with a goofy feeling he carried with him all day, the way he felt when he went to school without under-wear. No one had any idea he was one layer shy, and imagining what they would think if they knew thrilled Stanley for reasons he couldn't reframe as ordinary when he looked over them years later. It made him feel like a serial killer walking around in public with a victim's head in a knapsack, daring the world to have a look. Stanley as a man excused himself for being a child. Children have no organic secrets, so they have to carve them out of what-ever is at hand the way prisoners make weapons. What would Mrs. Frobisher or Martina McDougall do if they knew his dick was loose in his pants? What would they think if his mind had a glass bottom or transparent lid, his thoughts swimming free as fish beneath their purview?

When he arrived at her house later that day, Stanley hoped Martina would see on his face some of what the dream had left him with, something she would understand and respect without requiring an explanation, something that would ideally make her his servant until his parents loosened up and let him walk home from the bus stop by himself. Until then, there were endless sand-wich cookies, bottomless glasses of chocolate milk, and a Sega

Genesis to help him pass the long, dark winter afternoons in a house he didn't like, with other children he didn't care for. He'd ridden Martina through his internal landscape like Hannibal bestride a war elephant, shared it with her, made her sing at the end of his whip like a field hand as the land he loved flew apart, its pieces lost against the horizon she'd helped to raise. She was the only person to see where he spent his nights, to travel there with him, and to love it, he imagined, the way he did. He sat beside Wendell on the bus to her house once again, trying to remember if his mother had been naked in the dream. Stanley seemed to remember his hands against Martina's bare skin. So maybe, he decided, as the bus dumped them and the other children on her doorstep.

He tried to picture Martina in a studded leather harness when she appeared in the doorway to welcome them, but it didn't work. She wore an oversized brown t-shirt that broke at her knees and a pair of orange leggings with stirrups. The outfit reminded Stanley of the Thanksgiving turkey decorations hung around the school. He was disappointed; she'd looked much sleeker running around on all fours. No matter. There were other things to look forward to. He slung his jacket over a hook, and drifted down the hall toward Wendell's room to fire up the Genesis, but her voice called him back.

Have some snack, Stanley, she said. I'm not hungry, he replied, his hand on the knob of Wendell's room, the gaming system nearly within reach. No Sega today, she said; come eat your snack. I don't want any, he repeated; I want to play it. You let me yesterday. It was your first day, she said, appearing then in the hallway, rearing into the arc of the dining room light. Everyone is out here, she continued. You can't spend all your time here on that thing. It's Wendell's anyway. I'll ask him if he wants to let you.

She withdrew to wherever Wendell was in the house. Stanley realized he was in the midst of a charade of evenhandedness, the sort of egalitarian mirage his parents summoned up whenever they made a decision for him they knew he wouldn't like. He began rolling back his expectations. As much as it hurt to do, it was almost a reflex at this point in his life, a response to watching the things he wanted spin suddenly away in the undertow generated by those with his best interest at heart. Stanley knew Wendell would do whatever his mother told him to do. By the time Martina reappeared, Stanley was at the snack table in the dining room, glumly helping himself to cookies and chocolate milk. He almost expected her to roll that back too, so when she snatched half the cookies from his plate and distributed them among the other children sharing the table, it didn't blow him away.

Too many, she said. You shit-assed fucking dog whore, thought Stanley, toying with a new word or two he'd picked up from Dean Koontz. A volume of his had recently slipped in among the paperbacks at the school library, maybe by accident; but there it was, a thick-bodied tome with a suggestive cover, the kind of thing Stanley always noticed whenever he was in line with his mother at Price Chopper. Stanley found Mr. Koontz could offer his hatred a voice all its own. He read the book in a rocking chair by the window, watching the field across the road, while thinking: fuck you each time Mrs. Frobisher peered around her office door to spy on him. Rooting sow with rot-colored nipples, he thought, as Martina swooped in to dump his chocolate milk in the sink before he was finished with it. Time to play outside, she said. I don't want to play outside, said Stanley; It's cold. Put your jacket on, Martina suggested.

He put his jacket on. It might as well have remained on for the entire season that year. After a promising opening, the routine had established itself; Stanley saw that now. Two sandwich cookies, a half-glass of chocolate milk, and down the throat of the snowbound yard. The house sat in a copse of tall dark evergreens. Unlike Jean's house, the yard was unfenced. It reminded Stanley he could theoretically run away if Wendell didn't squawk like a klaxon whenever he approached the edge of the forest. It seemed Stanley had been given over to his care once again, this time by his mother. Keep an eye on Stanley for me, she told her son, adding another consequence-free chore to his growing list of symbolic responsibilities. It was all the same to Wendell; Stanley was just another milk to be monitored.

Stanley mapped the border over the next week, probing for weak points and finding none, until he knew exactly how far he could go from the house before Wendell would make a racket, just as he had once known how long it would take Jean to claw him off the top of the slide. He studied the timing as if he was planning a heist; as soon as the toe of his boot met the spindly shadow of the large pine tree beside the garage, the tether would snap like the whip he cracked into Martina's side in his dream, and he'd be drawn back by Wendell's reedy semitone calling his mother to come see what Stanley did. And what had he been doing? Sitting under the pine tree, sheltering in the partial cover of the snow-hung branches where they brushed the ground, watching the other children play, not like someone wanting to be included, but warily, but like an outlaw, watching the king's guard pass by.

Stanley mistrusted the other children. There was Wendell, of course, but also three interchangeable, hyperactive boys a grade below him, whom he'd seen throwing rocks at a cow that had escaped the field across from the school; one of them had advised the others to aim for the udders. Another of this bunch got in trouble for taking his milk into the bathroom and peeing in the carton; no one knew why. There was a spindly, dark-haired girl who came only on Tuesdays and Thursdays and was allowed to sit inside reading serialized young-adult novels about easily solvable middle-class problems while everyone else was shoved out the door. Stanley noticed this, and asked Martina if he could stay in and read too. Did you bring a book? she asked. Stanley hadn't, but said he did, hoping she'd forget about the whole thing after he'd plunked down on the couch and flipped on the TV; it was just after 3:30PM, still plenty of time to catch Darkwing Duck. He hadn't counted on Martina searching his backpack before his lie had even left the nest. Lying is wrong, she said, her voice cold and dark as the yard she tipped him into. The other children already out there, watching all this take place. Don't you ever lie to grown-ups again, Martina added loudly enough for them to hear before slamming the door.

Dirty apple-assed bumpkin snatch-kisser, Stanley thought, trying out something he'd picked up from John Saul, but his heart wasn't in it. He knew he'd blown his one chance to avoid the other children, and was furious with himself. Meanwhile, the other children were entering the ring cast by the porchlight, closing in. Stanley had begun to notice cruel impulses developing in his peers. He always remembered Abigail as the first person to teach him what laughter at his expense sounded like. They were in the same class at school, and also neighbors; her parents lived across the meadow from his. Their families weren't friends, but Stanley assumed the proximity of their homes meant she was well-disposed toward him, or comfortably indifferent, at the very least. The logic of this assumption was collapsible as a beach chair, but he didn't realize it until the first snowball hit him in the back of the head. When he turned around, another hit him in the face, knocking his glasses into the snow, and blurring the rest of it. When Abigail and the others realized he couldn't see, they grew bolder, and circled further in, not even bothering to throw snowballs, just walking up beside Stanley and clapping handfuls of snow to the side of his head until his ear canal was clogged with ice and slush.

This was their goal, he realized; giving him a hearing aid, as Abigail called it. Stanley remembered some things about her then; her house had burned down a year earlier. He'd seen the flames at night through his kitchen window, pulsing across the meadow. No one had been injured, and she had a new house now in the same spot, but everyone at school still treated her like she was living out of the charred foundation of her old dwelling, scavenging her meals, and bedding down each night amid the ruins of her possessions. The sympathy she engendered appeared bottomless and irrevocable. Stanley had seen her spit on another girl over a seating dispute in the lunchroom, and slap a boy who wouldn't give her a crayon he was using in art class. It didn't matter. Abigail had a tragedy on her side.

Martina loved her, no doubt about it. At first, Stanley enjoyed watching how jealous this made Wendell until he realized it also made Wendell police him more vigorously outside. Misery trickles down because cruelty drifts up, thought Stanley, though not in those words, as Wendell tromped after him through the snow, loudly warning him away from the property line.

During his first hearing aid, he swung out blindly at the sound of footsteps approaching, knocking one of the smaller boys into Abigail and creating a fuss. Martina passed the news along to Stanley's mother when she came to get him. He told lies and attacked the other children in the yard, said Martina, not bothering to conceal her lopsided version of events from Stanley, hidden behind his mother in the doorway, tugging her sleeve toward the Subaru idling in the driveway. Even the girls, added Martina, though there was only one; maybe she also knew about his breaks at school. They threw snowballs at my face, he said. That's not what Wendell said, replied Martina, as if that settled the matter; Stanley couldn't decide if she was over- or underestimating her son by assuming his incapability of lying, but it didn't end up mattering. When Stanley explained what happened to his mother, she said she would talk to Martina, but advised him to be the bigger person, and just walk away if it happened again. Stanley knew it would happen again, but he loved his mother, and did his best to follow her advice when it happened again the next afternoon.

Hearing aid! Abigail shouted as soon as he got outside, and the other children began packing snowballs. Stanley walked away, as his mother told him to, aiming for the trees, ignoring Wendell's warning shrieks. Snowballs fell around him, one clipping his ear. It stung enough to bring tears to his eyes, and he paused to wipe the tears off his cheeks before the others saw. This was a mistake, as it turned out. They were closer than he'd realized, the snow muffling their pursuit, and were now lined up behind him, each with a snowball prepared to mash into the side of his head. Two boys managed to get by him before Stanley slapped the third, who turned out to be Abigail. It was dark and his glasses were in his hand, so he had no idea it was who he'd hit until she began yelling for Wendell to go get help. Stanley took the opportunity to hide beneath the branches of the large pine by the garage, and remained there until Martina came to drag him out. She made him sit alone at the kitchen table in the dark until his mother arrived.

I did what you said, he told her once they were in the car; but they followed me. I believe you, said his mother; but you can't hit girls, Stanley. I didn't know she was a girl, he said; it was dark and my glasses weren't on. You can't hit anybody, replied his mother; It took a long time to find a place with an opening. I'm not sure where you'll go if you can't go to Martina's. I can't take any more time off work. Let me walk home from the bus, said Stanley; I won't burn the house down or play with knives or anything. I'm old enough. Your father and I aren't comfortable with that yet, said his mother; I'll look around for something else, but I need you to please not hit anyone or do anything in the meantime except walk away. I know it seems unfair, but please just ignore them. You're smarter than they are. I know you can do it.

Stanley could, he decided, entirely out of love for his mother. He gave up running or walking away, since movement seemed to encourage Abigail, and there was nowhere to flee with Wendell watching the trees. He settled into spending his afternoons seated on the back steps of Martina's house, his glasses safely tucked away in his jacket pocket, waiting to receive his hearing aid. He didn't cry, and tried not to wince when the snowballs met his face, and even hummed to himself while it was happening, angry, fortifying music he heard in the basement of the college library during his father's radio shows and carried with him; The Dead Kennedys, The Misfits, Black Flag. The other children soon grew bored with him. By Christmastime, hearing aids were a thing of the past. Stanley realized his mother had given him good advice, even if he felt like he was only marking time the way Jean probably had whenever he kicked her son in the balls.

Abigail and the others drifted away, leaving him alone to refine the scope of the revenge he would take on them. It had to be quiet and slow so Martina wouldn't notice, and would ideally take place at school where there was a crowd he could fade into. He saved a sandwich bag from his lunch, and used it store some toilet paper he'd wiped himself with until he found the right moment to distribute the sheets like memos between the backpacks of the three boys who acted under Abigail. Each arrived at school the next day with a different backpack, but it wasn't enough. He repeated this once a week for a month before moving on to Martina and Wendell. After using the toilet at their house, he got into the habit of circumscribing the bowl's corroded interior with the quiver of toothbrushes beside the bathroom sink. He rinsed everything off in the outflow, flushing only when Martina tapped on the door and asked if Stanley was okay; he said he was fine, as indeed he was, feeling nothing as he finished swamping out the crapper with her toothbrush.

Stanley saved Abigail for last. She took some thought. He wondered if he could set her hair on fire, remind her of times past. But there didn't seem to be a way to get the thing done without it being traced back to him. As a child, Stanley was closed-off enough to delight in the misery he caused without needing it sourced to him. Authorship was beside the point. He wanted his revenge to reflect the indifference of the universe as he saw it, to be without a pattern and empty of apparent motive. The scariest thing about the sky falling is that the sky is everywhere all the time; so in whatever he would do to make Abigail pay, Stanley sought to be the sky.

It made him impulsive. One winter afternoon, he crossed the meadow separating his house from hers and pissed on her family's woodpile after doing a not very thorough job of making sure no one was home. He had to run for it when a light flew on in the window he peed beside, wetting his leg as he fled back across the meadow with his pants undone before the gauze of steam he'd left behind had dispersed, drifting off toward the icebound lake like an echo of the fire that had claimed the house a year earlier.

Stanley arrived home unsure if he'd been caught, but certain he would be after noticing the door-to-door trail he'd made in the snow. It spelled out where he'd been and what he'd been up to there, no doubt about it. Doom loomed hugely then, adopting the shape of Abigail's father, a barrel-bodied woodcutting type who always seemed to be awaiting a clash of exactly the kind Stanley had laid the groundwork for by peeing on his woodpile. Slogans suggesting strong, one-sided ideas about liberty, sports, and arsenal husbandry speckled the rear of his truck, a trinity Stanley's own father had offhandedly trained him to associate with people who were a little out of control. Stanley read over the back bumper whenever he noticed the vehicle outside the general store, not understanding all of it, but getting enough of a thumbnail sketch of life at Abigail's house to figure out where her meanness actually grew from, or what the fire left behind. Stanley had to come by hatred on his own, slapping it together from whatever washed his way. But Abigail's father clearly loved her too much and too simply to let anything slide, so his hatred for the world became her inheritance, or what he loved her in spite of, or what his daughter made room for him to believe in; it could have been one or the other, or maybe both. Either way, she was the only unflawed thing in his life, and he made sure she knew it. He took her ice fishing, mudding, snowmobiling. They shot deer together, cheered for the same teams, used insurance money to raise horses in a paddock across from the house after it went up in flames. Stanley heard all about it whenever he stopped off at the general store to tank up between school and his parent's house years later, after Abigail left to go to college somewhere in Massachusetts. Her father was lonely, and took to parking himself beside the store's woodstove between beer runs to the ice-fishing shanty or deer stand he'd once shared with her, holding forth on a mélange of topics he'd scrubbed together into a kind of distilled sermon on the way things should be, simple stuff really, more or less in line with what he'd slapped on the truck at anchor in the parking lot. Stanley still had no good understanding of any of it and no real interest in learning more, so it was easy for him to be kind to Abigail's father whenever they ran into each other at the general store. Listening to someone who didn't need to be heard by anyone reminded Stanley of almost everyone he went to school with at the small campus down the road. When Abigail's father found out he was a student there, they were able to bond over a mutual dislike of the place. Why you want to go to school with those flower-climbers? asked Abigail's father. My dad has cancer, replied Stanley; it's nearby. That was the last time they talked about it, and the first time Abigail's father offered Stanley a beer from the case at his feet, but not the last. It was how men like him replied to things they knew might come for them too.

Stanley liked drinking beer with someone whose loneliness had an apparent center, a bull's eye at the heart of things; his own isolation had nothing to aim for. He remembered the decoy rolling past the school bus window on the way to Jean Bulow's house, and wondered if it was still in use, or what it would tell him if it was. His father said he had music in him, and now his father was sick. Stanley wondered if this made the music inside him sick also. He had his own radio show at the college now, 6AM to 10AM every second Saturday, the same slot as his father. The nicest thing he'd heard about his program was that it was unpredictable. His mother had said that. His father was usually asleep when it came on. He didn't know how to explain that he was still searching for what he'd been promised, his inheritance as he saw it, hoping to find it before it died with his father. His mother didn't need to hear that. Stanley kept it to himself.

Sometimes Stanley drove Abigail's father home from the general store if the clerk took his keys. They rode together down the back roads with open containers between their knees in all seasons, having nothing in common aside from loving their families too much to love the world along with them. Stanley learned sharing pain with another human being is a privilege. Abigail's father was divorced. The house was always dark when they arrived. The horses across the road were gone, sold long ago. A car hit the dog the week after Abigail left for school. The property singled out her father as the only survivor. Stanley took to walking him to the door in winter after watching him slip and fall in the driveway a few times. It upset the balance of neediness between them, but Stanley still felt bad about pissing on the woodpile so many years back, and figured he should try and make up for it, since it was easier than confessing. He still saw the footprints he'd been so afraid of Abigail's father following, running up and over the meadow dividing the properties, a urine stain at one end, his front door at the other.

Fortunately, a winter storm rolled in a few hours later, blanketing Stanley's tracks, and earning everyone in his school district a snow day. It gave him time to regroup, consider his options. Abigail had to pay. That was clear. The only remaining question was how dearly. It was winter, so there was no poison ivy to harvest from the yard, and replant in her desk at school. Road kill, likewise. With the others it had been easy. He wanted whatever he did to Abigail to be special. Maybe he could poop in her room somewhere she wouldn't immediately know about. Stanley actually spent a good part of his snow day considering this plan, watching her house through a pair of his father's binoculars from a stand of trees in the meadow, hoping for the right moment. It never came. Abigail's mother appeared topless in an upper window for a moment with a cigarette in the corner of her mouth. She was a gaunt, spindly woman with breasts like the cones Mrs. Halloran used to divide the gym during dodgeball, and the first woman Stanley had ever seen naked in real life. It formed the basis of no proclivity he knew of later on, but disturbed him enough at the time to send him into full retreat, back across the meadow, his snowshoes thumping the fresh cover as he wondered if he might be a little gay, maybe even hoping for it, anything to keep him from having to one day crack his lance on the gristly dragon Abigail's mother represented. There was no slaying her in his memory.

It sucked the wind out of his sails so thoroughly that he nearly abandoned ship, flinging himself and all his unkind plans for Abigail overboard into the dead calm waters seeing her naked mother had left him in. He hoped the storm in his heart would pass as the one that cloaked his footprints had. He could barely recall how his life was before needing to hurt someone became part of it. It seemed hatred was now his hobby.

The trees he walked toward on the other side of the meadow were already walling off the last of the sunlight, and he knew he'd wasted the day. His father made him a grilled-cheese sandwich when he got home. He ate it beside the fire, wondering if any part of Abigail's mother tasted this way, and was barely able to finish. His father asked him if something was wrong. Stanley said nothing was wrong, and made a little show of enjoying the sandwich until his father went away. What could he say? Stanley couldn't ask his father how a vagina tasted just to set his mind at rest. And even if he could, there was still the lingering bad feeling left behind after spending all day spying on Abigail's house so he could poop in it. Thinking about that made him feel the way he did when he was sick with a stomach bug on a sunny spring morning, with all the windows in the house open for the first time, warm breeze aerating the rooms shut since winter, and the land outside beckoning him like a crone from the candied egress of her cottage, all of it lost forever as sunlight crept down the walls, tepid Ginger Ale burned his tongue, and The Price is Right tailed off on a small black and white set his parents set up beside the couch where he napped in small moist bursts as the hours closed off, one by one.

Days like that, or the one he'd just spent shoeing around the meadow behind Abigail's house, made it seem like life was always ready to skid off if you didn't set your hook the way Titus always did when they were out in the boat; it scared him to death as a child, and even more as an adult, still trying to head it off years later in Chicago. He ran down the shore of Lake Michigan each day in the middle of winter, imagining a wall of flame chasing him over the ice and frozen sand on the empty beaches, eating up everything it fell upon; he told his wife about it after she told him about something that seemed equivalently vulnerable in her own day to day life, but turned out not to be after it was too late to take it back, or pretend he was joking. Their love was the kind that made room for damages, he knew that well enough, knew she would forgive him for giving her something more or less new to worry about in addition to finishing up grad school and a tooth she'd recently chipped on a popcorn kernel. He tried to reassure her by saying he didn't think the flames would ever catch him. She seemed to cry without crying at that; her face buckled the way the land still did in his dreams. Fortunately, they were eating in a restaurant and she was sensitive to the way she appeared in front of strangers, so that was as far as it went. Chicago bored them both; it was a city like a funny story about someone else's child. The Midwest came to eat and eat and eat here, watch the ball game, float in a boat. The apron of the lakeshore where they lived was a swamp paved over. Murals in Rogers Park showed all the things that used to live there before the place was cleaned up; birch trees, lake trout, Indians. Stanley looked it all over one night while peeing on one of the cobblestone sections of Glenwood Avenue, the bar door he just spilled from glowed like the mouth of an oven at his back. The red line clattered by overhead, southbound; the wall of flame moved at about the same speed. He wouldn't share that with his wife. Details like that were not his friend at the moment. Meanwhile, he couldn't decide if he was more at war with himself or the world as it was; one of them was getting in his way, while the other appeared to be his resting state.

He didn't immediately recognize this as an updated form of the same question he'd puzzled over as a kid until he directed his stream onto the door of a parked car with a saying he didn't like affixed to the bumper. That brought back Abigail's father first, then her naked mother smoking in the window, then the wood-pile, last for some reason. Was this still how he lashed out? With piss and shit like a monkey? The gravity of what hasn't changed is sometimes strong enough to pull the universe aside like a curtain on a window to what is most worth regretting about yourself. Wild light suddenly flooded a dark and narrow room long closed. Stanley could forgive himself for what he'd done as a child, the dirty toilet paper in the backpacks, the toothbrushes in the toilet, peeing on the woodpile. This kind of revenge came easily to him because it was all he or anyone his age had for ammunition. As children, they had no real rights to anything beyond those grant-ed on consignment by their parents, teachers, or whatever other adults they were given over to. Their bodies didn't belong to them. They were dressed, doctored, and educated as others saw fit. Their tastes were curated. Their activities monitored. Their choices chosen. All this was given up in exchange for the promise, not the guarantee, of a childhood free of molestation, battery, murder, or neglect.

So, aside from those that bite or are good to eat, Stanley realized, children have the same rights as most animals. It had pretty much worked out, he had to admit. No one sent him to work in a garment factory or diamond mine after school. He knew no child soldiers when he was growing up. No adult had ever asked him to board a commercial flight after swallowing a condom filled with cocaine. He had grown up safe and powerless, engineered in what he was told was the first world, a world that gave him no anchor for his hatred, poor him. Back when Abigail was giving Stanley hearing aids, social media didn't exist as a way for people to join conversations that scared them in real life. School shootings were not popular yet. Bullying was considered a normal part of sharing the first world with assholes. It left Stanley and the kids he grew up around few choices when it came to settling differences. Poop and pee were natural outlets, the only things you made yourself that everyone was scared of and no one could take away from you. And the bathroom was the one place grownups always left you alone; Stanley still did most of his plotting on the toilet.

Children are lazy, he decided; so are adults. Which of them is lazier depends on how angry they are. But at the end of the day, the difference between peeing on someone's woodpile and a mass shooting is a difference of resources and imagination. As a kid, Stanley knew he could act on his worst impulses with impunity, because he assumed the worst he could do was the worst he could expect in return; his imagination reached no further than that. He considered sharing this with his wife as an early example of empathy, something to offset the thing he'd said about the wall of fire chasing him through the park and throw her off the trail for a while. But he wasn't sure he could fit it into the kind of conversation he wanted to have without revealing what he'd eventually done to Abigail. He couldn't comment on the rug without pulling it out from under his feet. Empathy would just end up beside the point.

It took him a week to figure it out, or for the afterimage of Abigail's naked raw-boned mother smoking in the window to burn off and scab over. Stanley couldn't focus with that fresh in his mind, the horrors it seemed to promise. He refreshed himself with his father's magazines, centerfolds unfolding in soft focus to reveal breasts like fishbowls, hips like the dunes at Cape Cod, orderly, seashell vaginas that didn't look like they were about to roar, or shout at him for taking too long in the bathroom. He knew these women were exceptional, and out of reach. That was okay. They taught him he had to establish his lows to earn his highs. He had never appreciated them more.

5.

"Nihilism had no bottom."

—Henry Adams, *The Education of Henry Adams*

Abigail got new shoes for Christmas. She was very proud of them. They were the kind with small red lights in the sole that blinked when she walked around. Her classmates complimented them. Even some of the teachers thought they were pretty nifty. Abigail loved this kind of store-bought attention; most people do. And why shouldn't they? Few emerge from a first-world childhood without the right to feel special at any time. Now it was Abigail's turn, once again; she'd engineered many. A dear distant relative of hers seemed to kick the bucket every other weekend; sympathy noted, cards force-written in class, to be delivered when she returned from the service. Or maybe one of the horses was sick again; those noble animals had terrible luck. If not that, then there was always the cool snowmobiling jacket she just got, or a new Lisa Frank Trapper Keeper. Abigail's shoes were only the latest. They gave people a light to follow; people like following lights. And it gave Stanley an idea. He watched Abigail prance around the classroom like one of the horses she had at home, glad something she loved was finally within reach. The only thing left to do now was destroy it.

It was still winter outside, so Abigail changed into the shoes when she got to school, and out of them again when it was time to board the bus for Martina McDougal's house. The only other moment they were off her feet was during recess. Here, Stanley found his window. He studied the timing for a week before making his move, watching Abigail exchange the winking blinking footwear for her snow boots in the hallway outside the classroom, using her movements to map it all out the way he'd once used Wendell sounding the alarm to chart the boundary of his mother's yard. Recess clocked in at a half an hour, with a five-minute buffer on either side. That left Stanley about twenty minutes; more than enough time, as it turned out. When the day came, he feigned a stomachache shortly before recess, and stayed inside with his head on his desk, watching the other students pass the classroom window until he saw Abigail. He waited two minutes by the clock above Mrs. Veitch's desk before asking her to use the bathroom; his teacher assented with a look that said she already knew he had diarrhea, and to just go if he needed to and leave her out of it, inadvertently sweeping the last hurdle aside.

There was suddenly nothing to stop him. It was like stepping from a shadowy dream into daylight.

Out in the hallway, Stanley went to his backpack and removed a pair of latex gloves he'd taken from his mother's first aid kit, and a doubled grocery bag of furzy turds he'd excavated from the family cat's litter box the night before. Abigail's shoes were paired just so under the hook where her backpack hung, as always. He lifted the insole of each, and arranged the cat shit beneath it before pressing it back into place, making the lights in the heel blink on and off as he did his best to smooth out any lumps or bumps. He finished up, dropped the gloves in the empty bag, balled the entire thing up and stuffed it in his pocket. He checked his time on the clock above the door to the playground; the entire operation took less than two minutes. That gave him ten or so more in the bathroom before Mrs. Veitch came looking for him. Stanley knew he wouldn't need it. He was back in the classroom with his head on his desk no more than three minutes later. Mrs. Veitch asked if he needed to visit the nurse. Stanley said maybe to cover what remained of his tracks.

The bathroom in the hallway was unisex and served a few other classrooms, so there was no way to know who was the first to see what he'd written above the sink. But he noticed ripples of it passing between the children later that afternoon and over the following days; whispers, giggles, eyes sliding toward Abigail, striding around in her light-up sneakers like a majorette. Stanley did a good job of packing everything down; she had no idea what she was walking on. He couldn't tell if there was a smell yet, but figured there would be sooner or later. It didn't really matter. The other students would smell what they wanted to smell, the same way they'd lined up to praise the shoes. The suggestion he'd planted in the bathroom was enough. Everyone already hated

Abigail. All they needed was a reason to let it show, something to seize upon, a drop of blood powdering the water, a little heave-ho to send them all waltzing in for the kill. Stanley had created nothing. He'd only given his classmates a different light to follow. He asked Mrs. Veitch to use the bathroom once more before the day was out just to admire the way hatred had taught him to share it. There it was on the wall above the sink: ABIGAIL SMELLS LIKE CAT POOP.

Over the next week, Stanley reproduced this slogan wherever he could; in other bathrooms, on tabletops in empty classrooms and the cafeteria when no one was looking, but also in books he flipped through in the library during his breaks under the not too sharp eye of Mrs. Frobisher. He even added it to Abigail's drawings of ponies and whatnot where they hung in the hall outside the art room, attaching SMELLS LIKE CAT POOP to her signature; she always dotted the i's in her name with flowers or hearts, the sort of thing that invites target practice from the goblin-minded, even at the best of times, which this certainly wasn't.

What Stanley didn't predict was that the slogan he'd saddled Abigail with would reproduce itself independent of him. There it was, freshly scribbled beside her coat hook. SMELLS was missing the last S, but that was beside the point; Stanley hadn't put it there. And outside, on the playground beside the swings; someone had paced it out in the snow in letters large enough to only be seen from the top of the slide. And again, on her desktop, not written, but carved into the pressboard surface, perhaps with the business end of a compass from geometry glass, singing out between the stickers of unicorns and other nonsense Abigail had slapped all over the place. This last one represented a risk Stanley never would have taken. It left him feeling outdone, and somewhat awed by the way hatred emboldens people, especially when shared out in the open like a picnic. No one tried very hard to hide what they thought of Abigail anymore. The boy she'd slapped, the girl she'd spit on, the fat students she always reminded of their fatness; they all held their noses when Abigail flounced past, her shoes blinking like a rescue beacon long unheeded.

Stanley never joined in the nose-holding; it would have been redundant as the actual cat shit he'd put in her shoes. It didn't matter now; that had been mostly for him anyway, a gift gesture. He was happy enough watching the raw form of the monster he hadn't created, only released, as it shambled after Abigail, trailing its claws along the ground the way he'd always imagined Jean Bulow's husband did when he wasn't in a hurry. There was no putting the beast back now that it was out, but the adults at school did their best. The custodians scrubbed the bathroom walls and lunchroom tabletops each week, blanking the tablet for Stanley's classmates to begin it all again; somewhere, it had been decided that no flat surface looked right without ABIGAIL SMELLS LIKE CAT POOP embellishing it. Sometimes words were missing or the phrase was abbreviated, but the meaning was always clear and present. Teachers and classroom aides checked student's pockets for markers and pens before they went to the bathroom or anywhere else below the horizon until some of the more libertarian oriented parents got wind of it; angry phone calls, hollow but numerous legal threats, and allusions to Nazi Germany were made in turn, all of which combined to give Mr. Dux a pretty good idea of the thickness of the ice he loped upon. That didn't stop him from hiring monitors for the halls and watchers for the bathrooms. Whatever corner of the school budget he'd needed to hollow out to do it couldn't have been great, so no one complained and maybe it was a compromise; the new employees were mostly seasonal laborers working for beer money or retirees needing something to do during the day, even if it was only sitting on a folding chair outside the bathroom and keeping a log of its condition whenever someone went in or out; student name, time of use, and a checkmark if everything looked good. Simple enough, it seemed, almost errorless if you didn't take cigarette breaks, naps that needed to happen, and long lunches into account, which Mr. Dux hadn't. By the time he did, it was too late to do anything about his mistake except see it through to the end. The team of incompetents he'd hired were under contract, the teachers union would skin him alive if he let them do anything other than continue leaving the bathrooms and halls unguarded, each in his or her own fashion, while the obscene slogan they'd been hired to forestall ran through the school like shit through a goose. Just that morning it popped up in one of the faculty restrooms, a sure sign that things were out of control. Calling a staff meeting and demanding the culprit come forward would be correctly seen as an announcement of weakness. All his plans were bad; he saw that now. If he did nothing, it wouldn't matter which was worst. This idea left Mr. Dux feeling peaceful. His secretary appeared, reminding him he had a call in fifteen minutes with the district superintendent. The whiteboard on the back of the door rattled as she closed it on her way out, drawing Mr. Dux's attention to what was printed there in the black erasable marker he normally used to write notes to himself or chart out his day. Nothing he hadn't seen before, and nothing he wouldn't see again, most likely. Mr. Dux realized he'd reached his middle years without knowing how to lose any way other than all at once. He calmly pillowed his sport coat against his face and sobbed into it until the district superintendent called.

Meanwhile in the hall outside, Stanley sailed past the principal's office like a world-ending asteroid, on his way to a break in the

144

library, oblivious to the span of the crater he'd made in the over-head doings of the school even though he occupied its apparent center. His mind grazed elsewhere. He was thinking about Abigail. He noticed she was pretty the first time he saw her cry. That was this morning, during show and tell. She'd gone first out of habit; a mistake, it turned out. As soon as she took the floor the other students held their noses. Tears barred Abigail's cheeks. I don't even have a cat! she shouted before fleeing the classroom. Nothing was shown or told. Mrs. Veitch pursued Abigail, remanding the class to the care of her assistant, Mrs. Olaf, a full ground stop, in airport language. Mrs. Olaf kept a napkin to spit in, and her breath smelled like a kerosene heater. She seemed to be always in the process of moving, no one knew where. Stanley had seen her car in the parking lot; all the seats she didn't need to drive were crammed with boxes of what looked like knickknacks and baby clothes. Her son had either died or gone to jail; the differ-ence was indistinguishable from the way she spoke about him. She watched Mrs. Veitch leave the classroom as if her moment had come, as always. No one knew what to expect; Mrs. Olaf encouraged speculation like an old map. She was a mountain whose peak was forever clouded, an island in the fog, a house abandoned with all its furniture. The students awaited her open-ing remarks like the start of a parade. When my cat died his eyes were open so I didn't know for a few days, she told the class, adding: I think the Jamaicans upstairs might have dug him up to make one of those soups they make. That was at my old place. I don't live there anymore. I've moved a few times since then.

She paused, and a chickadee smacked the classroom window, leaving a smear on the glass, but managing to flap unevenly away, to die somewhere far from the school building. This was one of Stanley's omens. Whenever a bird hit the window, he asked for a break, no matter what. If he didn't, it would be bad luck. Mrs. Olaf didn't seem to understand the question. Stanley gets to go to the library whenever he wants so he doesn't hit any girls, supplied one of the other students. That appeared to get through. My son hit a girl once, warned Mrs. Olaf as he left the classroom, adding: we all know how that turned out for him.

The near memory of Abigail crying rattled around Stanley's head like a penny in a drier as he walked past the useless monitors cluttering the hallway, earning their health insurance, and oldsters dozing outside the bathrooms, their clipboards lying askance across their knees, the sheets unblemished. He didn't know what he wanted from her. He knew he'd made her an object of ridicule to some, so she was also now an object of pity to others. Both meant she was the still the center of attention, the thing she seemed to crave most from other people. All he'd managed to do was swap out the lens they saw her through, and set her on the other side of the glass. And now she was also on his mind, so he also knew he'd failed. True revenge would have been making her invisible, irrelevant, or boring to others, impossible to do unless you have something better to distract them with, a thing to dangle or brighter lights to follow. Stanley had no lights of any kind, only the beacon of hatred he'd paid forward, and now lost sight of as it outgrew him. But he'd learned that Abigail had nice blond hair, and pretty blue eyes. When she cried, she looked less like the bitch he remembered, and not all like the fairytale monster her mother had turned into. Maybe Abigail would end up in one his father's magazines someday. Who could say?

The future suddenly unrolled from the present like an endless carpet stretching from the mountains to the sea. It made Stanley wonder what age he needed to be before his new feelings for

Abigail found a proper context; fourteen, as it turned out, nearly fifteen. They were both in ninth grade by then. She was the prettiest of her friends, a bad sign, at that age. Stanley had no friends, but was thought of as wanting it that way by everyone. He wore a Fugazi t-shirt to school three days a week and liked skateboarding, Wheel of Time novels, and horror movies. He had no idea what she liked; evidence of it never stuck with him. But they were now friendly enough in a neighborly way for her to diddle him during an eclipse after he'd walked over the meadow to her house one mushy spring afternoon. How had it happened? He could remember the schematic, but the nuts and bolts slipped through his fingers. A vague invitation at the base of the lake, where the bus dropped them off on Friday afternoon; that was how it started. They walked the mile home together often enough to make some kind of gesture inevitable, some acknowledgement of the social middle ground they shared opposite corners of at school, a sign that they would give settling for each other a try. So when Saturday rolled around, Stanley found himself coiled beside Abigail on a futon squeezed against the furnace in her basement, while one of her less pretty friends narrated a film about affluent bored teenagers throwing their lives away in the communicating room, where the stairs were; if the narration ceased, that meant it sounded like Abigail's mom was coming and they better put a good face on whatever they were up to in there. This was a hand job, on her end, and not a good one. Stanley tried to give back by probing her breasts like fruit he might buy. She fended him off when he tried to go lower. That was okay. He told himself whatever was down there would open up when the time was right, the way the land always did in his dreams. He had to believe this because it saved him from needing to pretend he knew what to do in that event. He could imagine no equivalent for whatever

Abigail was doing to him, a motion that reminded him of trying to squeeze the last bit toothpaste from the tube. Attempting to picture anything more mutual sent deliquescent tongues of dread trickling like rainwater through the bedrock of his wall-to-wall ignorance. He assumed they were kissing to keep from talking. That part felt normal to him. Her lips had a glossy finish and tasted like cider or cinnamon, maybe applesauce. Her spit hung from his chin like a sneeze. It was dark in the boiler room so they occasionally missed mouths, their heads wetly passing like planets in close orbit. It gave him time to breath. When Abigail finally said she thought she heard her mom coming, signaling the coda, Stanley was too lightheaded to get off the futon, and pretended to lie there in glee beside the furnace long after she had giggled off to the other room.

They parted ambiguously before the movie or the eclipse or the hand job was over. He called her the next day to see if she wanted to do it all again and she said no. He understood the bench test had failed and didn't take it personally. Later, he heard she told several people his dick was too small. He wondered how she would know, but measured it on his own time anyway with a tape from his mother's sewing basket. He realized Abigail fractured his pride without wounding anything essential about him, the way he had done to her years ago, so they were finally even, as he saw it. Pride held the whip, wore the chevrons, told you where the line started. It made him measure his penis like he had some basis for comparison as it had once prevented Abigail from throwing the shoes away despite the cat shit he'd larded them with.

Or so Stanley thought, until he'd checked it out on his way back from the library an hour or so after Abigail hadn't shown or told. It was recess. The hallway was empty. The students were outside. The watchers were at lunch. The shoes were there, paired beneath her coat hook, as usual. Stanley lifted the insole of each. The turds were there still, mummified by the heat of her feet. Seeing this was like having someone tell you a joke they've forgotten you told them first. He felt ashamed by what he'd done without feeling sorry for Abigail, a tricky fence to straddle. But he didn't want to think a girl with cat shit in her shoes was pretty, so he scraped out the desiccated turds, repatriating them in the backpack of the wiseass busybody who made the crack about him hitting girls to Mrs. Olaf earlier that morning. Doing this was regressive, but taking no joy in it felt like progress; his hatred had been circumcised, sent off in the rain without a hat, free to circle back after it had considered its crimes. Stanley washed his hands in the unisex bathroom down the hall, the place where it all started. The custodians had recently painted the walls; there was nothing to look at but newness, closing in on all sides.

6.

"Look up to something, yes, do that, because that is right for you, you're young, terribly young . . . but always admit to yourself you despise it, the thing you're looking up to with respect."
—Robert Walser, Jakob van Gunten

Sue Halloran came with spring. Not like a flower, or the showers that draw it up; like a section of road collapsing after a thaw, swallowing everything that swims above. A bottom-feeder gulping toward the light, that was her. The house was situated like a primitive keep, hidden in a dark pine grove at the peak of a tall hill, with gray fields falling away in every direction. Stanley could pick out his mother's Subaru coming for him when she was still a half-mile out. Emptiness held each window he looked out of like a porthole; he had never been in a place that made him feel so alone. Past the fence were the pines, and beyond the pines, only farmland socked in by mist that never entirely dissipated, as if the ground it rose from was under some enchantment. Things howled from the fogbank; tractors maybe, he hoped. Stanley never saw one, so he didn't know. His view was limited to what he could see through the fence, and his fear made bottomless by it, or by what he imagined dragging around out in the mist.

He was filling an opening; that was what his mother had said when she finally pulled him out of Martina McDougal's at the end of March, just as things had begun to get good there, mostly because of Paul, who showed up at Martina's after Christmas. Paul was few years younger than Stanley, and used to getting his way at home. He turned into a wild animal when Martina took his Game Gear away for playing it at the table during snack. Paul called her a fucking bitch, and threw his chocolate milk against the wall. She told him to go to timeout after he cleaned up his mess. Paul did neither of these things. Instead, he said he was going home. I know where my house is, he shouted; I'm leaving and you can't stop me because you're not my parents, you fucking bitch! Sit down, and be quiet, right now, hissed Martina, closing in; any more language like that and I'll wash your mouth out with soap. If you touch me, I'll kick your ass and then you'll get arrested! said Paul; My dad's a cop! You'll go to jail! Don't talk to my mom like that, said Wendell, crisply. Shut up, you fat retard! replied Paul. Martina made a grab for him at that, but Paul ducked her arm, grabbed his Game Gear off the kitchen counter, and ran straight out of the house.

He was already on the road by the time Martina made it to the porch, and well into the woods by the time she made it to the road. All the children watched her through the window, all except Stanley, who took the opportunity to fill his pockets with cookies in the kitchen, and was sitting in the bathroom with the door locked eating them one by one on the toilet by the time Martina returned and threw everyone out in the yard while she made a phone call. Stanley overheard the whole thing from the bathroom, Martina misrepresenting events, or manhandling them until they fell in her favor, as she always did, saying she couldn't keep a boy like Paul at the same rate as other children. If he was going to stay, it would cost whoever was on the other end of the line.

This turned out to be Paul's father, who was the chief of the Barre City Police Department. He and three deputies turned up forty minutes later in two cruisers and fished Paul out of the woods, following the tracks he'd left until they found the boy playing his Game Gear in someone's deer stand. The convoy departed after that, and everyone assumed they wouldn't see Paul again. But he showed up the next day, and played his Game Gear all through snack, helping himself to as many cookies and as much chocolate milk as he wanted. Stanley realized this is what privilege can buy; freedom from idiots like Martina, and rights to their goods. She said nothing about it, even later that afternoon, after she'd tried to put Wendell in charge of Paul when everyone went outside. Paul caught on pretty quick and ran off into the woods in back of the house, daring Wendell to come find him. Come and get me, you fat ass retard! he shouted, over and over until Wendell went inside to his room. This became a regular enough thing by the time Stanley left for Sue Halloran's compound that sightings of Wendell around the house became rare indeed; the boy was like an endangered species in his own home. The only sign he was still there was the sound of pinging from behind the closed door of his bedroom as Paul screamed from the woods, daring Wendell to come outside.

When Paul grew tired of this, he threw stones at passing cars or chased the other children with a stick. He swatted Abigail once across the back, and she came in crying. Martina comforted her, and did nothing; whatever she was paid to ignore Paul was clearly worth more than she got for paying attention to the other children, including her own, declining in his room like a Latin noun at that very moment. It taught Stanley that evil needed to be allowed before it could flourish; watering it with miserliness and overall stupidity helped. From the kitchen table, Stanley surveyed the wreckage of the household. Martina sat blankly beside Abigail rubbing her back, drying her tears, as video game sounds pinged from the end of the hall where Wendell sheltered, and the three indistinguishable boys streaked past the living room window pursued by Paul, stick held high. I'm coming you fags! he howled with glee. Paul had blown life into certain terrible things Stanley recognized in himself, things he would never do because he feared their consequences, but had often wished to do. But now that he saw these same wishes granted for Paul, they seemed no more special than the long afternoons he'd spent kicking Aiden in the balls at Jean Bulow's house. It was just more meanness to move the day along.

Stanley's disappointment disappointed him enough to take the stick away from Paul and kick him the balls for hurting Abigail, who always looked prettiest when she cried. Stanley still didn't know how to feel about that. But Paul was smaller than he was, and hurting him was easier than asking Abigail if she wanted to go to the movies or get an ice cream. The policeman's son lay on the ground, crying while the other children looked on. Stanley went inside and ran Paul's Game Gear under the faucet in the kitchen for a few minutes. Martina watched him do this, saying nothing, looking a bit war-torn as she combed Abigail's hair with her fingers. Stanley helped himself to some cookies and played video games with Wendell until his mother came for him. It was a weird afternoon. But the upshot was that Martina, Wendell, Paul, and everyone else left him alone after it. Paul had a new Game Gear within the week, but stuck to playing it far from wherever Stanley was. This was fine with him. He was no longer encouraged to interact with the other children, and was allowed to read on the couch or watch Darkwing Duck until he got picked up. It took some time, but things appeared to have worked out for Stanley. Then his mother shipped him off to Sue Halloran's house.

The couch he would have liked to read on there always had Sue and her three daughters socking it in, basking beneath the eye of daytime television. There were two robust and villainous sons as well, usually tinkering with one of the four or five blocked-up cars out front when they weren't mingling with the schoolchildren out back. They and their sisters all lived at home with Sue, and didn't appear to have any place they needed to be during the day. It made her house a little like a kennel or den, all howls and yips and dominance displays, with Sue perched at the top, and her children sliding in and out of favor beneath her like tranches of the same dubious investment. Fur flew like rice at a wedding.

Two of the daughters were hugely pregnant. Stanley imagined the sons had done this, the both of them, between rounds of striding shirtless around the playground out back. They were always a little sunburnt and angry, maybe because of it. One had a port-wine stain blotting the upper half of his torso like a volcanic map. The other seemed to take heart from this, his brother's firemark, and the lead as well, in everything they did together.

Stanley heard they liked to take kids like him for walks outside the fence, and make them fight with sticks in the pinewoods; if you won, you didn't have to fight the next day. He waited his turn in the shade of a play structure that swayed when the wind blew, and atop which children were sometimes trapped for hours when the same wind blew the ladder over, or one of the brothers ran off with it. No one who got stuck up there seemed to mind. You were off the ground, out of sight and out of range of whatever awful thing preyed below.

Who knew how his mother found out about this place. Maybe from Sue's sister, Mrs. Halloran. She taught gym class at Stanley's school. He had no idea what her first name was; he didn't have any reason to learn it. Nothing Mrs. Halloran represented was related to his interests; dodgeball, popcorn parachute, or Jump Rope for Heart, wherein Stanley and his classmates were made to believe the fatness of America could be skipped away in an afternoon. He used his breaks to avoid all of this, slipping out of the gym to the library down the hall to read whatever offhand pornography he could find in the spinning cassette of mass-market paperbacks by the back wall. Mrs. Frobisher still dogged his movements, even after all the time they had spent together. Stanley began imagining that she was the last of her kind, and he was witnessing the final moments of a species soon to be struck from the record. This made him feel comfortable and occasionally lucky. And putting up with the silent scrutiny of a living fossil like Mrs. Frobisher was always better than whatever nonsense Mrs. Halloran had brewed up for the day, he could be sure of that; hula hooping, juggling scarves, capturing the flag. Who cared? Not Stanley. Mrs. Halloran always looked a little sad when he said he needed a break during the opening of her class. But you haven't even heard what we're doing today; she would usually say something like that, her voice lonely as a glacier shedding itself into the sea. Stanley would have felt worse about this, her need for him, if most of the grownups he disappointed didn't seem lonely to begin with. His ability to haunt the same common ground they did and sympathize with people like Mrs. Halloran had been fatigued into torpor long ago, wearing out its usefulness like an old horse hitched too often to the same plow. As it was now, loneliness in the adults around him might as well have taken place on the moon.

That was maybe the big difference between Mrs. Halloran and her sister. Sue was never lonely. How could she be? Three lazy daughters, two deranged sons, not to mention the tide of children washing up on the doorstep of her hilltop compound five days a week. Her house straddled a few districts, so she got kids from all over. Stanley knew almost none of them; he was just glad there were enough to hide among. The yard was large enough to keep them all strangers, and there were enough playhouses, amusement nooks, and other structures for Stanley to narrowly pass each afternoon by himself, watching treetops nod in the mist above the yard like the masts of ships grouping at port. The nearest he came to making a friend was when a boy named Timothy asked him to come see something behind one of the playhouses, and exposed himself to Stanley when they got there. This left no impression on Stanley, even after he heard Timothy telling everyone what Stanley made him do behind the playhouse. The other children were too dispersed and listless to care overmuch about who showed who what dick where. Everyone was just trying to avoid seeing Timothy's penis themselves, or having to go into the woods with Sue's sons, or getting their mouth scrubbed out with dish soap for saying something she didn't like, a thing she was in the habit of doing to pass the time during commercial breaks.

They were studying American government in school. Mrs. Veitch explained what a democracy was to the class, and told them they lived in one, that they were free. Stanley wondered why he saw no evidence of this. He and the other kids he knew spent most of the day bored or living in fear. So this was democracy then, he decided, looking around Sue's yard at the children sheltering in place; another rhetorical byway for the very few to practice and refine their cruelty toward the very many. Mrs. Veitch had thrown in a few words about equality as well; this made a little more sense to Stanley. Everyone he knew suffered equally and as well beneath the mantle of powerlessness they shared; it was hard to imagine being better than anyone else when they were all waiting for the same shoe to drop. But Mrs. Veitch really lost him when she capped off the class by encouraging her students to be proud of their country. How could Stanley be proud of something he took no part in? It was like being proud of the bus he rode to Sue Halloran's house each day, acting like it was the best bus ever when it was barely average, dirty, smelly, cold in winter, like a breath of hell in the summer, captained by a hog-necked alcoholic with hay in his hair.

Later on, Stanley learned that cheering on the inescapable parts of American life is how most people get through it; that was why folks always went crazy when they actually had something to get excited about, rioting their way through holiday sales after Thanksgiving or flipping cars over when their favorite sports team won. Even waging war lost some of its glamour when you realized how badly people needed to see their leaders victimize someone else for a change, someone without as much to be proud of, less to cheer for. It feels good to crunch around the sand in boots with the weight of a weapon in your hand and the flag snapping over fresh ruins; this is because war is sports mated to progress. As a child, Stanley associated sports with Mrs. Halloran, and progress, the manifest sort, with her sister; all the rights to life, liberty, and the pursuit of happiness Mrs. Veitch assured him of each day at school were swept away as soon as he arrived at the compound on the misty hill, where each new development in Sue's household rolled his personhood back like a retractable awning.

Lately, there had been a problem with the plumbing in the downstairs bathroom, the only one the twenty or so children under Sue's care were allowed to use; upstairs was reserved for family, or friends, if she had any. The outcome was that anyone caught flushing away the paper they'd wiped themselves with instead of throwing it in a receptacle beside the toilet would lose snack and/or outdoor privileges, depending on Sue's mood. It had already happened to Stanley, an error he'd made out of habit rather than malice and realized too late, almost stooping to dredge the spitball of used tissue out of the toilet's porcelain throat with his bare hands before one of the gravid daughters started hammering on the door. You were supposed to let them see the bowl before you flushed to make sure it was clear; that was the system Sue had worked out. Stanley spent the rest of the afternoon at the snack table, first watching the other children eat, and then listening to them play outside, forbidden to move from where he was, but moving anyway after Sue and her litter abandoned him to go watch television down the hall. He raided the snack cabinet first, gorging himself like a cursed Greek, feeling neither satiety nor joy, only the foundational sense of obligation hatred towers over when all roads suddenly lead to it.

But there was more to be done. Before Sue went off to watch TV with her daughters, Stanley saw her transfer a load of bed sheets between the washer and dryer in the alcove off the kitchen. The cycle still had twenty minutes left when he opened the door, probably long enough to dry the cup of pee he threw in before restarting it. Stanley knew he was regressing in a way he wouldn't feel bad about until later on, after something newly dehumanizing had reared up to overshadow this regression, or call attention to how nothing had really been changed by it. Tonight, Sue would bed down on the sheets he'd soiled to dream up fresh torments for him and the other children the next day, the same as every other night. Going forward, Stanley would always remember pissing in her laundry when election season rolled around and voting came up; remember rinsing out the cup and setting it in the dish rack before resuming his post at the snack table, exactly where he'd been when she told him not to move before leaving the room.

Stanley's tenure at Sue Halloran's house came to a close the day her swimming pool opened up. It was an aboveground job with a deck erected around it, the kind of setup that makes poor people feel seasonally rich. The day was warmish, humid, and unusual. Sue's daughters, pregnant and otherwise, were deployed in a fertile crescent around the yellow water in oversized t-shirts and bikini bottoms, all loudness, soda slurping, and thighs fanning out of deck chairs like they were preparing to give birth on the spot. Even though he didn't care about swimming pools, it made Stanley want to get closer, to sit with his eyes just above the water like an alligator, taking in the littleness the girls had to offer. They weren't pretty, but they were real enough to reproduce their kind, which was good enough for him. The women in his father's magazines never carried anything they couldn't do without, diaphanous shawls, large straw hats, baskets of fruit. The sort of ugliness he lived with was unsheddable, so it made sense that its attendant furies would represent choices it was too late to walk away from.

Children splashed around in borrowed swimsuits. He asked Sue if she had something he could wear. She went into the house and reappeared with a one-piece leotard that would have looked exactly right on a girl about Stanley's age. He thought she was joking; she wasn't.

You ain't gotta wear the straps, she said; just fold it down and no one will know. I think they will, said Stanley, thinking: my dick will fall out the bottom of that, you lunatic whore; I can just swim in my underwear. Nope, replied Sue, already looking a little put out, a sign she was probably about to double down; you wear a suit in my pool or you don't go in. And you gotta have a pair of these since I don't know if you can swim. She produced a set of neon floaties from somewhere nearby. Stanley imagined himself flapping around the three or so feet of lukewarm water in a girl's swimsuit with floaties engirdling his arms, trying to steal a glance at the cloven vacuity beneath the overbite of each engorged womb at the waterside like a spelunker cutting turf. I can swim, he said. Show me, said Sue, proffering the girl's swimsuit. She had him there. Stanley said nothing, and returned to the yard, just as Sue's shirtless sons appeared. Children scattered like minnows, up to the top of the swaying structure, into the playhouses, off to wherever seemed out of reach. All the hiding places were suddenly taken. Stanley had nowhere to go. His turn had come.

The boys led him and four others into the mist, the pines swishing and swaying like sails. No one spoke. Fun sounds from the poolside faded as they followed Sue's sons deeper into the woods. Timothy walked beside Stanley, looking nervous. Whipping it out wouldn't solve this, so Stanley figured Timothy was out of choices. They stopped in a clearing, one side of which let out onto the curtain of empty field Stanley's mother always hove out of when she arrived. You go first, said Sue's son, the unstained one, handing Stanley a stick. He turned to face his opponent, who turned out to be Timothy, looking unchallenging without his dick to cover the balance. Stanley knew he could win this round easily, and have tomorrow off, but it wasn't enough to make him want to. He was big for his age. Sue's sons were probably around sixteen or seventeen, bigger than him. But Stanley had a stick. Fight, ordered the one with the port wine stain. Stanley turned and smacked him in the side of the head with the stick instead of going for Timothy. Blood descended from a cut above the boy's brow ridge like rainwater rolling off a roofline, blending with the pigment feathering his shoulder and chest like war paint. Stop you faggot! ordered his brother, advancing the way his mother did when she was about squirt dish soap on someone's tongue for saying no or darn or jump up your own ass you round-heeled hillbilly squaw. Stanley lashed out again with the stick, dividing the boy's upper lip and stripping a tooth from his jaw, all in one motion. The sudden pain Stanley had caused distracted everyone momentarily from the matters at hand, but he knew he was in trouble immediately. He dropped the stick and ran off into the mist.

Kill your leaders. That was all he thought then, the lion's share of the lesson he took away from Sue's house that day. Those who lead must be destroyed. Kill them, and move on; wait for the next to slide into place and kill them too. The violence Stanley participated in haunted him only because it felt incomplete without Sue standing by to receive her end of it, a kick in the ass or stick to the tit. He'd seen fear in the brothers' eyes before he'd dropped the stick and run away. That was how he knew he'd made the right choice. It was what watching Paul had taught him: evil must be allowed in order to flourish. He'd ended up having to kick Paul in the balls for more or less the same reason he'd hit Sue's sons with the stick, but the takeaway from watching him tear apart Martina McDougal's household still held. All power draws fire. Stanley would be the fire.

Both boys needed stitches, and one of them some dental work. His mother related all this after Stanley was recovered over by the district high school, where he ended up when the fog lifted. A security guard found him loitering around the parking lot, and lured him to the front office after saying he would have to call the cops if Stanley didn't call his parents. He chose his mother, knowing she would cycle through the descending order of confusion, anger, and sadness faster than his father after the story about why he was calling in the first place came out. Sue actually saved him the trouble. Stanley's mother had all the basic details by the time he got her on the phone. Gratitude at him turning up unharmed replaced confusion in the order of operations. There was no way of shouldering anger out of the way, but Stanley knew his mother would wait until she had him in the car to let it rip. He had about an hour before that happened, and the nice ladies who worked in the front office allowed him to wait it out in the library across the atrium.

The library had all the books he liked to read through on his breaks and many more, a previously unimaginable harvest of one-sided sex, flashy violence, and gutter talk. Stanley set to reaping as much of it as he could while he waited for his mother to arrive. She could take all day for all he cared. Without Mrs. Frobisher creaking around, casting her warped shadow over the pages he read, munching like a dromedary through her lunch in the back office, there was nothing to distract him. Stanley had become so used to something hostile or repulsive greeting him whenever he glanced up from the page that the older girls flying like figureheads through the atrium outside almost seemed grotesque in light of what they stood against in his mind, like naiads at a public pool. Most of them wore shorts and halter-tops; it had been an unseasonably warm day.

The place Stanley held then, a low chair in a glassy, out of the way corner, was a spot he would return to years later, when he was a student at the high school with a low B average, a short, knotty string of hit-or-miss girlfriends, and no car. His teachers all agreed that he was smart, but not nearly smart enough to explain how bored he appeared to be in their classes; he would have had to be troubled or slightly retarded to really pull it off, so the low-achieving genius tag never stuck, fluttering off instead to alight on the shoulders of a boy named Phil who lived with his mother in a motel up by the airport. Phil spent his weekends playing trading cards games in the back room of a comic book store in Barre, and was making a suit of armor in the school's metal shop. He ended up studying philosophy at Swarthmore and then at Stanford, and then having some kind of wild breakdown that prevented him from continuing. He was shipped home to live with his mother in a brand-new block of low-income housing by the food coop in Montpelier. Stanley sometimes saw Phil puttering around the railroad tracks in back of his mom's unit with a loaf of day-old bread from the food coop's dumpster, tearing pieces off and throwing them to birds that weren't there. It reminded Stanley of Wendell, or the damage people do by empowering whoever they decide needs it without checking to see if they do or not. If Phil had fewer mentors in high school, people to drive him to test-prep classes, guidance counselors managing his scholarship portfolio, maybe he'd still be casting spells and slaying dragons at the comic shop in Barre, happily mediocre, like the rest of us, instead of whatever he was now, a low-achieving genius all grown up; in other words, a low-achiever.

Seeing the wreckage doing everything right had made of Phil left Stanley glad he'd chosen to spend most of his high school years hiding out in the corner chair in the library. It was where he went when he was either in trouble or about to be, the place he came to skip a test he hadn't prepared for, avoid a study hall he'd been assigned for skipping the class he needed to prepare for the test, or a meeting with some well-meaning career fraud who wanted to explain why the test was important if Stanley wanted to graduate, a thing that always seemed to hang in an unstrikeable balance between outstanding achievement and absolute failure whenever it was brought up, as if the school administration would tolerate nothing greater or less. It was the only leverage anyone had, Stanley realized later, after he emerged from high school with his diploma and a scholastic resume free of accolades of any kind, no sports, no chess club, not even an editorship on the school newsletter; his life on paper might as well have barely begun. Stanley fiddled around comfortably and unremarkably for a year before entering the comfortable and unremarkable liberal arts college where his father had a radio show on weekends, mostly because being a student seemed like an even-handed way to live at home for a few more years. People he'd graduated with were buying houses, starting families, and founding dynasties, judging by the way his mother talked about it. Stanley only missed the limbo high school represented when he saw how hard his parents had to work to find something to be proud of about what he'd done since leaving it behind; not enough time had passed for him to forget what it felt like to have his future be something they were excited about.

In general, parents teach their children how to do great things, and children teach their parents how to settle, in that order. Shortly before starting his freshman year of college, Stanley overheard his mother talking to a friend over the phone, praising the way he'd helped her stack firewood that morning as if he'd just graduated from law school. Stanley was mortified. He wanted to dig a hole in the yard in which to inter himself and all signs of his earthbound existence, to give his parents a chance to start over from scratch, or maybe just with Titus. But his father had just mowed the lawn and was obviously proud of how it came out; Stanley didn't want to disturb that. This was the only time the stuff his mother always said about owning his own home really sunk in.

The high school library was also where he went when things were a little disorderly in his life. It had the convenient and sacrosanct feel of a roadside shrine. No one bothered him there. He was free to mope away the day over the soccer captain who said his Cure t-shirt was gay, or a girl who'd told him he was too clingy to take seriously, or another who wouldn't leave him alone, and had begun leaving pictures of herself with E.E. Cummings poems written on the back in the door of his gym locker; he had no idea how she'd smuggled herself in there. The library was where he spent the morning after his father had returned from Dartmouth-Hitchcock with some not so great news. That was the tail end of Stanley's senior year. Everyone around him was excited to be moving on; Stanley knew he wasn't going anywhere, especially not now. How could he? He had a feeling his parents were lying about how much he should worry. He might never do anything spectacular, but he would always be on hand. He missed the time when he'd first sat where he was sitting then, when it seemed like all the bad things that happened could be hung on the raft of low-grade personalities overseeing him each day rather than the swirling, top-down indifference of the universe. He didn't think he would ever be happier to be in trouble than that first day in the high school library, waiting for his mother to retrieve him.

What were you thinking? That was first question she asked him after they were in the car. Kill your leaders, Stanley thought. He didn't say that. His mother didn't wait for an answer. She was summarizing what he'd done, or the lopsided version Sue had given her over the phone after her sons returned from the forest without him. The details were all there, but the specifics were missing. Maybe Sue didn't know them. Stanley was willing to give her the benefit of the doubt on that. She probably thought the best of her shitty kids, the same as every other parent. You're seeing a therapist, said his mother; your father is looking for someone for you right now. Oh, fuck no, thought Stanley. You can't keep up this kind of thing with other kids, continued his mother; you really hurt those boys. Now we have to pay for the stitches, the dentist, all of it. And I know you're probably thrilled that you don't have to go back there, but I don't think you understand how hard it was to get you that spot in the first place. And I have to take work off until we can find another placement for you. I'm not sure you're aware of any of this, Stanley, and I'm sorry if hearing it makes you feel bad, but you need to know how doing this kind of shit affects us as a family.

Aside from the medical details, Stanley was aware of all this already, and felt bad for his mother. He knew she had done her best to get him out of a crappy situation at Martina McDougal's house. It was too bad his mother's best had landed no higher than Sue Halloran, a woman who raised idiots like sweet corn, wanted him to cross-dress for her amusement, and collected filth like a storm drain. He remembered the basket in the bathroom, piled high with shit paper; you couldn't even wipe your ass at her place without looking over your shoulder.

Stanley didn't want to get into any of this with his mother. It would only make her feel bad. He would see a therapist, whatever that was, and accept however else his parents decided to punish him. Maybe no TV for a week or something; he could live with that. Your father and I decided you're going to write a letter of apology to Sue and her family, said his mother; it will give you a chance to think about what you did and why you can't do stuff like this anymore. You can start when you get home.

This was too much, far more than he'd predicted or bargained for. He could fake his way through a verbal apology; the kerfuffle with Astrid had been no sweat. But putting it down on paper and handing it over gave it realness and permanence, the weight of a trophy, something Sue could refer back to whenever she wanted, evidence that someone somewhere had done her wrong and was now paying for it. It was like peeing in her laundry, only worse; nothing would change because nothing had to, now that there was written evidence to support her continuing to be an autocrat harridan slutbag. Kill your leaders, Stanley thought; I am the fire that power draws. With that, concern for his mother's feelings slid off his conscience onto the chopping block.

They made us fight with sticks, said Stanley. What? asked his mother; who did? He explained. She listened. By the time they got home, she wasn't angry at him anymore. She called Sue, and the two of them had a long discussion. His mother took the phone into her room and closed the door, so Stanley couldn't hear most of it. She looked tired when she came out and noticed him sitting on the couch in the living room, looking expectant. She gave him a hug, said he wasn't in trouble, and asked if he was okay. He said he was, and asked if she still had to pay for the stitches and dentist. His mother shook her head. So do I have to go back there now? His mother looked appalled at the thought that this possibility still existed somewhere in his mind. Shame you didn't kick them in the balls like that dweeb at the other place, his father piped in across the living room, rattling his newspaper emphatically. Enough, said Stanley's mother. Did you get kicked out again? asked Titus, who was tying flies at the coffee table, bent over his work, steady as a bomb-maker. Yes, said Stanley. Maybe I'll get kicked out too, continued Titus; then we can go fishing after school. Okay, said Stanley, glad to be part of the harmless amorality that reigns over all happy families. It fed and settled him like bread soaked in milk. Since I'm not going back so Sue's house, said Stanley; can I just walk home from the bus stop tomorrow? Not a chance, said his father from behind his newspaper.

7.

"No doubt about it, this apocalypse provided a magnificent spectacle."
—Albert Speer, *Inside the Third Reich*

The landscape in Stanley's dreams had developed. Platforms stood in the water in the far cove that had opened like a mouth when Martina McDougal sang to it, houses on stilts, walkways between them hung with lanterns, bunting, Christmas lights. An island rose from the skin of the lake like a wart, a hotel or car-avansary of some kind topping it off. People skimmed the sur-face of the water in motorless launches, canoes, and on rafts, ignoring Stanley as they went about their unclear business. Who were they? He never knew. He floated through all this invisibly, unnoticed as he rested his elbows on the rails of the catwalk between two houses, watching the sun drop into a crack between the hills across the lake, something he had never seen here before. The land no longer rippled like a mirage or rose to meet the sky; whoever these people were, they had settled it, driven out the wildness he had come to rely upon. The camps he knew were cleared away or refurbished until they were unfamiliar, converted to shops, markets, apartments; the shore was a bolus of activity too thick and rangy to swallow.

It looked like they'd run out of room at the water's edge and started building out into it; all the structures perching on the surface and linked by bridges like the one he stood on, watching the sunset, were fancy. Whenever Stanley came here, there was always something new going up; the sound of hammers hammering and saws coughing reached him no matter where he was, seated at an empty table in one of the cafes on shore, digging through books in a shop tucked in the elbow of the far cove, or watching a woman undress in her bedroom. Stanley noticed her shopping in one of the markets on shore, and followed her home. She lived in one of the newer houses; it hadn't been here the last time he was. Her bedroom was on the top floor. She stood naked against a paned window framing the unpeopled hillside across the water like an aiming site. Stanley knew it wouldn't be long before the progress she represented found its way over there too. That was the pattern, how things got done. Cruelly and inevitably, so beautiful people like the naked woman before him could have what they wanted, fun places to shop and eat and walk their dogs. Was her nudity enough to make him forget what he was losing in order to see it? She was perfect in a way Stanley was familiar with from his father's magazines. He occupied a wing chair beside the mirror she looked herself over in, and left the house after realizing he was bored by how beautiful she was, the same way he was bored by the destination location she and all the people like her had built over the shifting sands of his hermitage. She cupped her breasts speculatively, her bottom lip pouting like a half-shut drawer; he saw it from above then, the roofs of houses overlaying the water, blotting it out until the lake was lost forever, and he knew he would never forgive these people, whoever they were, for the way they'd ceilinged his dreams and made him an alien in his own head.

He passed her husband on the stairs, the kind of straight up and down stooge he would later come to know from Chicago's municipal recreation paths, flying by in a spandex costume aboard a precision bicycle, whistling people out of the way so his kilometer/time ratio wouldn't droop. For now, he was only a mediocre enemy, another intruder living out a quitclaim on holy land. He worked at the islanded hotel, a place Stanley hadn't visited yet, but had seen people with uniforms like the woman's husband paddling out to and away from at sunrise and sunset. Who stayed there? Stanley never found out. The island was out of bounds. The current always drove him away, or the wind was too strong; whatever craft he commandeered to get out there either swung wide of its mark or had to turn back. He'd tried swimming and been carried by a volley of small, gentle waves back to the beachhead as people in kayaks and rowboats flew past without a hitch. He settled for observing the island from a pair of coin-operated binoculars the town council had installed on the promenade he'd once ridden Martina McDougal down when it was a still a dirt road banded with empty seasonal homes. The hotel looked more like a B&B job, an overlarge Victorian house with a mansard roof and circular tower off to one side, a yawning porch, fussy landscaping, the sort of place that ends up looking a little haunted all year round no matter what you do to dress it up. Nothing about the hotel on the island suggested why Stanley couldn't go there, or that it was even a hotel; he never saw anyone who looked like a guest, and didn't know where the idea of it being a place to stay had come from. But he went on thinking of it that way since it was all the dream had allowed him to think about it, so he settled for what he already knew like the indolent college student he would one day become.

In point of fact, the hotel was only a house, a house on Cliff Street in Montpelier where, several years later, Stanley would lose his virginity to a classmate after going to see her paintings at the bar and grill that had agreed to hang them for a munic- ipal art walk. His feelings about the art and its authoress were mixed, but he went home with her anyway, thinking of himself as charitable at the time, big-hearted even, since she wasn't too pretty, slipping easily into the mold most men never stray from of imagining the standards they imagine for themselves as a sort of red carpet, rolled in and out according to how generous they feel toward the women they see, judge, and disappoint. He didn't recognize the house then, or not as the hotel from his dreams, but the sense of déjà vu stayed with him, long after he and his classmate had gotten the thing done, said their goodbyes, and she had kicked him out so he wouldn't be there to incriminate them both when her parents got home. Still, he hung around outside afterward, gawping up at the façade like a tourist ma- rooned before a marvel, guidebook in hand, trying to see what all the fuss was about. His classmate eventually noticed Stanley lingering beneath a streetlight, and told him to buzz off from her bedroom window, which he did, snapping his guidebook shut on an entry that would maybe have written itself widely across his memory like something written in the sky if he hadn't been con- vinced he was now a man. He walked back toward town to meet his mother for a ride home; maybe she would buy him something to eat on the way.

All that was to come. For now, the land he loved was filled with things he hated, making his dreams about it as routine as the reality he previously tried to escape from. Stanley learned hatred kept regular hours, checked its watch, was never late for dinner, no matter what existential plane its bearer occupied. Knowing this made Stanley feel unlucky and vulnerable. He tested the parameters of the cheerful, middleclass settlement in his head like a prisoner pacing out the dimensions of his cell, trying to trip someone's child on the lakeside playground, throw rocks through the windows of the nicer houses, scuttle the boats lined up on the beach with an awl he'd filched from an untended toolbox. The child ran on, the windows winked merrily in the setting sunlight, and the boats floated as they always did, easily out to the forbidden island on water black as wine and smooth as silk, a surface that roused itself from placidity only when he dipped a toe in it. Stanley sensed witchcraft but couldn't source it. He had the feeling the people were laughing at him whenever he turned his back on them. He always awoke from the dream relieved to find himself back in a world that wore its evil like an armband. Still, he had to make sure it was all still there as he remembered it. He left the house each morning after breakfast and slipped down to the lake through the meadow, beneath the apple orchard, and out of the palisade of trees studding the property line, just to assure himself that it hadn't changed into something horrible while he slept.

It was summer, so the water was busier than usual with boats and swimmers, but nothing like what he'd spent the night trapped in. His waking life had become his only refuge from his dreams, a reversal he couldn't explain without acknowledging that things were pretty good at the moment. School was out; there was no Mr. Dux, Mrs. Halloran, or Mrs. Frobisher cluttering up his weekdays with their mutualized need for hollow order, shallow obedience, and nominal respect. And his father was a teacher, so Stanley got to spend the warm, bright summer days with him, swimming, hiking, and fishing instead of getting yelled at in the fenced-off yard of some redneck hag's doublewide; he hadn't seen the inside of a house he didn't want to be in since his mother pulled him out of Sue Halloran's back in April, and it was almost July now. What else? His parents got him a Discman for his birthday a few weeks ago. Stanley took it with him each morning when he went down to the lake to make sure idiots hadn't overrun it during the night. He owned three compact discs, as they were called, and kept them in constant rotation; *London Calling* in the morning, on the water, *Power, Corruption, and Lies* in the afternoon, riding around in his father's Isuzu, looking for something to do, and *Unknown Pleasures* after dark, while he was lying in bed, trying to get himself excited about what dreams would come. Ian Curtis' voice reminded Stanley of the song Martina McDougal had sung as he rode her bareback, the music he suspected might live somewhere inside him. He hoped that listening to it each night before he fell asleep might swing everything back into place; the stilted houses and their thin bridges would sink beneath the surface of the lake, the forest would crack open to swallow the eateries, condos, and boutiques on shore, and the ridge across the water would crack open, sucking the island and its goddamned unreachable bed and breakfast or whatever it was out to sea and over the horizon, never to be seen again. It never worked, leading Stanley to the conclusion that he couldn't exist without something nearby to hate, and in the absence of this in real life, his mind would compensate and betray him, raising bitterness and malignancy like a flag of quarantine wherever he laid his head.

Had Stanley declared war on himself somewhere along the line? It seemed that way, a feeling he would revisit many years later while dodging walls of flame in the Midwest. For now, he settled for the parts of it he enjoyed, the same as he did in real life; browsing in the bookshop in the far cove, shooting a pellet gun at paper targets in an arcade that sprung up one night on one of the piers, following pretty women home to watch them undress, even sometimes ones that weren't pretty, just to establish his lows in order to earn his highs. There were plenty of each that summer for Stanley. While riding his bike on the back road, he was chased by dogs and barely got away. He caught a fish Titus admired for the first time in either of their lives. He shot the state bird with a pellet gun in the apple orchard behind the house, and watched it tumble to the ground in a mess of feathers and blood instead of folding politely in on itself like the paper targets in his dreams; he buried the bird and swung the gun against the side of an apple tree until it split in half, seeding the grave with silver pellets from the shattered breach. He nearly drowned trying to masturbate beneath the surface of the lake, imagining buxom mermaids swirling nearby, egging him on in Martina McDougal's voice. His father showed him 'Stand By Me' one night when his mother was out of the house, and described it accurately as the perfect summer movie; Stanley longed for a crew of misfits to pal around with and a bully to point a gun at for a week afterward. He read a trade paperback edition of *The Unlimited Dream Company* he picked up at yard sale with his mother, and found enough of his own life in it to make him sure not so much that god existed, but that god was probably interested in the same things he was. He had a wet dream in a borrowed sleeping bag at friend's house after watching too much soft-core porn on cable, and ended up having a too-long conversation about it with his father after his friend's mother caught him trying to jam the thing into her washing machine at three in the morning and thought he'd wet the bed. She spoke to his father about it in the morning while Stanley waited in the car. Everything okay? his father asked when they were on the way home. Yes, replied Stanley. It happens, continued his father; but if it keeps happening, we should probably get you checked out. It wasn't that, said Stanley; it was the other thing. Oh, said his father, clearly relieved; that's way more normal and to be expected. Don't worry about it. I'm not, said Stanley. Good, said his father. He made Stanley an omelet when they got home, and took him and Titus to the circus in Montpelier. They ate cotton candy and got to pet a python. It turned out to be a good day.

The summer ended as it always did, with a family trip to Cape Cod. They rented a bayside cabin between the dunes. Stanley slept on the couch, and stayed up watching 'Picket Fences' on the TV after everyone went to sleep, the waves concussing outside. He and Titus rode bicycles through the beach forest, past the saltwater lagoons, scattering seabirds and dragonflies. Drag queens prowled the streets of Provincetown, men holding purses like gym bags, beautiful in their own needy way. Stanley ate ice cream on the town wharf and listened to The Smiths on his Discman, something new he'd picked up and was confused by. Titus was beside him, scratching at the bench they sat on with a Swiss Army knife, and reading through a book about pelagic fishes he'd found somewhere on Commercial Street. Their parents were off in the galleries, hunting down a respectable souvenir amid the seaside kitsch, smartass t-shirts, petrified blowfish, bottled ships. Can I have some of your ice cream? asked Titus. You spent your money, said Stanley. I know, replied Titus; I wouldn't have to ask you if I could have some if I didn't. One bite, said Stanley, handing it over. Titus took two, and handed it back. What are you listening to? asked Titus. Stanley took the cone back and handed over the headphones. Sounds like someone crying in a silo, said Titus; no wonder you have bad dreams. How do you know I have bad dreams? asked Stanley. I hear you walking around, said Titus; even here. You wake me up sometimes. Sorry, said Stanley. It's okay, said Titus; what are they about? It's hard to explain, said Stanley; it's like the end of the world except the world doesn't end. It just goes on without you, but you get to watch. Can I have some more? asked Titus, after thinking this over. Stanley passed him the cone again.

The week wound on. The family played mini-golf; Titus won. They had a fire on the beach, toasted marshmallows, drank cocoa. They ate at an Italian restaurant on a wharf at the eastern end of town. Stanley's father told him most of what was on the menu came from the boats moored outside. Stanley imagined a line of fish and crabs and cockles and whatever else marching up a gangplank through the restaurant's back door to a reedy tune played on a kind of pan pipe by a large fat man with a black bushy mustache and a chef's toque, the sort of stock character you normally expect to find ennobling a pizza box.

Stanley spent all his money the first night in town, so he haunted the leather shops and adult novelty stores until the clerks booted him out. He saw braided bullwhips, padded handcuffs, a mask with a zippered mouth, something he would have liked to throw on just about every adult he knew back home. He asked the woman behind the counter for the price and she asked him where his parents were. He wanted to tell her sixth grade would begin when he got home, and he could use something like what she sold to keep everyone in line, Mr. Dux, Mrs. Halloran, Mrs. Frobisher, whoever his parents were going to put in charge of him after school; this last part was still unclear. But he ran out of the store instead, and down Commercial Street until he found his parents and Titus having dessert in a Portuguese bakery they all liked, espresso cups, cake plates, and a painting wrapped in brown paper on the table. They asked where he'd been. Back to school shopping, he said, a little too emphatically. Find anything we can help you with? asked his mother. I doubt it, said Stanley, shoving something sweet and bulky from Titus' plate into his mouth so he wouldn't have to say anything else.

8.

"If you offer a sacrifice and are pleased with the result, both you and the sacrifice will be cursed."

—Wittgenstein, *Culture and Value*

Irma Ritter lived in a big blue house beside a big blue barn, part of the farm that had been parceled off a hundred years earlier to make the village now standing at parade rest around it, the baker's dozen of New England capes, community center, and general store that bore her name: Ritter Corner.

The titular corner was actually down the road from all this, landmarked by a red brick tavern that had once served stage-coaches clattering along the County Road to or from Montpelier; it was now a museum and occasional art gallery that was never open. Up the hill from the tavern stood a whitewashed church where Stanley and his family came to sing secular hymns on Christmas Eve. The church was heated by a single woodstove lodged in the narthex, and had no electricity or plumbing, just as it didn't when it was built in 1823, a fact the acting caretaker and self-appointed local historian of the place never wearied of sharing with out-of-staters who sometimes got lost on the back roads during foliage season. He was known to flag down cars with plates from Connecticut or New York cruising aimlessly up the hill from the direction of the tavern, waving the bewildered occupants to the shoulder to offer them a feeless tour of the church, as if he had Chartres or Mont Saint-Michel on his hands. Visitors often mistook the caretaker for someone the town had paid to appear in costume for their amusement and edification; his wife made him one new set of clothes per year and patched them as needed, which left her husband looking a little like a deserter from the Continental Army. A tricorn would have set everything off perfectly, but the caretaker favored a forage cap in bad weather, a straw hat in good, and a lustrous mutton-chop beard all year round; his face would have looked just right on enemy currency.

Stanley often saw him from the window of the school bus, stalking across the empty yellow fields behind the houses in Ritter Corner, or emerging from the purple stand of evergreens uphill from the museum as if he'd just escaped from one of the ante-bellum daguerreotypes exhibited there. The caretaker seemed to never use roads to get where he needed to go, waltzing across property lines, over fences, and through backyards with apparent neutrality, often singing shape note hymns in a strident baritone as he trespassed, sometimes with two or three neighborhood dogs trailing him. A few weeks after Stanley started taking the bus to Irma Ritter's big blue house after school. The church steeple was struck by lightning during a late summer storm, and the jack the town council got to appraise the damage gave them an estimate that was too great to keep a caretaker on the payroll.

He kept busy anyway, turning up here and there over the years, delivering firewood to Stanley's neighbors, conducting hayrides during the Ritter Corner harvest festival, setting out chairs for Thanksgiving dinner at the community center across the road from Irma Ritter's big blue house.

The last place he turned up was in a field beside the church. Some hunters crossing from the trees to the road found him lying in the shadow of the refurbished steeple, his straw hat on his chest. It was a stroke; a big one, Stanley heard. He was dog-paddling through his sophomore year of college at this point, trying to graduate on time and sleep with a girl named Jill who wrote poetry most people seemed to think was really something. Jill had a problem with her legs, a result of a childhood accident, and needed a wheelchair to get around. Stanley hoped this evened out the attractiveness differential between them. While wheeling her back to her dorm the night of the caretaker's death, he asked her how sad it was reasonable to be over the passing of someone whose name you didn't even know. Jill knew his father was sick, and assumed the question was somehow related to that; it was a topic Stanley didn't talk about much, and she was always trying to get him to. Maybe it's like a grief rehearsal, said Jill; in case things don't go well. What things? asked Stanley. You know, with your dad, she replied. I don't want to talk about that, said Stanley. Maybe you should start, she said; it's good to know how to talk about these things before they happen. Nothing's happening, replied Stanley; and even if something did, languages appear out of necessity all the time. Sure, she said; but not the kinds you need to write poetry.

Narcissist psychobabbler, thought Stanley, fighting back the urge to steer the wheelchair into an active roadway. Instead, he bonked Jill a little roughly up the steps outside her dormitory and left her there without saying goodnight. He intended to go straight home, but ended up drinking beer and driving his parent's car in circles around the lake with the windows down and his music turned up way too loud. A girl he knew from high school, Anna, had just moved into a rehabbed chicken coop down the road, so he decided to see what she was up to at this time of night. Stanley hoped to feel better by sleeping with Anna, and she seemed to read this plan loud and clear when he appeared on her doorstep, swaying in the porch light with an almost empty six-pack dangling from the end of his arm like a storm lantern, grinning with the eternal hope of an inveterate sleazebag; he looked how he felt, so this made sense.

Anna brewed him a cup of tea, spiked it with the honey she made for a living, and listened to him talk slushily about the dead caretaker for a few minutes before interrupting. You mean Phil Windsor, she said. I guess so, said Stanley; is that his name? Yup, said Anna; did you know he had a habit of accidentally locking tourists in the church and then losing the keys? Pretty girls mostly. He liked to watch them through the windows. Last summer, he kept some girl from New Jersey in there for an hour, basically until the state police showed up. The keys appeared before they had to kick the door in. I thought he lost his job because of the lightening, said Stanley. That was just an excuse to get rid of him, said Anna; The town council had been waiting for one for years. They didn't want to step on any toes, but they also didn't want a weirdo on the payroll. The Windsor family owns a lot of land in Ritter Corner, the museum, a couple houses, some lake frontage; they could do a lot of damage if they wanted to. I guess they had Phil there to collect rent, and manage the properties. I always figured he was just a local seasonal laborer type, said Stanley. He was, in a way, said Anna; but he didn't need the labor. My dad says he just did it to blend in, and appear normal so he could take the kind of risks he wanted to take. He had to stop delivering firewood because a customer found him in her bedroom after he asked to use the bathroom. He said he got lost. Shouldn't he be in jail or on a registry somewhere? asked Stanley; I mean, if he wasn't dead. There was barely anything to prosecute, said Anna; Too much reasonable doubt, folks from out of state. And even if there wasn't, his family would have bailed him out. Don't feel bad for him, Stanley. He was a creepy shitbag who got to spend his life doing exactly what he wanted to do without ever worrying about the consequences. He probably died very happy. Sounds nice, doesn't it? Stanley figured showing up at Anna's house the way he had, expecting service like a motorist at a filling station, probably answered the question for him. Her dad was a state's attorney of some kind, and had likely trained his daughter to keep an eye out for people like Phil Windsor; or Stanley, for that matter. He felt foolish, penitent, and unlucky, all at once. He gave up wishing to take back parts of the way the evening turned out; the only thing to do was try again tomorrow.

Anna took his keys, and threw a blanket over him, saying she had to work in the morning. He slept on the couch, wondering where the rest of his self-mythology began and ended; it was hard to tell so far down the pipeline. He had gotten into the routine of idealizing his past to avoid the present, always harder to do after some vibrant aspect of time gone by and fondly remembered suddenly loses its soft focus. When fed with too much context, his favorite memories always crash-landed with no survivors. This had been happening a lot lately; the caretaker was only the most recent. It left Stanley feeling like someone watching their house burn, going over what they'd left inside and would never get back. He missed the manifold ignorance of his childhood, a time when he didn't know anything about people like Phil Windsor. But it made him wonder what else he didn't know back then. The question no longer had a ceiling. Maybe Irma Ritter trafficked child sex slaves out of the big blue barn in her big green yard. Maybe that was why she was always telling him and the two other children she oversaw not to go in there. They'd gone anyway, of course; Stanley, Gardener and Anders, scrambling across the exposed beams like rats, climbing all over the cloaked and useless farm machinery, peeing in the hayloft. They'd realized early on that supervision wasn't Irma's strong suit; she was elderly, and couldn't remember her own warnings, so she wouldn't punish them for disobeying her. She kept boxes of Pop Tarts under the kitchen sink beside the cleaning supplies, and let them watch The Disney Afternoon until talk shows came on. She and her husband Varner would appear then, on the stroke of four as if summoned from a magic lamp, two people Stanley never saw move at more than a shuffle suddenly settling into their respective armchairs as if they'd been waiting since dawn to see what Sally Jesse Raphael had to say about things, and Stanley and the other two boys would go outside to tear through the big blue barn like treasure hunters loose in a pyramid's lumber room.

When the barn got old, they dug around in the other outbuildings, the sugar shack, the stables, the garage where Varner kept his car, a 1954 Cadillac with a raised commercial chassis, finned and black as a sea wolf beneath a jacket of yellow dust. Varner never drove it, as far as anyone could tell. The boys took turns behind the wheel, tugged the shifter, mashed the pedals, wrote: FART WAGON in the dust on the hood. The noise they made sometimes drew Irma's son out of the apartment he sometimes lived in behind the garage, a tall, thin, mild man in his mid-thirties who spent most afternoons playing solitaire on a television tray, and staring ambiguously out a window at the back bay of Curtis Pond that drew up on one side of the big green yard. In nice weather, he might take his game to a derelict dock listing out over the water, sitting in a folding chair with his television tray beneath a red and white striped beach umbrella. These two locations comprised his range and seemed to fulfill all his needs. He was kind to the children, never getting on them for messing with the car or being too loud, and didn't use their confinement on his mother's property for the afternoon as an excuse to talk about himself, something adults were always doing, Stanley noticed; trying out their wisdom on kids who couldn't escape. How many times had he sat quietly while some lonely or bored grownup forked over an advisory personal anecdote for him to chew on, like a second helping forced on him at a barbeque? People whose moral compass had no magnetic north couldn't pass him without suddenly believing they had something vital to offer, dropping to one knee to impart some limp adage about doing good in school if Stanley was reading a book in plain sight, being kind to Titus if he and his brother were arguing in public, or the wide, uninteresting world of sports if they caught him anywhere near a playing field. Who were these people? Stanley wondered then. Hunters of small game, he decided, later on; pedophiles of the soul.

Irma's son never had anything to say about himself. He just asked the boys questions about school, what they liked to do, commented on the weather, stuff like that, before returning to his room behind the garage. It made him a kind of human lacuna in their minds, something worth investigating. They spied on him a few times through the back window of his apartment, took turns watching the room where he sat all afternoon flipping over playing cards, glancing out the window toward the pond, sipping from a smudged glass of tap water. There was nothing to see here; they realized that pretty fast. The single room Irma's son lived in held one chair, a twin bed, a television tray, but no television, no books or magazines, no pictures on the wall. There was a gym bag at the foot the bed, presumably for clothes. The scene was set and invariable. No matter when the boys peeked over the windowsill to have a look. Eventually they stopped looking and started speculating.

Maybe he's a queer, said Gardner. You're a queer, said Anders. You're both queers, said Stanley, with joy, liking this new word the other two had taught him, though its meaning was still murky. Gardener said it meant you were the opposite sex. That didn't seem so bad to Stanley; the opposite sex puzzled and intrigued him. It made him think the word was all about how you said it instead of what it meant. It reminded him of how Mrs. Veitch and the other teachers said his name when they were angry with him. The boys stood on the dock where Irma's son sometimes sat, throwing rocks at a dead chipmunk they'd launched into the water on a log, trying to sink it.

My dad says queers go to hell, said Gardner; his dad was a pastor and an area bigot. My dad says hell doesn't exist, said Stanley. Your dad's wrong, said Gardner. Your dad's a queer, said Stanley, giving the word another trial run, not really meaning anything by it. Gardner punched Stanley in stomach and told him to take back what he said. Stanley kicked Gardner in the balls and left the dock. Anders didn't seem to know whose side he was on, but ended up trailing Stanley, maybe because they had been friends back in fourth grade. Stanley stopped inviting Anders over after Anders peed on his basements steps as a joke. Anders had a dog named Blackie. He always said Blackie was his best friend. Stanley had no trouble believing this. Anders lived on the other side of Curtis Pond with Blackie and his parents, an arrangement that didn't end up changing much over the next twenty years, except Blackie died of dog cancer and Anders' father moved out. His dad sold fire extinguishers and ran the local Boy Scout troop; whenever Stanley saw him, he always had spit in his beard. Anders would get his picture in the paper a year or so later for successfully extinguishing a fire he'd accidentally kindled on the roof of his own house by burning trash on a windy day; he wore his Scout uniform and held a fire extinguisher, exhibiting both prongs of his patrimony for the photograph. He ended up in the paper again eight years later for breaking into the Ritter Corner general store to finance an oxycodone habit that culminated in facial reconstruction surgery after he tried to rob a drug dealer in south Burlington. He moved to Wisconsin, had a kid, hawked shady home loans for a living. Stanley was in Chicago by this time, so he and Anders were almost neighbors. The thought of Anders dropping by crept up on Stanley when he ran short of other things to worry about.

Gardner met them by the flagless flagpole in the big green yard after he'd recovered. The spot overlooked the community center parking lot, where the high school bus dropped off the two or three older girls who lived in the neighborhood, so it represented a zone of neutrality for the three boys, since they all met there to see the same thing. Gardner had tears on his shirt; his eyes were pinkish and a little puffy as he watched the girls disembark the school bus. There was nothing remarkable about these young ladies, except that they were developed and unfamiliar as private islands; that was enough. Stanley would have preferred to watch them alone. He didn't like the idea of his fantasies crossbreeding with those of the other two boys, mongrelizing his wide-awake life until it resembled the chimera he slept with each night and was gradually becoming bored by, all the beautiful, upright people carving out a merry lakeside community for themselves while he looked on, wishing for some unnatural disaster to sweep them all away. Sitting between the two boys watching the three girls by the flagstaff, Stanley saw himself as an impossible mountain range dividing two distinct biomes of complimentary idiocy; hopefully, the cobalt clouds occluding his peaks would rain shit and fire on any who dared to make the ascent from either side. May they never mingle, that seemed important; people with good ideas rarely agree, people with bad ones always seem to. Watching people he didn't respect get along was becoming just another part of life, but Stanley remembered his hearing aid, and was wary of morons joining forces. He would do whatever was needed to keep Anders and Gardner from eating off the same mental placemat, at least when he was around.

I'm going to pee in that one's butt someday, announced Anders, already showing signs of being the fruitless crackup he would one day become. He pointed out the lucky damsel passing on the road below. Don't point, scolded Gardner. Why not? asked Anders. It's not polite, replied Gardner, almost like it was a punch line. Out of the two of them, Stanley decided he had the most hittable face. He turned out not to be the only one who thought so. Gardner barely lasted six months in middle school before his father pulled him out and packed him off to an institution more in line with the family way of thinking. Gardner fell from sight like he'd been swept off by an outgoing wave, but not before school picture day. The photographer had done what he could to touch it up, but the preacher's son still stared out of the yearbook from behind a raccoon mask of twin bruises empurpling either eye. He looked like he had trouble at home; he didn't. All of Gardner's trouble was at school. Stanley was there when some of it happened. Boys a grade or two ahead of Gardner pushed him into lockers in hallway, or out of chairs in the cafeteria, threw his bag lunches out of windows, stole his homework and flushed it down the toilet. Pretty standard stuff really, nothing some eternal misfit doesn't find himself in the middle of year upon year for his hand always being first up in class, dressing a bit too nicely, or reporting the wrongdoing of fellow classmates to teachers, all things Gardner did with a kind of self-destructive Calvinist glee, like he was hand-picking the nails he would use to crucify himself. Young people are always cruel because they're always bored; Stanley already knew that. Watching Gardner learn it brought him no joy, mostly because it only seemed to buttress the other boy's belief that he was better than everyone, and for all Stanley knew, he might have been. The school was a gallery of half-grown beasts; howls came from the lunchroom, toilets overflowed with the torn-out pages of textbooks, the halls smelled like chewing gum and farts. Students strode around in beaded hemp collars, vo-luminous JNCOs, puffy Airwalks. Stanley wanted these things without knowing why, and felt he was betraying himself when-ever his mother took him clothes shopping at JC Penny. He sought something to admire in the surly know-nothing scowling back at him from the dressing room mirror, easily able to rec-ognize the raft of sub-average nobodies from school in what he saw. This was success, on a certain level. The only other choice was to be more like Gardner, who spent each school day waiting for someone to pin a kick on his ass like a tail on a donkey; even the teachers he tattled to didn't feel bad for him when they saw the joy he took in getting other students in trouble. Gardner's tormenters were counseled not to snatch at the low-hanging fruit the boy represented, but schools operate more like jails than monasteries; forgiveness sets you on the same level as what you forgive instead of elevating you above it. The students who locked him in a custodial closet, or spit in his yogurt at lunch, or kicked a soccer ball into his face in the atrium, the source of the goggle-like bruises in the school photo, probably felt they had no choice but to act on what they'd been given, the same as the teachers Gardner reported them to. He came to exhaust the patience of everyone around him like a car alarm. Bullies and those who oversaw their bullying shared a sense of relief when Gardner was finally pulled out of school; it saved them from having to admit he'd won.

When Stanley had settled into himself a bit more, he envied the preacher's son for the early start he'd gotten on being at odds with the world; it seemed to have helped him thrive in it. Gardner turned out to be good with computers. He made a boatload developing a line of digital products to help employers spy on their employees. This blended with Stanley's expectations enough to mean almost nothing to him until he came home for Christmas from the Midwest, and was driving through Ritter Corner with his mother. The big blue barn and outbuilding where Irma's son had spent his days quietly in crisis had been converted to offices and labs after she died, and the property went up for sale. Gardner lived in the main house with his wife and their daughter, who had been born back in November, while Stanley was still imagining walls of flame eating up Chicago. A new Volvo sat in the driveway beside a newer Audi; the sort of vehicles that transported people who had it together. Gardner also had a speedboat, and owned a summer home on the lake beside Stanley's parent's house. His mother didn't know which one, and Stanley got tired of guessing. He was relying on Christmastime to make his perspective generous, but envy appeared to be taking the wheel on this one. Gardner had purchased a part of Stanley's landscape and its history out from under him, something he thought was only possible in his dreams, where the worst things always showed up fully formed. As it turned out, all worlds were open to progress and piracy alike. Happiness was buying the property as an adult where you were kicked in the balls as kid; Stanley saw that now, and it made him wonder if part of the way his childhood kept sidestepping his idealizations was his fault. He wanted some part of his life to have once been perfect; it was easier to scroll through the past for evidence of this, than hunt the imminent horizon.

But had things really been so great at Irma Ritter's big blue house? Maybe they were okay in daylight, but the place gave him the creeps after dark, when Gardener and Anders had been picked up by their parents, and Stanley was left to wait for his with Irma and Varner. The two of them looked like mummies in the light from the television, and breathed like whales under pack ice. They said not a word to Stanley or each other as the three of them took in the lurid subject matter on screen: out of control teens, AIDS, the Ku Klux Klan. Sometimes drag queens appeared, making Stanley feel briefly at home from his time among them on Cape Cod. It was evidence of a world existing beyond the living room where he seemed to have been forgotten by his caretakers. Meanwhile, other things around the house unsettled him. Irma loved owls, and her house was stuffed with various characterizations of them; large eyes, sharp beaks, and expressions of judgmental astonishment hooted from every nook and cranny whenever Stanley looked away from the television, as if the birds ornamenting the house couldn't believe he'd made it this far. Though ignored by Irma and Varner, the inanimate parts of their home kept him under constant observation. Stanley sometimes wondered if the house had a ghost in it, and when it would come for him. Through some odd remodeling quirk, the stairs to the second floor were located through a door in the bathroom. Stanley had mistaken it once for a closet while hunting for a spare roll of toilet paper. Now whenever he used the facilities after nightfall, he heard the stairs creaking, as if something was descending toward him from above. He peed all over the seat numerous times watching the door for movement over his shoulder, imagining it swinging wide to reveal red slanted eyes glaring out from the shadowed landing, claws spreading like wings, a mezzaluna mouth lined with teeth like the oxidized saw blades out in the big blue barn. But what frightened Stanley most of all was the possibility of Irma and Varner dying while he was there, and his mother not showing up. He lived in fear of being abandoned with their corpses, feeding off the dwindling supply of Pop Tarts beneath the sink as the house sailed through the impenetrable night outside, drawing further and further away from everything he knew and cared about until it was just a speck adrift in an unforgiving void, one boy, two corpses, together forever. Sometimes it actually seemed like they stopped breathing. Stanley listened clinically during these moments, waiting for respiration to resume under the withering gaze of the owls, too scared to breathe himself, afraid it might cover the sound he needed to hear to know Irma and Varner were still alive.

He shared an abridged version of this fear with his mother one particularly dark night after she picked him up, telling her Irma and Varner looked dead after the sun went down. They're just old, she said; old people have seen a lot. You should talk to them more. I don't think they know I'm there after Gardner and Anders leave, replied Stanley. Of course they do, said his mother; I'm sorry you're uncomfortable alone here, Stanley, but I can't get out of work any earlier. They say 'Sounds like somebody's here' when your car pulls up, said Stanley; they have no idea who it is, because they have no idea I'm still in their house. That's not true at all, said his mother, though Stanley thought she sounded less sure about it.

He ended up proving this to her in a roundabout way a few weeks later. Stanley didn't notice that Gardner and Anders weren't on the bus until he'd gotten off by himself at the foot of Irma's driveway. He briefly wondered where they were, and decided he didn't care; Anders always talked during The Disney Afternoon, an overloud, gapless string of utter nonsense that would have been the envy of any politician, and Gardner always took the chair Stanley liked to sit in. With them gone, he could watch Goof Troop in peace and comfort, and probably eat as many Pop Tarts as he wanted; Irma never counted, though Gardner always told her when Stanley took more than his fair share. The afternoon was shaping up to be free of interference from total assholes, a circumstance Stanley rarely encountered outside the woods, and had given up hoping for; he knew how to share his books and toys and compact discs with Titus, but was still learning how to share the wide-awake world with other people. You're not always going to be able to take breaks whenever you need them, his father said while they were stacking firewood last weekend. Stanley tried to weasel out of it the way he did with gym class at school. Try to get good at knowing when you're in the middle of one, his father added, meaning a break; doing something you don't like with someone you like is sometimes as close as you get. At the time, Stanley hadn't understood what his father was talking about, but maybe moments like this were what he meant. If he couldn't find the music that lived inside him, he could at least find the day-to-day silence where it wasn't.

Gravid grey clouds blocked the sky as Stanley walked up the driveway to the big blue house, and rain began curtaining the big green yard as he reached the door, and found it locked. He knocked, waited, knocked again, waited for what felt to him like longer, but was actually less time. He tried the handle once more, pushed at it, even kicked the door once or twice, before cupping his hands around his face and peering through the sidelight. Owls stared back enigmatically, but there was no sign of Irma or Varner. Stanley left the porch, and circled the house in the rain, looking in windows, trying the back door. He finally ended up at the garage behind the barn. Varner's Batmobile was gone, a bad sign. Stanley knocked on the door of the apartment where Irma's son sometimes lived, figuring he might have a spare set of keys, but there was no answer. Stanley hadn't really expected one. The boys hadn't seen Irma's son for a few weeks. Queers were always moving around, Anders had explained, after the boys looked through the window and found the chair and television tray empty, the duffel bag gone; that was why people got AIDS everywhere. No, said Gardner; it's because Africans have sex with monkeys and then each other. I hope you both get AIDS, Stanley had thought then, not really sure what AIDS was; Ricki Lake never clearly explained it, and the health classes at school hadn't gotten that far yet. But he wished they were there now, Gardner and Anders, if only to confirm that whatever oversight had marooned him alone at Irma Ritter's big blue house had taken place out of sight and beyond his control. Stanley's recent track record didn't really support this version of events. There were the permission slips he'd failed to deliver, school projects that slipped his mind, tests that sprung up out of nowhere like an ambush. He'd once spent all day at school watching Mrs. Olaf spit in a napkin while the rest of his class went swimming at an indoor pool in Montpelier. Stanley had no one but himself to blame then, and he hoped that wasn't the case now, as he sat on Irma Ritter's porch watching the cold rain fall through the untended trellis.

Stanley's mother arrived two hours later to find her son cold, wet, and sitting by himself in the dark. Why didn't you call me or your dad when you realized no one was home? she asked after the basic facts had been established; You could have used the phone at the store. I would have come to get you. I didn't want you to have to leave work early, Stanley lied. The truth was he had no idea how to reach his mother or father at work. They'd written their respective daytime phone numbers on an index card and told him to carry it with him at all times, a thing he never did. The card had been returned to the school library long ago along with the John Bellairs book he'd marked with it, and was probably filed in some flea-bitten annex of Mrs. Frobisher's office now, never to be seen again. You should always call us when stuff like this happens, said his mother; you can't just sit in the rain all afternoon like a homeless person. If you let me walk home after school, we wouldn't have to worry about it, said Stanley, swinging like a gymnast from the end of the knife in his mother's side. He knew she felt guilty, and saw his opening, a chance to finally get his way. You're right, his mother admitted. That might have settled it once and for all if she hadn't called Irma later in the evening to sort out what had happened. Apparently, Stanley missed an announcement a few days earlier: Irma had to drive down to Rutland. Her son's body had turned up on a logging road outside of town. No signs of foul play, toxicology pending, but it looked drug-related, probably an overdose. Not unusual down there on the border with New York State; a lot of stuff found its way in. Irma's son had been in and out of treatment for years. He was a gentle person, but always a little mixed up, she said. The last time he came around asking for help, she thought he meant it.

Irma hadn't told the boys any of this, but it came out on the phone with Stanley's mother. Irma had been in the car all day with Varner and probably needed someone else to talk to about it. She would have driven herself, she explained, but her eyes weren't so good. Stanley's mother delivered condolences and took a reasonable portion of what she'd sat through on the phone out on him after she got off. You need to listen when adults tell you things, she said; otherwise, we all end up having to run around picking up the slack for you. It's not fair to your father or me. This is little kid shit, and you're not a little kid anymore. So can I walk home by myself then? asked Stanley, knowing he'd encountered a critical setback, but trying to circumvent it anyway; this might be his only shot from here on out. We're not talking about that now, said Stanley's mother; images of himself strolling home from the bus stop after school collapsed like cakes in the rain.

Stanley returned to the big blue house the next afternoon, and might have returned there every afternoon until he moved out of his parent's house for all he expected of the future at that point, if he and his mother hadn't passed Irma walking on the road a few weeks later. Stanley had just been picked up when the figure of the childcare provider rose up in the headlights beside the old tavern on the corner bearing her name, there and gone again in an instant like the ghost he imagined haunting her house, but unmistakable, even so; Stanley was in the habit of looking at nothing except the television after Gardner and Anders went home, and didn't realize she'd even left the house. His mother turned the car around, and pulled up beside Irma, asking if she was okay, did she need a ride, that kind of thing. Irma said she was just going to check up on her son and got a bit turned around; she didn't acknowledge Stanley, or appear to recognize his mother. They corralled Irma into the car and drove her home, waiting until she got inside before they pulled out of the driveway. I told you she has no idea I'm here, said Stanley, trying to keep the glee out of his voice; he knew Irma's senility was probably his ticket to afterschool sovereignty, but didn't want to break his mother's heart by sounding overjoyed about it. I'll talk to your father about doing something else, said his mother; There's no way you can go back there. I'm sorry I didn't believe you. It's okay, mom, said Stanley, going out of his way to sound mature and magnanimous, easy to do when you expect to get everything you want.

9.

"The result, therefore, of our present enquiry is, that we find no vestige of a beginning — no prospect of an end."

—James Hutton, Theory of the Earth, 1788

Stanley walked home from the bus stop with Alexander. Alexander had red hair and always looked ready to play intramural soccer; these attributes made Stanley mistrust him. They were friends once, back before Alexander's parents got divorced; his father used to appear at the Ritter Corner community center on Halloween night dressed as Ichabod Crane, and try to read Washington Irving to the children gathered there to bob for apples and eat candy. It was way over everyone's head, even some of the parents. But they let him go through with it anyway, year after year, the kind of harmless perennial oddity people like to set their watches by, a dog no one owns, but everyone feeds. He lived somewhere in western Massachusetts now, and taught English at a private school Alexander's older brother, Augustus, attended. Augustus had been on the local news for organizing a student walkout at his high school, something to do with wanting longer lunch periods. He'd won, and immediately moved to the Berkshires to live with his father and attend the boarding school where he taught. This all came out when Alexander brought in a tape of Augustus' interview on WCAX for show and tell. Stanley remembered his dad from Halloween at the community center, the same as everyone else, and asked if he wore costumes to his English classes during the follow-up Q&A. Stanley wasn't trying to be funny; he really wanted to know. But some students laughed; so did Mrs. Veitch, despite herself. Meanwhile, Stanley recognized Alexander's expression across the classroom. It reminded him of the way his face had looked reflected back at him from the abyss of Jean Bulow's prescription skull glasses whenever she sounded off on something about him she didn't like; hatred, running downhill like storm water, finding its watershed. Their friendship probably ended that day, but it took a few more weeks to tail out.

After the divorce, Alexander changed in a way that suggested his parents had maybe overdone whatever affirming they needed to do to assure him their separation wasn't his fault; from that point on, nothing seemed to be. They'd fortified their son like a forward operating base, and turned him into a kind of monster. Alexander got in the habit of saying his parents named him after someone who once ruled the world. Early on, Stanley asked him if this included Vermont, and Alexander called him stupid; Vermont wasn't part of the world back then, he said. This hurt Stanley's feelings, and made him want to kick Alexander in the balls. He hadn't done it then because they were friends, but regretted missing his window later on, after their friendship faded, and Alexander continued calling him stupid, often in front of their classmates, and always when Mrs. Veitch wasn't around to hear. Alexander was careful to do this in way that made it sound like he was just presenting the facts of the matter rather than picking a fight with Stanley. I thought the mashed potatoes were ice cream for a second, Stanley might say over lunch in the swampy cafeteria. That's nice and stupid, Alexander might respond from across the table, turning his attention elsewhere before Stanley could respond. What could he say? Nothing really. The moment for it was long gone. Only naked aggression remained for Stanley, a kick in the balls or a swat with the sectioned tray he ate from. But the only thing that looks dumber than starting a fight is losing the fight you start, and Alexander was about his size, rangy, long-limbed, built to fly down fields toward unambiguous goals while people like Stanley dragged along in fruitless pursuit, chained to the kind of defeat that's mentioned honorably at best, if at all. The adults in Stanley's life taught him that failure didn't set them or anyone else apart; it was normal enough to be a kind of camouflage in low to middle-average company, the kind of folks you're likely to run into at most places. It made success seem less about talent, whatever that was, and more result of some mediocre person not doing their job, bungling a snappy comeback, failing to block a shot on goal, laughing at cruelty or entirely ignoring it, the way Stanley's classmates and teachers did whenever Alexander called him stupid.

Stanley decided this was a good thing, overall; it meant Alexander needed him more than he needed Alexander. The other boy's popularity at school had ballooned since he began calling Stanley stupid. People always appreciate having a target selected on their behalf, especially when it's someone or something they fear; most of Stanley's classmates assumed he was way out of bounds since the dustup with Astrid. He liked to hit girls, so he was unpredictable, maybe a little crazy. The other students treated him like a cursed object set down in their midst, something they would live with and occasionally sacrifice to if it meant they could go about their business; he was a minotaur who avoided gym class like the sword of Theseus by skulking off to take a break in the labyrinth that was the school library. So Alexander suddenly swooping in to call him stupid was like watching someone kick over a gravestone or spit in a temple or slay a dragon all at once. It was a little unholy and very exciting.

The other students may have seen Alexander as a liberator, which he was, having freed them from the tyranny of their limited shared imagination. Stanley knew he wasn't stupid, but he also knew whether he was or wasn't didn't matter to his peers. They trusted Alexander's judgment because he had been on television; a family friend landed him a bit part in a popular children's adventure show that aired on Nickelodeon. The class was forced to screen it one rainy Wednesday afternoon on a television Mrs. Olaf rolled into the classroom like a siege tower. Alexander wore a fluffy wig and shot a bow and arrow. Stanley thought it was a fascinating waste of time. Many students asked for Alexander's autograph when the program ended; Stanley fished around in himself for reasons they might want such a thing. He didn't come up with any until later on, when it was too late to kick Alexander in the balls without coming off like a psychopath, and Stanley's breaks had been rolled back to two per day, and only once a week during Mrs. Halloran's class. By then, the autographs seemed like party cards, a way to remind Alexander who in Mrs. Veitch's class had been shrewd enough to get in on the ground floor of his dominion. No one wanted to be singled out like stupid Stanley, who'd stood around counting birds flying through the rain outside the classroom window while everyone else was lining up for Alexander to inscribe their notebooks, Trapper Keepers, old homework, even a sweatshirt, in one instance. The birds were a way Stanley tried to tell the future; in this case, they failed him.

Oddly enough, all of this dropped out of sight when the two boys walked home together from the bus stop. There was no reason for it; they both seemed to know that. They spoke like people in a Laundromat late at night. Stanley didn't mind strolling along at the side of an enemy; it was better than being trapped at some redneck lady's trailer with him all afternoon. He figured if Alexander got out of hand, he could always walk faster, or push him off the embankment into the lake. It never came to that, but Stanley imagined the threat was there, hanging between them like a beaded curtain neither wanted to part. They were two young men alone on the road with only the woods, the hills, the lake to chaperone them; anything could happen, so nothing needed to. Imaging that Alexander vaguely feared him in these moments made dealing with what happened at school easier, as if he was one half of a charade kept up out of charity, so the other boy wouldn't lose face. They talked about girls. Alexander liked Astrid. That made sense. Great things were generally expected of them both. Stanley liked Astrid too, but said he liked Abigail to be different and open up the conversation. That makes sense, said Alexander, in a way that indicated this fit with his low-class expectations for what people like Stanley might want out of life. Stanley forgave Alexander for it privately, since this was a habit left over from when they were friends, and treating everyone as if they were his family's vassals didn't seem to be something he could avoid. Where did it come from? Stanley didn't know, but it always made him wonder if Alexander's family was somehow rich. He'd been over to their house many times, but never came away with an impression of vast wealth. Alexander lived on a hundred-acre former estate high above the lake, the kind of misty, crumbling property that betokens a fortune in heirlooms no one wants to buy, creaking stairs, lofty cobwebbed ceilings, statuary listing or keeled over in tall grass, a basement best avoided, and often gives shelter to at least one restless spirit. Instead, his mother haunted it, restoring illuminated manuscripts for museums in Boston and New York when she wasn't driving like a goddamned maniac along the back roads; she'd nearly run Stanley's mother off the road last winter. What else was up there? A model train set in the attic, the sort of typical American boy's toy Stanley knew he would never own. Alexander also had a hammock in his room and a mini-fridge with organic soda in it. He got a Playstation shortly before he and Stanley stopped being friends; they'd only played it together once. Did any of this add up to the kind of feudal relationship Alexander had with the people around him? Maybe it did, decided Stanley; maybe everyone is just one model train set away from believing they piss lemonade, shit ice cream, and fart concertos.

There was one moment when it almost got out of hand. Alexander and Stanley took a break from girls and were talking about books. Alexander liked science fiction, Bradbury, Heinlein, Harry Harrison, that sort of thing. Stanley liked books about bellicose talking animals; he had just reread the *Redwall* series for the fifth time, and was reading *Watership Down* for the second. Figures you'd like that stuff, said Alexander. Why? asked Stanley. It lets you be a little kid for longer, replied Alexander, not meanly. He just had no other way to say it; his feelings were a watery bottom sunlight never found. It's okay at school right now, said Stanley. What is? asked Alexander. The way you talk about me to other people, said Stanley; but we're going to be in a new school next year. And I don't want you to say that stuff anymore when we're there. What stuff? asked Alexander. That I'm stupid, said

Stanley. You are stupid, replied Alexander, proudly, like Stanley had walked into something; it was the first time he'd said this during their commute. I can hurt you, said Stanley, mildly, looking out at the lake instead of Alexander; I can do it now, or I can do it when we're in middle school. But I will hurt you if you don't stop. You can't hurt me, said Alexander, narrowly avoiding it being a question. I can hurt you really bad, Stanley assured him; I've been to your house. I know where your room is. I could find it in the dark. And I don't care about you at all. I live right down the road. I could walk over and hurt you in your sleep. But you can say what you want for now. I just don't want it to be something you keep doing when we're in a different school. I can say whatever I want about you, said Alexander, drifting off toward the far shoulder; you don't matter. Neither do you, said Stanley. It would be like nothing happened, only you would be hurt from what I did to you. All I want to know is if you'll stop when I'm asking you to stop.

Alexander looked afraid. Leaves drifted down around him; the woods belting the lake rusted behind Stanley. It was good to say these things here, he thought, to let them fall like leaves. The land was steadily dying off; Stanley felt bloody-minded after dreaming about it the night before. He awoke in the tower room of the hotel on the island, the place of his future deflowering. He knew where he was from the view through the window, a view that had always escaped him until now. The room was the studio at the liberal arts college where his father had a show; all the music that lived inside Stanley was catalogued and arrayed along the walls. He felt deeply grateful for it, the records, tapes, and compact discs, points of identity in a place that was no longer his. Out the window, the water was nearly obscured by the houses rising on stilts from the surface. The shore was an archipelago of lights, a mélange of happy sound, a cataract of joyful movement, the land upholding it all swallowed in a single throat. A turntable sat before him. He chose a record from the shelves along the wall, settled it down, watched the arm swing into place, the stylus falling into the trough like a finger sweeping a drain. Stanley didn't see any speakers. He wondered where the music would come from. It never came. The record spun on in silence until the first screams arose from the mainland.

Through the window, the land was changing as it hadn't for a long time. Mountains rose suddenly, like tall men in long coats shouldering aside the hills. Cafés on shore lurched and fell, boutiques dropped as if they were painted on glass and tapped with a hammer, a yoga studio disappeared into a crack in the surface of the earth, never to be seen again. People ran, swam, and begged for shelter. Their homes sunk below the surface, the stilts and palings cracking acutely like leg bones, the walkways between them buckling, the roofs sucked away as the shore opened like a blunted mouth to swallow them, uplifting as the ridge parted. The peninsula swung out, clearing the deck of whatever fell in its path, bookstores, wine shops, places to have your dog groomed. The water ran red with the blood of those who had made Stanley's dreams their home, or perhaps it was just the sunset spilling from a gulf in the far shore, feathering the water red. Stanley couldn't be sure, but he noticed the island was drifting out to it, receding through a split in the horizon as the world it gave perspective fell into chaos. The screams changed to crying, resignation, extinction sounds. The record stopped. He started it again, adjusted the volume of the silence he heard, wanting to see what else would happen. Stanley was overjoyed to see the world end. He knew then that the music inside him wasn't one thing; his father meant each song he carried along into the world cascading toward ruin before his eyes, but also the silence these songs fled when something Stanley loved or hated was destroyed. Horace Bulow buying beer on his good leg. Titus saying, we can go fishing after school. Irma Ritter's son stiffening into nothingness on the logging road where they found him after some time. Whichever of Sue Halloran's sons he'd blinded in one eye. His fiancée saying she would go through with it, while the sand turned to glass under the wall of flame flying down the shore of Lake Michigan like an elevated train. Phil Windsor with his arm flung out, appearing to reach for his hat. Martina McDougal calmly watching him soak Paul's Game Gear under the kitchen faucet. The way Abigail looked during the eclipse, or the way her father looked falling down in his driveway after Stanley dropped him off. The way his own father looked through the window of the dispensary, shopping in pain like most of America. Stanley's childhood ran like a river into the side of a mountain, lost below ground, slipping beneath the skin of the land without ever leaving it behind. It left him feeling like a villain in the wilderness, misplaced in the absence of something to prey on. He knew this wasn't true, or hoped it wasn't. Meanwhile, his father grew thinner, his mother grew sadder, and Titus swept the days aside like a bad cast. He and Stanley pulled trout the size of torpedoes out of the water in back of a sewage treatment plant when the brothers met up in Montana. A beaver as big as a bear cub strolled out of the reeds into the river. Stanley wished their father were there to see what hung on the end of his line. Titus told him to keep his tip up, or he'd lose the fish. A golden eagle swept in out of nowhere and yanked something out of the water, trailing filament. Stanley cried like he hadn't since the dispensary.

Okay, Alexander said. They kept walking.

****

Descent

RYAN KILLED CHRIS ON A FRIDAY in June. It was the last day of school. Everyone got out around noon. Ryan was a year away from graduation; Chris had been out of school for a few years. Two of his friends, Cole and Sheldon, saw what happened. Cole threw up on himself, and Sheldon wet his pants. Neither had a phone. They walked into town to report what they'd seen, Cole with vomit on his shirt and Sheldon with a dark stain shaped like North America drying on the front of his jeans. Both were treated for dehydration and ticketed for public intoxication when they arrived at the Montpelier police station a few hours later. They stopped along the way to drink some vodka at Sheldon's apartment and presumably get their story straight. By the time they spoke with an officer, Ryan was in Lake George merging onto I-87, and Chris' body had been discovered in the parking area of the town recreation field by a family out for a picnic.

On Saturday morning, Ryan pulled into a roadside concession stand outside Xenia, Ohio to get something to eat and take a break from driving. Heavyset families in big white sneakers sat on hay bales eating ice cream; a few broke off and stuck their heads through a board with holes cut in it to make their faces appear to belong to a pair of jaunty dairy cows. They shot a few photos of this illusion before returning to the hay bales. A miniature golf course suggested itself from around the side of the main building. Crates and cardboard boxes of variegated produce for sale stood against the wall with the most shade. Green cornrows sped away from the property line in all directions, fronds crackling lightly in a wet and sticky wind. Everything seemed upbeat and aggressively normal.

Ryan ordered a hamburger and some coffee and looked over a poster advertising a wooded basin beside a town a few miles down the road, a kind of preserve with walking trails and Indian burial mounds. Ryan had never seen a burial mound before and decided to check it out. The clerk behind the counter was a pretty girl in her twenties. She had smiled at him when he placed his order, and smiled again when she brought his food. He asked her for directions to the place on the poster.

"It's just across the street from where I live," she supplied, looking over his shoulder at his car, a navy Volvo wagon from the early-nineties with a bright green license plate. "I live in the dorms at the college. I run on those trails every morning. You'll sure like it there, it's real pretty."

Ryan thanked her and tried to take his food away, but she had more to say.

"Where are you from anyway?" she asked, pointing at his car with her chin. "I've never seen tags that color. Vermont? That's a long drive. You come to check out the college?"

"Sure," said Ryan. After driving all night, he was happy to have the reasons for him being where he was supplied by someone else.

"Well, I get off in a few hours, if you want me to show you around," said the clerk, writing something down on one of the souvenir postcards kept by the counter. The postcard was a picture of the concession stand and miniature golf course; if not for the full-grown corn in the background, it could have been taken that day. "Give me a call or just come by my room, if you want."

"Okay," said Ryan, as she handed him the postcard with her details. He glanced at it to get her name. "Thanks, Tammy."

She smiled again, and he took his food to his car.

The cornfields gave way to hardwood copses shading a few houses in the midmorning sunlight. Steam rose from lawns in town. A single blinking orange traffic light denoted the beginning of a small commercial district. Student types were out and about, sipping coffee from paper cups and having cigarettes on benches. A chorus line of motorcycles took up two parking spots outside a bar and grill. An antique shop had moved some merchandise onto the sidewalk for display. Ryan saw a spinning wheel, a cider press, and a pair of Adirondack chairs, items that reminded him of home. The college rose against the sky ahead like the loops and whorls of an amusement park. He found the street Tammy lived on. The campus had a lot of red brick buildings and big trees. The lawn needed to be mowed, and a naked flagstaff stood in the center of the quad. He parked in a small gravel lot across the road from a quartet of uniform two-story buildings that must have be dorms. Tammy lived in one of them. Ryan didn't know what to do about her. Killing Chris had left him with new ideas about himself, ideas he liked though he was struggling to understand them. Tammy seemed nice, probably smart; as he took the first trail down into the glen, he imagined her running ahead of him in shorts and sports bra. There was no way to disguise that kind of vulnerability; Chris had taught him that. Ryan wondered if he would now see it everywhere he looked.

He ate his breakfast atop the first of several tumuli arrayed along a limestone ridge. A small waterfall tailed out into a creek below. A nearby sign told Ryan some of trees shading him were over four hundred years old and to please not climb on the burial mounds. He considered the dead beneath him, how many bones there were down there, and felt nothing. Feeling nothing made him tired. He napped in the shade with the sound of birds and water rising and falling nearby, and dreamed he was chasing Chris on all fours down the trail to the burial mounds. Chris was naked, and begging over his shoulder as he fled from Ryan. From the dream, Ryan somehow understood he could catch Chris at any time, but was choosing not to. He hands and feet were paws with long claws, and he felt sharp teeth in his mouth. His sense of smell was also keener than it had ever been. As Chris stumbled across a creek ahead, Ryan stopped to see his reflection in the water. What he saw there thrilled and enchanted him.

Things began burning in June. Smoke blew through the canyons into the valley where Vernon lived, and the inversion from the mountains kept it there. He woke up one morning, and couldn't see his neighbor's house across the alley; the kitchen window above the sink was a sheet of ash gray fug. The wind sometimes blew it around, but the smoke never quite cleared. It stained whatever sunlight got through a sodium-vapor shade. A campsite cooking odor enveloped the town. The sky was cloudy at night. Smoke hung in street lamps. Choppers beat the air above trailing Bambi buckets of water or retardant. Folks walked dogs and rode bicycles in surgical masks. Vulnerable populations were urged to stay inside with the windows closed during the day. It was Vernon's first summer in Montana. He had never seen anything like it. The way the world looked outside his kitchen window reminded him of how the planet was depicted after the asteroid that killed the dinosaurs crashed into it. He imagined sauropods and theropods sweeping and striding out of the smoke in an unrelenting and hopeless march toward sanctuary. Fossils had been found of numerous animals doing just that a few hours east; maybe it happened here too.

The wildfire causing all the fuss had a complicated background. It was half on, half off a reservation fifty miles north of town, and was burning in a hard to reach corner of an already remote wilderness area. The steep and rugged terrain had sent burning debris down into lower regions, burning through about three hundred acres before the first Hotshot crew got to it. A few more crews were on their way. Kim was on one these. Vernon watched her throw things in a bag, readying herself for life at burn camp. She would be putting in twelve to sixteen-hour days for two weeks digging handlines. Then back for two days rest, then back to the fire. She would miss his birthday. That was okay. Vernon was turning thirty-five, not ten. This was her busy season, he knew that. She took him out for oysters the day before as a kind of early celebration. The restaurant was attached to a hotel overlooking the river. Several individuals in masks and goggles fished off the gravel bar below. The oysters and beer all tasted smoky to Vernon. Kim was preoccupied with her own thoughts, and their conversation limped along well-trodden lines. She took a phone call in the middle of the meal from someone she would see the next day, stepping out into the hotel atrium. Vernon took the opportunity to finish his beer, and order another. He managed to get the level in his second glass down to where it had been in the first glass by the time she returned, looking excited.

"Who was that?" Vernon said, a bit too brightly.

"Paul; a friend from work," said Kim. "He's going to give me a ride to the airport tomorrow."

"I can drive you."

"You'll just be getting up. Don't worry about it."

"I don't mind."

"It's fine. We want to stop for a drink on the way there anyway."

Kim dropped Vernon off at work afterward. Vernon worked weekend nights at a residential shelter for misled youth. He had gotten the job to fulfill the practicum requirement for the master's degree in social work he was pursuing at the university across town. The position had been advertised as a great opportunity for students. The agency recruiter promised Vernon unlimited study time. This was technically true. Vernon had much of the night on his hands. But he couldn't read without falling asleep, and the few papers he'd written reflected the general jetlag under which he lived most of his waking life. He'd gotten into the habit of having three to five drinks before coming to work, just to keep things a little dangerous and interesting. His professors would have diagnosed this behavior as a heightened form of self-sabotage, something the children Vernon watched over were always getting up to; practicing his own style of it made it easier to empathize with them on a day to day basis, and had the upright feel of a professional decision before the beer wore off, usually around 1AM.

The shelter was a split-level home with girls upstairs and boys downstairs, eight rooms for each. The downstairs was also where the staff office and common areas were. Vernon spent most of his time sitting on the couch in the living room playing video games and waiting for the sun to rise. Every hour or so, he performed bed checks to make sure the children hadn't absconded on his watch. He prepped meals for dinner the next day, pots of chili, trays of lasagna, loaves of zucchini bread for breakfast; the house garden had produced a bumper crop of zucchini so far, but the children would only eat it in pastry form. He mopped floors and did his laundry; Kim's house didn't have a washer or dryer. He folded her panties on the kitchen table where the children had their dinner and watched a reality television show in which fat people told stories about falling down. He wandered home at dawn and fell into bed like he'd been pushed off a cliff.

When he awoke that afternoon, Kim was mostly packed up. He offered to drive her to the airport again. He was still in bed, and didn't really mean it, but he didn't have much to say beyond suggesting things she didn't want or need. Paul pulled up outside before she could turn him down again. She gave him a kiss and skipped out the door. Vernon stood at the window with his eye pressed to a raised slat in the blinds, trying to get a look at Paul. He drove a nice big newish Toyota pickup, the kind of thing that could drive right over the top of Vernon's Honda without much fuss. The cab shadowed Paul's face, but a tanned and brawny forearm with a number of interesting tattoos rested on the edge of the window. Kim tossed her bag in the back, and off they went. Vernon returned to bed, and fell back asleep. He had a disturbing dream that he was lying in bed in the dark, naked and throwing a very long, very sharp knife into the air above him. He felt the impact when it landed on the bed beside him, and had no idea why he, in the dream, kept picking it up and throwing it again, but that was apparently what he needed to do. Vernon awoke at 9PM, and barely had time to drink two beers and eat a banana before going to work.

Tammy studied forensic accounting, but this didn't accurately describe her interests. Occultism was her cup of tea, and spookery her bread and butter. She was currently developing a thesis on the real property certain women of Salem stood to inherit or had inherited before they were accused of witchcraft. Ryan's eastern origins intrigued and excited her. He was a stranger sent to her from the land of ghouls and she wasn't about to let him go.

"When you said you were from Vermont, I knew we just had to talk," she said. "You ever visit Glastonbury Mountain?"

"I don't think so," said Ryan.

"What about Dudleytown? That's in Connecticut."

"No. What are these places?"

"The one's part of what folks call the Bennington Triangle. Five folks have disappeared completely, or almost; they did find one body, but it was too far gone to figure out the cause of death. There's supposed to be a monster in the woods, strange lights at night, stuff like that. I guess the indigenous folks wouldn't go near the mountain. They thought it was cursed. Birds don't sing there. The other's a town that was settled by a well-to-do family Henry VIII kicked out of England for bothering him at court. They apparently carried their bad luck with them to Connecticut, because everyone that lived in the town they founded there either went insane, got murdered, or moved away. Nothing's left of it now except cellar holes."

Tammy had clearly been holding onto this information for quite some time, awaiting the perfect audience for it. Ryan appreciated her enthusiasm for his homeland, though it left him no point of entry. That was fine. It was nice to make another person happy by just sitting there and listening. She spoke expansively of macabre occurrences, her eyes glittering in the light from a bonfire they shared with several of her peers from the college. An abandoned golf course abutted campus, and stretched darkly away from the flames in all directions; this is where Tammy brought Ryan when he awoke from his slumber on the woodland burial mound. It was early evening in Ohio. The lights from the dorms were visible through the trees. He bathed his face in the creek, and walked to his car. Tammy had apparently spotted it in the lot across the road from where she lived. A note reiterating the substance of their earlier conversation at the roadside snack bar was folded beneath the driver's side windshield wiper. Had he ever been wanted like this? He wondered about that as he tucked the note in his pocket and crossed the street to where its author lived.

"Most people back east came there because they were kicked out of England," said Ryan, sipping at a beer; he didn't like beer, but understood this was how to join things. "There must be more to the curse than that."

"Oh, I agree," she said. "In fact, I looked over some maps of the area and read through a couple almanacs. They were trying to grow corn, wheat, and flax in the shadow of two or three large mountains. My family's all farmers. You don't set up to grow those crops in a place without good sunlight. The town also didn't have a water source nearby.

"Sounds like bad planning more than anything else," said Ryan.

"I guess you could consider stupidity a kind of curse if it makes you and those around you unhappy for long enough," said Tammy. Ryan thought of Chris. It wasn't the kind of thing he expected her to make him think about when they met earlier that day. She asked where he was staying that night and he told her he expected to sleep in his car in the nature preserve parking lot.

"That's just across the street from where I sleep," she said. "Why don't you just stay with me?"

"Okay," said Ryan. He had expected something like this, but it still made him a little nervous. "If it won't make you uncomfortable."

"You don't seem dangerous to me," said Tammy giving him a once-over. "Besides, my brother's a cop in Dayton. He hurts people for money. You have none of the characteristics that interest him."

They left the golf course shortly thereafter. The fire had dwindled to a dull eye in the center of a diminished girdle of people and light. Folks began pairing off, or lurching away on their own. The time hadn't tipped toward earliness; it still seemed very late. A few lights were on in the dorms, but most of campus was dark and misty. Cicadas fizzed in the trees as Ryan walked beside Tammy. He liked her. She was smart in a way he was unused to, and confident in the things she knew about, even if those things were a bit kooky or spurious. He stood before the small bookshelf in her room, looking over the titles. There were many regional guides to the paranormal, several volumes of Hans Holzer's investigations, a few oversized books of photography of abandoned houses and towns, even some genre fiction with raised print. A nice collection, overall.

"You're really into this stuff," said Ryan. It sounded both bland and judgmental, though he meant it neither way. Tammy didn't seem to notice.

"It's just a way folks talk about things they don't understand," she said, taking his hand and leading him over to her bed. "There's usually something important behind it. I like to try and see what that is."

"I wish I knew how to do that," said Ryan, sitting down beside her. "Talk about things I don't understand, I mean."

He noticed a bottle of what appeared to be wine on the floor between his knees and realized he was a little drunk. He took a gulp anyway. The wine tasted odd, neither red nor white.

"This wine is different than other wine I've had."

"It's moonshine," said Tammy, taking the bottle away from him. "My daddy makes it. Best in the county. Don't tell anybody."

"I'm glad to have tried it. No one in Vermont makes moonshine. Some people brew their own beer. But I guess people do that everywhere."

"You didn't come here to see the college, did you?" she asked, stirring a finger in his hair, combing it out of his face. "No, I didn't."

"Where are you going?"

"I wanted to see my brother," said Ryan. "He lives in Montana."

"You must be in a hurry to get there. You looked tired today at the ice cream stand."

"I might not be able to see him for a while if I don't get there soon."

"Why?"

"I haven't figured out how to talk about that. Or how it made me feel different."

"I think you hurt someone back in Vermont."

"It felt like the right thing to do," said Ryan. He didn't understand exactly how she deduced this, but it seemed right that she had.

"Lots of people hurt other people," she said. "My cousin was in Afghanistan. He doesn't know how many people he killed. I think that bothers him more than killing them."

"They threatened my family," said Ryan. "That was why I did it."

"How many where there?"

"Three. I only got one of them."

"All least you know how many you got."

"He was the one I wanted most."

She rotated his face toward her and kissed him then, steering his hands toward her body, and hooking one of her legs over his. In her arms, he felt safe for the first time in thirty-six hours and allowed himself not to worry about what they had discussed. A window above the bed stood open. Cicadas filled the night with static. Ryan liked Ohio, so far. He would be sad to leave.

"It would be cool to see it," said Tammy, a bit later. "The old foundations and stuff in the woods. I like that kind of evidence."

"You're not going to tell your brother about me?"

"I talk about my family all the time. I understand what you did it for."

"But if you change your mind and feel like you need to tell him, please just give me a head start," said Ryan. "I don't expect to get away with anything. I expect to be punished. I just want to see my brother before that happens."

"I won't change my mind. Go to sleep," she said, tucking his face against her chest as if she was preparing to nurse him. Ryan did as he was told, and dreamed of Cole and Sheldon running around a bonfire as he chased them an all fours. They somehow knew if they left the circle of light and ran off into the darkness, he would catch them, but with each circuit around the fire, they grew slower and more tired. It was only a matter of time before Ryan caught them. That was fine. He could wait forever.

Vernon spent his birthday adrift in a kayak on the surface of Brown's Lake with a beer between his knees and binoculars pressed to his eyes, watching yellow-winged blackbirds thrash in the reeds and snowy grebes sprint across the water whenever a hawk blew out of the sagebrush and spooked them. A few campers and tents were set up on shore and one or two motorboats tooled around with people fishing out of them, but the place was mostly empty. Mountain ranges serrated the horizon on all sides, so huge and distant they appeared close and easily summitted, despite the snowpack helmeting their peaks.

The lake was seventy miles outside of town, and the smoke

was thinner here. Vernon figured Kim was out in it somewhere, making a difference alongside Paul. He wouldn't let any of that ruin his birthday. He watched birds as if they contained something vital he'd missed out on early in life. It was a thing he'd started doing after failing to make any real friends during his first term of graduate school. His second term produced the same result. Kim suggested that maybe he should try doing something on his own, instead of just going to classes and work and hanging around her whenever he wasn't at either of those places. That seemed like a good idea. He suggested getting a dog. She told him that was fine, but it would be his dog; she wanted no part of it. That sort of took the wind out of Vernon's sails, but he got into the habit of going out to animal control anyway to see who needed a forever home. The staff liked him because he took the dogs for long, aimless walks in the immediate area. The airport was across the road, and planes often came in low overhead. This scared some of the animals shitless, and made others aggressive, but Vernon enjoyed the way the noise kept him from lingering for too long on any one of the unpleasant topics on rotation in his mind; Kim, school, work. The order sometimes shifted, but the grist remained the same.

The staff at the pound seemed to think Vernon was going through something acute but harmless, so they allowed him to sit for hours in the kennels with some of the more traumatized animals, reading a book or doing his homework, sometimes saying a few soft words to the dog cowering in the furthest corner. It got better after a while, but would never be perfect; his studies had taught him that this was how trauma worked. The dogs had been beaten, starved, and abandoned. Some were tossed out of speeding cars. A few had their ears trimmed with scissors to make them better fighters. A lifetime wouldn't walk that kind of thing back. Some of the children he oversaw at the shelter were in the first stages of it. The odds of them living normally were low. He saw his role with dogs and children as essentially the same; not to prove that people were good and what they had experienced was an anomaly, but that occasionally they would come across a person who wasn't dangerous, and to tell the difference. That seemed like the only way to honor the futility of the whole thing without handing the keys over to it.

Vernon was stalking a belted kingfisher along the edge a scrubby peninsula on the far side of the lake when the wind picked up, rocking his boat in the current. Thunder issued from a gunmetal cloudbank off to the east. The storm had crept out from behind one of the mountains and was cruising toward the lake. The few fishermen already had their boats ashore, and were sitting in folding chairs beneath the awnings on their campers, watching to see if Vernon would make it back to land before things got serious.

He was within spitting distance of shore when lightning struck the water thirty feet away and knocked him out of the kayak. Fishermen dropped their libations and rushed to their boats to get Vernon out of the water. He was unconscious, floating on his back without a lifejacket. They wouldn't reach him in time. A second lightning bolt saved his life by blowing him out of the lake when it struck the water again. The event was unprecedented. Vernon arrived on shore unconscious, but alive, dreaming of Kim and Paul. They each had the head of a bird, and were flying over a large fire, shitting on it to put it out.

Ryan awoke with sun in his eyes. Tammy forgot to close the blinds. She got up to tug the cord. She was naked and okay with herself. Ryan thought she was beautiful; the thought occurred to him with a suddenness that made him wonder what he'd thought of her before; he couldn't remember. He was a little hung over and pretty happy. The cicadas were starting up outside and it was hard to get back to sleep. She offered to take him to breakfast before he hit the road, so they got dressed and walked into town. A marshy odor arose from the preserve and blew down the main street; he imagined it was the smell of aborigines decaying in their mounds.

Tammy took him to a place with character. Olive oil cans served as lampshades for the booths. Waitstaff were pert and tattooed. The menu was localized and confusing. She fed him off her plate and walked him to his car afterwards.

"Come see me again on your way back through," said Tammy. "If you don't get caught."

She kissed him and crossed the road to her dorm. He started his car and drove back past the cornfields and the snack bar to the highway. He wondered vaguely if Tammy would report him to her brother now that she'd had her fun, but it probably wouldn't matter much if she did. He crossed the Indiana state border not too long after saying goodbye to her, and was up to his waist in Lake Michigan by late afternoon, bathing in the shadows of high-rises stretching across the sand. It was Sunday, and the beaches in Edgewater were festive, packed with goers of all kinds. A band played renditions of AM radio hits from long ago on a stage erected between the bathrooms and a lifeguard station. Several volleyball games and barbecues were in progress. The water was warm, shallow, and calm.

Ryan had never been to Chicago before. He liked the city so far. Alison had said he should come visit if he could, and here he was. He knew from the way her voice responded to his voice on the phone earlier that the invitation had been mostly a rhetorical gesture. It made sense. They'd been dating for six months when Alison's father took some sort of high-profile administrative position at Northwestern and moved his wife and daughter to Illinois. Alison decided shortly thereafter that a long-distance relationship with Ryan wasn't for her, but that he should still come visit if he could.

That was about a year ago. Rather than hurt, Ryan had been secretly relieved. They tried to talk on the phone a few times since then, but it didn't amount to much. When Ryan called Alison from a rest stop outside Indianapolis, it took her a second to understand where he was and what he wanted. Her parents were gone somewhere for the weekend. Alison had the house to herself. She gave him the address. He planned to drive straight through the city, but noticed midway up Lakeshore Drive that he smelled a little strongly of beer, campfire, and Tammy. That wouldn't do. Dunking himself in the lake wasn't a perfect solution, but it was better than showing up as he was. It reminded him of deciding to stop at a self-service car wash in Montpelier shortly after leaving Cole and Sheldon at the recreation field, and hosing off some of what Chris had left on the bumper and tires. Small steps like this were important, he decided. They set the tone for what was to come.

Alison lived in a palace on the lake in Evanston. The ceilings rose high above Ryan's head, and his footsteps echoed in the tiled hall as she led him through the house and out onto a ribbon of private beach. They sat beneath a verdant pergola and drank pale yellow margaritas out of tall frosted glasses. Alison smoked now. That was new. She had gained some weight, as well. It looked fine on her, Ryan thought. She wore a swimsuit top and denim cutoffs. He watched the different way her body moved down the beach when she stepped away to take a phone call. He remembered swimming naked with her a few times back in Vermont, and looked out at the water, curious if that was a possibility here.

"Some people are on their way over," she said when she returned. "One of them is the person I'm seeing."

"Okay," said Ryan, refilling his glass from a pitcher between them; margaritas agreed with him more than beer, it turned out. "I'm sure it will be nice to meet him. And your other friends."

"I didn't want you to be disappointed," she said. "In case you had any ideas or expectations about things."

"I just appreciate you letting me stay the night so I don't have to sleep in my car or keep driving."

"Are you going to visit your brother?"

"Yes."

"How's he doing? I always liked him."

"Mostly good, I guess," said Ryan, though he wasn't quite sure how Charlie was doing. It had been a while since they'd spoken, and Ryan hadn't called ahead. They hadn't seen each other since last summer, when Ryan visited Charlie in Missoula. They went fishing a lot, and camped a little bit, did some hiking. Charlie had a girlfriend named Linda who sometimes joined them for meals and activities. They seemed like a good fit. Linda worked in the juvenile probation office downtown and had friends at the courthouse. Charlie directed programming at a private residential treatment facility for deranged youngsters way up in one of the canyons outside of town. He and Linda's professional interests shared a certain cross-pollination that appeared to check certain unspoken boxes between them. It made Ryan want something similar with someone like Linda someday, but he had no idea how people found each other and stayed together. He considered Alison before him, her swimsuit top and the half inch of ass cheek puffing out the bottom of her cutoffs; what would it be like to move beyond these attributes? He suddenly missed his parents; it was the first time he'd thought of them since leaving Vermont.

"What about your sister?" asked Alison. "She must be eight or nine now, right?"

"Lisa's eleven," said Ryan. "She's fine, too."

Alison appeared to have reached the end of the things she remembered about him. Ryan was okay with that. This kind of catching up didn't suit either of them. Having a drink and looking at the lake and waiting for her friends to arrive was just fine. He remembered Alison talking to Charlie a lot when they were dating. He was older and real handsome, and was preparing to set off for college in Montana; this had some peculiar allure for Alison that Ryan couldn't understand. To his knowledge, she had never attempted to communicate with his sister beyond a wave or a smile. This wasn't entirely Alison's fault. Lisa was deaf, but could read lips pretty well. Ryan and Charlie and their parents had all learned some ASL, but none of them were fluent. Ryan tried to show Alison some rudimentary things to say to Lisa, but she got bored with it fast. He never figured she was with him for the long haul, so this wasn't a problem, but it did surprise him. Most people wanted to talk to Lisa. She was cute and kept to herself, was always digging through tubs of Legos or watching things with binoculars from her bedroom window or drawing wild technical maps on graph paper at a little art table set aside for her in one corner of the living room. She often allowed people to treat her like a handicapped doll because she knew they didn't know any better, but Ryan knew she hated it. He was supposed to pick her up from school the day he left Vermont. Her school got out a little later than his, so he went to the rec field to kill some time at the skateboard park instead of heading home. He called the school after going to a car wash to say he couldn't make it, but he felt like shit for making her sit around, waiting for the adults in her life to get it together, once again.

Alison's friends began showing up as it got dark, like bats or the things they ate. Folks let themselves in, walked through the house, and came down to the beach. They seemed to know their way around the place. Her boyfriend was one of the last to arrive. His name was Brad. He was a sophomore in college, and already owned an impressive home in a noteworthy location. He drove over from wherever this was in a new car he insisted everyone leave the beach to have a look at. It was parked beside Ryan's Volvo in the driveway, a sporty sedan with a custom paint job and chrome-plated racing rims. Alison fawned over the vehicle like she'd never seen anything like it, and everyone else seemed to think it was pretty nifty. Brad got in to demonstrate the sound system. The concussion from the bass produced an odd rattle from the Volvo beside it.

"I'd turn it up all the way, but I wouldn't want to make your car fall apart," said Brad to Ryan, but loud enough for everyone to get a kick out of the remark. Ryan didn't say anything. He and Brad had each taken the measure of the other earlier when Alison introduced them. She referred to Ryan as a friend from Vermont, but it was clear Brad thought there was more to it; either that, or he was one of those guys who saw potential rivals at every bend in the road. Ryan sensed whatever was going on would become clearer after Brad had a few more drinks; the wisecrack about the car was just the tip of the iceberg. Brad was four or five years older than Ryan, taller and heavier, as well; he'd probably win any altercation that took place. But the same thing could be said about Chris, and Ryan had managed to even those odds without too much trouble. The key was to be prepared. He excused himself to use the bathroom, and wandered around Alison's house instead, searching for weapons or tools he could hide on himself and use on Brad if things got serious. Ryan found a few items that might work if it came down to it, but nothing he had complete confidence in.

This is probably why people buy guns, he thought to himself as he searched the kitchen drawers for something sharp and small enough to keep in his pocket, but not so sharp that he'd cut his balls off if he sat down wrong, and not so small that it would difficult to get hold of in a hurry. In the pool room, he tested the aft end of a cue against his palm; that could do some damage, but even if he snapped it in half, concealment would be a problem. He also needed something more difficult for Brad to get away from him.

The pool room window looked out on the back patio. Everyone was hanging around the swimming pool now, or sitting in a jacuzzi off to the side. Some tiki torches guttered in a breeze off Lake Michigan. Brad had shown up with a cooler of steaks and he was now grilling some of these with his shirt off at a barbecue terminal embedded in retaining wall beside the swimming pool. A few people were eating the finished meat off paper plates with their feet in the water. Seeing Brad shirtless confirmed that he could likely kick Ryan's ass without a problem. He looked like a former high-school athlete now living well off the fat of the land. He was also on his eighth or ninth beer, and his volubility seemed to be growing more circular and erratic. Ryan continued his search for something to defend himself with renewed vigor.

The music was cranked way up when Ryan came outside. Alison kept lowering it, and Brad kept turning it up. It was almost midnight and everyone had eaten, but he was grilling with sunglasses on anyway. A few paper plates were floating in the pool. Guests seemed to be giving the two of them a wide berth.

"Someone will call the cops if you keep playing this shit so loud," said Alison to Brad.

"Then cops can give my dad a call if they have a problem with it," said Brad.

"Your dad sells fucking real estate, idiot!" said Alison. "Is he going to find my family a new house when the neighborhood association kicks us out?"

"Why don't you take a swim and cool off?" said Brad. Before Alison could reply, he scooped her up and tossed her in the pool. A few people laughed experimentally. She surfaced coughing and paddled over to the edge. Brad turned the music back up.

"I had my fucking phone in my pocket, you asshole!" she said, her voice cracking a little. Brad ignored her and went on grilling food no one wanted. Ryan helped Alison out of the pool, and handed her a towel. She sat in lounge chair, drying her hair. A paper plate was stuck to her back. Ryan sat down beside her and pulled it off.

"I'm really embarrassed you saw that," she said, running a finger under either eye, smearing her makeup into a kind of bandit mask. "I miss Vermont sometimes."

"Come visit," said Ryan. "Bring Brad."

"I don't know what to tell you about him."

"Don't worry about it."

"My parents hate him."

"I'm sure they'll grow into him."

"You can still stay if you want. He'll pass out pretty soon, and you can just leave early in the morning. He won't even know."

"I don't think I want do that."

"Please," said Alison. Something in her voice shifted, but Ryan couldn't tell what it was. "I want you to."

"What are you guys talking about?" said Brad. He suddenly stood in front of them, listing a bit with a bloodstained paper plate of steaks in one hand and a beer in the other, his sunglasses askew.

"I was just saying my goodbyes," said Ryan. "Alison was telling me the best way out of the city."

"Probably starts with you heading out the front door," suggested Brad.

"You bet," said Ryan, turning to Alison. "Nice to catch up. Maybe I'll swing by on the way back."

"Sure," she said. "I'm sorry."

"What are you sorry to him for?" asked Brad. Ryan didn't hear Alison's reply. He'd left a few things in a bedroom upstairs, so he went inside to get them. People could act real ugly at the drop of a hat. You could even point it out, and they'd just keep going, tunneling to the center of their meanness. Sometimes they'd even invite you to join them. Chris had done that right before Ryan killed him. Ryan still felt bad about taking him up on it; he'd have preferred to kill Chris on his own terms. He couldn't go back and change things to do it better, but walking away from Brad felt like progress, or had felt like progress; when Ryan came downstairs into the pool room, Brad was coming in from the patio.

"I was just coming to find you," said Brad, pausing between Ryan and the hall door. "I wanted to make sure you were gone."

"I'm leaving now," said Ryan, trying to get to the door behind Brad. Brad stepped in front of him and laid his arm across the jamb.

"What did you say to her?" he asked.

"We were just talking."

"I fucking know that. But she was sad after and she wouldn't talk to me because of what you said to her."

"Maybe she was sad because you threw her in the pool in front of all her friends."

"Maybe you should mind your own fucking business," said Brad, giving Ryan a one-handed shove in the chest. It backed him up a few steps into the pool table. "You're not leaving until I say so. Now tell me what you said."

"I thought you wanted me to leave."

"That was before you made Alison sad."

"Move your arm, Brad."

"What?"

"Move your arm."

"What?"

Ryan swung out and smashed Brad's knuckles against the doorjamb with a pool ball he'd grabbed off the table. A few smaller bones seemed to give. Brad was too surprised to make much noise, but he kind of woofed when Ryan kicked him in the balls so hard his sunglasses flew off. He fell back into the hall, and tipped over onto his right side on the tiles, cupping himself and breathing hard. Ryan knelt beside Brad, patting his shorts until he heard something jingle in a pocket. He tried to reach for it, but Brad grabbed his wrist and wouldn't let go.

"The last person who acted like you did toward me ended up in bad shape," said Ryan. "Give me your keys, or I will hit you with the pool ball until you let go."

Brad let go, but didn't hand over the keys. Ryan hit him twice above the eyebrow with the pool ball, opening a small cut. When Brad noticed blood on the tiles, he didn't give Ryan any more trouble about the keys or anything else. Ryan pocketed them, and stood to go, making eye contact with two guests who had just come inside. They paused on the threshold, looking from Brad to Ryan and back again.

"He fell and hit his head," said Ryan.

"Should we call someone?" asked one of the guests.

"I don't think so."

"It looks like it hurt."

"He's pretty drunk," said Ryan. "I doubt he feels anything."

"He's bleeding a lot," said the other. "Maybe he needs stitches."

"It's just a small wound," said Ryan, turning to Brad. "Do you think you need stitches?"

Brad said nothing, but moved his head in a disaffirming gesture and stared at the space between his knees where blood had pooled.

"I used to know first aid," said the one who'd spoken first.

"Then I'll leave you in charge," said Ryan. He walked down the tiled, cavernous hallway and out of the house. Brad's car glittered in the moonlight. Ryan clicked the keychain and hopped in. He'd never driven a car quite like this. It handled like a frisky horse, jumping at the slightest prompt, ready to bolt at his command. And when he closed his eyes, the force of the car's movement through the darkness reminded him of the way he felt chasing prey on all fours in his dreams; that was pretty interesting.

Vernon awoke in clinic in Seeley Lake a few hours after being pulled unconscious out of Browns Lake. His awakening thrilled a doctor charting beside his bed.

"I was just sitting here trying to decide if you're the luckiest or least lucky person I've ever seen in all my years of general practice in western Montana," he said. The doctor looked younger than Vernon, so he probably wasn't plumbing too deep either way. "I'm Dr. Wolf."

"Nice to meet you," said Vernon, noticing a branching, lightening-like figure on the interior of his forearm as he shook the doctor's hand. "What the hell is this on my arm?"

"A Lichtenberg figure, apparently," said Dr. Wolf. "I had to look it up. Don't worry about it. Should be gone in 24 hours or so. How do you feel? Any pain anywhere?"

"I have a headache and my chest hurts," said Vernon, after thinking it over. "And I feel like I threw up."

"You swallowed a bunch of water," said the doctor, nodding as if he'd put money on Vernon's reply. "You're lucky there was a fire fighter on shore to pump it all out of you."

"With that truck they got?"

"What? No. With his hands. And his mouth. You know, CPR."

"Why was he on shore? Was there a fire?"

"He was fishing. He likes to fish," said Dr. Wolf, his zeal retracting a touch. "I feel like we should refocus on how amazing it is that you're awake, and talking to me. Folks in your position end up paralyzed, or with brain damage, been in comas. Other than that crazy scar, you don't have scratch on you. And you're awake and talking to me. Mind if I check you're reflexes?

Vernon didn't mind. He followed Dr. Wolf's finger and a flashlight with his eyes, wiggled his toes when asked, twitched when his tendons were tapped with a rubber hammer. Vernon liked all this just fine. It was more attention than he'd had in a while from another human being.

"Remarkable, like I said," said Dr. Wolf, making a few notes in Vernon's chart. "I'll have to run a few more tests before you leave. What is today? Saturday? The MRI guy won't be here until Monday. That'll give us a nice observation period until we can get a look inside your noggin. Depending on the results, you might be able to leave here by the middle of next week. Anyone you want us to call in the meanwhile?"

"She's not available," said Vernon. "I have to work tomorrow night."

"An employer would be an example of someone you would like us to call," said Dr. Wolf, sounding a little impatient. Vernon didn't respond, and Dr. Wolf wasn't sure what to say next. The two of them sat in silence, blinking at each other for a minute or so.

"It's hard to get coverage at my job," said Vernon, finally.

"What's your job?"

"I'm the weekend overnight person at a therapeutic group home for teenagers with difficulties."

"Then I definitely recommend you don't go to work tomorrow night," said Dr. Wolf. "For your sake, and the teenagers'."

"I don't think I can afford to stay here either way," said Vernon. "My insurance won't even pay for me to get blood drawn. They definitely won't cover an MRI, or probably any of the other tests you want to do.

"You can't put a price on your life."

"I make eighteen thousand dollars a year," said Vernon. That kind of put the breaks on things for a minute. Dr. Wolf studied him with his chin in his hand and his elbow resting on his knee.

"Your boat probably kept most of the electricity off you when the lightening hit the lake, but the concussion knocked you unconscious," he said after a wooden minute or two had ticked past. "You went under right as the second bolt hit. Lightening travels on the surface. If you had been up there even a second longer, you would be dead. And it hit the water in just the right way to blow you onto shore, where a first responder just happened to be spending the afternoon with his rescue gear in his truck. I know it's your birthday, but I've decided you're still the luckiest person I've ever encountered in all my time doctoring here in Montana."

"How do you know it's my birthday?"

"It's on your driver's license," said Dr. Wolf. "Why is that the first question you have after what I just told you?"

"I feel like there is something specific you want from me," said Vernon. "I have no idea what it is."

"Most people in your position would be happy to be alive."

Vernon studied the doctor like he was watching him through the end of a long dark pipe, but didn't say anything.

"Just out of curiosity, have you ever taken the PHQ-9?" asked Dr. Wolf.

"I don't mean to be rude," said Vernon, "but I'm graduate student in social work, you're a cowtown GP; I'm more qualified to assess my mental health than you are."

"Okay, Vernon."

"And the PHQ-9 was developed by Pfizer. It's useless."

"Well, great," said Dr. Wolf, standing up. "I guess my work here is done. Still, I need you to stay for some tests."

"I don't want any tests."

"It's medically necessary, for your safety," said Dr. Wolf, adding, almost as an afterthought: "And the safety of the children in your care."

"You can't prevent me from leaving."

"I can if you're incapable of making an informed decision that compromises your safety or the safety of others, like the children at your job, or anyone you might share the road with on your way home. It's just like taking someone's keys away when they've had too much to drink. That lightening might have cooked your brain for all we know."

"You need a mental health professional to determine that."

"The local headshrinker is a fishing buddy. His office is up the hall. You want me to call him in here to make it official, or will you agree to stick around?"

"I'll sue you."

"I'd be interested to see what kind of legal counsel you secure with $18,000 a year," said Dr. Wolf. "But maybe your natural charm will make someone want to take the case pro bono. For the moment, do you want me to explain what will happen if you try to leave?"

Vernon didn't say anything.

"Excellent. Since it's your birthday and you've agreed to let us proceed with the recommended course of treatment, I'd be happy to grab you a meal from somewhere in town, my treat. I'll send a nurse to take your order."

Dr. Wolf left. Vernon looked out the window. Past the parking lot and across the road, part of the lake was visible through a screen of evergreens that looked black under a gray and rainy sky. He liked the view and could probably hang out here for a few days. But Kim would be in town on Monday evening to take a quick break from the fire before heading back, and Vernon wanted to see her. That settled it. Her eased out his IV, and snuck into the hall wearing only a gown. His clothes and other belongings had been taken, including his car keys, but he kept a spare in a magnetic box under the chassis; Kim had bought it for him after he locked his keys in the car for the sixth or seventh time in as many months and called her for help. She'd been on a date and he'd had to wait two hours for her to show up.

He found a fire door down the hall from his room, and slipped out of it into the parking lot. It was mostly empty and his car wasn't hard to find. He retrieved the key from the underside, and let himself in, working the pedals barefoot as he drove onto the main road. The arm with the branching scar ached, and his ribs felt bruised from the CPR, but he felt fine otherwise. He was glad he had escaped Dr. Wolf and excited to see Kim. Hopefully, she wouldn't have anything lined up, and they would get to spend some time together. Vernon knew this was a long shot, but imagining the possibility raised his spirits.

He also knew Kim was bored with him, and had been for some time. He couldn't say how long. It had come on gradually. When he thought of how they met, it seemed they never should have been together in the first place. The housing he arranged remotely fell through shortly after he arrived in Missoula for graduate school. The address where he was told to pick up the keys to his new apartment turned out to be a popup cookie shop with a funny name that had only popped up a week earlier; it had been vacant until then, he was told by the confused looking teenager manning the place. Vernon's security deposit, first and last month's rent were gone, pocketed by some itinerant flimflam man. School wouldn't begin for another few weeks, and whatever financial aid he might receive would be held in abeyance until then. He ate his meals at a soup kitchen with lunatics and perverts who couldn't be anywhere else, and lived out of his car in a parking lot beside the campus library. Each morning, he went to the university housing office to see if something had become available, and if it had, to try and get the name of whoever managed it in order to beg them for a break, just a few weeks until his refund came through. But the term was about to begin and students were arriving in town each day from far and wide and snatching up whatever places were available. The staff at the housing office got to know Vernon pretty well, and took pity on him when they learned of what had happened. An employee there named Freda had a friend who just left town for work and needed someone to look after her cat.

"She's a firefighter," Freda told Vernon. "My friend, not the cat. Nasty one flared up just yesterday out by Superior. You probably saw the smoke. Anyway, she asked me to find someone to housesit and feed the cat while she's gone. I would but I'm allergic. I don't know how long she'll be gone, but it's better than sleeping in your car."

Vernon agreed. Freda gave him Kim's address and a spare key, and Vernon moved in. She had a nice place, a stucco duplex with a kind of frontier flair a few blocks from the Higgins Street Bridge, on the south side of the river. The cat was a black and white job with a trusting nature. Vernon couldn't tell if it was a boy or a girl, but they got along just fine either way. The bed looked nice, but he slept in a sleeping bag on the couch, made sure not to leave dishes in the sink or the toilet seat up, in case Kim got back unexpectedly. The uncertain nature of her work meant this was probably the only way she would return, Freda had told him. That turned out to be accurate. Kim showed up in the middle of the night two weeks later, pretty drunk and kind of a wreck. There had been some kind of accident on the line. The wind changed, and things got out of control before anyone realized it. Kim had lost a few friends. The fire had been so fast and hot that there was nothing left. They were just gone.

Vernon was a complete stranger in her house, but she told him all this in a drunken rush, getting closer and closer until she was in his lap and kissing him. This made him excited and uncomfortable. He helped Kim get ready for bed, and brought her something to drink that didn't have any alcohol. She asked him to hold her, she didn't want to sleep alone. He had been staying in her house for two weeks rent-free, so this seemed like the least he could do. Vernon kept his clothes on, and crawled into bed beside her. She thrashed around and woke up a lot yelling. In the morning, she was sober and hungover. He made her scrambled eggs and bacon with some fruit and toast on the side, and brought it to her in bed. She ate, said she felt better, and tried to seduce him again. It worked this time. Vernon remembered the next few months being some of the happiest of his life. He offered to get his own place when school began, but she insisted on him staying with her. He'd been there for her when she needed someone, she said; now she would be here for him. She took him hiking in the canyons outside town, on picnics beside Rattlesnake Creek, and out to the bars most nights. Vernon had never been with someone who made him feel special before; he had no idea this was something he could get from another person until he met Kim. He also met her friends. There were no obvious leading lights, but they seemed like a fine bunch. They had been pals for a long time and had goofy nicknames for each other. Mud Bike. Quiver Liver. Doctor Fingers. Bone Crone. The last one was Kim's. They reminded Vernon of a gang of stylized protagonists from a Saturday morning cartoon, the kind that solved mysteries while addressing salient issues of the day.

He saw less of them and Kim when classes began, and he started working overnights at the shelter. She was still going out on the weekends. It hadn't occurred to him that she might be seeing other people until he came home from work one morning and she was in bed with one, a puffy alcoholic musician from a popular local ensemble known for their eclecticism. Kim awoke, and apologized to Vernon.

"Sorry, you're probably tired," she said. "I told Archer he couldn't stay over because you were working all night, but I guess we drank more than I thought and fell asleep."

That sounded like an idea to Vernon. He left the house without saying anything, crossed the street to a gas station and bought a six pack of beer. He sat on the back porch drinking it until Archer emerged, combing his hair with a lit cigarette in his mouth. He nodded to Vernon, who stuck out a leg and tripped him as he stepped off the porch. Archer wasn't hurt, but he was angry, and loud little scene ensued.

"I'm going to attach your haircut to the bumper of my car and drive around until my beer is gone," said Vernon, advancing on Archer, who seemed unsure of his role here, despite his stage presence. Kim broke it up and sent Archer back from whence he came, and drew Vernon inside. She told him she loved him, and wanted him. But she also loved and wanted other people, too. Could he be okay with this very important part of her? He said he wasn't sure; he would like to be enough for her.

"It's why I like fires," she told him. "They're always new."

She also said it was how she learned about herself, making it hard to argue with. Vernon decided to move out that afternoon, but the enormity of the gesture didn't accurately reflect his feelings. Kim made him feel special. Without her, he wasn't special anymore. Besides, they'd never hammered anything out, and it was her place. Compromise loomed. He got her to agree to not bring people around when he was going to be there, and to try and confine her activities to places he wouldn't go. At the time, this felt like a triumph, but it didn't make him feel much better.

"Why don't you want to see me happy with someone else?" Kim asked him. There was no good answer. She took the opportunity to remind him that he could see other people too; he didn't have to hang around all the time, waiting to see just her. Vernon considered this idea, and got a little twisted on pumpkin beer one fall evening when Kim was out on a date and called up a friend over the line in Idaho. Caroline worked for the Forest Service and lived in a ranger station outside Pocatello. He'd met her at the soup kitchen. She served his meal, and had noticed the sore thumb he represented among the regular clientele. They went out for beers a few times and found out they had some things in common. Caroline was also living out of her car, waiting for the gig in Pocatello to start up. She had a camper in the bed of her pickup, which seemed like a palace after the weeks Vernon spent sleeping in the driver's seat of his Honda in the library parking lot. She invited him aboard the night before she left town to start her new job, but by that time, he was already living with Kim and assumed he was subject to all the regular obligations that entailed. The weekend following Caroline's departure, he came home to Kim in bed with Archer.

"I have to quit beer," said Caroline. She had been reading a book when he called. Vernon could hear her shuffling the pages.

"Why is that?"

"It gives me the farts."

They laughed about that. It was nice to catch up. Vernon explained why he turned her down on her last night in town, and asked if he could come down and see her sometime in Pocatello, make it right.

"Maybe," said Caroline. "Is Kim still in the picture?"

"Sure," said Vernon. "But she sees other people. Musicians, mostly."

"Is that some arrangement you guys have?"

"I guess. It is now."

"You know no matter how many times you come down here, it's not going to make you less fucked up about that," said Caroline. "I dig you, Vern, but I'm a big deal down here. I have suitors. Men come from town to cut my wood and make me soup, take care of my ponies. They know better than to treat me like a second thought."

"I'm sorry," said Vernon. "You're right. I'm embarrassed."

"Call me when you get free of her," said Caroline. "I got a nice place here to reset. Plus, I'll fuck your brains out. Just yours, no one else."

That was the last time they talked. Vernon had thought of her every day since then, but always in relation to Kim. Caroline was right. She deserved better than that. He hadn't called again. Instead, he accepted his love for Kim like a sentence. Between school and work, he didn't have time or energy to cultivate meaningful intimate relationships with anyone else. Instead, he spent weekends jumping at shadows at the group home, wondering who she was fucking in the place where he would lay his head in a few hours. Sometimes she changed the sheets, but not always.

Vernon arrived at the stucco duplex in Missoula without any clear idea of how he'd gotten there. The trip home from the clinic in Seeley Lake was a lacuna, like he'd driven into a black hole and out the other side. Perhaps this was what Dr. Wolf had been worried about. A quartet of ravens strutted along the roofline of the stucco duplex, honking and flapping as Vernon crossed the yard barefoot in his hospital gown. His landlord was out mowing the lawn. Vernon waved. His landlord returned the wave with a nod and a murmured word to himself, as if he had always expected Vernon to one day show up like this, on the loose from somewhere.

Inside, Vernon found Kim asleep in bed, alone. She smelled like smoke and sweat and the woods. His spirit soared. He removed his gown and got into bed beside her. She awoke for a second and looked at the arm draped across her, the arm with the Lichtenberg mark.

"Did you get a new tattoo?" she asked, her mouth mushy with sleep, before dropping off again. Vernon figured she meant Paul. That was okay. It was still his birthday and here he was. Vernon fell asleep, and dreamt he had arrived at the top of a tall black hill on a bolt of blue lightening, swinging from it like an ape on a vine.

The car was a trade, as Ryan saw it. Chris didn't have anything to trade, so he had to go. Brad had this silly automobile. It had to go. Ryan drove to a small lakeside park down the street from Alison's house, a place he'd noticed on the drive up from downtown. He bumped the car over a low parking divider and crossed a patch of lawn with the lights off and the windows down. He gave it just enough gas to get over the dune grass and across the sand when he reached the beach. The moon over the lake cast a fine milky glow across the water as it rose over the hood like a curtain running in reverse. Ryan popped the car in neutral and pulled himself out of a window. He hopped down into the shallows and splashed ashore. They keys were still in his hand. He dropped them in a sewer grate when he reached the street.

The music was off and the lights were low at Alison's house when Ryan returned to get his car. Alison was smoking on the front steps with the accordioned remains of several cigarettes between her bare feet. It seemed she had been waiting for some time.

"You can still stay if you want," she said when he appeared out of the darkness. "Nobody is coming. About the car or the other stuff."

"Thanks, I think I should go."

"Brad went to sleep."

"He seemed to be winding down when I saw him last."

Alison left the steps and walked up to Ryan, hooking a finger in the waistband of his shorts. She smelled like cigarettes, burnt steak, and pool water when she got close. It was an ugly, predictable odor.

"You don't take any shit from anyone," she said. "You weren't always like that."

"I don't have a reason to anymore," he said. "I can always do something worse to them than they can to me. When I realized that, it opened a lot of doors."

"Let's go for a swim in the lake," said Alison. "That used to be something we did."

Ryan thought of Tammy. He didn't need to knock anyone in the head with a pool ball to make her like him. She even knew about Chris. It seemed to make her like him more. He had a feeling Tammy would probably try to talk to Lisa if they ever met. Imagining it made him happy, even it would probably never happen. Alison thought his smile had something to do with her. She began tugging him by his waistband toward the steps.

"Maybe I'll see you on my way back through," said Ryan, gently removing her hand from his clothing and backing up a few steps. "I should go."

"Is it because I'm kind of bigger now?" asked Alison.

"I think you're really pretty."

"It's hard out here. Everything is either covered in melted cheese or gravy or cooked in beer."

"I like the way you look, Alison."

"Then what's the matter?"

"I just think I want to be somewhere else in the morning," said Ryan, turning away from her. He unlocked the Volvo and got inside, started everything up. Alison tapped on the window. He rolled it down.

"Can I come with you?" she asked. "I've always wanted to see Idaho."

"Montana."

"What's the difference?"

Ryan considered her question for a moment.

"I don't know," he said finally.

"I can help with driving and gas," said Alison. "We'll probably get there faster. Please just let me come. I want to be somewhere else in the morning too."

Ryan couldn't really argue with that. His money was running a little thin, and at some point, the credit card his parents had given him for emergencies would probably stop working. He tried to pay for most things with cash, but the few times he hadn't were enough to give someone a pretty good idea where he might be headed. He also wouldn't mind Alison's company, or the possibility of intimacy her company suggested after a long day of driving through the big empty spaces ahead. It was hard to sleep at night knowing how huge the sky would be in the morning, the way it seemed to reach out and down. He imagined hiding from the sky under Alison like a buffalo robe, looking out at the wide sunny world from the shade of her body. That mostly settled it for him.

"What about your friends?" Ryan asked her, nodding toward the house. He wasn't sure why he was asking about this stuff. It didn't matter to him.

"I'll tell them lock up when they leave," she said, brightening as the last obstacle to her getting what she wanted fell away. "Let me just grab a few things."

She was in and out of the house in less than ten minutes. They drove through most of Wisconsin in the dark, and reached Minnesota by dawn. The morning was wet and gloomy. Ryan stopped at an A&W in a town called Hayfield. Alison paid for their meal. The place was empty and didn't have all the lights on yet. A yellow mop bucket had been abandoned in the center of dining area; the mop was nowhere in sight. Ryan and Alison sat in a booth by the front window. A grain elevator rose from an otherwise empty field across the road, looking blurry and fortress-like in the rain. So far, the Midwest appeared to be full of these kinds of inexact figments; pylons, grain silos, water towers. They stood out separately from the landscape like mirages in the desert.

Ryan thanked Alison for the meal. She slid her hand across the table until it bumped his.

"I'm glad you let me come with you to Wyoming," she said, running a finger over his knuckles like she was exploring the contours of a seashell. "He was showing off for you."

"Who was?"

"Brad. When he threw me in the pool."

"Maybe."

"I never understood what he wanted. He never tried that hard to tell me."

"We don't have to talk about it."

"I saw you watching right before I hit the water. You looked like you were at the zoo."

Ryan didn't say anything. Alison wore an oversize flannel shirt knotted loosely over her swimsuit top. It fit her like a fresh pelt. He wondered if it belonged to Brad.

"I cried when you went back inside to make him follow you in there," she said. "I wasn't sad. I wanted to see what would happen to him."

"You were jealous."

"I'm sorry. I knew you'd be okay when I saw the way you looked at us."

"Like I was at the zoo."

"Right, and like there was nothing there that scared you," said Alison. "Are you angry with me?"

"No," said Ryan. "You're different than I remember."

"So are you."

That seemed to cover everything unspoken between them. They finished eating and hit the road. Alison drove so Ryan could rest a little. He fell asleep to the sound of rain pebbling the roof and dreamed of wearing Brad's skin the way Alison wore his shirt. He was alive and didn't seem to be in any pain. His face had been fashioned into a sort of hood that fit nicely over Ryan's head. Brad kept asking where his car was, making the hood wiggle and flap. This got annoying after a while. Ryan ended up feeding Brad's skin coat to a creature at the zoo, hood last. The creature was what Ryan had seen in the water back in Ohio when he checked his reflection. Ryan touched his hand to glass between them, and the creature mimicked this gesture. Ryan waved and smiled. So did the creature, after a fashion. Ryan decided to free the creature. He kicked the glass until it cracked. The creature did the same. The glass shattered. The creature was gone.

Vernon hit a dog on the way to work that night. It died instantly, or was dead by the time he located the carcass on the shoulder. Vernon hadn't been driving very fast, but the dog had flown through the air and out of sight when the car struck it, disappearing between curtains of smoke like bait on the end of a line. Its body made a short ugly sound against the grill, and off it went. There was a little blood around the dog's nostrils, but not much obvious damage otherwise. The dog's skeleton felt loose and fragmented beneath its coat when Vernon picked it up. It wore no collar, and its fur was waxy and smelled of smoke, like it spent a lot of time outdoors. Still, Vernon studied the row of houses along the street for one that looked like an obvious home for the animal. He decided to come back and put up signs, but he didn't want to leave the dead dog there on the street in the meanwhile, where the small children he imagined loving it would find the body when morning came. He wrapped the dog in a flannel shirt and laid it on the passenger seat of his Honda, unconsciously curling his fingers in the animal's thin gritty fur as he drove the rest of the way to work.

Kim had a date. She'd made that clear when they awoke, and he offered to take the night off to spend with her. She'd switched things around to come back sooner from the fire. Maybe he could do the same.

"I'll say I'm sick," said Vernon. He was feeling a little odd, but he figured that was from the lightening more than anything else. He hadn't told Kim about what happened at Browns Lake, and she hadn't noticed the mark on his arm; it was already beginning to fade.

"I have plans," she said. "Depending on how things go, I'll be here in the morning when you get off."

"I would like to get drunk with you and maybe fool around," said Vernon. It was the best he could come with on the spot.

"Some other time, Vernon."

She went off to take a shower, while he slurped a beer, considering the way his parade of expectations had just shrunk to a thin trickle of desperate, scavenging need, an emotional welfare line. How long had it been this way? Long enough to make the beginning hard to remember.

When it was time to leave for work, Vernon passed Paul's Tacoma idling in the driveway. Vernon had put away a few drinks at that point and his nerve was up. Let's get a look at that mug, he thought to himself. He approached the pickup and tapped on the driver's side window with a car key until Paul rolled it down.

"Can I help you?" he asked. He was pleasant looking, but not over the moon handsome by any stretch. Kind of resembled a redneck Prince Harry.

"Just wanted to get a look at you," said Vernon.

"You're Vernon, right? You live with Kim."

"You got it."

"You okay with this?" asked Paul, nodding toward the house

where Kim was. "She said it was fine, but this isn't anything I've done before."

This stunned Vernon. He had no idea how to reply.

"Frankly, the entire thing makes me a little uncomfortable," Paul added, as if Vernon had the power to make it all go away.

"It takes some getting used to," Vernon said. He hadn't counted on this kind of consideration from Paul. Hearing it aloud made him feel empty and purposeless. It seemed his work here was done. He turned to go and tripped over a sprinkler the landlord had left on the lawn; it made him do a kind of albatross run to where his car was parked. Look like shit, feel like shit, act like shit, he thought to himself as he drove off, glancing at his reflection in the rearview. Vernon was looking himself straight in the eyes when the dog wandered into the road.

He arrived at the shelter twenty minutes late. The kids were already in bed, and the kitchen had been cleaned up from dinner. The dishwasher hummed and sloshed. Beach towels and swimsuits rotated in the dryer. The general disarray children create had been combed together and put away. One of the day staff members was already gone. The other that had volunteered to remain until Vernon arrived was an uptight, witchy authoritarian who often attributed the children's problems to certain astrological contingencies at weekly staff meetings. Her name was Maggie. She reminded Vernon of something that would decorate the prow of a sailing ship. He had no idea what he reminded her of; something unpleasant from her past, he guessed, a foul-minded uncle who ruined one Christmas after another or maybe a grabby Gus from her college days. Vernon made sure to mention the dog before she could really lay into him for being late.

"That's terrible," said Maggie.

"Yes," Vernon agreed, slurring a little because of the beer.

"Did you find the owner?"

"No. I'm going to print some signs on the office computer and put them up tomorrow with my phone number. Maybe I'll knock on some doors."

"Good idea," said Maggie. Vernon was glad he hadn't had to lie to soften her. She briefed him on the events of the day. There wasn't much to report. They took the kids swimming at Frenchtown Pond, made cookies, and watched a movie about flamboyant teenage vampires and the petit bourgeois werewolves they did battle with. It was an easy group, three docile teenage girls and one twelve-year-old boy who slept with the light on. There wasn't much to do.

Vernon thanked Maggie and she left. He waited a few minutes before retrieving the dog from his Honda. It was still eighty degrees or so at 11PM. Even if Vernon cracked the car windows, he didn't think the animal's corpse would keep well in the passenger seat. He also needed photos for the poster. Vernon figured he should probably take them before the dog began to stiffen, in case he had to pose it. Things still felt pretty malleable, but who knew how long that would last.

Vernon laid the dog on the dining room table. It certainly looked dead like that, but maybe he could arrange its limbs in some way so it looked asleep. He tried this a few different ways, but none satisfied him. The dog's tongue kept flopping out the side of its mouth no matter how he tucked it in, splaying the jaws wide in a silent death yodel. Vernon used scotch tape to keep its eyes open, but this somehow heightened the effect, making the dog look like it had died in a state of abject terror. Vernon tried rigging the animal up to the ceiling with dental floss and duct tape, one big loop under its front legs and another smaller loop around its neck to make the dog appear to be sitting. This took some adjusting. The dog ended up looking taxidermied, but more alive than it had before. It would have to be good enough. Vernon didn't have all night to raise the thing from the dead.

He took a few pictures with the house camera for the fliers, and wrote some text on the office computer. When he finished, it was past midnight and time for the first bed check. The twelve-year-old boy slept soundly with every light ablaze. Upstairs, two of the girls were out cold, but the third was sitting on the edge of her bed in the dark with a hand pressed against her chest when Vernon knocked and opened the door. He remembered her name was Destiny. He turned on the light and asked Destiny if she was all right.

"I felt something go in me," she said.

"Like something broke in you?" asked Vernon, not understanding.

"No, not like that," said Destiny. "Like something went inside me while I was asleep. Like a ghost."

"Is it still in there?" asked Vernon.

"I'm not sure," said Destiny.

"Did it hurt?"

"No. But it felt like I couldn't breathe."

"Can you breathe now?"

"Yes," said Destiny. "But I'm scared. I'm native. My grandma told me all about what spirits can do if you're not careful."

Can of worms, thought Vernon.

"I don't think there's anything here now," he said. "But I'll look just to be sure."

"Okay."

"You can hang out downstairs for a minute. I'll make you a cup of tea after I finish looking for ghosts."

Destiny left the room and went downstairs. Vernon stood in the doorway, assessing for spooks. She seemed like a nice enough kid. She had pictures of her family taped to the wall above her bed. They looked like the cared about her, even if they couldn't get it together. Her caseworker had been going from reservation to reservation for a few weeks now, trying to tease out a kinship placement. Who knew what would come of it.

When Vernon came downstairs, the first thing he noticed was the dog he'd left lynched to the ceiling above the dining room table; the mistake hit him with the kind of adrenal immediacy he remembered from locking his keys in his car. The second was Destiny standing a few feet away from the dog, her arms crossed and her chin lowered with her gaze fixed on the creature suspended before her. Vernon had left the patio door open. The corpse swayed ever so slightly in a smoky breeze from outside.

"It's part of a project," said Vernon. "For school. I'm in college. Why don't you come sit on the couch while I clean up?"

He flipped on a television show about a jet-setting raconteur gourmet who travelled to war zones to sample the cuisine. Vernon hoped that would buffalo Destiny while he wrapped the dog in a black plastic garbage bag and stuffed it in the chest freezer in the pantry. The animal was starting to get rigid, and it took a little maneuvering to get it to fit among the packages of hotdogs and fish sticks and other things the children ate. The lid barely closed; Vernon had to weigh it down with a large bag of rice. Not a permanent solution, but it would hold until morning. He returned to the kitchen and made Destiny the cup of tea he'd promised.

"What do you go to college for?" she asked when Vernon brought her the steaming mug.

"I don't know," he said, misunderstanding her question.

"No, I mean what do you study."

"Oh, right, sure," said Vernon. "Social work."

"I have a social worker," said Destiny, glancing at the place in the room where the dog had recently hung. Vernon waited for her to say something else, but she didn't. Apparently, a dead dog dangling from the ceiling like a puppet squared with whatever her ideas and impressions of social work were before.

"I didn't find a ghost in your room," said Vernon. His voice sounded a little shrill and untrustworthy to him, but he didn't know how to fix it. "Looks all clear to me. I guess you must have had a bad dream."

"Did you kill it?" asked Destiny.

"I don't think you can kill a ghost."

"I meant the dog."

"No!" said Vernon. "It was an accident. I love dogs. I wish I could have one."

"Did you hang it up like that so it would look alive?"

"Yes. I thought it would be less scary that way."

"I wish you could have a living dog."

"Me too."

"It would probably be easier to explain."

"I'm sure that's true."

They sat in silence for a minute or two with the TV droning. The show changed to a serialized tale of teenagers who live by a lake and murder each other.

"Well, goodnight," said Destiny. She washed her mug in the sink and went back upstairs. A nice kid, Vernon decided.

Ryan awoke at a gas station outside Oacoma, South Dakota. He noticed Alison in the side mirror filling the tank with her hand on her hip. A sign across the road said the Missouri River was a couple miles east. Fishermen types stood around the parking lot in the drizzle, exchanging observations on the conditions. A few of them appraised Alison at the pump.

"There's a hotel over there," she said when Ryan got out of the car to stretch his legs. He looked in the direction she was looking. A Days Inn reared out of the gloom like the Bates Motel. "I wouldn't mind a shower, maybe some takeout and TV before we get back on the road."

"I'm not eighteen yet."

"I am. You can just stay in the car when I check in."

That sounded okay to Ryan. After what he and Alison talked about back in Minnesota, it seemed like they had more in common than he realized. Ryan wondered where that might go if they had a hotel room to themselves. Imagining the possibilities put a skip in his step as he walked inside the gas station to use the bathroom. Alison came along to buy cigarettes. When they returned to the car, a man was squatting beside the right rear tire, examining the sidewall.

"Can I help you?" said Ryan.

"This your car?" said the man, standing up and wiping his hands on his jeans.

"Why would I ask that if it wasn't?"

"Right, I see what you mean," said the man, plucking at some gray stubble on his chin and giving Ryan the up and down from beneath a faded orange baseball cap. He looked like he was in his mid-forties, tall and thin and not too clean. "Thing is I just pulled in behind you here, and I noticed your tire has what looks like a nice sized roofing nail stuck in it."

"I don't know how to change a tire," said Alison.

"I know how to change one," said Ryan. "But I've never done it before."

"I've changed plenty," said the man. "I don't mind giving you a hand. But you're going to need to move your car away from the pump before it gets any flatter. My name's Earl, by the way."

Ryan pulled the Volvo into a deserted corner of the lot and removed the tools and a donut from under the rug in the trunk. Earl finished gassing up and parked his truck behind Ryan's car. He had the tire off and the donut on in a matter of minutes. Alison sat on the curb beside the station entrance with her back resting against a rack of red and blue motor oil containers, smoking a cigarette and watching Earl work like he was raising the Titanic. Ryan didn't know what to do except offer him some money when he finished up.

"Job's not really done yet," said Earl, waving the money away. He peered at the hole the nail made in the tire and then at Ryan's license plate. "It looks like you two are just passing through."

Ryan nodded.

"Where you headed?"

"Missoula."

"Where's that? Wyoming?"

"Montana."

"His brother lives there," said Alison from her perch by the motor oil.

"Montana's a ways," said Earl. "I'd be amazed if you make it to the next exit on that donut. And the tire's pretty old and already been patched. I wouldn't trust another patch to hold if you're going that far."

"So, I need a new tire," said Ryan. Earl shrugged, nodded, and spit in the grass between the cars. He seemed to await another question.

"Is there somewhere we can buy one?" asked Alison.

"Not on a Sunday evening," said Earl. "Most everyone I know of is closed. And not too many folks around here work on these foreign jobs. They'd probably need to order something that would fit right. Could take a few days, maybe longer."

"We're in a hurry," said Ryan.

"Well, I might have one that'll work at my place," said Earl, plucking his stubble again and squinting at the Volvo's wheel well. "My shop's a few miles up the road. Might take an hour or two to find something and get it on, but I got a place you can wait and watch TV. Might take less."

"How much?" asked Ryan.

"I'd take $300," said Earl. "I think that's a bargain, considering the circumstances."

"Fine," said Ryan. That was more than half the money he had left, but there didn't seem to be any other choices. Either follow this yokel into the hills, or wait for another to come along. Or call his parents to come pick him up, like he used to do before he could drive and got stuck somewhere. That would certainly cut things short.

"Follow me," said Earl, getting into his pickup. "And take it slow on that donut."

"You want to come with me or hang out at the hotel?" Ryan asked Alison.

"Why would I want to hang out at a shitty hotel by myself?" she said, and got in the car.

Ryan drove through town, passing some shops, a library, and an urgent care clinic. There didn't seem to be much going on. He crossed a bridge over the Missouri River. A few people in slickers were on the water, fishing out of boats in the rain. Dense hardwood forest sprung up on either side of the road beyond town. Earl drove slowly ahead, and signaled a quarter mile before turning left onto a two-track that wound up the side of a small hill. Through the trees and rain, the river appeared below, resting against the land like a wing over a nest.

"Nice view," said Alison. "I hope this guy doesn't kill you and rape me."

"Maybe he'll rape us both," said Ryan, trying to keep track of Earl's truck; it had just disappeared around a sharp turn ahead.

"Seriously, do you trust him?"

"No. But I think this is the most immediate of our limited options."

The road ended at a dirt parking area around the next bend. Earl was out of his truck, raising the door of one of two bays in a large garage. All kinds of vehicles in various sates of disassembly occupied a weedy meadow nearby. Ryan saw parts from motorcycles and boats, even some that appeared to belong to a small plane. Everything together looked something like an elephant graveyard in the rain. Earl flipped on some lights inside the garage, and waved Ryan in.

"I like to tinker with things," Earl said when Ryan and Alison got out of the car. "I'm sure I have something that'll work here, but I might need a minute to find it. There's a room across the hall where you can wait. It's got a couch and a TV. Might even be some beer or sodas in the fridge. Help yourself. I'll let you know when it's all set."

Earl motioned them toward a door in the back of the garage. It let out into a hallway with a concrete floor and a lot of other doors. A narrow staircase led up at one end. There wasn't too much light. Rain swatted the corrugated metal roof and dripped down in a few places. The room Earl mentioned did indeed have a couch, television, and fridge. That was about it. There were no windows. The floor was a concrete slab with a patch of sandy green carpet in the center. Light came from a bank of fluorescent tubes attached to a girder overhead. Alison took a beer out of the fridge and asked Ryan if he wanted one. He shrugged and sat on the couch. She brought him one anyway.

"I'm definitely going to want a shower after this place," she said, sitting down beside him and throwing her legs over his lap. She turned on the TV. A documentary about trailer park denizens who believe they are the master race had just begun. It was starting to get good when Earl appeared in the doorway with a crossbow.

Vernon was drunk at the farmer's market. The time was somewhere around 9AM. He'd gotten off work a few hours earlier and come home to Archer asleep on his side of the bed. This surprised him. What had become of Paul? Perhaps his reticence carried the day. Or maybe Kim experienced a sudden swing in her proclivities. Either way, here was Archer, insensate and drooling on Vernon's pillow. Vernon went to the kitchen and got a beer and a bamboo skewer. He brought the skewer into the bathroom, and used it to spear a brittle turd from the cat's litterbox beneath the sink. He returned to the bedroom with this item held before him like a sword pulled from a lake.

Vernon scooted a chair up beside the bed, and held the skewered turd beneath Archer's nose to see if he would wake up. Archer wrinkled his nose, but didn't awaken. He tried to turn his face away, but Vernon tracked his nostrils like a tail gunner. He was better at this odd activity than he might have expected; it gave him an idea. He went to the kitchen for another beer, and back to the bathroom for a pair of scissors.

Archer had turned away when Vernon returned to the bedside. He used the cat shit kabob to lead Archer's face where he wanted it and set to work on his hair. Vernon had nothing particular in mind. Archer's haircut always reminded him of the kind of purebred animal that costs a thousand dollars and lives for year. Archer liked to toss it around on stage while singing his songs and plucking his guitar, as if it constituted a third element to the performance. He had seen Kim comb her fingers through it at the bar when she thought Vernon wasn't looking; it made her hands glisten. Snip snip snip went the scissors and glug glug glug went the beer; Vernon went through most of a six-pack before judging his work complete. Archer now had a kind of high-rise bowl cut with a long uneven skunk tail in back. Vernon thought it suited him. He left the scissors on the nightstand and the skewered turd in the interior pocket of Archer's leather jacket, where he kept his cigarettes and comb.

Vernon felt peaceful, but not very tired. It was as good a time as any to hand out the fliers he made at work. Just across the river, the farmer's market was in full swing. That seemed like a good bet. Vernon bubbled his last beer, belched roundly, and struck off across the bridge, the pages with the dead dog's photograph snapping in a warm, smoky wind blowing out of the canyon and across the river.

The farmer's market was a colorful place full of local wonders. Artisanal bread and rainbow chard held space beside a wide variety of place-specific handicrafts. Vernon managed to distribute most of his fliers before 10AM to bright young people well outside his weight and economic class. No one recognized the dog, but that was okay; he had done his duty, as he saw it. It felt good to be around people he didn't care about, to drift along on the current of their wants and needs without being responsible for their fulfillment. He could live like this forever if it he needed to, astray in public with all his vengeance for the day behind him; it was good to get that kind of thing out of the way first, to start the day with a bang. Kim would be mad. That was fine. Vernon remembered the lightening the way he hoped to someday remember his graduation from social work school. The scar on his arm was almost gone, but its lines would remain imprinted in his memory like a map of home. He loved her still, but there were other things now to make him feel special.

Vernon was nearly out of fliers and considering the possibility of more beer when someone spoke his name from nearby. He knew the voice: Professor Skip Varney, PhD., the chair of the social work department at the University. Vernon had just completed his class on working successfully with groups and communities. The class was mostly an opportunity for Skip to talk about his time doing group therapy with indigenous people in some far-flung region of Alaska, and the story of his eventual acceptance into the tribe after many good-natured, rascally tests and tribulations, all of which he passed with flying colors. These sounded to Vernon like the kind of souvenir experiences that really keep people going; he would like some of his own one day. He wrote his final paper on this very topic, and received a C- from Skip. This had been their last communication.

"How's your summer going?" asked Skip, shifting bags of watermelon radishes and jars of garlic scape pesto to shake hands with Vernon.

"I got struck by lightning at Browns Lake," said Vernon. Let's see what you do with that, Skippy, he thought, adding: "Twice."

Skip chortled, and released Vernon's hand.

"That's that sense of humor I remember from having you in class," he said.

"It was my birthday."

"Well, I guess I should wish you happy belated birthday."

This killed the conversation for a moment. Vernon remembered Skip having a gift for this kind of thing. The wind off the river changed and the professor's nose twitched as the scent of the beer Vernon was sweating off wafted over him.

"You're missing the point," said Vernon. "Just like you did with my paper."

"This really isn't the place to discuss it," said Skip, donning his departmental hat. "But I'd be happy to talk to you about your paper during my office hours. If you think your grade is unfair, I could suggest some revisions to bring it up."

"Forget it."

"Well, maybe you'll change your mind after a good night's sleep," said Skip, looking Vernon over with a kind of gleeful pity. "I remember when I was flying in by floatplane to work with folks up around Homer. Some days the flight was so rough I wished we'd just crash to be back on the ground."

Another of those weird silences passed between them.

"I don't understand what you're trying to say to me," said Vernon. 'Say' turned to 'shay' as it left his mouth.

"How about we talk it over during my office hours?" suggested Skip, his gaze passing over and then returning to the few remaining fliers in Vernon's hand. "You lose your dog?"

"No. This dog is dead. I hit it on my way to work. I'm trying to find the owner."

"How'd you get a picture of it alive?" asked Skip, taking one of the fliers and examining the photograph.

"I'm glad it looks alive," said Vernon. "It took some effort to make it appear that way."

"What are you going to do if you find the owner?"

"Give them their dog back."

"I see. So, you hung onto the body?" asked Skip. He seemed amazed.

"Yes. I did," said Vernon, realizing with the same keys-locked-in-the-car suddenness that the dog's carcass was still in the chest freezer at work. "I have to go."

Vernon left Skip amid the custom birdhouses and apple baskets and ran back across the bridge, trailing fliers. He arrived home just in time to see Archer leaving the house from across the street. He wore a wide straw hat that belonged to Kim and didn't go at all with the rest of his getup. Vernon ducked behind a parked car as Archer reached for his cigarettes; this was more than he could have hoped for. Archer removed his hand from the interior pocket of his leather jacket and sniffed it quizzically. He coughed once or twice, and choked a little, looking back at the house and yanking off the jacket. Archer walked off down the street with it folded over his arm, and the hand he'd reached for his cigarettes with held away from his body palm up, like he was expecting alms from passerby.

Kim had the sheets off the bed, and was sweeping up hair from the floor when Vernon walked inside.

"Leave," she said, without looking up from her work. "You're not welcome in my home anymore."

"I just came for my keys and my phone," said Vernon, grabbing these items off the dining room table. He turned to leave, thinking that would be it, but her voice paused him in the doorway.

"You need to learn how to treat people before you come back."

That made Vernon laugh.

"What are you laughing about?" she asked. "I'm serious."

"I know you are," he said, giggling his way to the door. His laughter built to a kind of crescendo after he left the house and got in his car. He drove way too fast up into one of the canyons howling hysterically with the windows lowered, barely able to see through the gleeful tears painting his cheeks as he angled the Honda up a forest service road, and drove along the canyon wall until he came to a turnaround overlooking town. He was slightly above the inversion the mountains created. The buildings, roads and people sat in a bowl of smoke below. A little rain stirred the dust his car had kicked up. Lightening mapped the deep blue distance.

Vernon was the happiest he could remember being since meeting Kim. He laughed himself to sleep in his car and woke up ten hours later, sweaty and disoriented with only twenty minutes to get to work by the dashboard clock; his phone had died during the night. On his way back into town, he realized the dog was still in the chest freezer.

Ryan stood up so fast he tipped Alison onto the floor and knocked beer everywhere.

"Don't make a fuss," said Earl, pointing the crossbow at Ryan. "If the TV or anything else in here gets damaged, we're going to have a real problem."

"What do you want?" asked Ryan.

"Well, I'm deciding," said Earl. "Put these on while I figure it out."

He produced a pair of handcuffs from somewhere and tossed them on the carpet in the middle of the room.

"There's a pull handle on the wall behind the couch. You can just loop them through that. One for each of you. Make it tight. I'm counting clicks."

"I'll give you more money," said Alison, from behind Ryan.

"Money's not really what I'm after," said Earl. "You a couple?"

They didn't say anything.

"I was wondering because you seem pretty comfortable with each other," he continued. "You like movies? When I noticed you two at the gas station, I thought to myself, there's a pair that belongs in the movies. I think I have a good eye for that kind of thing."

"If you let us leave, I won't hurt you," said Ryan.

"Oh, I'm sure you'd like to," said Earl. "I saw what you did to that boy with that car of yours. Left him pretty much a pancake."

"What is he talking about?" Alison asked Ryan.

"I'm not sure," said Ryan.

"I'm guessing you haven't been watching the news," said Earl. "Let me catch you up. Somebody was making a video of their dog chasing a ball or frisbee or something and ended up getting you driving over some fellow in the background. A couple big outfits picked it up. Evidently, I'm not the only person who thinks you could be in the movies. I got a good eye for that kind of thing, like I said."

"That's why you're in such a hurry?" Alison asked Ryan. He shrugged, but didn't say anything. "Who did you run over?"

"Chris Foley."

"Oh, good choice," said Alison. "I don't know why you're running away. The mayor of Montpelier will probably give you a medal."

"Cole Weeks and Sheldon Bisset were there too, but I let them get away."

"That's too bad. You could have really lightened some poor social worker's caseload."

"It seemed important to let them live to tell the tale," said Ryan. "Although if I knew someone was recording everything, I might have gone for a clean sweep."

"You two are quite a pair," said Earl, motioning them back toward the couch with the crossbow. "Now put on the fucking cuffs."

"What are you going to do to us?" asked Alison, stooping to retrieve the handcuffs from the carpet and weighing them in her hand. She seemed to be testing the idea of attaching them to her body. Ryan noticed she didn't sound scared.

"Well, I thought we'd make a little movie," said Earl. "I'll show you what I mean."

He reached behind him into the hall and entered the room with a tripod over his shoulder. It already had a video camera attached. He set it up on the patch of carpet facing the couch.

"Now, you two move that couch away from the wall a bit and you'll find a pull handle probably like on the doors at your high school," Earl continued, talking mostly to Alison. "The cuffs go through that. I'd like you on my right and him on my left. Don't bother yanking on the handle. I welded it on there myself. You'd need a tractor to pull it out of the wall."

"I think I understand what you want," said Alison. "It might be kind of awkward with the handcuffs."

"You both seem pretty clever," said Earl. "I think you can make it work. But don't worry. I'm going to be directing things anyway, and we're doing everything according to the script."

Ryan assumed this was just an expression, but Earl pulled an actual script from the back pocket of his jeans and flipped it open.

"Okay, first scene. A room with a couch and a TV. Check. A girl and a boy sitting side by side. The girl says 'What do you think he's going to do to us?' and the boy says 'I don't know' and then the girl says 'I'm scared' and the boy says 'Me too' and then they start kissing. I know this is our first time working together, but I feel like we can knock this one out in one or two takes. Wait, I almost forgot," he said, removing his orange baseball cap and tossing it to Ryan. "Put that on."

"No fucking way," said Ryan, kicking it back to Earl. The hat landed in a puddle of spilled beer at his feet.

"Okay. Let's try this a different way," said Earl, his features purpling. On the top of his head, a sallow bald patch the baseball cap had concealed was bejeweled with sweat. "Here's the deal. If you don't wear the hat and do everything else I say, I plug you with an arrow and then I call the sheriff to come up here and take your body away. I'll tell him you assaulted me when I asked you to pay for the car, and that'll be that. Maybe I collect a reward, maybe not. Either way, I'll hang onto your friend until the movie is finished, and then send her over to some people I know in Sioux Falls. They will put her to work. How does that sit with you?"

Ryan looked at Earl, but didn't say anything. He was remembering his reflection in the water in his dream. If he remembered it hard enough, he wondered if Earl might be able to see it too. The way Chris' face looked before the car went over him made Ryan think it was possible.

"I'm sure you're probably wondering if you can take me," said Earl, smirking a little. "Maybe you can, but it's not going to be as easy as running some dork over with your car. Now, put the goddamn hat on so we can get started."

Ryan continued staring at Earl in silence. They were about the same size. Earl looked like he had a lot of ropey muscle to him and probably a few nasty tricks up his sleeve. It wouldn't be easy, but Ryan believed what had looked back at him from the water would help get the job done. He took a step toward Earl.

"Jesus fucking Christ, Ryan! Wear the fucking hat," yelled Alison, crossing the room and kneeling down to grab the orange baseball cap out of the beer puddle at Earl's feet. She stood up with the hat in one hand and something small and black in the other. Ryan couldn't tell what it was, but he heard a sharp hiss. Earl shrieked and dropped the crossbow, reaching for his eyes and trying to grab Alison at the same time. He stumbled into the tripod, tipping it over. The camera hit the floor and broke into a few pieces. Earl tripped and landed on his knees on the sand green carpet, heaving and choking. An arrow seemed to grow from his back. He made a short ugly sound, and tried to get ahold of the shaft, but it was out of reach. Alison stood a few feet away, reloading; Ryan hadn't even noticed her pick the thing up off the floor. She fired another arrow into the back of Earl's left leg. He was able to grab it, but it seemed to hurt too much to pull out. Alison shot one more arrow at him. It went a little wild, ricocheting off the top of Earl's skull and up into the rafters after leaving a nasty gouge in his bald spot; it reminded Ryan of an interdictory circle.

"I'm out of arrows," said Alison, tossing the weapon aside and crossing the room to stand beside Ryan. Earl moaned and thrashed at their feet, like something hauled ashore from murky depths.

"You could pull one out and use it again," Ryan suggested. He toed one of Earl's hands experimentally, applying a bit of pressure to the back to see if he would notice. It didn't seem to register. "I didn't realize you had pepper spray. No wonder you were fine coming up here."

"My parents make me carry it whenever I go downtown," said Alison, gently tugging the arrow in Earl's back. "I don't think that one's coming out."

"You waited a while to use it."

"*I needed to get close enough.*"

"*I think you wanted to see if I went for him.*"

"*Maybe I did at first,*" said Alison, after appearing to give this some thought. "*But then he said the thing about taking me to Sioux Falls, and I got tired of waiting.*"

"*I'm sorry I put you in danger.*"

"*You're not afraid of anything. You didn't know. It's not your fault.*"

"You don't seem scared either."

"Chris Foley tried to drag me into his car one night behind the movie theater in town. It was before you and I got together. He had me by the wrist and told me if I screamed, he would break my arm. I screamed anyway because a cop car was driving past. Chris let me go, but he said if I told anyone he would kill me. I believed him. I never told anyone."

"He told me he was going to rape my sister," said Ryan. "He said she wouldn't hear him coming."

"That's really ugly," said Alison, taking his hand and poking Earl in the ribs with her toe. "It's good you killed him. Knowing you did that made taking care of this bozo seem like the least I could do for you. I know you had your own reasons, but I never stopped wishing Chris was dead, even after I moved away."

"I also believed him. I wish I did it without him having that kind of power over me."

"Would you still have wanted to?"

"Yes," said Ryan, after thinking it over.

"I'm sorry," said Earl, from below. They'd almost forgotten about him. He was bleeding a lot from the arrows, but remained somewhat lucid. The hand Ryan had been stepping on was now harrowing his ankle in a beseeching manner. "Listen. It was a mistake. I have money. A lot of money. Thousands of dollars in cash. If you take me to the clinic in town, I'll tell you where it is."

"Money's not really want I'm after, Earl," said Ryan, kicking his hand away. "You still have to fix my tire."

"Well, okay, sure. I can get that done for you," said Earl. "If you maybe want to help me onto the couch there and let me recover myself a little, I could give it my best try."

"No problem, Earl," said Ryan, taking one of his hands. Alison took the other, and they dragged him over to the couch. Ryan slid it aside with his foot to expose the pull handle Earl had mentioned. Alison looped the handcuffs through and closed them on Earl's wrists. He hung there in a kind of parabola with his face against the wall and his legs splayed out behind him.

"This isn't what I had in mind," said Earl. "Please, listen to me. You can't leave me like this. She won't have anyone to take care of her."

"Who are you talking about?" asked Alison.

"Upstairs," said Earl. It seemed to take most of what he had left. His head hung low between his shoulders and blood dripped from his mouth onto the concrete floor. His breathing didn't sound right.

"I think you might have nicked a lung," said Ryan to Alison, but she was already halfway to the door. Ryan followed her out of the room and up the stairs at the end of the hallway. The rain on the roof sounded like applause. The stairs let out in a small apartment where Earl appeared to have made his home. There wasn't much to it. Racks of antlers on the wall, and some pictures of the animals they came from. A few magazines about cars and women. Dishes were left in the kitchen sink. The television in the living room looked pretty new. A sliding glass door opened onto the roof the garage, which Earl had converted into a kind of deck by adding a few bench seats from old cars and a patio umbrella. Ryan expected this setup would perfectly suit the needs of the company Earl kept. There was also a kind of shed off to one side, which turned out to be a greenhouse filled with marijuana plants and orchids. The operation seemed fairly sophisticated, and was clearly attended to with care. Rain streaked the clear plastic roof; unlike inside of the house, none of it got in.

"This is interesting," said Ryan. "But I don't think it's what he was talking about."

"Neither do I," said Alison. "Let's finish looking inside."

They went back inside. Earl's bedroom was down a short hallway between the kitchen and living room. A red and black swastika flag hung above the bed, and the walls were lined with gunracks. The bed was neatly made. Ryan counted the weapons. Thirty-eight rifles and twenty-three handguns; also, six swords, three spears leaning in a corner, a compound bow, and two halberds crossed on the wall opposite the Nazi flag. They appeared to be guarding a bookshelf packed with fringe-oriented lunatic literature. A guide to raising hothouse flowers was on the nightstand, the pages marked with a pot pipe.

"I don't understand why Earl would use a crossbow when he has an arsenal upstairs," said Alison.

"Maybe they're unlicensed," said Ryan. "If he shot me with one, he wouldn't be able to call the sheriff."

"It makes me think he was planning on doing that no matter what we did."

"Maybe," said Ryan, noticing a doorframe peeking above the top of the bookshelf. "I think I found what Earl was talking about."

The bookshelf was on casters. Ryan rolled it aside. The door it concealed was painted to blend in with the wall and held shut with a heavy bolt. A light appeared behind it. Ryan noticed a shadow moving around in the crack by the floor. He glanced at Alison. She was also watching the shadow of whatever was inside. This turned out to be a girl a few years younger than them. She was sitting on the edge of a cot with her knees hugged up against her chest, staring straight at the door when they opened it. She looked fourteen at most. The room she lived in was a medium-sized closet with a single overhead bulb. There were some clothes and books neatly organized beside the cot, even a few makeup items. A plate with some partially eaten food sat on an upturned white bucket with a gallon jug of water beside it. If the girl was surprised to see them, she didn't show it.

"Are you okay?" asked Alison.

The girl looked at her, but didn't say anything.

"Is Earl your dad?" asked Ryan.

The girl shook her head.

"Why don't you come with us?" said Alison, entering the closet and holding out a hand. The girl shrunk from her. Ryan noticed she was looking past him, into the room with the weapons and Nazi flag.

"Don't worry about him," said Ryan. "He's attached to the wall downstairs."

This seemed to be good news. The girl immediately stood up and took Alison's hand. The three of them walked downstairs to the garage. Earl took the donut off the Volvo, but hadn't done much else. None of the materials around the garage suggested he had been on the way to an immediate solution to the tire problem.

"I don't know how to solve this," said Ryan. His eyes wandered from the naked axel to Earl's truck standing out in the rain. The bay door was up, perfectly framing the vehicle. A video of the Volvo flattening Chris was on the news here in South Dakota. Ryan figured it was probably time to change horses if he wanted to make it to Montana.

The truck was unlocked, but the keys were missing. Alison waited with the girl in the cab while Ryan went back inside to find them. Earl was mostly the same as when they'd left him, except he was unconscious. Ryan checked for a pulse out of curiosity. There didn't seem to be one. He patted Earl's pockets in search of his car keys. This procedure brought Brad to mind. The night they'd met in Chicago seemed light years away.

The keys were in Earl's right front pocket. Ryan pulled them out and turned around to find the girl watching him from the doorway.

"She wanted to see for herself, I guess," said Alison from behind her.

"That makes sense," said Ryan, pocketing the keys and moving out of the way to give the girl a better view of Earl. "Come closer if you want."

The girl walked up and stood beside him. She reached out and touched the arrow in his back with her fingertip.

"Do you live around here?" asked Ryan. "We can give you a ride home."

The girl looked at him, but didn't say anything.

"You don't know where you are, do you?" said Alison from the doorway.

The girl shook her head, her attention elsewhere. She was gripping the arrow in Earl's back below the fletching and seemed to be trying to push it further in.

"We'll give you a minute," said Ryan. He and Alison walked back outside to the truck. The girl came out a few minutes later and joined them in the cab. She had some blood on her hands.

"Is that from you or him?" asked Alison as Ryan started the truck.

"Him," said the girl. Her voice sounded like a bell in the rain. Ryan threw an arm over the seat to back the truck up and noticed a yellow and black nail gun sliding around the bed. Seeing it there reminded him that the day had held nothing accidental, so far. He was glad they weren't leaving anything hanging.

"I checked some of the other rooms in the hall while she was in there with you," said Alison as they wound their way down the two-track to the main road. "He had them set up like the closet. With a cot and a bucket."

Ryan just nodded. The girl sat between them allowing Alison to clean her hands with some tissues from the glovebox. Her skin looked translucent and a little yellow, like she had a vitamin or nutrient deficiency. Ryan figured she probably needed to see a doctor. He remembered passing a walk-in clinic on the way through town. The place was just closing up when he pulled into the parking lot. The girl looked nervous, but Alison managed to coax her out of the truck.

"I'll go in with you," she said. She walked the girl beneath an overhang above the entrance and came back to the truck for her cigarettes. Ryan noticed her hands shaking pretty good as she lit one.

"Tell them exactly what happened," he said. "Except that I killed him."

"Sure," said Alison. "I think I might stay with her for a little while."

Ryan said that sounded fine. She would call him to pick her up when someone came for the girl. He would lay low in the meantime, maybe go check out the river, see if the fish were biting.

"We can get that hotel room tonight if you want," said Alison. She sounded a little shy; odd, after what they'd just experienced together.

"I'd like that," said Ryan. She touched his hand where it lay on the seat and closed the door. He waited a minute or two after she went inside the clinic before dropping the bag she'd packed in Evanston under the overhang by the entrance. He didn't see how she could miss it there.

Ryan skipped visiting the river and drove straight back to the interstate. Three and a half hours later, he sat in a booth at a Pizza Ranch in Spearfish, munching away an hour from the Montana border.

Animal control came for the dog while Vernon was still passing out fliers with the creature's picture at the farmer's market. The house manager discovered it in the chest freezer and made the call. No one could reach Vernon to get the specifics, but Destiny noticed the animal control officer on his way out with the black plastic garbage bag beneath his arm and asked the guy where he was going with Vernon's school project. The house manager overhead this, and asked Destiny a couple questions. She said it was sad that Vernon couldn't have real dog, but that he was good at looking for ghosts, so she was glad he would be a social worker someday. Maybe then he could have a real dog.

This alarmed the house manager enough to call the program director at home on the weekend. The program director was named Ken. He was a gentle, shy man who lived alone on several acres fifty miles north of town. He made wine from grapes he grew and kept far too many chickens for one person; he often handed out cartons of fresh eggs at staff meetings. Children perplexed and mystified him. He mistrusted their basic motives, and needed his weekends to recover from interacting with them.

Still, after speaking with the house manager, Ken was alarmed enough to make the trip into town and investigate matters himself. When Vernon arrived for work, Ken was seated on the living room sofa. He'd dismissed the day staff members, and the children were in bed. The house was silent, but a steady rain tapped like a finger on the windows, as if some third party sought admission to whatever was about to take place.

"I've been trying to get ahold of you all day," said Ken.

"My phone was dead and I was asleep anyway," said Vernon. He sat on the opposite side of the couch from Ken. "I'm sorry you had to come in. I meant to take the dog with me when I left, but I was tired and forgot."

"Are you okay?"

The question surprised Vernon. No one ever asked him that.

"No. Yes. I don't know," he said. His face had somehow come to rest in his hands. Vernon had no idea how it got there. "Thanks for asking."

"Sure," said Ken. "Why don't you tell me about the dog in the freezer."

Vernon obliged, unfolding the tail of the creature's demise the night before and his failure to find the owner at the farmer's market. Ken listened without saying much, only asking a clarifying question now and again. After Vernon finished his story, they shared a silence that seemed tailored, so well did it fit the occasion.

"How about you take tonight off?" said Ken. It sounded like a suggestion.

"Am I being fired?" asked Vernon.

"No! Not at all!" Ken assured him. "But you seem like you could use a normal night's sleep. And I'm already here to cover your shift."

"Thank you," said Vernon, a little bewildered by his sudden freedom.

"It's no problem. I have some breakfast recipes I'd like to try out on the children," said Ken, casting a glance toward the kitchen. Cooking ornate meals was also a hobby of his, Vernon remembered. "You know, I used to do your job. I was constantly out of step with the rest of the world. I kind of forgot how to treat people because I wasn't around them very much."

"How long did it take you to figure it out again?"

"I never did really," said Ken, getting up off the couch and walking toward the kitchen. "I didn't try to. I realized I liked not having to think about it."

"I've noticed it makes some stuff easier."

"Yes, some stuff," agreed Ken. He'd begun opening and closing cabinets and drawers, assembling tools and ingredients like he was planning a voyage of many leagues. "Other things got harder. I just moved away from town. Now I don't notice."

"Do you ever get lonely out there?"

"All the time. You can teach yourself to like loneliness. It's certainly peaceful."

That sounded like the right note to close out on. Vernon left the shelter and sat in his car in the parking lot. He was still somewhat astonished by his own luck. He'd never had an easier time getting a shift covered. Who knew all it took was a dead dog in the right place? The night's manifold possibilities seemed suddenly endless. Kim's house was off limits, but that didn't matter much to Vernon. If it continued to pour all night, she'd be out of work by morning, an ugly possibility. When people learned what Kim did, they often asked Vernon if he worried about her. He always said yes, of course, not knowing how to explain that he worried more when she wasn't working. A fire had defined outcomes you could count on. It burned in predictable patterns. It killed in a few ways. It wasn't always new, as Kim had said; she just liked the way thinking this made her feel. Vernon's life with her had been like that, newness scattered around for her to unearth and him to stumble over, a forced celebration of bantamweight novelties and anodyne local personalities. Since they met, he had attended more food truck inaugurations, pint night fundraisers, and local displays of creative expression than he could count. It was exhausting, but Vernon always figured you keep up with this sort of thing for the sake of someone you love, even if that just made more of it come. The lightning had changed something. It made Vernon feel lonely and superior at once. There was nothing Kim represented to compare it to, not even the fire.

Vernon drove to a bar he liked across the river. It didn't have a liquor license and live music was unwelcome, even on weekends. Habitués lined the room like topiary. Vernon noticed Carlos among them. Carlos was the closest Vernon had come to making a friend in graduate school. They sometimes drank beer together at a sports bar across the footbridge from campus during class breaks. While other members of their cohort were at lunch or the gym, Vernon and Carlos watched football highlights and discussed their hopes and dreams. Carlos was from Idaho, and worked for the Ag Workers Union in the next town over. He wanted a girlfriend. Vernon remembered him having one picked out, a mousy Catholic brunette in their psychopathology class, the class they went to after closing out at the sports bar. Her name was Nora. Vernon watched Carlos watch Nora in class. It was interesting to see how people put the eye to things they assumed were out of reach. Longing didn't quite describe it; neither did disappointment. Contentment came closest. Carlos looked at home watching Nora, like he would rather be nowhere else. No wonder Kim didn't like him; the self-containment of others always seemed to rankle her.

Carlos noticed Vernon and waved him over. Nora sat beside him, a glass of what looked like communion wine between her thin white hands. There were two other classmates at the table whom Vernon recognized, but couldn't name, even after going to school with them for years. Both were nice young women in their mid-twenties with similar interests and values. One was named Blair, the other was named Lauren. Blair asked Vernon if he would like something to drink, and Lauren filled a glass for him from a pitcher of beer they were sharing when Vernon said yes. Nora asked how his summer was going. Vernon told them about running into Dr. Varney at the farmer's market. Everyone got a big kick out of that.

"He's my advisor," said Lauren, generating groans and expressions of sympathy.

"He told me I looked tired when I met with him at the end of last term," she continued. "I said I was tired because I'm working and going to school full time and doing my unpaid practicum hours at a group home for psychopath toddlers that try to scratch my eyes out when I don't let them eat candy for dinner."

"What did he say?" asked Carlos.

"He said that sounded hard, but social work isn't for everyone."

"You're shitting me," said Nora. This turn of phrase coming from her startled and delighted Vernon.

"And that he works sixty-hour weeks as chair and just got a new pointer puppy," Lauren added. "So he understands what it's like to be tired."

"Is forgetting how to treat people part of getting a doctorate?" asked Blair.

"He showed me pictures of the dog," said Lauren. "It's real cute."

"It's like he lives on the moon," said Vernon, refilling his glass.

"Most of the PhDs at the University of Montana belong in a zoo," said Carlos.

"Not the petting variety," said Nora. "Have you guys had Advanced Research Methods and Program Evaluation with Casey Winkler? She's a real artifact. She nominated herself for an award given to individuals who make some sort of impact on the lives of indigenous people."

"Did she get it?" asked Carlos.

"No," said Nora. "Skip gave her tenure instead. Now she

spends the first forty-five minutes of every class doing mindfulness exercises with the lights off. Sometimes she lays on the floor."

"I'd rather have my tuition money used to make bombs than pay her salary," said Lauren.

"It's not so bad," said Nora. "I get most of my online shopping done in that class. One person brings a coloring book."

"The more time I spend around social workers, the less I want to be one," said Carlos.

"Maybe that's why Skip is always calling himself a 'gatekeeper of the profession'," said Vernon, enjoying himself. It was good to air his embitterment this way, alongside the embitterment of others who also felt they had earned it. Why had he never done this before? He knew the answer, of course; no mystery there. Vernon had gotten used to making himself available to Kim, clearing his schedule when it wasn't written for him by work or school in order to go where he was bidden; eighties karaoke at the VFW, trivia night at the cidery, maybe a standup comedy competition featuring an array of local crackups, who knew what wonders the evening might hold? After a long day of listening to Skip Varney delineate his exploits among the natives of Homer or Casey Winkler apologize every few minutes for holding her class on Indian land, who wouldn't want to kick back with Mud Bike, Doctor Fingers, and Bone Crone at a favorite watering hole while they reviewed the non-events that made up their lives? Somewhere along the line, Vernon realized, he'd forgotten he had choices. He didn't directly blame Kim for this. The economy of scarcity she created between them meant he had to do what she wanted to see her. That had been fine for a while, or better than nothing, he thought. And yet, here he was, enjoying nothing just fine. Ken was right. Loneliness, of a type, was certainly peaceful.

Ryan was reading a book in a lawn chair under the cherry tree in Charlie's backyard when he got home from work. Charlie spotted his brother through the kitchen window, got two beers from the fridge, and went out to join him.

"Mom and dad said you might stop by," said Charlie, pulling a seat up beside Ryan and handing him a beer.

"I know they're worried," said Ryan. "I guess I wasn't sure how to do what I wanted to do without making them worry."

"Maybe give them a call today. They'd like to hear from you."

"Are they angry?"

Charlie liked this question. It reminded him that he was still Ryan's older brother.

"I don't think so," he said. "The video on the news really upset them."

"I heard about that, but I haven't seen it."

"It's not great, especially if you were hoping to tell people it was an accident."

"I wasn't planning on it."

"Did you have to go over him that much? It seems like once or twice would have made the point just fine."

"I didn't want to feel him under the wheels anymore," said Ryan. He noticed the change these words wrought in his brother; it was like Charlie took a step back without moving. "Are you angry?"

"No, Ryan. I remember Chris. He was a piece of shit. If it hadn't been you, someone or something would have got him eventually. I just wish it hadn't been you."

A flock of crows blew out of a nearby standing tree and began circling the house, as if Charlie's wish had summoned them. The rain overnight had thinned out the smoke. The black, animate shapes cruising against the patches of blue sky above reminded

Ryan of watching Lisa draw or write on the colored paper she liked. It made him feel okay about telling Charlie what Chris had said about her.

"He also said he knew where we lived," Ryan added, watching his brother frown at a patch of dry grass between his sandals. "I remembered we went to elementary school together for a few years before he got pulled out and sent somewhere else. We rode the same bus. He saw where I got off. I believed him."

"I don't understand why he was bothering you in the first place," said Charlie. "You never had a problem with anyone I knew about. You were always good at avoiding shit like that."

"Chris was in front of me at a light. I had no idea it was him. It turned green, and he was just sitting there fucking around, so I tapped my horn. He drove in front of me until I turned off at the rec field and then doubled back."

"That's not normal behavior."

"He didn't look right when he got out of the car, like he'd taken too much of something. He kept asking me if I had a problem and saying that no one honked at him in his town, he wasn't going to tell me twice. He also kept telling Cole or Sheldon to get something out of the trunk. I don't know what it was."

"Probably a paintball gun," said Charlie. "Dad told me about it. Police went through the car. They turned one up. Apparently, Chris and the other two boneheads had been doing drive-bys with it around town. But they also had a katana and some fireworks in the car, so who knows."

"I keep waiting to hear something that will make me feel bad about this," said Ryan. "That isn't it."

"Well, consider that it's being characterized on the news as an unprovoked attack, on your part. You might want to clean up your attitude about it and get your side of the story out there before much longer. Linda and I will get you started. She works with people that can help you."

"That's fine. I don't expect you to keep me hidden or anything like that," said Ryan. "I just wanted to see you before things got rolling."

Charlie didn't say anything, but he put his hand on Ryan's back. They had another beer, and ate a few cherries off the tree, talked about what the fishing had been like so far. The wind out of the canyon had picked up and the sun was intermittently visible. Ryan wondered how Charlie would feel if he knew about what happened back in South Dakota. Even if Alison didn't say anything, the car was still there, jacked up in Earl's garage. It wouldn't take a master sleuth to notice the Vermont plates and put everything together.

Linda didn't seem surprised to find Ryan in her house when she arrived home. She and Charlie grilled bison burgers for dinner and went over the practical aspects of what would come next. None of it surprised or frightened Ryan.

"You're far from home," Linda told him. "So, not a flight risk. I know the judge who you'll see. I'm pretty sure I can get him to give me your case. If you promise me you won't run away, I think we can avoid having you wait around in baby jail while the paperwork gets sorted out."

"You arrived at a good time," said Charlie. "The countywide trend at the moment is in keeping kids in homes rather than cages."

"Cheaper," said Linda.

"Can I stay here?" asked Ryan, glancing around the property. He noticed this question made Charlie smile.

"We'd love to have you, but I'm already toeing the line here by getting involved in this," said Linda. "I think that might be pushing it with the court."

"Can I know where I'm going to go before I promise not run away?"

"I don't know if you're joking or not," said Charlie. "But Linda is putting a lot on the line for you. So am I. We both care about you. Please don't make us look like fools."

That settled it, more or less. Ryan cleaned up from dinner while Charlie and Linda made some calls. A social worker friend of his brother's would come for Ryan in the morning, and take him to a group home where he would await extradition by the state of Vermont.

"It's possible they'll allow mom or dad to fly out and bring you back," said Charlie, as he made up the sofa for Ryan. "But we'll have to see. Did you call them yet?"

"No. I will tomorrow."

"Please do, they're worried," said Charlie. "Where's your car, by the way?"

"Down the street," said Ryan.

"Remember to leave the keys here so I can move it when the streetsweeper comes by," said Charlie. He wished Ryan goodnight and went upstairs to go to bed. Earl's truck was parked in the weeds behind an abandoned service station over by the university. Ryan had found a tarp mixed in with some tools in bed and thrown that over it, weighting the corners down with rocks. It looks like what it was, something left behind. The keys were in Ryan's pocket. If he was going to leave, now was the best option. He felt safe and happy with his brother and Linda, and knew they were doing the right thing. Still, the right thing sounded like a drag. Ryan expected he would have to spend a lot of time listening to people talk about what had happened to Chris, and answering their questions. It would be boring and pointless. He was already tired of thinking about it. He would probably have to pretend he felt bad and somehow project this so others could appreciate the depth of his contrition. It all sounded like the typical lumbering process behind everything people believed in, even smart people like Charlie and Linda. Ryan had noticed that humankind was usually either at war or developing crummy little chores for itself to pass the time until the next war. He could leave now and avoid the entire circus. It would hurt his brother and disappoint Linda, but the stakes were different for them. Ryan hoped they would understand this in some way, but didn't feel any sense of responsibility for their edification. At a certain point, he knew he was on his own.

Ryan hadn't slept much since Oacoma. He needed some rest before driving anywhere. He set an alarm for a little before dawn and slept straight through it, dreaming dreams of chewing through different parts of his body to get them out of traps. First his hand, then his leg; he was working through the wrist of his other hand when Charlie woke him up. The social worker had arrived. Charlie asked Ryan for his car keys again before he left. Ryan handed over the ones that went to Earl's truck. Charlie didn't notice. It seemed like things would be mostly symbolic from here on out.

Vernon walked Lauren home from the bar. It was late, but they were having a nice conversation. The streets didn't have too many lights, and some people had sprinklers going in the dark. Vernon and Lauren got caught in the sweep a few times; it gave them something in common to laugh about. That was good, and most of what he wanted, he realized, after bidding her goodnight and aiming himself back in the direction of his car. Lauren offered her couch after learning of Vernon's circumstances, but he was used to sleeping in the Honda by now and imagined he would rest better there. They had a beer on her porch and called it a night.

Vernon was bit too looped to get back up into the canyon, but he found a nice enough spot down by the old train depot beside the river, where he could hear the water with his windows down. Smoke feathered the output of the distant lights along the bike path; the rain hadn't entirely finished things. Perhaps Kim would be heading back to work tomorrow, and he could grab his belongings from the house. He didn't have much. Some clothes and books, a few toiletries, maybe a dish or a cup or something. It would all fit in the trunk until he found a place to live. Maybe he'd stop in the campus housing office tomorrow to see Freda. The options might not be great, but they had to be better than sharing a bed with Archer and whoever else followed Kim home.

Vernon wondered if he would miss her; it had to be possible, but he just couldn't imagine it for himself. It would be like missing a black hole or a crack in the earth's surface, a void that things dropped into and never came out again. Maybe sadness would hit him later on; for now, he felt nothing. The lightning felt like it helped him feel this way. Vernon didn't know how exactly, but he believed it was still with him; he sometimes felt it in his chest or his head, like something trapped under glass. Dr. Wolf had wanted Vernon to feel amazed and lucky to be alive. Instead, he was a little angry with the lightning for not arriving sooner. He dreamt of it almost every night now, of swinging between high dark peaks on one bolt after another, striding up and down the white-hot branches like steps or climbing them like a ladder. Sometimes he tugged a bolt to earth like he was drawing a blind down from the sky, and watched as it eliminated what it touched; Archer, Dr. Skip Varney, Paul before he and Vernon actually met, but most often it was Kim turning to ash in the belly of a fire he had ignited around her. The lightning was telling him to use it, Vernon suspected. He trusted the lightning, so that's what he would do.

The next morning was smoky and drear. A chopper somewhere overhead awoke Vernon, beating the haze as it flew toward the sun. Perhaps Kim was on it; things appeared to have picked up during the night. He drove back to the house. Her car wasn't in the driveway and the door was locked. Vernon backed the Honda in and popped the trunk. This seemed like a good opportunity to miss her; still, he felt nothing, only a becalmed emptiness within himself where whatever the lightning took had once been. Vernon didn't have boxes or containers. He walked in and out of the house with armloads of his things and dumped them in the truck until it was full. Was that everything? Vernon had no idea. He went back in the house to do a final sweep, not sure what he was looking for. Kim's cat threaded his ankles, mewling and vibrating. Vernon picked the cat up and held it against his shoulder like a baby. He liked this animal. Its needs made sense to him. It ate from a bowl, slept on a pillow, and shit in box. Those were its variables and considerations. The door opened and the cat's vibrato changed against his shoulder. Vernon knew what that meant; Kim was home.

"I just came for my stuff," he said, setting the cat down and looking for something that belonged to him to pick up. There was no immediate escape. Kim blocked the door. She looked natural doing it. "I thought you were at work."

"I was dropping off Archer," she said. "We should talk."

"No thanks," said Vernon.

"I'm sorry I told you to leave. I was mad at you for what you did to Archer's hair."

"He looks better now."

"He said you put shit in his jacket."

"I think he probably put it there himself and forgot."

"I don't understand why me being able to love more than one person makes you so angry."

"You're like something from one of my classes."

"That's a really horrible thing to say to a woman."

"It's bad no matter how you parse it, I agree."

"You think just because you're getting a master's degree in social work that you get to diagnose me?

"Yes, I do."

"So what's your diagnosis?"

"You're a fucking selfish nutcase."

A glass smashed into the wall beside Vernon's head. He hadn't even seen Kim pick it up. She had a broom in her hands now, the one they kept beside the door to sweep up the crap they tracked in. She got him pretty good on the side of the head and once in the eye before he got it away from her. Vernon's eye was already starting to swell when she flung a handful of potting soil from one of the plants in his face. He could barely see what he was doing now, but he heard Kim coming and it spooked him. He ran for where he thought the door was and collided with her. Something gouged his forehead and opened a wound along his hairline, and Kim made a sound he'd never heard before. Vernon's vision cleared enough to find the doorknob. He fled to his Honda and sped out of the driveway with his trunk open, trailing sweatshirts and textbooks.

There was blood in Vernon's eyes from the gouge on his forehead, but he didn't stop driving until he felt like he was out of scampering range of Kim. He pulled off into the parking area of a grocery store, and looked himself over the rearview mirror. A deep, narrow cut edged his scalp, and bled a bit when he squinted to get a better look at it. How the fuck had Kim done that?

Maybe not stitches, but definitely a large bandage was needed. Vernon wrapped t-shirt around his head like a turban and went inside the grocery store to gather doctoring supplies. The cashiers eyed him. It was slow and there wasn't much else to look at. The store radio played Bach, and then Paganini; it made the shopping experience seemed like a grand venture. Kim ruined it by calling Vernon in the middle of things. Because he was reading through one eye, Vernon misread the number as Ken, and thought it was his boss. He answered a bit too jauntily.

"You knocked my fucking teeth out!" shouted Kim; she may as well have been on speakerphone.

"Which ones?" asked Vernon.

"The two in the front!" said Kim. Her voice had taken on an odd slurry whistle with the change in her dentition.

"Your incisors."

"I guess so."

"Sorry. You should have just let me leave."

"You're done in this town, Vernon," whistled Kim. "People know me around here. You won't even be able to go to the shitty bars you like. You're going to be the guy who knocked my teeth out."

"It was an accident and you know it."

"It doesn't matter. I'm a hero. I keep this fucking cowtown from burning to the ground. What the fuck do you do?"

That was a good question. Vernon didn't have a good answer. It was hard to imagine a world in which he gave a shit what Doctor Fingers or Quiver Liver thought. He had never planned on making this his home anyway. If Kim wanted to cast him as the man who had broken her heart and unseated her fangs, what did he care? He would let the lightening do that talking in the meanwhile.

"I'll go toe to toe with any crap-jacket you send my way. There's no one in this town scarier than you."

Vernon hung up and continued his shopping.

The social worker's name was Jenna. She wore cat-eye glasses and a variegated scarf with an imported look to it. Ryan found her attractive in a number of ways that were new to him. The way she pronounced 'process', as in 'child welfare process', gave him a tingle he couldn't figure out. There was nothing ornate about it. He just liked the soft sound the word made leaving her mouth.

Ryan also liked the way Jenna drove him in her Subaru to the shelter for aberrant youngsters where he would await the over-head movements of his punishers. She sat straight in her seat with her hands at ten and two, eyeing the road for hazards or other developments like she was testing for her license. After all the driving he'd done recently, it was nice to be a passenger watching someone else do it. Things were generally out his hands now. Jenna tried to make him feel better about that as she drove.

"I think you'll like this place," she said. "It's run by people that really care a lot about the kids and they do everything they can to make it comfortable and fun. You'll have your own room, and get to go bowling and swimming and hiking all over the place. They even have pizza and movie night every Friday!"

"Excellent," said Ryan. It sounded like the dream of a disadvantaged ten-year-old come true. That was okay. The shelter had to be better than the juvenile detention center, which was across town behind a Target store. Ryan knew he would probably end up someplace like that eventually; he didn't see a way around it once things got rolling. The thought of being locked up scared him more than anything he could imagine. He'd put it off as long as possible.

Ken answered the door when they arrived at the shelter, and led Ryan and Jenna upstairs to a conference room with a window overlooking a small park in back of the house. While Jenna exchanged his details with Ken, Ryan watched a sloppy fistfight between two inebriated transients in the park. They were too messed up to seriously hurt each other, but their mutual will to do so was strong enough to keep them trying. One of them got hold of a small stick about the size of a relay baton. The other had an umbrella. Each time the one with the stick advanced, the one with the umbrella rapidly opened and closed it to fend him off. It was a noisy and interesting display. A small crowd had gathered to watch, and seemed to be rooting for the guy with the umbrella; a clear underdog, in Ryan's opinion. Four police officers in two patrol cars arrived just as Jenna called him away to sign some paperwork. The outcome would remain a mystery.

The documents she slid across the table were essentially different iterations of the same general pledge to behave himself and not run away. Ryan signed and initialed where he was asked, feeling like he was getting pretty good at participating in these kinds of symbolic rituals. His keepers looked pleased, at any rate. Jenna excused herself shortly thereafter; she had other cases to attend to. She left her card and told Ryan to call if he needed anything.

"I have to ask you a favor before we do anything else," said Ken, after Jenna had gone. Ryan noticed his hand rested on a heavy packet of papers that was probably some sort of rulebook to be reviewed. "We ask all our residents not to discuss why they're here with each other. If they need to talk about it, they can talk to staff. If residents break this rule, they get a small consequence. However, things are little different with your case. I agreed to let you stay here with the understanding that any mention of what happened in Virginia gets you sent to jail. No warnings, and only one consequence. Can you live with that?"

"Do you mean Vermont?"

"What did I say?"

"Virginia. I've never been to Virginia."

"I suppose I meant Vermont then," said Ken. "Sorry. I've been up all night, so I may be a little groggy."

"Why were you up all night?"

"The overnight person had something come up. His name's Vernon. You'll meet him tonight."

Ken looked down at the rulebook like he wished his hand was big enough to hide it from sight.

"Why don't we save the rules for later," he said. "Would you like a tour?"

They went downstairs to see what there was to see. It was a nice enough place. There were a lot of potted plants and photographs on the walls of teenagers engaging in age-appropriate prosocial activities. The living room had a comfortable couch and a large television with gaming system and selection of movies to watch. There was a not too bad library with a foosball table and a couple of computer terminals with their browsing capacities dialed back. A glass door looked out on a patio with a grill and a few picnic tables. A large garden screened the house from the park where the bums had skirmished. Ryan's room was at the end of a long white hallway. There wasn't much to it. The room held a bed, a desk, a lamp, and a chair. The window looked out on the side of the only clinic in town offering abortions. It was surrounded by a ten-foot-high fence topped off with garlands of concertina wire. If Ryan stretched a bit, he could catch glimpses of a small band of protesters holding signs and distributing leaflets out front. These people and their priorities intrigued him. He couldn't imagine caring about something the way they appeared to, and wondered what it must be like. Probably annoying, he guessed. Making people aware of all the silly shit you believe takes time and work. Ryan couldn't understand why anyone bothered.

He heard a sound in the hall like an old dog wheezing. It turned out to be Ken snoring. The program director had fallen asleep sitting up on the couch in the living room with his chin on his chest and the rulebook splayed on the next cushion over. Ryan sat down beside him and had a look. He'd noticed Ken handling the pages with the same talismanic regard Earl had for his movie script, and was curious to see what kind of boilerplate lurked within. The opening page warned Ryan that he should expect to have fun and work hard going forward. That somehow came off sounding like a pain in the ass and also impossible. What else? The house functioned on a level system, with residents moving up or down based on general behavior and overall compliance. As an entering freshman, Ryan would begin at level two. This entitled him to use of the television and computers, snacks with sugar and/or caffeine, and a bedtime 9:30PM on weekdays and 11PM on Fridays and Saturdays. Receiving one or more consequences in one or more of the categories spread across a double-sided, horizontally printed matrix containing every possible combination of nuisance behaviors could drop him to level one, wherein bedtime arrived earlier and privileges were reduced. Further misbehavior would land Ryan what was called 'seat time'. In this event, he would be asked to 'take a seat' by staff, and consider his crimes. Where this seat was would be determined by one of the youth counselors, as well as the duration of his stay there. Reasons for 'seat time' included smoking tobacco products, skipping school, or running away. Ryan was astonished what a human mind could produce with limited oversight. Sending people on trains to a death camp made more sense to him.

From the rulebook, Ryan also learned that he could leave the shelter at any time. The doors were always open, and staff would never prevent him from walking through them. Ken allowing himself to doze on the couch made a little more sense now. Vigilance held no incentive. It provoked Ryan to toy with the idea of the running off. He had little money and no vehicle. Even if that wasn't the case, where would he go? Maybe the hobos in the park could mentor him, share their ways and wisdom from lives adrift. No, Ryan would stay, if only for Charlie and Linda, though there was only so long he was willing to entertain that consideration; at some point it would grow stale and crumble like something lost at a picnic.

The front door opened and Ken awoke with a start, smacked his lips and gazing around the living room until he noticed Ryan beside him with the rulebook open in his lap. The program director's eyes silently begged Ryan to say nothing about his nap as the sound of children returning from some outside venture filled the formerly silent air. Destiny and the other two girls appeared on the stairs alongside the boy who feared the darkness. Maggie and another counselor named Henry brought up the rear carrying a cooler and beach bag. All of them shared a pause when they noticed Ryan on the couch. Ken swallowed a yawn and introduced him. A few greetings and names were exchanged. The children dispersed to various activities and Ken shut himself up in the office with Maggie. Henry went off to the kitchen to begin dinner preparations. The boy who feared darkness asked Ryan if he wanted to build a Lego set with him. That sounded fine. They sat side by side at the dining room table assembling bricks for the next few hours, not talking much. It reminded Ryan of spending time with his sister. He wondered how things would be explained to her. It made his heart hurt to imagine her knowing what Chris had said, but not what Ryan had done to him because of it. Out of everyone in his family, he thought Lisa understood things best.

Charlie stopped by after dinner to see how Ryan was settling in. They sat out at one of the picnic tables behind the house. Bums yowled in the park on the other side of the garden as the sun began to set. Charlie seemed troubled. It didn't take long to find out why.

"I need to know who these belong to," he said, placing Earl's car keys on the table between them. "I couldn't find your car and I know these don't go to it."

"I had some trouble with a tire on the way here," said Ryan. "I left the Volvo to get fixed up and the mechanic gave me a loaner. I told him I'd drop it off on my way back."

"Why are you lying to me?"

"Because I'm not sure what you already know."

Charlie looked appalled and maybe like he was about to cry.

"A detective from Sioux City called dad," he said. "Your car was found at crime scene. The detective said he couldn't share too many details yet, but he told dad someone got killed."

"Why did he call dad?"

"Because the car is registered to him and he pays the insurance on it. His name is all over the documents in the glovebox."

"I wish that hadn't happened."

"What did you do, Ryan?"

Ryan shrugged, but didn't say anything. Charlie waited for him to speak, probably the way he did for the deranged and wild teens he worked with at the place up in the canyon. When he realized nothing was coming, he got mad.

"Ryan, this is fucking serious," said Charlie. "I see this kind of shit all the time and so does Linda. You can't fool these people, or weasel your way out of anything. But if you make it easier for them, they might do the same for you. Someone from Sioux City is coming up here to talk with you about what happened. Dad said the detective told him the vehicle you stole might be a key piece of evidence. I tried to find it based on the description he gave dad, but this town is full of old pickups. Whoever they send is going to want to know where it is. If you cooperate, and he shows up with that part already done, no one has to waste their time and we can all focus on finding the best possible outcome for you."

"I think I'll wait and see what the detective has to offer."

"I'll leave the keys for him in the staff office," said Charlie. There was a tremor in his voice, but he managed to keep it together. No goodbye or promise to visit again soon though. Ryan knew he'd hurt his brother in a way that they might never fully come back from. It was tough to watch Charlie leave that way, but Ryan figured this would make whatever came next easier on him. He watched his brother hand off the keys to Maggie. She put them in a labeled plastic bag and dropped it in a red metal tool box with a cheap combination lock, the kind you could easily knock off with a hammer or a rock. Ryan's cellphone was in there too. Opening the thing wouldn't be a problem, but getting ahold of it would be tricky. Nighttime was probably his best bet. Ken said someone named Vernon was on shift tonight. Getting a crack at the lockbox depended how he sized up. Ryan didn't want to threaten or hurt him, but this might be his final chance to flee whatever was in store for him. He slept through his last opportunity. That wouldn't happen this time.

Vernon arrived for work happy and sober, but looking like an absolute nightmare from his run-in with Kim. One eye was bruised and swollen, the other was red and irritated from the potting soil. The gash in his scalp from her teeth was covered with a moist, overlarge bandage that looked like a sanitary napkin. A few of the children were still settling in getting ready for bed when he showed up. They asked what happened. He told them he hit a deer.

"Your car looks fine," said Destiny, eyeing Vernon's Honda through the kitchen window. A few of the other kids went over to have a look.

"I was on a bike," he said, adding: "It's antler scratched my face."

Maggie corralled everyone to their respective hallways and dismissed Henry for the night. She asked to speak with Vernon in the staff office.

"We have new one," she said. "He killed a kid with his car somewhere back east. The others don't know. If he mentions it, call youth court. They'll take him to jail. That's the deal."

"I didn't know we took murderers," said Vernon.

"It's some kind of special arrangement. He's important to someone over in the juvenile probation office. I told Ken I didn't like it, but he just said the same shit he always says about how important it is to give people a chance."

"He said that about the kid who lit the fire in his room."

"And the one that like stuffed animal porn."

"And the one that killed the baby after he went home."

"And the one that got his jaw shot off in the high school parking lot after trying to rob that drug dealer."

"How's he doing?"

"It's hard to say."

They both chuckled about that. Maggie took her leave, and Vernon settled into his first round of chores. The smoke had started to clear in the afternoon, and the evening was cool and comfortable. He switched off the air conditioner and popped open the patio door. The people in the park were pretty quiet tonight. Every so often a red or white bicycle light cruised through the darkness. Progress seemed to be in the air. Vernon had spoken with Freda after patching himself up. She had a few things that might work. If any of them did, he could move-in as soon as next week. He'd also talked with Caroline. She wasn't too happy. An ATV flipped on her, and she had been peeing blood for a couple days. Her doctor said she would be okay, to take it easy for a while, and gave her something for the pain. She was still pretty uncomfortable. Vernon asked if he could come down to Pocatello and see her, maybe fix her some good meals and help out with the horses and whatever else needed to be done until she felt better. He had some time off saved up. He said he would like to see her and she said she'd like that. Vernon didn't say anything about Kim, and Caroline didn't ask. She seemed to understand something had changed. He filled out the forms for requesting time off, and tucked them in Ken's mailbox. For his reasons on paper, Vernon had checked the box beside family/medical; after the incident with the dog, Ken probably wouldn't see this as a stretch. It had been a while since Vernon had something to look forward to; the feeling was unfamiliar enough to be almost unpleasant.

Maggie was planning a barbecue for dinner tomorrow; burgers, hotdogs, watermelon, and ears of corn. There wasn't much prep for Vernon to do. He'd offered to make potato salad, and she seemed to think that was a good idea. He put some water on in the kitchen and started a load of towels in dryer. He emerged from the laundry room right on time to see someone he didn't recognize enter the staff office. Probably that murderer, Vernon figured. Going in there without permission was a big no-no, but new kids usually made that mistake once or twice. Who could blame them? There were a lot rules to remember.

Vernon figured the murderer probably needed a toothbrush or something, but two sharp metallic reports from somewhere inside the office suggested trickier motives. Indeed, the new kid had the lockbox open and was putting something in his pocket when Vernon walked in.

"You must be Ryan," he said. "Anything I can help you find in there?"

"I don't think so. I'll be out of your way here in just a second," said Ryan, turning so Vernon could see the hammer from the house manager's toolbox in his hand. The combination lock lay in two pieces at his feet. Vernon had been sent to a few trainings that said you should never block a door during moments like these. He duly stepped aside and sat down at the desk to give Ryan a clear flight path.

"Taking off?" Vernon asked.

"That's the idea," said Ryan, retrieving his phone from the box and closing the lid. "Sorry about the lock. I was going to ask you to open it, but you weren't here."

"It's my fault. I left the office door wide open. You mind telling me what you took out of there? I have to write all this up after you go."

"Just my phone and car keys."

"Sounds good. Bon voyage," said Vernon. Thunder rumbled outside. He heard the screen door to the patio open and close. Now what? he wondered, standing a little too fast. It made Ryan tense up in a way that gave Vernon a pretty good idea what was at stake here. "It's fine. I'm just going to see what's going on with the door. Be on your way."

A man was sitting on the couch in the living room when Vernon walked out of the office. That wasn't entirely unprecedented, especially during the summer. Folks camped out in the park would get inebriated or confused late at night and head toward the house lights or walk through any door they found open. The guy looked rough, but not in a homeless way. Social work school had taught Vernon that nobody ever looked like anything, so this made sense.

"If you want a sandwich or some water, I'd be glad to help you out," he said. "But I'm going to need you to wait outside."

"Thanks, I'm not hungry," said the man. "What I would like is to speak with one of your residents. I believe his name is Ryan."

"Ryan, you have a visitor," said Vernon, over his shoulder. Ryan emerged from the office and stood beside Vernon. He was still holding the hammer.

"Hi, Earl," he said. "When I heard about the detective calling, I wondered if you might show up."

"Your dad was very helpful," said Earl. "I just came for my truck. Your brother said the keys were here."

"Right here," said Ryan, drawing the keys out of his pocket and dangling them from a finger. "Come grab them."

"What's your name?" Earl asked Vernon. Vernon told him. "Okay, Vernon. Ryan here is going to hand you the hammer he's got behind his back and then toss the keys to me."

"You got it," said Vernon, reaching for the hammer. Ryan stepped away from him, still dangling the keys from his fingertip. Earl lifted his shirt and removed a handgun from the waist of his jeans. He held it loosely in his hand without pointing it at anything. Drawing it out appeared to cause him considerable discomfort. The thunder sounded closer now.

"Ryan, we been through this," said Earl. "The difference now is that before I had a little more on the line. All that's gone now, because of what you and your friend did. Now, I think we can agree, I have been more than patient with you so far, but if you test me, I will pass with flying colors."

"You need me alive if you ever want to find your truck," said Ryan.

"That's true," said Earl. "But I certainly don't need you in any kind of shape. I will make Vernon pick which of your nuts I blow off first. And he'll do it if he wants to keep his."

Ryan seemed to be chewing this over.

"Ryan," said Vernon, his voice sounding a little reedy. "Please hand me the hammer and toss the keys to Earl."

The keys hit Earl in the chest, and the hammer dropped to the carpet with a muted thud. Ryan looked disappointed. Vernon was on the verge of crying with relief. He kicked the hammer beneath the foosball table.

"Good choice, Ryan," said Earl. "Now, we're going to take a drive."

He stood up and motioned them toward the door. He walked with a limp that looked painful to Vernon, and seemed to struggle to keep his breathing regular, even on the short walk to the parking lot where Ryan's Volvo awaited them. It had started raining. The trees in the park were dark, but the sound of them moving in the wind sounded like low conversation.

"Thanks for finally getting around to changing the tire," said Ryan.

"Don't mention it," said Earl. "I swapped out the plates too. Didn't want anyone bugging me on the drive over. Now, I know you don't do so great behind the wheel when you're angry, so Vernon's going to drive. You sit next to him and give directions. Don't either of you let me feel like you're taking me someplace I don't want to be."

Ryan and Vernon got in the car and took their places. Earl sat in the back with his hands folded over the gun in his lap. He appeared at ease during the drive to the derelict service station where Ryan had left the truck. It was still there beneath the tarp, looking a little ghostly in the headlights as Vernon parked.

"Now, Vernon, you seem like a person who cares about the welfare of others," said Earl.

"I suppose I am," said Vernon. It sounded like a guess.

"Why else would you work at a dump like that place?"

"You've got me there."

"Now, as a person that cares about the welfare of others, there are some things you should know. I want you to sit tight here with the engine running in case anyone comes along. In that event, I'm a disabled person and you two are helping me get my truck; it's here because I lost my housing while I was in the hospital and had nowhere else to park it. You with me so far?"

Vernon nodded. Earl continued.

"If you do that, I will bring you back to work as soon as we finish up here and the children won't even know you were gone. If you don't do that, if you pull away as soon as I step out of the car, for example, I will spill this twerp next to you straightaway, and then I will go back to where you work to see what I can get into there. Despite what people may say afterword, it will be your fault. Do you understand me?"

Vernon said he did. Earl and Ryan got out of the car. Earl yanked the tarp off the truck and unlocked it. The operation clearly taxed him. Ryan thought there might be an opportunity there, but Earl seemed to sense this.

"Don't even think about it, you little weirdo," he said, raising the pistol and tossing a canvas grocery bag at his feet. "You and your girlfriend did quite a number on me."

"The girl helped," said Ryan, toeing the bag, but leaving it where it landed. The rain had really picked up and the thunder was louder and more frequent.

"Well, it's a good thing she isn't too strong. I kept her meals light."

"How did you get loose? I've been wondering that."

"Well, that was a lucky thing," said Earl. "A customer stopped by a little after you took off with my truck. You went through my place so I'm sure you noticed I have several different income streams."

"Your flowers were nice."

"Those were just for me," said Earl. "Anyway, the customer happened to be a vet. He helped patch me up and get the tire on your car. He also gave me a few things he had on hand for the pain. Again, it was a lucky thing. He was on his way back from the race track at Fort Pierre, and had some of what he'd been peddling left over. I'm mostly here now because of the wonders of equine amphetamines and oxycodone."

"What did you say happened?"

"I told him the little shitbird maniac from the news assaulted me and stole my truck when I realized who you were. He was sympathetic."

"I bet he probably didn't know about the girl in your closet."

"Nina and I have a very private relationship. It's not anyone's business."

"Now it is."

"And who do I have to thank for that?" said Earl, pointing at the canvas grocery bag with the pistol. "Now, pick that up, and get in the fucking truck."

Ryan did as he was told, curious to see what Earl had in mind. He told Ryan to flip up the bench seat in the cab and put what was under there in the bag. This turned out to be three sizable bushels of plastic-wrapped dollar bills. There wasn't enough light to see the denomination, but Ryan figured it was probably significant. No one would have come this far to get a crummy old truck back.

"Toss it over," said Earl. Thunder roared overhead and lightning lit everything up for a moment. Ryan saw Benjamin Franklin's face peering out of the bag in his hands. He heard tires squeal and an engine moan under the rain and looked up. The Volvo was closer than it had been and Earl was on the ground, having what looked like some kind of convulsion in the rain. One of his hands slapped the surrounding area, searching blindly for the pistol. It reminded Ryan of the way Earl looked after Alison pepper-sprayed him, only a little worse, probably something he wasn't going to walk or stumble away from. Vernon finished it in time with the next bolt, as if he'd been waiting. Ryan didn't bother checking for a pulse. He got in the passenger seat with the bag in his lap, and off they went.

"What's in the bag?" asked Vernon. He sounded more relaxed than Ryan would have expected.

"A lot of money," said Ryan. "We can split it."

"I think you're going to need it more than me. I'll just take out my security deposit. You keep the rest."

"I wondered if you'd do it," said Ryan, after they'd driven for a while and were almost back at the shelter. The storm had moved out over the mountains and was lighting up the distant peaks. "Earl didn't think you would."

"He didn't know about the lightning," said Vernon. He suspected this is what it had prepared him for. That was clear now. Ryan had enough respect for the hazy motives this implied to not ask anything further.

"I need to go back inside," said Vernon when they arrived at the shelter. "You don't though."

"How long until you have to call it in?"

"I can give you an hour, if you leave now."

"That's not much."

"The house manager will show up soon. I don't have a choice."

Ryan opened the bag and looked at the money.

"I don't know how much this will help me," he said. "There's only so many places I can go with it."

"Where do you want to go?"

"I'd like to see my sister again," said Ryan. He opened one of the packages in the bag and handed Vernon the first inch or so of bills. "Is that enough for a security deposit? I've never paid one before."

"Probably," said Vernon. He put the money in his pocket without counting it and got out of the car. Ryan got out too, and came around to the driver's side. Vernon was already on the front steps, fiddling with his keys.

"It felt like if I didn't kill him, he would live forever," said Ryan. "Is that how it felt for you?"

"Yes," said Vernon, without turning around. He got the door open and went inside and Ryan drove off. Vernon lay down on the couch where Earl had sat not long ago and flipped on the television. He watched a show with the sound off, something about predatory birds that hung the things they killed on thorns and branches for all to see. The sun rose through the living room window and light crept up the wall behind the television. There was no sign remaining of the storm that had swept in overnight.

Vernon had the report written and faxed to the city police desk by the time the house manager arrived. He had moved the hammer out from under the foosball table and placed it beside the broken lock and open lockbox to provide the appearance of a stepwise order of events. The house manager hadn't had much to say to Vernon since finding the dead dog in the chest freezer. That didn't change now. Vernon left and drove up into the canyon to get some sleep. He dreamed he was driving through the night to Pocatello to save Caroline from something ferocious and inevitable. The sky was empty and the road ran between black evergreen spires. The centerline stretching out into the darkness beyond the headlights reminded Vernon of the lightning in his dreams, something he would ride from top to bottom until he reached her.

Nina's family lived in a suburb outside Rapid City. Ryan got the address from Alison. She wasn't too upset about being left at the clinic in Oacoma, especially after he told her about Earl showing up in Montana. She asked if he was going to stop by Chicago on his way back. He asked if that was okay with Brad. Alison said she hadn't seen him since she got back from South Dakota. She didn't mention the car in the lake.

The house was an average rambler in a nice enough street. Nina's mother answered the door looking curious and worried. Ryan explained who he was and handed her the bag with the money in it.

"Where did this come from?" asked Nina's mother.

"From him," said Ryan.

"Will he come for it?"

"He's dead."

"Did you do it?"

"I helped."

"She said he never touched her," said Nina's mother. "The hospital said so too."

"I'm sorry I made you think about it anyway."

"I just mean it's good you helped. I still wouldn't have been able to forgive him."

Nina was visiting a friend. Her mother asked if Ryan would like to wait for her, and if he was hungry. He thanked her for the offer, but said he had to be moving along and to give Nina his best. As her mother closed the door, Ryan noticed a hefty crucifix on the wall behind her, the bejeweled kind you might carry in a procession or smite a sinner with. Whatever it had been before, it was now a house where forgiveness was important, but not always possible, the same as most houses.

On his way out of town, Ryan went to have a look at the faces in the mountain. The place mated the tackiness of a roadside shrine with a resort area's sweaty summertime footprint. Ryan understood this was one of the totem locations where those who would see him punished for what he had done derived their symbolic ideas about things like power, justice, and the necessity of order. It wasn't much different than any other fetish object, as he saw it; its power was mostly in its bigness, like a bully. He imagined the faces were frowning at him, urging him to receive his comeuppance with their stern rebuke. People snapped photos and posed before the disembodied heads. Perhaps their compound majesty was meant to thrill and humble onlookers, but it mostly seemed like the same old mythology with a waterslide attached. Still, he knew they would come for him.

Ryan stopped off to see Tammy on his way home. They spent a nice couple of days together. It was hot in Ohio. They slept late and lay around beneath the fan in her room for most of the afternoon, talking about ghosts and drinking her family's moonshine. When things cooled off in the evening, they walked in the preserve beside the campus or went into town for something to eat. He told her about the money in the bag he'd given to Nina's mother. Tammy asked where it came from. He told her about Earl. She said the bad things people like him do live way longer than the good things other people do, even after both are long gone. She also said she saw the video of Ryan killing Chris after he left. It made her wish people knew the whole story. That reminded him to get in touch with his parents.

Ryan called from atop one of the burial mounds in the woods near Tammy's dorm. His mom and dad were glad to hear from him and said to come home. He said he was on his way and apologized for the trouble he'd caused. They said he shouldn't worry about any of that right now, to drive safe and they'd figure it out when he arrived. He said he loved them and hung up. Earl's pistol was on the ground between his feet. It was hard to sit with it in his pocket or waistband, so he set it down there before making the call. Ryan felt like he had no more limbs to gnaw off, but in his dreams, he still ran on all fours after whatever he wanted.

❋❋❋❋❋❋❋❋❋❋❋❋

About the Author

Josh Amses lives in Vermont. This is his fifth book with Fomite Press.

More novels and novellas from Fomite...

Joshua Amses — *During This, Our Nadir*
Joshua Amses — *Ghats*
Joshua Amses — *How They Became Birds*
Joshua Amses — *Raven or Crow*
Joshua Amses — *The Moment Before an Injury*
Charles Bell — *The Married Land*
Charles Bell — *The Half Gods*
Jaysinh Birjepatel — *Nothing Beside Remains*
Jaysinh Birjepatel — *The Good Muslim of Jackson Heights*
David Brizer — *Victor Rand*
L. M Brown — *Hinterland*
Paula Closson Buck — *Summer on the Cold War Planet*
Dan Chodorkoff — *Loisaida*
Dan Chodorkoff — *Sugaring Down*
David Adams Cleveland — *Time's Betrayal*
Paul Cody — *Sphyxia*
Jaimee Wriston Colbert — *Vanishing Acts*
Roger Coleman — *Skywreck Afternoons*
Stephen Downes — *The Hands of Pianists*
Marc Estrin — *Hyde*
Marc Estrin — *Kafka's Roach*
Marc Estrin — *Proceedings of the Hebrew Free Burial Society*
Marc Estrin — *Speckled Vanities*
Marc Estrin — *The Annotated Nose*
Zdravka Evtimova — *In the Town of Joy and Peace*
Zdravka Evtimova — *Sinfonia Bulgarica*
Zdravka Evtimova — *You Can Smile on Wednesdays*
Daniel Forbes — *Derail This Train Wreck*
Peter Fortunato — *Carnevale*
Greg Guma — *Dons of Time*
Richard Hawley — *The Three Lives of Jonathan Force*
Lamar Herrin — *Father Figure*
Michael Horner — *Damage Control*
Ron Jacobs — *All the Sinners Saints*
Ron Jacobs — *Short Order Frame Up*
Ron Jacobs — *The Co-conspirator's Tale*
Scott Archer Jones — *And Throw Away the Skins*
Scott Archer Jones — *A Rising Tide of People Swept Away*
Julie Justicz — *Degrees of Difficulty*
Maggie Kast — *A Free Unsullied Land*
Darrell Kastin — *Shadowboxing with Bukowski*
Coleen Kearon — *#triggerwarning*
Coleen Kearon — *Feminist on Fire*
Jan English Leary — *Thicker Than Blood*
Diane Lefer — *Confessions of a Carnivore*
Diane Lefer — *Out of Place*

Rob Lenihan — *Born Speaking Lies*
Colin McGinnis — *Roadman*
Douglas W. Milliken — *Our Shadows' Voice*
Ilan Mochari — *Zinsky the Obscure*
Peter Nash — *Parsimony*
Peter Nash — *The Least of It*
Peter Nash — *The Perfection of Things*
George Ovitt — *Stillpoint*
George Ovitt — *Tribunal*
Gregory Papadoyiannis — *The Baby Jazz*
Pelham — *The Walking Poor*
Andy Potok — *My Father's Keeper*
Frederick Ramey — *Comes A Time*
Joseph Rathgeber — *Mixedbloods*
Kathryn Roberts — *Companion Plants*
Robert Rosenberg — *Isles of the Blind*
Fred Russell — *Rafi's World*
Ron Savage — *Voyeur in Tangier*
David Schein — *The Adoption*
Charles Simpson — *Uncertain Harvest*
Lynn Sloan — *Midstream*
Lynn Sloan — *Principles of Navigation*
L.E. Smith — *The Consequence of Gesture*
L.E. Smith — *Travers' Inferno*
L.E. Smith — *Untimely RIPped*
Bob Sommer — *A Great Fullness*
Caitlin Hamilton Summie — *Geographies of the Heart*
Tom Walker — *A Day in the Life*
Susan V. Weiss —*My God, What Have We Done?*
Peter M. Wheelwright — *As It Is On Earth*
Peter M. Wheelwright — *The Door-Man*
Suzie Wizowaty — *The Return of Jason Green*

Writing a review on social media sites for readers will help the progress of independent publishing. To submit a review, go to the book page on any of the sites and follow the links for reviews. Books from independent presses rely on reader-to-reader communications.

For more information or to order any of our books, visit:
http://www.fomitepress.com/our-books.html

www.ingramcontent.com/pod-product-compliance
Lightning Source LLC
Chambersburg PA
CBHW030346200726
48286CB00013B/372